Praise for the short fiction of Tanith Lee:

"In *Red as Blood,* Tanith Lee rewrites a number of well-known folk and/or fairy tales. . . . These are not just rewritten stories, they are retold. And the retelling is good enough that many of them ring as 'true' as the originals."
— *Science Fiction & Fantasy Book Review*

"Lee's 'Tales from the Sisters Grimmer' retell these classics with unique, insightful, often terrifying twists."   — *Kliatt*

"Here is a book worthy of the real Grimm's fairy tales. . . . Like those older tales, these stories pull no punches, and end up being thoroughly fascinating."
— *The Intergalactic Reporter*

"Lee's entrancing and vivid style makes what may seem a minor exercise into a collection of essentially new stories with some of the resonances of folklore."
— *Publishers Weekly*

"She turns some familiar fairytales inside-out, investing them with an unearthly aura. . . . Very satisfying and highly recommended."   — *Library Journal*

"Lee has conceived something unique and executed it superlatively well, displaying gifts as both a fantasy writer and a folklorist."   — *Booklist*

TANITH LEE

Redder Than Blood

DAW BOOKS, INC.

DONALD A. WOLLHEIM, FOUNDER
375 Hudson Street, New York, NY 10014

ELIZABETH R. WOLLHEIM
SHEILA E. GILBERT
PUBLISHERS
www.dawbooks.com

First Printing, April 2017

1 2 3 4 5 6 7 8 9

DAW TRADEMARK REGISTERED
U.S. PAT. AND TM. OFF. AND FOREIGN COUNTRIES
—MARCA REGISTRADA
HECHO EN U.S.A.

PRINTED IN THE U.S.A.

TABLE OF CONTENTS

Redder Than Blood

1

HE FIRST HEARD of her when he was a child. Some called her the Red Queen, though she was not; others had titled her the Red or Scarlet Lily—or the Ruby That Sings. So many names, so much eccentric description hiding what it displayed. By the age of nineteen he was familiar with her history, and by twenty had read several esoteric books concerning her. Seventeen years after, he stood on a street, gazing at the Palace where she had lived.

He acknowledged he had been blindly if intermittently seeking her all that intervening time. And now he had arrived. But he was no longer a romantic of twenty. And she was almost four centuries dead.

My name is Edmund Sanger.

No doubt you will know my father's name, William Joseph Sanger, the actor-architect, whose memorable performances (Hamlet, Cesare Borgia) left audiences fainting or abject with joy; whose small herd of elegant buildings still dominate certain little towns of the north and west of England.

I grew up in a crazy household. I don't use the term lightly. William had long since driven my pretty, unclever mother mad. Their three daughters copied, or rose against her. I was the late son, appearing when everyone else was old enough to know better. I led a lonely, and perpetually astounded life, reliant on witch-like nurses, and drily erudite, if sometimes pederastic, tutors. At sixteen I escaped and took ship for France. The first book of my travels, which I then wrote, I was lucky enough to have made into a great success. *Conqueror's Road*, was and is my only truly popular work. But still in print, even now, it set my sails for me, both financially and in the sense of preference. I could go where I wished, and travel so often very happily alone (yet frequently involved in brief if exotic adventures with other human things). I could live almost in any mode I desired, save that of richman. I could escape from whatever bored or horrified me. I was able to become—not my father's son, or my family's irrelevant annoyance, let alone any villain's plaything—but Myself. God bless the written word, Amen.

How did I first hear of Cremisia Ranaldi? No doubt from one of the better tutors. But rather than being some tidbit of intriguing history I was lessoned in, it seems more to me that her name fell like a pearl seed into my mind and heart, and there grew of itself into a glorious tree. She, unlike my at-one-time ever-present jailor family, was my verified connection to the world. Of course I fell in love with her, soon with all the raw sexual energy of my youth, and next with my even more voracious brain. She was desire incarnate, genius rising like Venus on the waters of imagination. If it ever entirely came clear to me, in my very earliest years, that she, as had I, had needed to elude enslaving family chains, I don't think I was aware of it fully. Rather than the flag of rebellion, she was the sunrise that ends the dark.

And she was safe as sun and star, too, miles off in the past.

"Ah, you are a lover of the Red Lily," he said to me, my sudden traveling companion on the long, hot, near-noon road to the old city of Corvenna.

All about were the round hills, with their groves of somber cypresses, and topiary poplars like rounded, curled-into-a-ball black-green cats. High up, rock and burned grass flared an extraordinary topaz. Sometimes colossal shadows, like sorcerous flying machines from some unthinkable future (hawks), swept over the slopes, and down, hunting across the wide, white, throat-of-dust road. They reminded me, such shadows, oddly of the decapitating passage of a guillotine's blade, even to the airborne *swish*.

I glanced at my companion, who had attached himself to me in the day's beginning. A fellow walker. They were not always suspect, or to be swiftly sloughed. And he looked so like a rogue, I mostly doubted he was one. It was his role, his act perhaps, to keep *him* secure (whereas my disguise was only, and often truthfully, to look very shabby and poor). Curled hair he had, black as oil, eyes the metallic ochre of old bronze. But young, rather less than my own age, I surmised. An Italian, native to the area? Why not. The earring in his right ear was a gold coin rubbed smooth of its identity. He wore the typical red scarf at his throat tight enough to strangle him, I thought—practice for others? His name, he had instantly told me, was Anceto.

"I have met many," Anceto said, "who were deeply enamored of the Lady Cremisia Ranaldi. Yet how can a woman keep such influence over our sex for so many years after she has left the mortal state? What can you hope for? She's dust in a tomb. Nothing to embrace. Nor anything at all to see. Her voice, which they say was better than the voice of the harp, or the nightingale, no longer to be heard. Only her poetry remains, cold as soot-marks on the yellowed pages. What use, my young sir, what profit in such a desire, or in faithfulness to such a reclusive muse?"

"Her verses are superb," I answered quietly.

"So they say," he murmured. "I have never read any—for I *can* read. Never dared. Where I have heard some ancient song composed by her begin to be played, I stop my ears. I've no leisure to be bewitched by the dead, Signore."

All this came about because he had asked me if I went to the city, and when I told him I did, he guessed why.

Fairly canny by now, generally I didn't obscure such ordinary matters. Except, maybe, where I suspected some thieves' ambush might be arranged.

We walked on in silence, but for the chorus of cavallettas, and presently an inn occurred at the roadside, as if conjured specially for our benefit.

We ate a lean meal, cheese, olives, herbal rice, and drank some wine. In turn he told me of his own interests, which included a farm he yearned to possess somewhere in the hills, an old priest he was fond of, his wife, who was 'not unkind' to him, and one or two other succulent women he now and then also enjoyed. On this issue he was flattering but decorous.

After the afternoon pause, during which the crickets sang

on, he slept, and I wrote up some notes on my journey, we continued along the road, still together. The evening began to gather in the distance, while the sun blinded us as it westered, a smashed egg of liquid gold. The gates were in sight by then, and we believed we might make them before the city police closed up for the night.

He said, as we climbed the last stony incline, among some carts and donkeys also hurrying to arrive before the lock-up, "Do you know where she lived?"

"Who? Oh, Cremisia Ranaldi. The Palazzo Ranaldi, am I correct? I've never been quite certain where it lies in the city."

"Lucky for you then, my friend. For not many now *do* know, but I do. It's not, this house, where most might expect it, though always it was there."

Then we were in at the gates, the sky seemed to breath out blue and smoke itself to deepest darkness in a succession of moments. Stars burst in static fireworks, and an answering gust of lamps opened from the ancient alleys and towers of Corvenna. So close about us they drew then, the city buildings, like a crowd—less of men than smooth-furred beasts, silent on vast soft paws, their claws sheathed and invisible, their eyes pretending to be merely narrow windows.

Cremisia's mother, Flamia; she herself made some kind of magic, so the story had it, in the last months before her daughter was born.

Flamia's maiden name, as with her married one, had been Ranaldi. They were a near-packed family, noble enough and rich enough to demand legitimacy in all its forms. She was, plainly to be seen from that alone, used to order and the rights of a dynastic will.

Since she must bear this child, she would have, Flamia Ranaldi stipulated, a daughter, both beautiful and gifted— not only with the female virtues, but the skills and inspirations more normally associated with males.

To this end the girl must have the assistance of perfect looks. Hair ebony-black as a night wood, eyes jet-black as a night river, lips as red as fire, skin white as new-fallen snow.

Once delivered, the mother would know her other requests had also been granted, through the medium of these extreme china and stained glass pigments.

When the hour came—midnight, it was said, to match the wished-for color of black, and winter-snowing also for the white (and too in a sea of blood that might be compared, though wrongly, to the red of fire)—Flamia's daughter was born. They carried her, washed and new, before her mother. Flamia was too weak, they say, to hold her. But, and again who can be sure, it seems the dying Flamia remarked: "They have done all I asked. I had forgotten that the price could be so very high."

She died, evidently, within the next minute.

Motherless then, the child was left, flower of night and snow and flame, to flourish or to perish in that house of the God-ordained masters, the male Ranaldis.

The night's shelter was suggested to me by Anceto, a kind of hostelry of sorts; I suppose I had been doubtful. But curiosity won out. It was in fact a decent house, so far as I could tell, nothing extravagant, but all clean enough and to hand. I had the impression the woman who provided the beds was one of those succulent women Anceto treasured. But the two of them were modest in front of me.

I slept well, and woke up as the cocks crowed in some of the little yards round about. In the low-beamed dining-room below, we ate sweet polenta.

"If you are still set on it," Anceto said, "I will take you today to see the true Palazzo of the Red Queen."

I said I was.

My famous father, I'm sure, would have mocked me for a gullible fool. This rogue would lead me to some half-way convincing sty, regale me further with his opinions. Perhaps pick my pocket as I stared at the crumbling walls. If Anceto had done the last, of course, he would have got very little reward.

We climbed up and down through the hilly city, through thin streets strung with banners of washing, down flute-skinny defiles with only blind yellowish stone either side; so into broad avenues and squares whose floors were paved green and pink and black as if for dancing, or gigantic games of chess. Tangles of architecture passed by. Now and then I asked him what this or that might be, that church, this tower. He told me, seeming to know—or inventing—everything. But at least the lies made sense—few writers do not value that.

"You see, Edmondo," Anceto said at length, "there are a great many old houses and other buildings men will tell you are the Palazzo Ranaldi. Even your English guide-books weaken to confusion on the subject."

"I had noticed that," I said. "Strange, when her reputation was so great."

"Ah, but you must understand, my friend, she spun a kind of web about the place. Few after all did not believe her a sorceress, so mighty was her charm and bright her talent. Take her riddle, the riddle none can, either way, answer. You know of it, too?" I nodded. "No wonder she can veil her dwelling, if she has a wish to."

"But you have uncovered the palace."

"I, and others. You now shall do so." I looked aside at him, aware abruptly of a deep intensity in his gaze. His eyes had darkened, it seemed to me. He said, "What you will make of this only you will know. I brought a man here once. He fell on his knees and wept. He told me he had lived before, an earlier life in the time of the Borgia Pope, and met with Cremisia then, and loved her. But she loved only one."

"That was her second husband. The dwarf."

"Ah yes, Edmondo. The handsome dwarf, Loro, Loro Ranaldi, since he took her name on wedding her. She said of him he was a giant among men. Just as others said *she* had dwarfed all the powerful male tyrants in her own family, even her first husband."

I was giddy. His eyes seemed to have hypnotized me. I found I nearly stumbled, and caught at a wall. Habituated once more, I looked about, and was rather startled to find we seemed to have entered, unnoticed by me, an entirely different street. Ancient, as so much of Corvenna was, if not especially ruinous, it stretched itself out along the two high banks of a canal of dark jade water. Directly across from me, on the canal's farther side, lifted the tall shapes of mansions, palaces, each separated and skirted about by walls and palings, steps and terraces.

"There, Edmondo," said my guide.

There. It was as if I knew it, though for a fact I had never seen even a sketch of the Palazzo Ranaldi, let alone that modernly marvelous instant portrait known as The Photograph. But I might have walked here often, once, just like the crazy man, real or invented, who knelt down crying. It swelled up, wave-like, on a terrace above a stair, and a garden, this overgrown and wild, and spilling soberly over its high, yellow-amber walls. Trees had raised themselves to hugeness inside, reaching out for air and light, and they clouded round the palisades of stonework and windows. A pane, sun-struck, flashed golden, and with it some edges of masonry. In the water below, the reflection hung like a gilded mask.

Some three hundred and eighty-one years since she had been here. Since she had existed.

I did not quite believe in what I saw. The actual house was a mirage—less, itself, like a reflection in water than a mirror. Or else, some clever effect thrown by sudden light upon a blank void. But sun and shadow flickered, separated. A bird flew out from the trees into the church dome of the sky.

2

He led me to another tavern. I have no memory at all of getting—or of being got—there. In the vine-screened courtyard, he made me drink half a pitcher of water, and then some of the local rough and earthen wine.

I thought I must have taken too much sun—odd in itself, I had credited myself with being fairly used to the climate by now. Or, I wondered a little if he had lightly drugged me. (The lessons of my father: Trust none, *love* none, use *all*, had put me, early in life, in shackles. Scorn and hack them off though I had, to break that ever-reiterant hold was often hard.)

But Anceto said to me, "Never fear, Edmondo. You are only under her spell. I have seen it before, now and then. No shame to you. Nor will she hurt you. And I am here."

"So I see," I said. My voice was cooler than my head.

Both of us slept after, under the purple awning. When I woke in the sinking afternoon, some pretty insects—dragon-flies I thought them, but he gave them another name and pedigree, were dancing to and fro. They seemed to weave a fine and glistening net over the court.

"Be easy," said my companion. "Nothing needs to be done till sunset comes. Not even then. When the moon stands high."

"And then what?" I muttered.

"We return to the Palazzo Ranaldi. There you will bribe the old custodian—he's amenable and not expensive. We'll take him some wine, too."

"Wine, money—what makes you think I'm so rich?"

"But you are, Edmondo," he murmured, gentle as a lover. "If only alas, in the bounty of your elegant mind. You see," he added, as he poured for us a little more red delight, "she haunts the Palazzo. Or so they say. At this time of every month, when the moon is almost full, almost a perfect round like the mirror of a lovely woman . . . Then."

"Why?" I said.

He smiled at me. He was my brother, my best and dearest companion. Had I been able, ever, erotically to love a man, I think. I should have yearned for Anceto. But that extra element has never been a part of me. And besides, I did not trust my brother and friend. Of course, he would mislead me, perhaps even with some spurious and vulgar show put on for my benefit by mountebanks in the secret rooms of the Palazzo . . .

I laid my head on my arms and fell once more asleep. He would rob me, if he hadn't already, while I slept. Naturally.

Instead, it seemed, he himself paid for our late luncheon and woke me kindly at midnight. (Midnight—for I heard certain clocks and bells chiming in Corvenna, all out of pace with each other, so that the whole jangling farrago lasted well into six minutes.) And what anyway is Time? Save some fool's notion of ongoing existence. As if always we must walk sternly forward, onward—While instead we drift in circles, or flow backward, as does the sea. Or else we stay entirely still as any stone. As they say in France, *J'y suis. J'y reste*. Here I am, here I remain. But there I did not remain. Anceto guided me once more into the city, and toward the green canal. And the moon, indeed almost full, stood high.

The way across the canal was over a lumpy little bridge. I did not remember to have seen it there before. Perhaps it had not been.

The night water below, no longer green, blacker than the sky. But the moon lay in it, white mirror reflecting into mirror.

Approaching the Palazzo it seemed now only a huge, gaunt, forlorn old house in darkness. Among the other mansions distantly grouped along the bank, here and there the faintest light was showing. If some of these, I noted as our footsteps rang on the cobbles of the near shore, were timorously put out.

Anceto let us through an arched gateway in a wall, leading into the garden, which had become, as it had already looked, a primeval forest. The talons of trees clawed at us, thigh-high grasses whipped and little things skittered away. Once a pair of glowing eyes—some nocturnal bird or beast—or a demon—beamed icily down on us, turning red before they were gone. However, here was a side-door, lean and shut, but with a lamp burning somewhere behind and within, so every crack and undone seam in the door's wood gleamed. The moon by then too was beginning to fill up the garden, which seemed to me then suddenly like a drawing, or a woodcut, two-dimensional.

Anceto tapped delicate as a mouse on the thin door. Which after a moment was undone. "Is it you, Anc'o, my dear?" A tiny creature, the caretaker. Perhaps it had even been he, eyes ablaze, up the tall tree in the garden . . .

Anceto spoke softly in the accent of the city. And the way was made wide for us.

I found I did not want to go in.

Despite William Joseph's threatful warnings, it was not I feared a den of thieves. In fact—I feared nothing specific. Not even the ghosts it seemed I had been promised a sight of.

But it was too late for retreat. Will-less, I had already entered. Coins were changing hands, soft as bread. (Anceto's again, not mine.) The caretaker picked up the lamp, and led us through into some kind of anteroom. It was his bivouac in the huge wilderness of the house, not uncozy in its cramped and impoverished manner.

I had forgotten all my Italian. I could no longer tell what Anceto and the little weasel-man said to each other. Instead I seemed to hear a sort of murmuring, like far-off music—a mandolin, perhaps, a pipe—through the low-lit wall a flush of other brightness bloomed somewhere. Not cool and pale like the waxing moon; richer, yellow, hot gold. Only for a second. An aberration of the eyes?

"Come, Edmondo."

Anceto led me out again by another slight door. Stairs, probably a hundred of them. About halfway up the flight, a side window abruptly flaring, a searing line of light.

"Follow her," he said, or I believed he did. "The moon will lead you. No, I shall not attend you. Not for me, this. I've said, I do not dare. But for you, no choice. I envy you, my friend. And fear for you. Go now. Waste no more of your night."

Cremisia's father had been a prince. He ruled the house, as he did his estates about the landscape beyond Corvenna, and was the recipient also of endless wealth from other properties and concerns scattered elsewhere on the globe.

A large man, too, this Raollo Ranaldi, well over six feet in an age when five feet seven was the average height of a fit and well-nourished man. He was besides raven-haired, with small slippery frost-gray eyes that—certain scribes reported—seemed able to cut men who offended him, like knives.

Raollo's brother (the uncle of Cremisia) was broad-built and almost as tall. *He* had—reportedly—the dark cunning eyes of a rat. Although rats, of course, are intelligent animals, self-serving only through the laws of survival. Uncle Marcaro was a drunken lack-wit, vicious because he might be, and so greedy that, by the age of twenty, they said, he must needs be carried in a chair by six poor menials, his own bulk by then being already too much for him.

To this pleasant guardianship Fate had given Cremisia.

She had two brothers also, half-siblings to her, borne to Raollo's previous wife, a poor blonde lady who, according to further gossip, Raollo had murdered one night, out of inebriated peevishness, since she had accidentally spoken well of an enemy of his.

The twin brothers, Giuseppe and Giacobbe, had flaxen hair like their mother, and her large blue eyes. Otherwise they were all from their father's stable, big and tall, crass, cruel, and crazed. They fought duels and won them by strategies—such as having several of their own men run out and stab an opponent through.

When Cremisia was born, these lads were just seven years of age. But within four or five further years they had already attained much of their undainty reputation. They would pay their small half-sister scant attention until she, at the age of twelve, began herself to flower into adulthood. Then, at some eighteen or nineteen years, the princely youths mused on their 'quaint sisterling.' Such talks were neither brotherly nor choice.

The fifth male figure of note, whose shadow so far only hung upon the horizon of Cremisia's life, was her cousin, also a Ranaldi, Thesaio. And he was unlike all the rest, being in his nature fastidiously priestly and cold, lacking appetite for anything, and very conscious of the sins of Humanity, himself possibly excluded. For the sake of the precious Ranaldi dynasty, it had long been determined that any female child of Raello's must be wed to Thesaio. When she was three years of age and he nine, Thesaio and Cremisia were therefore duly betrothed, in the chapel of the White-Hooded Virgin at Corvenna.

Believe this or not, once more I was, and remain, unsure how I reached the next stage of my evening. I recall the stairs, and the moon's rim at the window, which silver-coated the steps' dulled marble treads. Then a space of vague shadow. And *then* there was a picture.

For a minute I thought it hung on a wall before me.

A wide and heavily gilded frame contained a grandiose

canvas, in dimension some seven feet (upright) by twelve
feet in length. Yet this must be like the night garden, which
I had interpreted as a wood-cut. The framed painting was no
less than a living, moving scene, the frame itself the surround
that was like that of a window. Light and color, sound and
motion, these were in the picture. (In recent times, I have
watched moving pictures on a screen. When first I saw such
things I asked myself if my memory of the framed living
painting were the same. But it was not.) There was music too
I could hear, the very melody I had caught the essence of
before, mandolins and pipes, the chirruping of small drums,
and then the clear-water genderless voice of a singer. The
words were not Italian, but Latin. I understood them immediately.

> *Come, bite the apple, my beloved,*
> *Pierce through the crimson skin into the sweet*
> *and firm green heart.*
> *How can it harm you? The Snake recommended it!*
> *It will make us strong and wise, and valiant in love.*

The scene, as I began to be able to focus on it, floating
there in a thick broth of candlelight, was of a banquet. On the
sumptuously caparisoned chairs and couches nobles sat, or
part lay, decadently, in the antique classical Roman pose.
Their costly garments (beyond the Sumptuary Laws), the
coverings of furniture, the swathed drapes, seemed generally
of a garnet red, or vermilion, or that red-magenta still often
called 'purple'. The long tables were a clutter of fine wood,
gold metal and silver, of gemmed knives for eating, and large
peculiar long forks—reminiscent of the killing tridents once
used in gladiatorial arenas—here presumably facile in the
skewering of meat or pastry. From metal ewers flowed fountains of scarlet wine to tall goblets, all those of a sheer green-
ish glass. Little boys—pages—scurried to and fro carrying
delicacies to this or that lord. Few women, I noted, were present. And the ones that were had a slightly unruly look, however glamorously got up. They wore makeup too, the ladies, a
sign in such days, when used so overtly, of the whore. (Please

don't think I speak in criticism of such women. It is one of the four oldest professions on earth, the generous selling of one's own body for sex. The other three professions being, of course, war, robbery, and murder. Of these four, prostitution is the only one that should be respected, and that fully. Those who preach otherwise are blind arrogant fools or shysters. These women are more than worthy of honor, protection, and wealth. They save minds. Perhaps even souls.)

Nevertheless, one was conscious this particular feast had a spurious air, a dubious component. For at the high place Raollo the Tyrant sprawled, and nearby his gormandizing brother Marcaro, deep in dishes. Elsewhere, glancing about, I failed to find the twin brothers, but they would at this date have been thought too young perhaps to attend. How did I know this? Because exactly then into the aureate soup of hall stole a little slender girl, some seven years of age, clad in a white dress, with her long black hair streaming down her back, much as did the locks of the lady guests, if hers more prettily, not being interrupted by combs and flowers and so on.

You could not help but see the child's skin was peerlessly pale. It glowed to rival the candles' gold. Her eyes were dark as darkness, and partly lowered with a modesty that nearly shocked, when seen in that cacophony of loudness and gluttony. Her mouth was soft red as a poppy. On a small gold dish she held carefully and steadily, this child, a single deep-red apple—redder than her lips. Let alone the painted lips of the ladies, the smoldering hangings, cushions and clothes. From the apple a soft steam lifted. I found I could smell its perfume, as—perhaps luckily—I could nothing else there. Cinnamon and ginger, a touch of sugar so brown and intense it too was like a spice. And through this the aroma of the fruit itself, both fresh-cut and baked.

The song came then again. *Come, bite the apple, my beloved*—

Raollo was sitting upright, pushing off, with typical boorishness, his female companion. He was laughing though, and not unpleased.

I had by now identified the scene. Any who had ever attempted to research the history of Cremisia Ranaldi has probably read of it. A poor book that left it out. She was indeed seven years of age. But, as I once was, it seemed, she had been given over to the care of witch-like nurses. And one of these, it transpired, was not unkind, and also an actual mageia, gifted in the arts of her calling; able also to effect the odd and genuine spell. She loved Cremisia like a mother, a stepmother, maybe, with a good heart. And her magic it was too that made her direct the child to tonight's act. 'One day,' the nurse-witch said, 'this step will render up a flower. Even if none remember or know why. So such rituals may work.'

Cremisia carried the unfaltering apple up to the dais, and her father. The nurse, soberly clad, a crone old and narrow as a hundred-year sapling, remained modestly below in waiting.

Raollo spoke to his daughter. I could not catch the words even to try to grasp them. But he grinned, and ran his doubtless meat-and-syrup smeared hand over her raven feathers. Then he gripped the platter, and using a silver spoon, berried with red jewels in its hilt, he mercilessly ran the apple through, and ate it in evident enjoyment.

The hall applauded. Politic to do so.

And then he spoke again, and I *heard* his words and what they meant.

"We thank you, Daughter, for this tender offering. And though you should, at this hour, be abed, no reprimand shall be returned to you. A charming gift. Now. What will you have in return?"

The hall laughed with jolly scorn. If the child were silly enough to ask for something, inevitably it must be infantile and vacuous. More likely she would be lost for words.

Cremisia spoke.

"Nothing now, honored sir. But one day I may ask for something."

The chairs and couches fairly rocked with mirth at this, Raollo's high seat too. And after that the musicians struck up another tune, and the witch-nurse, wrapping the child in a fold of her robe, led her swiftly away, out of the burning light, under the shadows beyond the picture's frame. At which the entire image sank like a dying fire.

*   *   *

Other paintings, scenes, pictures (mirages) occurred after this. They were up on walls, in doorways that appeared impenetrable, or over the ceilings, the floors.

I seemed to myself to be wandering the Palazzo, but always with inexplicable slight gaps between this step and that. Up stairs—marble, wooden—I went, and down. I found myself in open vacant rooms, with not a stick of furniture—or maybe one tiny stool, upon which the most miniature foot (perhaps of a child?) might be placed. Or they were stacked with chairs and tables and chests, like a restaurant (that had been closed), if rather finer than most. There was the occasional courtyard, very much in the pre-Christian Roman style. Here troughs shallowly rose, no longer freighted with flowers but overgrown by some form of laurel or ivy; each space was supplemented by a pool or fountain, now dry as the night had become. Hot yet heatless, pale though dark, the stars faintly overcast in rifts of invisible cloud. The moon, which had been so luminous and nearly full, was misty and far over to the west. Had so much time elapsed in my confused excursion?

Once I shouted down to Anceto, from a gallery all slit with smoky lightless windows, calling at least twice through the house. Which building seemed then hollow as a flute that no one played upon. Nor could my English voice do so. I called, and thought I had made some noise—but perhaps I had not. And for sure, not even a solitary echo replied. I felt I was tired. I wished to leave, could I but find the exit. I neither understood nor any longer cared what went on. I wanted to escape, to sleep. But the thing was the pictures every time galvanized me.

I think they didn't frighten me, but conceivably they did. I never believed them to be due to legerdemain. Or if they were, the sort occasioned by modern photography—then before its hour, or some older device that used a hidden mechanism and so played (apparently) color and animated form upon the mansion's stones. Finally there was another empty room, and in it a single chair, upright and of some historic value, unless being a cunning copy. I sat down in it, exhausted and affronted. I had, whatever else, been duped. (No doubt when the sun rose Anceto would negotiate my release, on payment of some suitable 'gift' which, naturally, I did not possess to be robbed of.) It seemed to me I next heard a clock chime, all alone, the fourth hour of morning. But God knows if I did. Everything was out of synch—moonrise, and set, my own progress, the night itself.

The world of the city was any way completely dark by then, while the golden images had all gone out and nothing new replaced them. What had they shown? Fragments of Cremisia's childhood, youth, young womanhood. She, about twelve, clad in crimson, rode a white pony in a procession, seated side-saddle. Or in a dull house-dress, perhaps thirteen, in a garden of hedge-sculpture, she was almost cornered by the two blonde half-brothers—a steward coming to call them off. Though she had seemed quite cool. There was, in these scenes, no dialog at all, no sound, no scent. But there were two other vital moments, *glimpses*—she turned her head at a window, her hair like a sea-wave of ravens—was she sixteen? Seventeen?—or she lay in a doll-like bed, only four or five years of age, sleeping. My eyes, as well as I, grew tired. The result of the constant irregular flux of blackness to candlelight, torchlight, or of a sun so long set it might have ruled another world than ours.

"Enough," I said aloud. Or supposed I had.

And then, instead of another of the fiery surges, I heard a voice lift out of silence. Male, it seemed to be, if rather distant. It spoke in English. It seemed to read to me from one of those books I had read in the past.

"And to her husband, Thesaio, she said this: 'I have denied you a husband's rights to me, for your own fastidious sake. Love and congress are not for you. God forbids it you, sir. I shall never bear you a son, nor shall I ever bear a son, nor any offspring to any man. For that is not either for me.'"

And at this, rather than be shown a picture, I seemed to imagine one inside my own head, and how Cremisia, now clad in deepest scarlet, and in a bedchamber, presumably her own, spoke the words very mildly and reasonably to her unpleasant husband Thesaio. And I saw, or imagined I saw him slink away, vicious but inept.

"Therefore," the voice quietly explained, "she dwarfed the them all, these six male giants (one even unborn, never to be conceived, her son). They, who should by rights have ruled and quelled and crushed her life, and she herself. With some she managed them by her manner alone, as with the vile Thesaio. With others by cunning games and subterfuge, sometimes aided by her witch-nurse step-mother, a very old woman by now, yet still paramount in Cremisia's household. The wicked brothers were diffused and held off, they say, by use of witchcraft itself. And her foul incestuous Uncle Marcaro easily — through pandering to his greater love of cuisine. And, as she had sidestepped the threat of pregnancy and further service ever after to a son, so she evaded her father, Raollo. They say that in one way she hypnotized *him*, for he could never make sense of her, nor properly grow angry with her. While in the end, as the story has it, she defeated him utterly by use of a riddle."

I had opened my eyes. I sat in darkness and waited, almost obediently, for another illustrating picture. Or for the voice to resume. The riddle: The Riddle.

What had I thought — felt — so far? I had no notion. I believed myself also under some spell. If not as profound as the witch's, nevertheless effective.

You fool, my father soundlessly, voicelessly repeated. I had learned the tenor of *his* lessons well.

In my own youth, I was in love with Cremisia, as one can only be inside the separating safety of time. For she was centuries gone, and her history, aside from written facts, unprovable. She had been lucky, that was all. Everything else — embroidery, exaggeration, and invented fairy tale.

She was twenty-six years old, Raollo's daughter, when she met her predestined lover and spiritual husband.

Until then, among her closest male acquaintance she had known only moral and intellectual dwarfs. Now she encountered a giant.

Loro. (His patronymic is generally uncertain — although some have guessed at it: he may have been the bastard son of a lower prince of the d'Estinis, or the Calcapuas or a legitimate child born to a skilled blacksmith known only as 'Roman'.)

Edmund Sanger knew of this, it goes without saying. His extensive reading had seen to that. How strange it is, however (perhaps), that most of those who learned about Cremisia. Ranaldi, poet and sorceress, came to her history *after* they had read her work and gladly drowned in it. That she was a powerful woman, able often to get her own way in an age when, as a rule, women weighed in the balance no more than 'a flower upon a soon-snapped stem' is remarkable. Frankly her success seems to say less therefore of her character — than of Fate. Only the lucky stand a chance, regardless of ability or worth.

So then, she met Loro d'Estini, or Calcapua or Romano, at the age of twenty-six. By the day of her death, when she was at least one hundred years of age, her lover-husband had been dead some decades. Even so he had lived long, having not been expected to. It was, in those days, unusual that he made old bones, since Loro, the mental giant, was physically a dwarf much under four feet in height.

The stories of their meeting are various. (Edmund himself had written of it.) Some other tales barely hold water — literally: Involved in an accident on the city river, Loro had leaped in and saved her. Or, she drowning in some lake in the hills, Loro, fortuitously in a boat, had raised her up. One other account had it she fell from a tower, perhaps at the push of one of the evil twin brothers, and Loro caught her in his arms. Though he was strong reputedly as a young horse, the very unmatch in their sizes would seem to deny this. (A man of six foot would have had trouble, though Cremisia was light and slender; the tower was some fifteen stories high.)

The apocryphal aside, it seems most likely Cremisia met Loro at one of the many places she by then frequented. She had long since wrested a lot of freedom from her father, let alone her overmatched husband. Quite how she did this remains, as demonstrated, something of a mystery. (Fate; the witch.) Her talents as a poet do seem to have enabled much of it. (By the age of twelve her poetry had escaped the confines of the house, and was feted everywhere in the city, even in the palazzo of the Duke himself. Indeed, before her six-

teenth birthday, her verses were read and sung far beyond
Corvenna. In France they spoke of her, in Spain, the Ger-
manian kingdoms. To Persia it was said many of her words
had been smuggled, where, of course none could agree any
female should ever be able to write such marvels.)

Wherever she went about the city, undeniably, she was accompanied by servants and guards of the Ranaldi. 'So
crowded round was she by her escort,' ran a comment of the
time, 'barely could a single petal of this rose be noted within
the red-uniformed hedge.'

Nevertheless, one close summer evening in the Pallina Bi-
anca Square, Cremisia was honored by the city, at the ending
of a festival, with a reading of her verse. Which feat was performed, ably and with exquisite beauty, by Loro.

Despite his lack of height, the dwarf's head and throat
were large and sculptorally formed, the rest of his body muscular and limber, and his barrel chest like a 'sounding bell'.
(He had lungs of the finest Spanish leather, some would tell
you, their easy expansion enough to put to shame those of
the best actor or singer in town.) Loro's hair was long, shining, in color like new-poured honey. He washed it, and his
body, every day, with sandalwood soap from the East. His
eyes were green as spring leaves. His teeth were strong as the
rest of him, and snow white, save for one, just to the right side,
knocked out in a battle he had had with three great dogs, set
on him in malice by some enemy. Loro had won the battle,
claimed the dogs as his prize of victory, and taken them to his
lodging (funded by the Duke). Here, loved, well-treated and
respected by Loro, they changed their ways, and became
playfully docile with him as puppies, if standing as tall as he.
But woe betide any after who meant Loro harm.

When he had read her poem through—the popular view
is it was her *Morning Devotion*—a silence hung like a trance.
After which applause split the air, the very sky. Loro smiled
and bowed. He was neither vainglorious nor servile. A prince
among men was Loro.

A little later in a quiet private garden above the square, he
and Cremisia met. None detailed quite how, or what they
said, but some had views and invented their language, florid

and enamored. The nearest shot came from the pen of Andoros, another poet, a man of taste and generosity. 'Never
since the Golden Era of Virgil, or Homer, or the Luminous
Sappho on her Isle of Maidens, has any possessed the Divine
Cremisia's gift, she who created her verses as a god of the Old
World created lands and seas. And the excellent Loro, recit-
ing, himself like a young god, caught every eye and heart and
mind, even hers, in the net of his brilliance. Oh what a meeting then was theirs. The piffling matter of height, between
such deities, is not in question. Be sure, before the sinking of
the rose-red sun, their hands had grown together, as soon
their lips must do. Not two separate souls then, but twined
together life-long, inseparable and complete. And if one of
them should speak the words of love, both speak them, in one
voice. But never listen! Only gods can bear the beauty such a
song. We should fall dead on hearing it, as the moth perishes
in the lamp flame.'

3

Others would have locked her in a coffin of glass. But Loro
kissed her awake.

I had read of their meeting in several versions, some extravagant. I think perhaps it was even less dramatic than that
which Andoros refers to. Loro had simply been employed to
entertain at the Ranaldi Palace, where by then Cremisia again
resided. He spoke her poetry (flawless, flawlessly). It was the
Morning Devotion, or the *Star Prayer*. She listened. Afterward, somewhere, sometime, authors of their own destiny,
they contrived to meet. But following that start, were not to
be parted.

(How she eluded her husband during this is conjecture.
Most likely is the idea Thesaio had retired elsewhere into seclusion.) At first also, the affair was secret. But both the caring and the cruel will gossip. Through what else is the bulk of
history retained?

Raollo learned. He upbraided his daughter. She stood

before him (so some texts have it) like a slender willow that is made of steel.

Loro was barred from the palace, the city. Given the scandal, even the Duke could not prevent this. It rather appears Raollo's assassins may have been set on Loro's heels. His dogs assisted him, and he and they fled unscathed.

"He is Nature's aberration," Raollo had bellowed, wine-full and drunk as the wine-skin, dangerous as life. "And you, you mindless minx, are already married to the noble Thesaio. Despite his parting from you, which now fails to astound me."

"I am married to Loro," *she* seemingly replied—was she really so extravagantly foolish?—"He is my husband in the sight of every god, and of God Himself also."

Accordingly, or merely in passing, Raollo imprisoned her in her suite at the Palazzo. After some months, she must have persuaded her way out.

They contend the witch-nurse was dead by then, but maybe, having been so powerful, she was able to visit, armed with advice.

And thus. And so.

The next picture was before me. It was large as a wall. And presently, now without any trepidation, I found myself in the midst of it, as if inside an actual chamber of three dimensions, and formed of tactile stuffs, light and sound, scents and vibrations. I was there, standing upon the floor, the walls about me.

Another Banquet Hall, with all the correct appurtenances. This time too the feast was being conducted more selectively. Not courtesans but respectable wives, or at the worst respectably accepted mistresses, sat by their lords.

Veni morde malum amor mi.

They were playing that again the old melody, the clear exalting lute of a voice, neither male nor female, to offer the Latin words: Come bite the apple, my love . . . the Snake recommended it! How can it do harm—

Cremisia is credited with the words of this song, in their mellifluous Latin. Which seems to suggest she wrote them—a Latin scholar!—in her sixth or seventh year. Perhaps possible.

She did write as an adult sometimes in good Latin. And was like no other.

Nor was she now in the Hall of the feast.

I myself seemed to have my own body about me, and no camouflaging period costume had been put on it. I seemed to myself, as I had half an hour before, tattered and tired, a misplaced visitor from the future.

It was true, none of the busy stewards or servitors collided with me. Yet neither did they pass through me, nor I through them. Where I stood, at and on the edges of the tessellated floor, whose pattern showed ivory dolphin leaping and merry, russet gods with green garlands and purple grapes, I could stare about freely, apparently, a disturbance to nothing.

I did not think I was dreaming. No longer did I reason I was under any sort of spell. I had, somehow, very intimately been enabled to witness the past. Look then, carefully, and take note.

She did not enter in the fashion she had when a child. Instead there came a pause in the song, and next the soft warble of a pipe, less a fanfare than the eerie signal of a goddess straying from a grove.

I had seen her in hallucinatory white and imagined scarlet. Now her gown was black as a widow's, though ornamented with threads of gold and silver. A single smart man, her personal steward, paced after her. He seemed as composed as she, while two maidens moved just behind him, they dressed in smooth bluish-gray, like the darker doves.

Raollo was, what else, drunk. And older now, no doubt in his fifties, wore it even less well than previously. But too, trained in and used to drunkenness, he was lucid enough.

"Ha, my daughter!" he exclaimed. "What now?"

Did he recall the scene of her childhood, the spice-filled, flattering apple which the same song had once heralded? If she interrupted his feasts, she must, obviously, perform some sort of show or act to flatter him. (The books do say that now and then she had been called in to recite some suitable verse, her own or another's. She had a beautiful voice. And she was by then famous, after all.)

No music, it had left off. Maybe an intense quiet, as the revelers, 'respectable' as they might be, craned to hear.

"I have come, sir," said Cremisia, "to ask you a riddle. And if you cannot answer it, to claim a boon of you. Do you allow this?"

What did he do, Raollo? Some accounts have it he glared suspiciously and was loath to agree, and only the intervention of some powerful other, then present, persuaded him to go along with the 'Fair lady's request'. Protocol, such as existed at most of the Renascence aristocracy's public occasions, might also have bound him to acquiesce. This had, after all, a classical ring to it. But other retellings of Cremisia's life declared he was only too swinishly jolly then not to comply.

"What else, my little duck? Ask away. Let's see if we can fathom your little feminine conundrum."

And so I reach the instant of the riddle. How frequently through the centuries it has been quoted. For needless to tell, that night none solved it, thinking it at first too simple, and after that obtuse, insane even, nonsensical. "My riddle, my Lord, is this," said Cremisia. "What is redder than blood?"

"Why—" he vehemently began again. Then stopped, his mouth ajar, contemplating somewhat, at last. Lamely he added, after a moment. "Why, girl, many things."

"I request," she said, "their names."

At which, finally scowling in concentration, irritation, he reeled off some inevitable and trite list of subjects and objects. About the hall, too, his men, and perhaps a few of the less modest ladies, added examples.

Cremisia waited, flawless in her glittering black. She was herself, ever and always, composed of three colors, black and white, and red. Flamia, her wise and lunatic mother, had seen to that. Cremisia waited, and the hall, flush-faced, barked and fluted and yelled its suggestions. And then silence returned, and Cremisia nodded to her steward who, calling out himself in a deep, carrying tone, caused the hall doors again to open. At this, in was borne an enormous silver salver, so huge it took sixteen strong youths to bear it. As it passed each table, each bench and chair, as it mounted the steps to Raollo's dining platform, every person there gazed and pointed. Some laughed, some jeered, some applauded, some shook their heads. And I—the future phantom at the feast—I peered long and hard at the flat gigantic silver tray and what it carried. They were all, not astonishingly, red things on it, some bright, some dark, some of a succulent medium mellowness. Apples lay there, berries, plums, other fruit, even vegetables—legumes, shoots, leaves—roses, flowers of many types, both real and formed from cloth; bowls of wine from different regions; gems—garnets, rubies—combs of deep-sea coral; scarves and girdles of velvet or sheer Florentine silk; leather dyed and burnished; metal goods, weapons with copper opulent inside them; feathers of birds; skins of creatures that had been deer or serpents, or dragons or frogs; pots of ink, of paint, of rouge and carmine; Arabic spice; glassware from Venice, sacred candles from Rome, plate from China; shoes and gloves; chess pieces; dolls; and other stuff, so much, unquantifiable, a chaos, a crowd of sights, and of *red*. And at the center of the tray, firmly enough fixed it did not shift about, there was a hollow red bowl in which burned coals with a somber red glow, and now and then a tiny snake-tongue of flame licking out; a red, these, as clear as water . . .

Dazzled, dizzied by the afterimage, I glanced up. The tray had gone by, it rested now on the dais, about the height of Raollo's knee. And he pored over it, as if counting, laughing still, at a loss, superior in his ignorance and carefree in his limitations.

"Such red," he remarked soon enough. "We must vaunt my daughter for her artistic collation."

And the ignorant and limited feasters again applauded.

And back came silence, on its cue.

"What, there," said Cremisia, and her trained voice fell silver-sure in even the thickest ear, "is redder, then, redder than blood."

The cries, like a brief little hail—"That!" "That!" "The apple!" "The sash!" "The comb!" "The girdle!" "The fire!" "All and any of it," drawled Raollo.

"But," said Cremisia, calmly, "it is not. Let me show you."

And from her sleeve she took the smallest tiniest blade, a

miniature tool for the trimming of a thread or a polished nail. When she slit the pad of her thumb with it there was, it was true, a shallow gasp of shock—thrill or disapproval, who could say.

That done, she stood above the salver, and let her pure young blood, red as blood, slip down and dot everything, like a fragile yet hellish dew.

Some got to their feet at this. They came along the hall and pressed near, straining to see. I was myself among them, they neither touching me nor I them, yet mingled. Each of us, it seemed, strove to judge between the blood and every other persona of red. Did this surpass it? Or *this*—surely—that, just there—or . . . that . . . or . . . not.

Cremisia had herself moved away by now. The knifelet was once again concealed. She had, invisibly and accurately, staunched the wound to her thumb.

It was not she who spoke at long last. Nor, come to that, the Prince-Tyrant Raollo. Some other anonymous voice broke through the re-clotting of soundlessness.

"Great Lord—I cannot see a single thing that is *more* red."

"Nonsense," said Raollo, but he was sluggish. All at once he *seemed* like the drunken sot he was. Slowly then he added, "She has outwitted me, the bitch." And the merest whispers of censor at the term spirited around, like steam.

He rose from his chair, and with his boot as he did so, deliberately or in mere drunk clumsiness, he tipped the tray, which clattered down, and each item slid and rolled off, even the dish of fire, and there was some needed scurrying then, to stop and stay, to prevent the catching alight of draperies and staining of garments. But Raollo held to his chair-back and glowered upon his daughter.

"You have ensnared me before them all," he said. "No, I can't answer your excrement of a riddle. *Is* there an answer?"

Level as any duelist she met the swill of his gaze with the clean blades of her own two eyes. "Yes, my lord. There is an answer."

"God hack-split it then, for I can't come at it. You've won, you bitch-cat. *So what do you want?*"

He did not need to ask. He knew.

Conceivably all of them did.

But she, who had not revealed the riddle's reply, answered this other redundant question. "What do I want: That I may go free of this splendid place, my Lord, and of my renowned and honored family, and live my own life as I desire, in some other spot."

"And play there a harlot to a rancid dwarf," growled Raollo, his tone muddled with saliva and malice and rage. Yet he could not deny her, of course. The most corrupt of such courts as his, in those enlightened and overlooked days, would not risk any ostensible denial of the bargain he had agreed to. He had been unable—all of them had—to say what was redder than blood. He must give in. "Go far off then," he snarled. "And be orphaned of me and damned by me, and accursed of Christ. Take nothing with you but the clothes you have on your body. Nor ever come here again to beg another mote of me."

"I promise that I will not," she said.

And turning she walked from the hall, through all the lavish golden light, and the spillage of reds—none of which was redder that the blood of woman or man or child or beast. Away she went, and as she did, the whole picture abruptly sank and faded. And I lurched backward—snatching at a wall to save myself from a fall into the lightless, bloodless dark.

4

Veni morde malum amor mi

In the time of pre-Christian Rome, *malum* meant an apple. In Christian times, certainly from the reign of Nero, and allied to the Older Testament of Genesis, and the Temptation in the Garden, *malum* might still mean an apple—but also *Evil*. Thus the world runs.

As I saw a hint of faint general lamplight ahead of me along the passage, in the staggering dark and night-chill of the house, great relief laved me over. Anceto, after all, must have come in. Despite his scarer's words—*dare not*—Thank God.

He had, obviously, a lamp; had maybe brought some beer or wine—or hot coffee, even better. Best of all, genuine human company. It was not I reckoned I had gone mad. I'd read of such ghostly adventures as had beset me in the Palazzo. But the notion of relief from it all, of actual *ordinariness*, was more than welcome.

Two big doors of carved blond oak hung ajar. I pushed one wide, and there the new room lay. It was much smaller than the others I had been shown, or entered. A salon for conversation and intimate sociability, not feast and flamboyance.

The lamplight was paler too, a melon-lemon glaze.

Two figures only were present, neither of them Anceto. One I had beheld before, the other only in my mind. He sat on a low chair, a book, huge as in those days so often they were, across a pedestal before him. He was handsome and young. I surmise he looked, maybe, either a touch younger—or more mature—than his years. I noticed then a tawny silky hound leaned relaxedly against his very short, very strong leg.

She however was stationed by an open window, though which faintly drifted the night aroma of jasmine, and other fragrant nurtured plants.

As before, she was clad in red. Blood red, if not a red any more red than blood. Her loose raven wings of hair were wound with pearls—white, and chains of jet-stones—black.

She had been looking out, and now she turned. In age, I guessed she was about thirty-five, which in her era generally would seem older, though she did not.

I had, and have seen, close to, many women of great loveliness, and of many differing types. But none like her. Her beauty surely held a dagger's edge that did not cut, a soft caress that stung. Or, she was only peerlessly beautiful, perhaps, only that. The previous sights I had had of her here, in the palace of her forebears, had been paintings on glass. This alone was real.

My weariness sloughed from me, leaving me light-headed and adrift.

I knew, back in the 1500s, Raollo had sent his men also after her, despite the bargain of the riddle. But they failed to find her, or else they refused to do so. And Loro quickly spirited her off, as he had done with himself, hundreds of miles away to some area that has never been satisfactorily defined. Some even declared the lovers visited England, or the Eastern Lands, India . . . A decade after, when Raollo and his fellow tyrannical masters of the Ranaldi had, one way or another, sunk in graves out of history's sight, Cremisia reinherited the Palazzo in Corvenna.

By that time, Thesaio having himself died from some plague, Loro and she were wed. Loro took her name, a reverse of custom unheard of and barely managed. Until his demise, and, finally, in her hundredth year, Cremisia's own, they resided at the palace. And, it seemed, as Anceto had described, on nights of the near-full moon, they did so still.

Loro—who but he—glanced at me only, nodding politely, as though to a known and trusted acquaintance, always acceptable, if seldom a visitor. But she held my gaze, and it was impossible to look away. There was nothing flirtatious about her. It was a kind and affectionate air she had, it seemed, for me. I was a distant cousin, perhaps, largely unknown, but familial none the less.

I did not, I swear to this, imagine such a welcome. Doubtless, it was how she would seem to very many, who found themselves able to behold her. She was patient with the living.

Then she spoke. To begin with, I think it was the Italian of the Renascence. Soon—I have no idea how—gradually her words altered to an English I assimilated at once, as most speech eventually, if unconsciously, must have done, when I watched the pictured scenes.

"Be seated, good friend. Will you try some wine?"

How in the world could I sit upon this uncertain couch, or drink the wine of ghosts? Or was *I* the ghost—for them, being not yet born?

"Yes, yes, thank you, Madonna. Gladly. You are generous."

And I sat, quite securely. And she it was who brought the cup to me, ready-filled. It was Venetian glass, the palest green, like fresh cucumber altered to crystal. The wine was the shade of a noble sherry, and—when I tried it, expecting anything— empty air, *poison*—of a pleasing mellow taste.

It eased me too.

She took a glass also to her husband. She did not drink. She said, "So you know of the riddle I coined to trap my oppressor?"

What could I say. "Yes, Madonna."

(I am always reminded that the old Italian honorific *Madonna*, means not only 'my Lady' but also the Virgin Maria. The discrepancy, with Cremisia, was less.)

"Then," she said, "Signore, shall I reveal the answer? Or have you already guessed it?"

I took too much of the wine. I coughed.

The beautiful dwarf spoke his baritone from the chair:

"That vintage always catches me just the same, Signore, at the first glass." But the silken dog had opened its elegant mouth and I could see it laughed at me, if not churlishly. Under Loro's chair was too another such dog, this one stretched out and dreaming, if ghosts can dream. Momentarily I fretted as to where the third hound was, but soon enough it sprang in through the open moonless window, and dropped from its mouth, at Cremisia's red-slippered feet, neither a dead shrew nor a mangled rabbit, but a single unspoilt spray of jasmine, white as the sinking stars. Which she lifted, and smoothing the canine head, put into her hair.

Ah, but I was happy in that room with them. If I could have remained, or some next time gone back—but plainly even the least sensible supernatural laws of this world would never allow that. Cautiously I sipped my wine.

"Madonna, *Sua Excellenza,* merely to sit with you—I am privileged. Yes, if you will, explain the riddle. I don't understand it. I never have."

Now she laughed. Her laugh was music. And he smiled at me. "Some," he said, "make out they do. Few have ever had the proper answer."

"Which is very simple," Cremisia said. "So simple one can miss it, like the darkened coin left in the sunflower's heart in the old story."

Beyond the window I saw then, suddenly, the very last cloud-veil of the moon slipping into the darkened city.

In my hand the glass was cold.

"What is redder than blood," said Cremisia Ranaldi. "Nothing is redder than blood. Nothing at all. *Proprio niente. Nihil.* The answer therefore is: Nothing."

A great bell had struck. Deafened by it I sat. "But Madonna—"

"Nothing, Signore, is *redder* than blood. Yet, if the answer *is* Nothing, then what does Nothing signify?"

She waited. I set down the glass, afraid I should drop it, ghost-crystal or not. I said, "Nothing is—the lack of anything—No Thing—the absence of *all*—"

Cremisia said, "No, Signore. In this we have misunderstood. Nothing is the absence of *anything we may understand*. It is invisible in this world, has no presence or substance, neither sight nor sound, touch nor taste, not even, usually, any feeling of itself. It is the vast and unknowable sea that rings us round and lies beyond the physical reality of life, and out of which fly amazements and miracles unforetold. It is what awaits us, just as it is the fount from which we sprang. And being Nothing, we cannot here remember it, just as, here, we fear to enter it again. It is Un-ness, it is Death, it is the empty and unknowable ending. And yet, and yet, in fact it is only perceived in this way since we have here no words for it, no channels of our clever physical minds able to capture and convey its being, either to others or ourselves. It is—here—so *unlike* here, and what we too *are when* here, that we find no method to visualize or reclaim it. Or—if some great poet or mystic somewhat may, he, being lost for words, can only resort to symbols, architypes most others will dismiss. Only before, or after life, do we know it. When we are one with it, with Nothing, nothing at all, *Nihil.* Only then."

I was glad I had put down rather than dropped the goblet. I said, stammering a little, "Your words, Madonna, fill me with terror and depression."

"Never let them," she said. "If they do, you have not grasped what I say. Nothing is *Everything* that is not in the world; nor ever could be. *Nothing* is the name that has been given to the Truth."

Another silence then. My teeth chattered. I was so cold. We hold to our flimsy hopes and beliefs, our prayers—our

dreams—To have one of the dead inform me that only anni-
hilation waited—

She shook her head. The pearls and jets made music with
the jasmine in her hair.

"No, no," she gently said. (She had read my thoughts?)
"Ah, Loro, my darling, shall we show him? It is partly possible
to us," she said, "as now we are."

And he nodded. And my heart, I believe, stopped—and
then—before I could protest or run away, the room turned
to the color of blood, than which nothing was more red. And
in the vastness of its scarlet I was subsumed. Lost. Over.

I awoke in his arms: Anceto, strong as a lion, was carrying me
across the bridge on the canal.

Behind and around his head, the dawn singed the sky, not
red now—could ever anything be red again?—a sort of stony
blue.

"What—" I said—"why—"

"Fear nothing, Edmondo, I have you safe."

"Did I die?"

He smiled down at me, his expression just visible in the
gloaming. "No, Edmondo. You fainted, or you slept. Just inside the little side door the caretaker found you, and called
to me."

How had I got there? I seemed to have tramped the whole
of the Palazzo through. The dark had drowned me. But before
the dark—

Dully I said, "You waited all night."

"Hush," he said, "rest now. I have seen all this before, you
must remember. And you are my dear friend. We'll talk later,
at the inn."

Not meaning to, I drifted. From my mouth came a scatter
of dreamlike words. "You're too young, Anceto, but still like
the father I never had . . ."

"Rest then, my dear son," he answered.

And so I did.

We were at another inn, a little taverna at the core of three
twisted streets, with a distant architectural church—a view

only, high on a hill, as unrelated to us as the sky to a cave. I slept all that day, or I must have done, and in the evening we ate and drank in the usual nicely vine-hung yard. Moths came to our candles, then flew upward, more intent on the unguttering flame of a full moon.

"Tell me nothing," Anceto said. I had not uttered a revealing word. "Remember what I have told you of my cowardice and prudence."

"How do I seem, then?" I asked him, as midnight struck creakily and all round in seventy different voices, that night taking well over ten minutes to establish itself on all sides.

"A man worn to his bones. Yet—" Anceto paused—"as now and then also I have seen, uplifted. If so, I am glad for it. But you must reveal no word of why."

"I know the riddle's answer."

"Hush."

Stubbornly I added, "I saw her. Near as you."

"Of course you did. I never doubted you would."

"She is beautiful."

"Of course she is."

"The rest is madness."

He said, with playful sternness, "As your English Shakespeare has it, The *rest* is *silence*."

And then I laughed. It rang around the court, making one or two remaining drinkers glance up. But I was docile enough. They let us be.

And Anceto wagged his finger at me, then put the finger over his lips.

"You've been," I said, "the best guide and the most loyal friend to me. How, Anceto, can I repay you?"

"I know you have no money," he said, and grinned.

"Not much—but yet—"

"I will take nothing," he said. But then he leaned across, and in the muted moth-light of the candle, he kissed me on the mouth. It was the most decorous kiss, but nevertheless, a lover's.

After which, calmly and separately, we repaired to our cramped and rickety beds.

The next morning he was gone, but our lodging and supper, even my breakfast, had been paid for.

To this hour I am unsure if he was quite real, or also some form of physically perfect ghost. But God knows, I shall never forget him, Anceto. Never. Here . . . or anywhere.

Epilogus

Then what is the answer to the riddle? If it is Nothing, then what does *Nothing*, in this context, mean? How I wish I might tell you. But, evidently, I don't know. How can I *know*? What then, in the storm of Red, did I see? Or after the tempest altered—for alter it did—did I see *then*? Again, I wish I might tell you. How I wish I might. But I cannot, cannot remember. Only this can I relate.

Something there was. Something that apparently we call *Nothing*. I can neither speak of it nor remember it. Not a sight, not a sound do I retain. Although the ghosts of the Palazzo I summon, at any moment to my memory, my voice and pen, and present them to you. But that second sequence—or that glorious abyss beyond my conscious awareness—*that* I can never call back, for either myself or any of us. Why should you therefore credit that eccentric Edmund Sanger, son of the illustrious actor-architect Joseph William, ever received a vision of utter and pristine Truth he cannot, even in a dream, recapture? Why indeed.

All I can offer is this (without a single remembrance or image, or even incoherent wisp of correspondence), even so I *knew*, in those eradicated moments, and I know still: That there, *there* outside the gates of any physical state or world we may inhabit, something is—which, being so unlike, so beautiful and radiant and eternal—can never be transported into living life, not even by a word. Brighter than fires, more soft than fur, better than the best—nameless, non-communicable, absolute. And, without a bookmark in our hearts or brains to enable us to find it while here, yet *there—there* it nevertheless is, and will be ever. There is nothing to fear or to regret. There is no end. Only always a Beginning—that not even the most lucid scripture, or most transcendent art (even that of the Scarlet Lily, Cremisia Ranaldi) can recreate. We touch upon it, yes, I believe we do, in our greatest poets (which is why, if only as a ghost, she could undo the door). In the best of love or joy, that too—but all of this is a shadow. The shadow of the Nothing which is Everything.

Years after, in a little French town, an elderly lady spoke to me of this, which she had come across in my more obscure writing. I can't now, after so many years, recollect exactly how we got to it. But I tried to tell her—untellably, as I do you. And finally I left off, apologizing. "I wish," I said, "I might show you what I saw. For that matter, I wish I might again show it to myself."

She said, "Oh, but, though you cannot, nor can I understand it, even so, now we meet, I see it."

"How?" I whispered.

"Ah, mon cher monsieur," she answered. "I see it in your eyes."

The author is indebted for the Latin translation to Aline Lonneville.

Snow-Drop

CRISTENA'S HUSBAND LEFT her after a month of marriage, and went away on business to a distant country. She had known, when she married him, that this would be the arrangement, that she would frequently be alone. Her function was to live in the handsome house above the lake, like the blue center of a clockwork eye. The house cleaned and scented itself, cooked meals to order from the groceries which were delivered twice a week, did the laundry, even kept the sweep of garden, pruning the trees, digging the earth and planting, and offering up cut irises and denim roses to match with Cristena's bright blue clothes. Cristena, her blond hair wound about her head, was a physically lazy, mentally active woman. She liked to read, watch television, listen to music, and sometimes she would write a slim wild novel without any effort, which would sell well for a year or two, and then slip from view. The house suited her ideally. She had always wanted such a house, and such a life. Even the long absences of her husband were actually perfect. They left her time for herself, and would give every homecoming excitement, every leave-taking the drama of high romance.

However.

Before he had married Cristena, her husband had lived with another woman, in the house. This woman, some years his senior, had been dark, passionate, and energetically creative, an artist. She had died alone in the house, under rather dubious circumstances of wine and pills. She left behind no trace of her being, for the house had fastidiously washed and redecorated itself after the funeral, and given her clothes and treasures to charities. All that remained were some small water-color paintings, very graceful and fine, and in fact worth quite an amount of money, for the artist had been highly esteemed. These paintings were to be found in every room, along every corridor. The subject was virtually the same in each of them. It was a young girl, about fourteen years of age. She was slender and eloquent, sometimes depicted sitting, and sometimes standing, often in an expanse of pure snow. Her skin was white as that snow, and her long smooth hair was black as wood. She had a pale red mouth.

At first Cristena barely noticed the paintings. They did not interest her very much—she preferred landscapes—and besides were all so alike that it seemed if you had looked at one you need never look at any of the others.

As the summer days passed, though, the lake darkened and the birches in the garden turned mellow, the coldness of the pictures, like little oblongs of winter brought indoors, began to annoy Cristena. They ached at the edge of her eyes, distracting her at her books and her Shostakovich. In the roomy passageways, they went by like white sentinels. They reflected in mirrors, duplicating themselves. They were even in the bedroom. Cristena removed them from there and hung instead two warm violet prints of hills.

The initial homecoming of Cristena's husband was not so astonishing as she had thought it would be.

He brought her a sapphire ring, which was very nice, although it did not quite fit, but rather than ardent he was tired and irascible. He spoke of business throughout their candlelit dinner. In bed, he kissed her, turned away and fell unconscious. He snored. Cristena found she could not sleep. At last, near morning, when she had managed to doze, her husband woke her up with insistent lasciviousness. He made love to her in a sort of drunken somnambulism, and while he did not hurt or distress her, he gave her no pleasure either. He fell asleep again on her breast, and she almost smothered until eventually she had prized herself out from under him. She achieved an hour's slumber on the brink of the mattress, where his bulk had gradually pushed her, for he too, apparently, was more used to sleeping alone.

At breakfast, a very ornate and sparkling one she had arranged for the house to prepare, Cristena's husband read papers and documents and made verbal notes on his pocket recorder.

Finally he looked up.

"Where are her paintings from the bedroom?"

"Oh, I didn't think you'd seen . . . I took them down. The prints are much more in keeping with the colors of the room."

"Maybe, but not a hundredth the value. She was famous, you know."

It was only in this way that he ever referred to his previous liaison, her fame. He did not like to discuss her as a person.

"Well, if you want," said Cristena, "I can put them back. Personally—"

"Yes, I'd prefer that."

Irritated, Cristena said, to irk him in turn, "They're all the same, aren't they. That girl. Self-portraits?"

Her husband grunted. "She wanted children," he said.

"You mean it's the fantasy portrait of a daughter she couldn't have?"

He frowned and did not reply.

He was quite ugly in the morning, Cristena thought, and he had put on weight which did not suit him.

She took the two pictures of the artist's unborn daughter out of the house storage, and set them back on the bedroom wall. Now she stared at them a long time. They had assumed a macabre importance, expressions of barren desire. No wonder they were capable of projecting such a horrid animation of their own.

That night Cristena wore her hair loose and a low-necked dress of midnight blue. Her husband seemed bemused, but nevertheless he made love to her on the rug before the fire, knocking over a brandy glass in the process, which the following day the house would have to clean with an odorless acid preparation. Cristena found after all she was not going to enjoy this sexual union any more than the first. In contempt, she pretended, and her husband floundered into a relieved climax. In bed they both swallowed sleeping capsules. Cristena woke at dawn with the white pictures shining above her head like two slices of ice, and all the covers pulled off her, leaving her peculiarly vulnerable in the draughtless room.

*   *   *

Cristena's husband only spent ten days at the house, before he had to leave the country again. On the afternoon of his departure Cristena did indeed weep. They were tears of nervous thankfulness. But he was enraged by the scene, shouting that he did not want a clinging vine. He would be gone five months.

In the weeks which followed, winter came. The garden and the landscape, the road which led to the city, and up which the delivery vehicle still beat its way on heated runners, turned snow white. The lake froze to a silver tray. The daylight shrank, and by night the sky flickered with luminescent coils of phantom hair.

The house was of a faultless temperature, airy and bright, all its mechanisms performing helpfully. But Cristena began to feel threatened. She was anxious, and found it difficult, for the first time in her life, to concentrate on her books and music. A novel she had begun grew sluggish and contrived, and she left it.

She tried not to look at the pictures of the artist's unborn child, but they glowed on the walls and in the mirrors. A snow girl, nivea skin and ebony tresses and red water-ice mouth. As Cristena sat in the rooms of the house, she felt the pictures watching her, and when she walked through the corridors, the pictures blinked past like eyes.

Cristena removed the two pictures from the bedroom again, and the larger picture from her bathroom, and all the pictures from the living room. She put them into the house storage and ordered other pictures from a catalog, and hung up those.

But now it seemed to be too late. The artist's paintings had left an imprint on the atmosphere of the rooms where they had hung, and in the places where they hung still they seemed to have amassed a greater strength.

The winter light too, which shone in penetratingly through all the clear windows, left drops of whiteness as if fresh watercolors depended there.

There was nobody to talk to. This had never before mattered.

Cristena took down all the paintings, every one, and put

them into the storage. The blank marks on the walls where they had been glimmered like candles.

Cristena kept the blinds lowered and the curtains drawn and the lights burned day and night, and television fluttered and sang in every space. She had to be stern with herself, as she went along the passageways.

On the morning that it happened, Cristena was making up in her dressing room.

She had decided to travel to the city in an automatic hire car, to shop, eat her lunch in a restaurant, visit the theater. The idea of going among people nearly frightened her, she had been alone so long, but also she was exhilarated, and she had poured a little vodka into her tea.

The dressing room was very attractive to Cristena. It was hyacinth with accents of gold. In the tall cupboards hung elegant dresses her husband had bought her, and in the drawers, folded among perfumes, undergarments of bones and lace, stockings embroidered with flowers, erotic items that once she had put on eagerly to please him, when he had been her lover. Cristena ignored these articles, as she ignored the jewels her husband had given her, especially the sapphire ring which was too small, and so almost insulting.

She dressed her face carefully, and it was as she was applying her dark blue mascara that she glimpsed behind her—something. Something white and slim and girl-shaped, standing between the mirror and the wall, there, on the carpet, visible.

Cristena lowered the mascara with a painful slowness. She glared into the mirror through a blue hedge.

The snow girl was about three meters away, over Cristena's shoulder. She was quite distinct. She wore the same white, seamless, vaguely form-fitting garment she wore in the paintings, and her snowy skin that matched it, and the long glissade of wood-black hair. Her lips were red.

Cristena screamed. She jumped up and spun around.

The room was empty of the artist's unborn child. Only a white gown gleamed from a half open door, with a mass of dark shadow above and a transparent scarlet rose sewn on its sleeve.

Swinging sharply back, Cristena took up a steel ornament and smashed the mirror. Fragments of glass tore off and flew about the room. The house would clear it all up.

Cristena pulled the white dress off its peg and crumpled it into the disposal shoot. It was carried away with a disapproving hiss.

She was trembling but angry. She realized the anger had lain dormant in her and now it sought release. She ran out of the dressing room, through the bedroom, along the passage and down the stairs. All the way, flashing razor glimpses, like a migraine attack, assailed her eyes; the spots where the pictures had hung of the artist's daughter.

When she reached the living room, Cristena pressed the button and the blinds flew up with the noise of furious wings.

Outside was the unearthly snow, and there in the garden under the birches stood the snow child, the dark of a pine her hair, a single red berry her mouth.

At that moment the door called tunefully.

Confused, Cristena flung up her head. There was no delivery today.

"What is it?"

"A man is at the door. He carries no weapons."

Cristena drifted in a trance into the hall. She signaled the door to open. Beyond the security bar stood a large and powerful young man, who beamed at her. He was incredibly ordinary, and real. Cristena had no notion as to who he was, or what he was doing there, but her awareness fixed on him voraciously. He was here for a purpose: Hers.

"Lady," he said directly, "I'm a photo-hunter. Look at this."

And into the hallway over the bar leaped a wolf, which stood looking at her with its beautiful eyes. It was a holostet the young man had constructed from photographs taken in the woods the far side of the lake, so he explained. It could be hers for a reasonable sum. For a fraction extra, it could be fixed to run about the house and howl.

"I can't buy the wolf," said Cristena. The young man looked sorry. "But come in. There's something you can do."

After she had plied him with alcohol, and resisted his amorous advances, which plainly were what he supposed she

wanted, Cristena, lit by vodka and hot tea, had him pile up on
the lawn the many water-colors of the artist's daughter. The
house was programmed not to harm its own possessions, but
he, with a large gardening implement, smashed these pictures
and mashed them. After which, together, they burned them
all, and the yellow flames rose glamorously up into the winter
sky. When it was done, not a crumb remained of the snow
child, not a flake or shard. The young photo-hunter dug the
snow over the black wound of the fire. Cristena gave him
some money, and he went whistling away along the road, with
his holostetic wolf leaping about him.

And that was the end of it. The end.

And that night, Cristena's husband called from a sky-
scraping mansion countless miles off, having clinched some
deal. He was a little drunk, too.

"I've destroyed them," said Cristena. "All of them."

"Good. All what?"

"The icons of her bloody child that she never had."

"What icons?"

Cristena shrieked into the phone: "The ice maiden. *Her
pictures*. I burned them."

Cristena's husband was in the wrong place to make a noisy
fuss. He told her she had lost him thousands of international
dollars. Cristena laughed. He should have, she said, all the
royalties of her next novel.

When he had rung off, she put on a disk of Shostakovich and
filled the house with it. She let the windows blaze toward the
lake. She sat late working out a scenario for the house to redec-
orate itself again, in saffron and blue. All the furniture should
be moved around, and she would buy new drapes in the city.
When her husband returned, he would wonder where he was.

In two weeks the house was changed to a gas flame, azure and
yellow. There were new pictures and prints in all the corridors
and rooms. Cristena had spent two or three days in the city,
choosing blueberry and primrose curtains. The contact with
people, of whom the photo-hunter had been the herald, hard-
ened and revived her. At length she was ready to withdraw
again into her mental vase of music, books and television.

Outside, the world stayed obdurately white, the lake shiny black beneath its ice. Cristena had had the berries stripped off all the bushes.

Cristena had almost finished her novel, the first part of which she had limpidly and easily rewritten. She sat working on the couch she had had reupholstered, her back supported by flaxen cushions. The television fluted faintly in the corner of the room. Something about the picture summoned Cristena's attention, and she looked up. The snow had filled the screen. It was utterly white. Cristena frowned. She was about to press the adjustment control when the whiteness opened out into a petal, and so into a single flower, and then the camera sprang back and there was a girl dressed in white and holding the white flower. She bowed low, and her long black hair, smooth as poured ink, fell forward to the ground. Cristena sat bolt upright, and her writing smacked on the carpet. Without knowing what she did, she turned up the volume.

"And here is Snow-Drop," said the voice of the television, "one of the stars of the circus."

The girl wore a short white costume and white tights that covered her from neck to toe to wrist, but described every inch of her young pliancy. The whiteness was coruscated by spangles. When she sprang suddenly over in a somersault, she glittered like a firework, and her hair sprayed out in a fantastic smoke.

Seven small figures ran across the space, which seemed to be that of a large arena. They wore red and black. Cristena thought they were children, but their thick dark hair, muscular faces and forearms, enlightened her. They were dwarfs. They formed a pyramid and tumbled down, rolling expertly to the white satin feet of the girl called Snow-Drop. She then arched over backward, making a hoop, and they trotted in a train under her. Next they lifted her up high and raced along carrying her, in the way ants carry a leaf.

There was a familial resemblance. Cristena wondered if Snow-Drop was related to the dwarfs. Although perfectly proportioned, she was very slight and petite. She looked about fourteen years old.

The dwarfs set Snow-Drop down. She coiled herself up into a cross-legged snake, while her seven companions bounced into position about her. In tableau, the dwarfs grinned. They had poised, good-looking faces, and seemed quite composed and happy with their lot. The girl also smiled.

This image was replaced by a garish sign, the fiery neon of the circus, which was performing in the city. Snow-Drop and the dwarfs were to be seen every night.

The television reverted to a rather sedentary play. Cristena switched it off.

She walked uneasily about the room. She felt a strange excited dread. For it was as if she herself had conjured up Snow-Drop in the mirror of the television. As if, by breaking and burning Snow-Drop's image, she, Cristena, who had never wanted children, had given Snow-Drop life. For Snow-Drop was the artist's unborn daughter, correct in each detail, even to her pale red mouth.

Every evening, for several nights, the same advertisement came on the television, and Cristena watched it. Sometimes other circus acts were shown as well, a man who swallowed clocks, a woman who danced extravagantly on the head of a pole. But Snow-Drop was always there, bowing, somersaulting, making herself into an arch, carried by the ant-like dwarfs, sitting in their midst. Beyond her name, which was probably any way false, no information was given.

It seemed to Cristena that a net had been cast for her and that slowly she was being pulled in to a snowy shore. It was useless to dissemble. She knew she would eventually go to the city, to the circus. There was even a vague fear that if she delayed too long, the circus might have moved on, and she would have missed it. At last this fear got the better of her.

An automatic hire car drove her along the frozen road, back into the icicled city, and delivered her at the entrance of the theater where the circus was resident.

Cristena took a gilded seat at the front of the auditorium. She was nervous, and as the spangled performers swung or pirouetted or leaped past, she imagined they stared recognizingly into her face with eyes as cruel as knives.

When the moment came for Snow-Drop's act with the seven dwarfs, Cristena was trembling, and she took some large gulps from a golden flask.

The dwarfs came springing out like seven sable cats. Snow-Drop appeared ethereally, wafted down on wires from the roof of the stage. She was dressed like a princess, in a long alabaster gown and diamante tiara. But she peeled off the dress and wires, to reveal her sequined second skin, and turned a series of cartwheels. At each revolution she went by one of the dwarfs, who in turn began to cartwheel. The eight forms twirled about each other until Cristena was giddy and shut her eyes.

When she opened them again the dwarfs were busy raising a body mountain up which Snow-Drop walked, and next they became a body sea on which she swam.

The dwarfs made Snow-Drop the axis of every pattern. They were landscapes over which she traveled and buildings into which she went and from whose windows she looked out. By prancing off each other's shoulders, they made her seem to juggle them—the audience laughed and clapped—and at one point they became an animal, a dwarf for each leg and three dwarfs composing a body, head, and waving tail. Snow-Drop sat on its back and it cantered to and fro, at last rearing up and catapulting her away into a scintillant triple spin.

Unlike all the other acts, neither the dwarfs nor Snow-Drop seemed ever to glance into Cristena's face. As they went through their plasticene antics, their eyes were fixed wide and brilliant and far away.

Cristena's nervousness gradually left her. She observed the acrobats with condescending interest. She began to want them to notice her. She wanted beautiful Snow-Drop, white and black and red, to look at her, to *know* her. It was not possible realization should be only on one side. It occurred to Cristena they were actually ignoring her, cutting her, but that of course was absurd.

Finally there was a *danse macabre*, during which three of the dwarfs stood on each other to fashion a tall man, with whom Snow-Drop waltzed. But Snow-Drop grew dizzy and fell down and died. The dwarfs bore her to the center of the

stage, where they described a funeral, and buried her in their
dark bodies. Then a spot-light sun shone on the mound, and
a white shoot pierced up through the earth of dwarfs. Snow-
Drop dived in graceful slow-motion up into the air and was
reborn like her name flower, to great applause.

As they bowed, Cristena stared at them, the seven handsome dwarfs and Snow-Drop. But their faces were like
enamel masks. When they darted off the stage, anger flushed
through Cristena, hotter than the vodka in her flask.

Soon after she was outside the theater, standing back
among some bare trees below the Stage Door, while across
the street, the hire car waited like an obedient ghost.

A group of other people had also gathered here, and a
number of children with autograph books. Artists emerged
and were beaming and gracious. Presently the dwarfs came
out all together in wonderful fake fur coats. They were jolly,
and teased the patrons and scared the children. In the street-
lamps their eyes were now wicked and wise. Long after they
had gone, when the autograph hunters had become impatient
and many drifted away, Snow-Drop emerged. Unlike the
dwarfs, she wore a skimpy black jacket and ankle boots. Her
hair was done in a long plait. She spoke to her admirers solemnly and signed their books quickly, like a thief. Cristena
watched, and wondered what she would do. But when Snow-
Drop's fans had melted away, she walked directly down
toward the trees. Cristena stepped out as if on cue.

"Hallo, how are you. Perhaps you remember me?"

Snow-Drop did not seem startled although she had halted
at once. In fact an immediate slyness was apparent, a vixenish
glaze of evaluation passing over her eyes. Then she smiled
without opening her mouth and shook her head.

"Your mother . . ." said Cristena. She added patronizingly,
"You would have been too young to recall."

"I'm older than I look," said Snow-Drop primly. Her voice
was flat and unpolished, and the statement offered its own
obscure meaning, redolent of something murky.

"Well, would you like to see the house?" said Cristena
boldly. She had planned nothing, but the words came as simply as in one of her novels.

"The house? Your house?"

"Yes, naturally mine. And we can have some wine, and perhaps dinner. The kitchen's fully automated."

"That would be nice," said Snow-Drop, in her cheap little voice. Only the under-pavement heating must have kept her slim legs from the cold in that short skirt and those unsuitable boots.

Cristena walked across the road, and Snow-Drop followed her neatly, docile. Under the lamps her face was just the face of the paintings, and her mouth had been lipsticked an even redder red.

There was no one left by the stage door, the street was empty, and Cristena did not think anyone had seen Snow-Drop come with her to the car. She was glad, for after all Snow-Drop was a little embarrassing. Yet, as the car drove them away into the countryside, Snow-Drop's awful loveliness filled the atmosphere like a low buzzing. Cristena felt the need to talk. She lied sumptuously.

"Your mother was so fond of you. I haven't seen her for so long."

Without protest or overt cunning, Snow-Drop announced, "I never knew my mother. I was brought up by the troupe."

"Are you close to them, the seven—"

"Oh, they don't like me," said Snow-Drop, reasonably.

The house glowed at them from across the lake, and when the car brought them to the door, extra lights flamed on in welcome. Cristena could see Snow-Drop was impressed. A nasty complacency had thinned her lips.

They went into the living room. Here, where the watercolors had hung in such abundance, Snow-Drop made a living sculpture. Cristena tensed for the house to respond in some way. But, when it did not, no poltergeist activity took place of any sort, she decided that she had already exorcized the architecture.

They drank a fresh yellow wine.

Cristena asked Snow-Drop questions about her life, and rather to her surprise Snow-Drop responded without either reticence or verbosity. She laid out events in bleak rows before Cristena. It was a sordid unjoyful existence which the Snow-Drop led, out of all keeping with her looks. And it had made her mean and ordinary in spite of herself. She had not ascended to tragedy or grotesqueness, but plummeted to the mealy-mouthed and the dull. Only glints of acquisitiveness distinguished her, and it was obvious she reckoned she would get, was getting, something out of Cristena. Otherwise she dwelled in the shadow of the circus and especially of the dwarfs. She was their slave, seeing to their laundry by hand, shopping for and cooking their meals on those occasions they demanded it. Cristena suspected that Snow-Drop was also their sexual toy. For that matter, almost anyone's, maybe. There was a metallic fragrance of willingness, which grew stronger as the wine left the decanter and filled instead their bodies.

"Offstage, do you always plait your hair?" asked Cristena.

"Shall I undo it?" asked Snow-Drop.

"Yes, why not? I've got a marvelous comb that perfumes the hair. We can go up. I'll show you my dresses. You might like to choose some. They'd be too big for you, but we can always have them re-tailored."

They went up the stair and along a passage where the artist's paintings had hung, and into Cristena's dressing room.

Cristena threw open doors.

"Look, that crimson silk would suit you. My husband bought it. I never wear red. And this black one with sparkles."

With a studied unselfconsciousness, Snow-Drop slipped off her tawdry skirt and top, and stood in faded under-things, dim pants and tights, and, since she did not wear a brassière, only a thin little cotton bodice to conceal her bosom. Her acrobat's body was perfect, firm slim muscle lightly padded by white satin, and the symmetrical rounded young breasts bobbing in their vest. She tried on the dresses greedily. Cristena pinched in material to show how well they would suit Snow-Drop once they had been altered.

From its case she brought the magic comb and switched it on. When it had heated up, she combed Snow-Drop's amazingly long tendrilly hair. A scent of warm roses, jasmine and cinnamon throbbed in the room. They drank more wine.

"There are some gorgeous underclothes too," said Cristena. "I never use them."

She opened the drawers, and let fall a shower of black and white silk corsets, black stockings sewn with orchids, garters of crow lace with silver buckles.

With no apparent modesty or reluctance, the Snow-Drop pulled off her drab tights and pants, and up over her delicate head in a whirlwind of hair went the inadequate bosom-bodice. She sat on a chair and drew the embroidered stockings along her dainty legs, and fixed on the garters. She flexed her thighs and her firm, curved stomach moved, and her breasts quivered like smooth white birds. Cristena assisted her into the black corset shot with ivory silk. She fitted it round the swaying stem of body and tilted into the bone cups the birds of the breasts, so the candy pink tip of a nipple rose just above each frill. Cristena laced up the corset severely. "You must wear it tight."

Snow-Drop posed before the mirror. She raised her arms artlessly, and the pink sweets rose further from their black froth containers. Between the silky limbs, under the corset's ribboned border, Snow-Drop's private hair, dark and thick like the fur of a cat, seemed the blackest thing in the room.

"That's very pretty," said Cristena.

She felt heavy, languid, tingling, mad. She put her hands around Snow-Drop's body and made a small adjustment to the corset top. Her fingers brushed an icing-sugar nipple. Snow-Drop giggled.

"Now, you mustn't be ticklish," said Cristena. She tried the nipple again.

Snow-Drop squirmed, pressing back against her.

In the mirror, Cristena saw, the beautiful doll with its bosom popping from the frills, its hands-span waist, and its naked lower limbs, wriggling. Snow-Drop's eyes were shut and her red lips parted.

Cristena pulled the girl backward against her body. She caressed her breasts, sought the V of coal-black fur. She watched in the mirror. Snow-Drop writhed. She parted her legs and thrust her buttocks into Cristena's belly. She uttered tiny shrill squeaks.

Fire engulfed Cristena. She pinioned Snow-Drop, rubbing, tickling, squeezing, choked by the perfume of roses and cinnamon, hair and skin, drunken and furious, and the girl was screaming, in the glass a demon of black and white and red.

Cristena felt the climax roll up between her thighs, turning her inner life, her soul, over and over in blind ecstasy, as Snow-Drop wailed in her grip and the room exploded.

When Cristena came to herself, Snow-Drop was sitting cross-legged on the floor. She sucked her thumb and played with the ribbons of the corset, like a spoiled child which knows it has been naughty, but that this will not matter.

Cristena told herself it would *not* matter, over and again, as she assisted the kitchen in the preparation of a lavish supper. Never in her life had she experienced such alarm. It was not shame, more terror. For Snow-Drop came of a dangerous, scurrilous race. Who knew now what she might do? For the moment she sat on the couch, still in the corset and still half nude, drinking wine and looking at the television, in whose speculative lens she had first appeared. Later it was possible she might be persuaded to go back to the city. But then again she might want to spend the night here. And after tonight, how many other nights? What payment would she exact, in emotion or hard cash? How luminous her eyes as she glanced about her at the furnishings of Cristena's husband's house.

Cristena put the last touches to the food and drink. Her hands were shaking, but she pulled herself together and made herself survey what she had done. It was a meal of red, white and black, although she doubted the Snow-Drop would take this in, let alone appreciate it. White soft rolls and creamy cheeses, slices of palest chicken in an almond sauce, caviar, fat grapes as black as agate, pomegranate seeds, burgundy apples whose crisp hearts were the shade of virgin ice. In the decanter now a rich ruby wine.

As she followed the service trolley into the living room, Cristena wished there had been someone to pray to. But there was not, she must deal with this herself.

"I hope you're hungry."

"Oh yes. I like my food," said the Snow-Drop, who had looked as if she lived on honey-dew.

She began to eat at once; alcohol and orgasm had evidently stimulated her appetite.

Cristena observed. She was prepared to say, if pressed, "No, I had dinner earlier. You have it all." But Snow-Drop, gobbling up everything in a prissy yet vulture-like way, did not bother with Cristena, did not seem to notice that her hostess ate nothing.

As more and more of the food and wine was consumed, Cristena's shaking increased. When Snow-Drop plucked up one of the gleaming red apples, Cristena flinched. Of all of the feast, she was afraid she had taken a chance with the apples.

Snow-Drop put the apple to her mouth and bit into it. Then, quite slowly, her jaw dropped. Cristena saw inside her mouth, to the piece of white and red apple lying on Snow-Drop's tongue. Snow-Drop turned to her. Snow-Drop looked mildly inquiring. "Mmr," she said. Then her eyes turned up in their sockets and she slid down the couch on to the carpet.

She lay there half an hour, motionless. Then there was a small spasm, which did not wake her. Crystal urine flowed out and wet the rug. A thread of scarlet slipped between Snow-Drop's lips. That was all. She was dead. She could not be anything else. Cristena had crushed twenty tasteless soluble sleeping capsules in the wine, and in the sauces, meat, fish, cheese, and fruit, had gone the odorless soft corrosive cleaning acids of the house, the unsmelling garden pesticides. She had burnished the apples with a vitriolic substance employed to polish the mirrors.

The house buried Snow-Drop's body without any difficulty in the garden. After the job had been done, the digger took up deep snow from the lawn and packed it in above the grave. But in any case that night new snow came down and covered everything.

If there were reports on the television of Snow-Drop's disappearance, Cristena, who studied the screen closely, did not see them.

Presumably no one knew where Snow-Drop had gone on

the night of her vanishment, and perhaps ultimately nobody cared. The seven dwarfs had not liked her and would probably find it challenging to locate and train up another beautiful lost child as their helpmeet and victim.

Cristena felt no compunction. She had had to protect herself. She settled down and completed her novel, then put it into the machine to be typed. By the time her husband returned to the house, the book would be in the hands of her publishers, and she could present him with the advance, which would humiliate him.

He came home some weeks early, when the snow was still down across the landscape. Calling her from the airport, he told her that he was bringing two of his business associates, and in the background she heard their hearty, stupid and inebriated voices. Cristena was not pleased, but she made believe she did not mind, sure he would bring the men to upset her and she could ruin his trick by seeming unconcerned.

She went about the house behind the automatic dusters. For months she had thought of it mostly as hers. She did not suppose he would like the new color scheme, and he was capable of having it changed. Cristena braced herself to be merry and careless.

The men arrived in the afternoon and came swaggering up to the house. Her husband was in the lead. He had put on yet more weight, and she had never seen him look so ugly, as if he had done it on purpose.

For an hour or so the male colleagues sprawled in the living room, eating things the kitchen prepared, and drinking beer. Cristena's husband had greeted her with affectionate uninterest, and now largely ignored her, but neither did he remark adversely on the redecoration. Indeed, he abruptly praised it. "The house is looking good. But wait until you see what I've brought for the garden." And somehow he made it obvious he had deliberately not brought a present for Cristena, who did not deserve one, but for the house.

They went outside, into the freezing twilit day.

With the help of the house porter, Cristena's husband trundled a large lamp-like structure into the garden, and set it up among the birch trees. He threw a switch and the lamp began softly to hum. From its bowl a yellow light streamed out and bathed the slope. It became warm. Strange scents shot from the ground, the trees. They were the smells of spring.

"The snow will be gone in minutes," said Cristena's husband. "The plants start coming up in half an hour. You can have a spring and summer garden in the middle of winter. Expensive, I'll admit, this sun-lamp, but wait till you see."

They waited, and they saw. And presently, after they had been splashed with snow and mud from the broiling, roiling earth, they retreated into the living room again, and looked on from there.

The garden was in flux, in tumult. Snow rushed in avalanches from the trees and along the ground. A kind of seismic activity thrust up huge tumuli, which seemed to boil. And on these peculiar black mounds, the porcelain flowers of spring bubbled through.

"You see?" asked Cristena's husband excitedly.

Cristena did. It was only a case of time, and already she was leaden and self-possessed.

Finally, after only twenty minutes, sabotaged by the sun-lamp, the lid of dense snow had melted off and the sides of the grave gave way. The upheaval in the earth pushed from below, and the Snow-Drop came out once more from the dark.

The cryogenic cold had preserved her flawlessly. The pressure on her spine made her sit slowly up in the grave to the astonished wonder of the three gaping men. And she was as ever white as snow, black as wood, and her pale red mouth opened and the bit of apple, also exactly preserved, fell out. And so she sat there exquisitely, with her lips parted and her eyes closed, dead as a door-nail, until the men turned to Cristena with their questions.

Magpied

(Translated from the Germanic-Alurguric
Poem of the Same Name)

His clothes were those of the magpie—
Black and white.
He entered the town with the brown sky
Of first night.

The traveler, in garments of white and black, enters the elegant and stone-built town at evening, but discovers the streets are full of rowdy youths and children, running and shrieking, drinking alcohol copiously, and doing battle with each other. Unable to pass through the pack, and sometimes receiving blows, he stands staring:

Like casques and masks, lacking all mind,
Their faces.
So much red-pride-flushed and drunk-gushed blind.
No traces

Were there, of care, or sanity,
Living shells—
Unlike births of Man, humanity;
These—From hells.

A man then rushes out of a house, and drags the traveler back inside with him, locking the door once they are within. He warns the traveler that these young persons rule the town after sunset, breaking into stores for purposes of robbery, hunting for stray older people in order to attack them; vomiting on the roadway:

You, stranger, such danger were in
On the street,
The hordes of these young—you among—spin
And retreat!

Beware of their arrogant slights,
Dirty words,
Their scuffles, each trick, broadcast sick, fights,
Scattered turds.

The traveler remains that night in the comparative safety of the man's house, whose windows—as are all those in the town—are shuttered up after dark.

Sleep though is constantly disturbed by the screams and yowls of the young outside. And once some of the creatures get up on the roof, hurling first stones, then feces down the chimney—a regular urban occurrence, his host assures the traveler.

The next morning:

When pale the sail of the dawn rose,
Fair and gold,
They broke the first fast, tumult passed; close
The host told,

In low tones, slow, how the anthem
To loved boys
And girls—as if royal—did so spoil them
They to noise

Went, vile deeds, while—in enough time—
They ruled all,
And nightmared each night, till new light climb
The day's wall.

By day the young, it seems, sleep off their excesses in various purloined roosts. None go home, for which their former parents and guardians are very grateful. A modicum of business and normal life resumes in the town daily, but interrupted always by the necessity of cleaning the streets and byways of the stinking mess in which the town's children nightly have left them.

At the traveler's request, his host then takes him to the house of the Mayor. This fellow, to begin with, makes excuses, but in the end breaks down and weeps. Hundreds of adults gather, also in tears. From adoring them the townsfolk have come to hate, loathe, dread, and be terrified of their young. They have been driven half mad and have no idea any more what to do.

The traveler then, flexing the snow and ebony magpie wings of his sleeves, makes the Mayor and the townspeople an offer.

He can play upon a magical pipe and:

> *This reed with speed, such is its sway,*
> *Will subdue,*
> *And mesh in a net like a debt they*
> *That harm you.*

> *To wit, each chit and child uncouth,*
> *Snared in steel,*
> *And locked as in jail, each most bale youth,*
> *Till earth reel.*

For some subsequent hours the town debates with itself a dilemma many parents must perhaps, now and then, acknowledge, whether they wish their offspring good or ill—or elsewhere entirely, and forever.

But eventually the sun tilts toward the west, the sky flames, and bothering sounds once more start to filter up from round about, reminiscent of wild beasts waking. Although it is a fact *no* beast, however maddened or savage, can approach—let alone surpass—the sometime evils of mankind.

Then the townsfolk hurry to the magpie traveler and entreat him, giving over everything into his hands—before once again dashing into their homes, putting the boards and shutters up at their windows, and bolting fast their doors.

Left alone upon the thoroughfare the piper, standing then

in the evening's final rays, seems not quite as he has been. He
is taller, perhaps, and his face less evident, and his garments
both blacker and more white, while in his hand, the pipe he
has spoken of gleams with a thin and silvery sheen, though it
was surely only of wood, and nothing at all special in its looks:

> *Then lout and loutess, ever quick,*
> *In a crowd,*
> *Come armed with their flasks and dark tasks sick,*
> *Laughing loud.*

Nevertheless, immediately, before even the road is properly filled up by the horde, a peculiar music commences:

> *So soft that often, sure, none hears,*
> *Faint as sighs,*
> *Yet thundered like drums, still it comes; ears*
> *Burn—and eyes.*

> *Each walk all talk has lost; all sound*
> *Now quite done.*
> *A massive full tide, vast miles wide, ground*
> *And air—one.*

Those that squint through shutter-cracks or keyholes *hear
and see* a miraculous gleaming, which accumulates. And they
see, too, how the demonic young are instantly snared inside
it—as promised—and made and *kept* dumb. There they stand,
unvocal and motionless, unprotesting, gazing, and gaping like
things mesmerized by the glare of a colossal snake, or some
unthinkable sorcerous spell, which supposedly it *is*.

And when the magpie traveler, the piper piping on, moves
off and up the street, the horde parts to let him by, as never
would they, or have they for years, any creature other than
themselves. And when he *has* passed by, stupefied as som-
nambulists, they troop after him. They do not speak or call,
they do not screech or fight or throw up their drink. There is
no upheaval. Only the flagons and bottles fall from their
hands and bleed stolen liquor on the lane.

So, as the shadings of night begin to seal the avenues, the town's children ebb away after the piper, away through the town and out of it, up into the high hills beyond:

> The skies, their size with darkness lave,
> Fill the jar
> Of town, closing black, front to back, save
> Just one star.

> Void is all this, and no last noise,
> Single form,
> No roaring girls reign, no profane boys.
> Speechless storm.

The troublesome young are never seen again. Never heard of. They have vanished, like dried rain, or blown dust. Not even a chip of bone, not a footprint, to mark their passing, or their *being*. Only the dropped flasks for a while spilling wine.

Perhaps there are maybe one, or three, nine or thirteen children left, sons, daughters. But these are those that never went out to join the nasty revels. *These* would drink socially among their own families, indoors, and sing there, or read, or discuss proper matters, properly; unusual children old beyond their years and having, perhaps, parents more than usually lovable.

After the filthy sea of the miscreants is gone, these few thirteen or so children and young people are respected and reverenced in lieu of the rest. They are held up as examples, and accept this modestly, and kindly.

As for any of the adults who thereafter pine again to produce offspring, they guard sternly against the desire, saying it is a brutish one, and they are not "mere" animals, and will resist. Which they do. Instead they breed and adopt intelligent and pretty rats, whose playfulness, geniality, and warm fur entirely satisfy any parental urge:

> With red and bred black coats, or white,
> They give joy,
> And yearning hearts fill through furred skill, bright
> Rat-girl, —boy.

As for the Magpie, the traveler, the piper, he too is never heard nor seen there again. Except in legend, or the mind's eye. Yet. . . .

> *Well hid; where did he send clod, bitch,*
> *To their doom?*
> *To some cliffs high brink? The sea's sink? Which*
> *Unworld tomb?*

> *Or to a new world, tolerant*
> *Of vile youth.*
> *To hearts, much too wise more to prize rant—*
> *Than love truth.*

> *For where—foul, fair—is childhood lured,*
> *By what?—Fuss?*
> *Or pipe's shadow sob, perhaps obscured:*
> *Jealous, us?*

Centuries after, it seems, when taxed by other communities on the disappearance of its children, the town lied, and blamed an itinerant, magpied piper, who—they said—had spirited the perfect youth of the place away, from sheer meanness.

But it is a fact, they still love their rats the best.

She Sleeps in a Tower

THROUGH THE DARK wood, the man rides on his horse. Birds sing sometimes in the heavy boughs, among the brackish leaves, but he is not looking out for birds. Nor for hares, though once a pale one ran across his path.

Then, he reaches the clearing. It is as they had described it. The fallen tree and beyond, the stone sundial, and there the ruined garden, in which still the tall and somber roses grow; and from which they have mounted up into the trees. Up the walls of the towers the roses have risen also, among the black-green ivy. Roses with terrible thorns.

And presently, the old woman, the hag, comes creeping out in her gray old mantle.

She bows low. "Good day, sir prince. Do you know where it is you've come to?"

"The tower," he says, the man on the horse.

"And do you know the story?"

Excited, the man twitches in the saddle.

"Tell me, old dame."

"A young girl, little more than a child. A princess. Bewitched. She lies in the tower, sleeping a sleep that may not be broken—save by her true prince."

"I'll wake her," says the man. He swings from the horse. "If she's *young*, and beautiful."

"Oh yes. There is the way then. Through that door. You must cut your path with your knife."

As he passes her, the man puts a silver coin into the old woman's hand. It is the usual amount.

Sex isn't for women. I always knew. My mother told me first. No, sex is for men. But women are the vessels.

You have to survive. God says you must, and then God tests you by making it very hard.

My father used to beat my mother, she was always black and blue, and sometimes he'd lay into me, but never so much. My uncle, my father's brother, used to protect me. "Get behind me," he'd say. Or, "Run to the well-house. I'll tell him you've gone into the wood."

When I was ten, and in the well-house, a year or so after my mother had died, my uncle came and sat beside me.

He told me I was a pretty girl and he played with my hair. When he put his hand on the little mound of my coming breast, I knew at once what he wanted and what would happen ... and I knew it was only what must always happen.

So when he suggested it, I lay down, and first he put his finger inside me, and then he put his penis in. It was agonizing, but I didn't cry, and he said afterward I was his special little girl and he'd never let any harm come to me.

He did protect me, too, from my father. But one day my father broke his leg, and it went bad and he died. I was nearly thirteen by then, and my uncle was losing interest in me, so he married me to a rich man's son, but the son wasn't right in the head, so no questions were asked.

That was how I came to live in the grand house with the three towers, which belonged to my husband.

My husband, who was a booby, was also hearty in bed, and very big, so I was glad I had already been with my uncle.

Inside a few months I was in the family way, and when I gave birth to a daughter, the rich man, my husband's father, cast us off, saying I was a slut and worthless. My husband, though a fool, would often beat me as my father had. However, because he had no mind, I could now and then outwit him and keep the baby safe.

In the next two years I had another two, both girls. By then the house was going to wrack and ruin, the roof leaking and ivy growing in through the walls. Great stones had fallen out, and all the servants had gone away, but for one old woman. She hated me, and usually tried to poison me. In the end, she made a mistake, and poisoned my moron husband instead. Then she ran off, and I was all alone with my three little girls.

I lived as best I could, but I found the only way I could pay for anything was by opening my legs. And so I did. A great many men had me, and every year I grew thinner and more wrinkled, and my hair turned gray and was like straw.

But my little girls were bonny. They were dressed only in rags, but their hair shone like copper and their skins were fresh and white as milk.

One night there was a storm, the rain rushed and split the leaves and in the house it rained too, and up in the three old towers the rats rattled in the leaves and thorns that had broken through the walls.

A stranger came knocking near midnight. When I let him in, he stood before the poor fire and said, "I'd heard there was a woman here served men. But you're an old crone. Where is she?" I said, "I fear she's gone away, sir." Just then my eldest daughter, ten years of age, came into the hall. She had been out gathering sticks to dry for the fire, and rain hung like crystals in her hair. "What's this?" said the man. "This is nice. I'll take her."

My first thought was No. Most mothers would think this, although it wasn't wise. But then he took out a silver piece and put it on the table. "I'll give you that for a go with her. But I like it a particular way."

What he wanted was that she go up and lie on a bed and pretend to be asleep. And then he would slip in and mount her, and at the end she would wake up and fling her arms around him and cry out he was her long lost love.

I could see she was listening carefully, so I took her aside. I told her it would hurt, but that she must pretend to be happy, and praise him. She was always a good girl.

When he came down he was sullen, but many of them are, after they've come, so I didn't worry, and indeed he let me keep the silver piece. My daughter had survived, though she bled for a week. She was cheerful, however, and boasted to the other girls that she'd been clever. Then they wanted to do it, too.

Well, their chance came for that, though not right away. A month later another man came knocking. It was afternoon, and he was pleasant enough. He said he'd heard a girl lay asleep who could be woken by a kiss—that was the story which had gone round apparently, rather like some of the old legends of the wood. And he said that the girl was in a tower.

So I asked my eldest if she'd go up into the west tower. She agreed, and she lay on the old bed there that had been my husband's mother's bed. She said, my girl, she was glad when the traveler came up, because, lying so quiet as she had to, the rats were skulking out. But he scattered them with his boot, and cut the thorns away from the bed—in a fortnight, they were back again.

It went on from there. And the story became a little more elaborate. And, as time went by, my other girls ... well, they know the way of it, how life is.

I come out to them in the garden, and I ask, do they know where they've come to. And they don't say, "The brothel," no, they play along, these kinky fellows. They say they've come to the tower. And some of them even say, "Is she sleeping here?" And, of course, she always is. Three shes. One in each tower. I go by how they talk of her youth, whether they want the youngest now, who's ten, or the middle girl of eleven, or my eldest, who's just twelve years.

We never have any trouble, and I've never been short-changed. Once even a rich man came and gave me a piece of gold. Perhaps he thought that was the fee, and I, obviously, didn't say No.

The man climbs up the stone stair of the east tower, his heart hammering. He lops the deadly murderous thorns with his long steel knife, but he breathes fast from hope, not exertion.

At last he reaches the wooden door, and thrusts it wide. A mad skitter of rats.

He takes the chamber in. Even in the summer light it is damp and chill, yet the roses have blossomed in the walls, and all about the mildewed bed. And on the bed she lies. Oh ... but she is lovely.

Slim as a wand, upon a cloud of dark red gleaming hair. Her skin like cream. Her hands crossed below her bosom— and oh, she is so young, only the faintest swelling there, like two sweet kisses.

She wears, she princess, a dress, of white silk, a little stained and worn, but this he does not see. In any case, she has been sleeping years—decades—perhaps a century, awaiting the true touch of love.

He goes to the bed and pulls away her skirt—easy, it might have been arranged for him to do it.

As he enters her pliant body he can barely wait. Such joy. She must feel it.

And she does. Her eyes fly open. She clasps him with her slender little girl arms.

And in her bird's voice, ten years of age, she softly cries: "At last! My prince!"

Awake

THAT FIRST NIGHT she woke up, which was the night after it had just *happened*, Roisa had been surprised. She'd been upset. She knew something had previously gone terribly wrong—exactly like when you have a bad dream, and you wake and can't remember what it was, only that it was awful, and the *feeling* is still there.

Now, of course, she was used to waking like this. She looked forward to it every night, near morning when she lay down to sleep again.

She sat up, threw back the light embroidered cover, and slipped from the bed. She slept clothed always, in the rose silk dress she had been wearing the evening *It* happened. Yet the silk was always fresh as if just laundered and pressed smooth by hot stones. She herself was also always fresh as if just bathed and scented, and her hair washed in the essences of flowers. She had long ago ceased to puzzle over that, though before That Night, keeping oneself so perfect had been a time-consuming daily task.

Roisa was sixteen. It had been her sixteenth birthday, the day it happened. Now she was still sixteen, but she had done and learned such a lot. She knew that the cleanness, and everything like that, was simply because of Great Magic.

By the bed was a little (magically) new-baked loaf, with apples and strawberries (magically) just picked, and a china pot of mint tea, (magically) brewed and poured.

Roisa made her nightly breakfast.

Then she left the attic room.

Outside, the narrow stairway was as it always was, dirty and cobwebbed, thick in dusts. But when the skirt of the silk dress brushed through the muck, nothing stuck to it.

She was used to that also.

As she was to the people standing about lower down, absolutely stone-still, as if playing statues in some game. There were the ladies-in-waiting first, the three who must have meant to follow her up to the attics that evening. Unlike Roisa, webs and dust *had* gathered on them, spoiling their gorgeous party clothes and jewelry, and carefully arranged hair. It was a shame. Roisa still felt sorry for them, if in rather a remote way.

The first time it had really shocked her. She had shouted at them, pulled at them, tried to make them move. Then worse than these, the other things—for example: the cat that had become a furry *toy* cat on the lowest landing, the bird that stood on the sill with its wings fanned out—never lowering them, never using them to fly off. And the young guardsman she had always liked, standing motionless, already dusty in his splendid uniform, his blue eyes wide open, not seeing her at all—

Worst of everything however, had been to find her parents, her funny pretty mother, her important grand father, sitting there like two waxworks, in the carven chairs from which they'd been watching the dancing in the Hall. The dancing from which Roisa had escaped, actually to meet secretly with the guardsman—but somehow she had missed him—and then—then, instead she had, also somehow, gone up into the attics of the palace . . .

Roisa had cried, when she woke that first night. She had felt no longer sixteen, but about six. She had put her head into the lap of her mother's dress, clutching her mother's body, which felt like a cold rock. Sobbing.

That was when *They* came.

They—the ones who told her. The ones with the magic.

When she got down to the palace hall tonight, Roisa did pause, only for a minute or so, to dust her mother.

She always did that. It seemed essential. Because of Roisa's attention, her mother (the Queen) still looked glamorous, her hair shining, and her necklaces.

The King Roisa didn't try to dust. She would never have

dared, because, in the past, he had seldom touched her, and then only with the firmest of hands, the coolest of kisses.

Beyond the hall lay the royal gardens, into which, her dusting done, Roisa ran.

Oh—it was full moon tonight.

Once wonderful scents had drifted here from lilies, and from arbors overgrown by jasmine. A gentle breeze blew this evening, and not one of the now-scentless flowers, not one of the tall, graceful trees, stirred. Not a single leaf moved, nor even the wind-chimes hung in the branches.

By the fountain—whose jetting water had stopped in a long, faintly luminous arch, like rippled glass—the two white doves sat, as they had done now for years. The doves didn't move. Nothing did. Not even the moon, which lived in the sky—at least, it never did when she saw it. Only the night wind, the breeze, only that ever moved.

Roisa glanced about her, by this time no longer worried over the time-frozen gardens. Not even the fish in the pool, still as golden coins, concerned her any more. There was nothing she could do about any of this.

Just then something seemed to ride straight out of the moon.

They had come back. As they always did.

With the brilliant flutter of sea-spray, thirteen white horses landed on the lawn. On the back of every one sat a slim, clever-faced lady, with flowing hair, each of a different color—and these tints ranged between apricot and copper, between jet and mahogany and flame and pewter and violet. Everything sparkled—horses, ladies—with gems, beads, *fireflies*— Then the thirteenth horse came trotting forward and the thirteenth rider swung from her gilded saddle, light as air. Even though, by now, she knew this person so well—better, probably, than she'd known her own mother—Roisa never quite stopped being surprised by her.

She was a Fey, of course. One of the Faery Faer, the Elder Ones.

"Awake, I see," said the Thirteenth Fey, whose name was Carabeau (which meant something like *My-friend-who-is-*

good-looking-and-has-her-own-household). "Up with the owl, my Roisa. Come on, let's be off."

So Roisa mounted the horse behind Carabeau, as she always did.

After which the thirteenth horse, and all the other twelve horses, lifted up again into the sky. They weren't winged, these faery steeds—it was just that they could, when they or their riders wanted, run as easily through the air as over the earth.

In seconds, the great palace and its grounds became small, far off and far down. It was possible to see, all round them, the high wall of black thorns that kept out all the world. And beyond the thorn-wall, the deserted town, the deserted weedy fields and ruined cottages, from which everyone had, over the years, dejectedly gone away. For the palace was under a curse that would last a century, and everybody knew it.

Roisa laughed as the horses dived up and up. The moon was like a huge white melon, hung on a vine of milky clouds. The shadows of the horses ran below them over moonlit forests, over looking-glass lakes and gleaming, snake-winding rivers, over sleeping villages and marble cities that had also intended to stay wide awake.

"Look, do you see, Roisa?" asked Carabeau, and she pointed with her long, ringed finger at an open courtyard in one of the cities. There was torchlight there, and music, and dancing—but all stopped utterly still. Exactly like the scene in the palace they had left behind.

"Do you see the banners?" asked Carabeau. "The lights and the colored windows. Look at the girls' rich dresses and the fine clothes of the men. Look at that little dog dancing."

And the little dog *was* dancing, up on its hind legs, cute as anything. Only right now, it didn't *move*.

Roisa sighed.

"What, my dear?" asked the Faery.

"I wish—" said Roisa.

"Yes? You know you can say to me or ask me anything, my love."

"Yes, I know. I'm only—sorry I can't ever see—what it's *really* like—I miss it, Carabeau. Only a little bit. But I do."

"Your old life, do you mean? Before you fell asleep and then woke up with us."

"Yes."

"Before the Spinning Wheel and the Spindle with its pointed tip."

"Yes. Oh—it's marvelous to fly about like this, to see everything, and all the foreign lands—the towers and spires so high up, the splendid rooms, the mountains and seas—I remember that forest with tigers, and the procession with colored smokes and elephants—and the great gray whale in the ocean, and the lighthouse that was built before I was even born—"

"And the libraries of books," said Carabeau softly, "the treasure-houses of diamonds, the cathedrals, and the huts."

"Yes," said Roisa.

She hadn't known, before she began, that she would say any of this. She hadn't known she *felt* any of it. (Nor did she think if Carabeau might be testing her, in order that she be sure of this very thing.)

"Is it because," said Carabeau, "when you visit these sights with us, time has always stopped?"

"Yes—no—"

"Because, Roisa, one day that may change. How would that be for you, if the people moved and the clocks ticked?"

"Of course—of *course* I wish everything was like that—so I could see it properly *alive*. But . . . it isn't only that. I want—to live *inside* it—not outside all the time."

"Even if you are outside with us, who love you so well? Even with me?"

"Oh," said Roisa.

Not long after that the horses dipped down. They galloped between scentless streamers of low cloud, that should have carried with them the smells of spices or fog or rain. They brushed the unmoving tops of trees with their glittering hoofs, and skimmed over a wild night valley.

This time they landed in the courtyard of a vast old temple. Though some of the building had come down from enormous age, still lines of carved pillars upheld a roof whose tiles, blue as eyes, remained.

In the past, they had often come down into the places of human life, and walked the horses, or walked on foot, among markets, and along busy highways, mingling with the people and the beasts who, 'playing statues', like everyone in the palace, and everywhere, stayed motionless as granite.

That very first night—so long ago it seemed now—Carabeau and the other twelve Feys, had explained to her. How, while Roisa and her palace slept their magical sleep, the rest of the world went on about its usual affairs. And how, when she woke up each night, it was inside a timeless zone the Faery Faer could make, and carry with them. And then, though she and they might spend all the hours of darkness traveling to the world's four corners and back, no time at all would pass in mortal lands.

"It isn't," Carabeau had said, "that we stop their time— only that we move aside from the time they keep. For them, less than the splinter of a single second goes by—for us it is a night."

"But the *wind* moves—" Roisa had cried.

"That wind which blows is not a wind of the world, nor subject to the laws of the earth. That wind is magical, and its own master. But the moon doesn't move, and the sea doesn't. The clouds don't move at all."

Astonished, Roisa had never really understood, which she saw now. She'd only accepted it all.

Of course she had. Thirteen Faeries had told it to her.

Only one thing. That first night she had asked if the other people in the palace—her parents—the guardsman—if they could wake up, too, as she had done. Because, as she knew, now the curse had fallen, they, like her, were meant to sleep for a hundred years.

"They won't wake," said Carabeau. "Not until the proper hour. Or else there would be no point to any of this."

Tonight, they dismounted from the horses in the ancient temple courtyard. It was full of the (magically raised) perfume of myrtle bushes, which had once grown there. Faery lamps of silvery amber and catseye green hung from spider silks, or floated in the air. An orchestra of toads and night-crickets made strange, rhythmic music. Invisible servants came to wait on the thirteen Feys and Roisa, bringing a delicate feast of beautiful, unguessable foods and drinks.

They picnicked, while the temple bats, caught in that second's splintering, hung above like an ebony garland thrown at the moon.

Roisa once more sighed. She'd tried hard not to.

Carabeau looked into her eyes. But the eyes of a Fey, even if you look in them back, can't be seen into.

"Do you recall, Roisa, what happened that evening when you were sixteen? Then tell it over to us."

So Roisa told Carabeau and the others what they all knew so well. They listened gravely, their chins on their hands, or their hands lightly folded on the glimmering goblets. As if they had never heard any of it before.

But this story was famous in many places.

At Roisa's birth, twelve of the Faery kind had come to bless the child with gifts. These gifts were just the sort of thing a princess would be expected to have and to display. So, they made her Lovely, Charming, Graceful, Intelligent, Artistic, Weil-Mannered, Dutiful, Affectionate, Patient, Brave, Calm, and Modest.

But all the while they were giving her these suitable gifts, the Twelve Feys were restless, especially the two that had to give the baby the blessings of good manners and dutifulness, and the other Faery who had to make her modest.

Every so often, one or several of them would steal closer, and stare in at the cradle. The court believed they were just admiring the baby. Of course she was exceptional—she was the King's daughter.

Eventually the Feys left the room, leaving it loud with congratulatory rejoicing. By magical means they'd called to their own Queen, the Thirteenth Fey, whose name was Carabeau.

Now this was unusual. And in the town which then thrived at the palace's foot, people looked up astounded to see the Queen Fey ride over the sky in her emerald carriage drawn by lynxes.

When she entered the King's Hall, courtiers and nobles stood speechless at the honor. But Carabeau looked at them with her serious wise face, and silence fell. Then she spoke.

"The princess shall be all that's been promised you. You'll be proud of her, and she will fulfill all your wishes. But first she shall have time for herself."

At that a hiss had gone up, like steam from a hot stone over which has been flung some cold water.

The King frowned. His royal lips parted.

Carabeau lifted her hand and the King closed his mouth.

"The Spinning Wheel of Time shall stop," said Carabeau, "because this child, by then sixteen years old, shall grasp the Spindle that holds the thread time is always weaving. Then she shall gain a hundred years of freedom before she becomes only your daughter, and the wife to the prince you approve for her."

The King shouted. It wasn't sensible, but he did.

The rest—was history.

When Roisa finished recounting this, which was all she knew, and all the Feys had told her, Carabeau nodded.

"You remember too that night, and how you went to meet the guardsman—you, always so dutiful, but not then—and somehow you missed him—as we intended, and climbed into the attics, and found me there. And when I offered you the chance of a hundred years of journeys, of adventures—of freedom—you gripped time's Spindle, and the Time Wheel stopped."

"I don't remember that—I never have," said Roisa, doubtfully. "Only—going upstairs, and perhaps finding you—But when I first woke afterward, I was frightened."

"But now you are not. Understand, my love, for you this wasn't a curse or doom. It was my gift, the thirteenth blessing. And anyway, at last the hundred years are at an end. This night is your final one among us. Let me tell you what has been arranged for you, when you return to the world. Tomorrow a powerful and handsome prince, even more handsome than the guardsman, will hack a way in through the thorns. He'll climb up through the gardens, the palace, mount the attic stair, wondering at it all. He'll find you asleep, as always you sleep by day. He'll wake you up. You'll fall in love at once, and so will he. Then everyone else will wake. The birds will fly about, the cats will purr, the earth's own wind will make the leaves rustle, the sun and the moon will cross the sky. You will live happily till the end of your days, you and your prince, admired and loved by all. The life that, perhaps, now you long for."

The Thirteenth Fey paused. She waited, looking at Roisa.

Roisa realized that something was expected of her. She didn't know what it was—should she thank the Faeries excessively for all the pleasures and travels, the feasts eaten and sights seen? Or for their care of her, their kindness?

Roisa didn't know that the Thirteenth Faery was actually waiting to see if Roisa would say to her, *But I don't really want that!* For Roisa to burst out that No, no, now the choice was truly hers, really she wanted to stay among the Faery kind. Providing only they could lift the spell from those left in the palace (as she knew they could) then she would far rather become one of their own—if that were possible (and it was). Even if it lost her a princess's crown, and all the rough romance of the human world.

But Roisa, of course, *didn't* want that, did she.

She wanted precisely what she had been supposed to have, before the magic of the Spinning Wheel and the hundred years waking Sleep.

And so, when Carabeau murmured quietly, "Are you glad your century of freedom is over?" Roisa sprang up. She raised her head and her arms to the sky. She crowed (not modestly or calmly) with delight, imagining the fun, happiness, glory that was coming.

And then, startling herself, she found she was crying. Just like on that first night. Just like then.

And when she looked down again at the Feys, they seemed pale as ghosts, thin as shadows, and pearls spangled their cheeks, for the Faery People can't cry real tears.

Then they kissed her. The last kisses of magic. The next kiss she would know would be a mortal one.

"Shall I remember—any of *this*?" she asked as, under the static moon, they rode the sky to her palace.

"Everything."

"Won't anyone . . . be jealous?" asked Roisa.

The Thirteenth Faery said, "You must pretend it was all a dream you had, while you slept." And in a voice Roisa never heard, Carabeau added, "And soon, to you, that is all it will be."

Love in Waiting

THE PRINCE AND PRINCESS met and fell in love at first sight. It was arranged he would marry her following her sixteenth birthday.

Unfortunately a curse had ensured that, on her sixteenth birthday, she was cast into a hundred-year sleep. The prince, by then eighteen, was desolated.

Yet his life was unusually long.

Aged one hundred and eighteen, the prince returned to her castle, and ripped through all the ensorcelled, disbanding thorns. He found her, still sixteen, and sleeping.

Only a kiss of true love could wake her. It was. It did.

She knew him, despite the cobweb netting of time.

"My prince," she whispered.

"My beautiful love," he answered softly. And fell dead at her feet.

The Reason For Not Going to The Ball

(A Letter to Cinderella from her Step-Mother)

TO THE PRINCESS, Wife of the Prince
Madam:

The girl will have brought you this, the one you trust. Before you tear it into pieces, remember, never before has she done you a disservice. Rather she has helped you. And, I must tell you now, she has been a friend also to me. This is not to make you hate her. It is to make you pause for a moment. To ponder that, if I have sent her to you, and she has aided you, can *I* have tried to aid you? Please, therefore, read a little further. Perhaps, say to yourself, you will read until I am cruel or insult you, or ask you for something. That is fair, I think. Of course, you suppose, as how should you not, that I have given you only evil. Your world is colored now by trouble, which seemed to begin, I would imagine, with me. But, beautiful Princess, let me have a little time. I promise, I will at least invite your thoughts. And if you read here a word of mine against you—throw this letter in your fire.

Where to begin then, conscious you may lose patience. Shall I provoke your pity? No, for how could you pity me, the wicked step-mother who thrust you from your adoring father, raised her two ugly daughters over you, exiled you to the dungeon of the kitchens to sweep up the dirt. And finally, worse—withheld you from the famous ball. But then, you went to the ball, despite my efforts. Consider that. Consider what that glorious night has brought you, and read on.

When I was thirteen, my father, a gambler, sold me to a man who offered to pay all the debts. I was very beautiful—so I can speak of she I was, for she was another and not I. The rich man wed me in a modest clandestine service, and then, for a month, he set about me. You know of rape. Naturally you do. I knew nothing. I was terrified. And before I had even grasped what he had done to me, I was with child. When I grew big he was encouraged. He thought I carried a son. But no, it was two daughters. Four days it took me, it took them, to free ourselves from each other. I almost died, and so did they. Probably from this cause they were so ugly. Or else, it was from their father, a hideous man like a gigantic goblin. But they did not have his nature. No, they were in temperament like my own mother. Sweet and gentle, full of laughter. And loving.

Well, you already think me a criminal. Why dissemble? I poisoned the goblin wretch in my twenty-seventh year. He had begun to beat me by then, as he beat his servants. When I could not hide them, he beat his—*my*—daughters. There was a clever groom. He knew how to procure certain drafts. It looked like a disease of incontinence, and indeed, my husband had given his favors everywhere, no one was surprised, not even he, though he railed against women for a month, before he died.

His estate passed to a brother and I was left with very little. I lived on sufferance in the house of a relation, and my daughters with me. This terrible woman, my aunt, would say to me, in the hearing of my children, "Even though you are poor as mice, and they foul as imps, some man will take you all on, if you act properly."

And to this end she conveyed me about and welcomed suitors. She told me frankly she would expect a gift when I remarried.

Then came your father.

He seemed, of course, like a dream-being, so handsome, so wealthy, so softly spoken and gracious. I was amazed, but even so, now I had the space, I put myself to learning his true nature. I had suffered before, you see, and my daughters had suffered. I did not want them again trapped in the house of a man who would knock them down and spit upon them, calling them pigs and monsters. Your father was, in fact, only courteous to the girls. He even brought them little presents, when he came to call on me—you know his excellent manners. A red rose for me, wound with a tiny golden bracelet. And for them—a sash of scarlet silk and a sash of yellow silk. As if they were pretty, and would soon be popular. I thought myself very mean of spirit to set my faithful groom to learn things of your charming father. But still, I did it.

And so, dear Princess, I learned. And what I learned made me grim but not uneasy. For I was quite selfish and perhaps still am. Me he could do no harm I would notice, and my children would be treated with kindness. Even so, I was loath to marry him—he had by now asked me—until the evening when I saw *you*.

It was, in its way, strange, for I beheld you by accident, going by in his carriage, just in the fashion my first husband had seen me in the carriage of my gambler father. There was only a moment, your pale and perfect face, the glimpse of your raven hair, and then you were gone like a spring flower.

Possibly you have never seen—how would you—that you and I resembled one another. Why that should be I have no notion, and probably now the resemblance is less, or is no more. But you, Princess, were like the girl I had been. And, being selfish, perhaps that is the only explanation for what I did next. Because you were like the child I might have borne. Because I knew—and, to my shame before had never troubled with it—what would become of you.

I wed your father, and I recall how first I met you. You were twelve years old, and came out to greet me hand in hand with him. You leaned on him, in utter trust and love, and his pride in you was evident. At me you looked not shyly, for you are not shy, but carefully, polite and reticent, yet not cold. You were ready, my dear, I saw, to be my friend, if I should prove worthy.

Even then, I appeared far younger than I was. I had been taken, in candlelight, for sixteen. That is an age he liked, as do so many men. We would sit then, do you remember, on the crimson sofa, you and I, and I would embroider and you would tell me stories. Oh, what lovely stories they were. You wooed me, did you not, with those tales of servant girls who won the love of kings. And I wooed you, tactfully, cautiously, with my embroidered scarves. And do you recollect too, my poor dulcet daughters, who admired you so and were never jealous, as they would no more be jealous of an emerald or the moon?

I told you stories, too. That was when you turned from me. I did my best, but patently, I did all wrong. In my tales the kings were not good and noble. In my tales most men were not to be trusted.

You did not believe me. Why should you? I had only the awful proofs I had been brought, evidence too disgusting to show you. Perhaps I should have done. To you, innocent and gracious and loving, his arm about you, his hand on your waist, the pressing of his lips over and over to yours—yes, even pressing with the lips a touch parted and moist—these were the normal attentions of a gallant father. But I had heard, I had heard and I had learned. How your mother had been privately dressed, and I was privately dressed, as a very young girl. How he liked best when we whispered girlish rhymes to him, and pretended surprise, even alarm, as he unlaced himself. That is no matter. There is nothing bad in that. But he had bastard daughters too. He had abused them all. There were three, and none a virgin, for each had had to endure him. He did not like them too young, that was the only saving grace. About fourteen, that was the age he relished the most. He had married me in truth not so much because I would play his games and in candlelight looked younger than I was, but since I must be grateful and, while I might please him until you were ready, would never blab once he had begun on you.

Yes, yes, I tried to tell you this, ever more explicit, ever more embarrassed, ashamed, as I have sometimes been, by the excesses of others. And you, naturally, jumped up in horror. You ran away from me.

Did I mention one other matter? Your father was insane. If you can credit anything that I have said here, and conceivably, still, you cannot, although I think you may have learned by now the ways of this world, then doubtless you can believe in your father's madness.

You must judge.

I went about my task a new way after your rejection. My method was—curious, I think a fearsome method. But what could I do? I had no money, and so no power, of my own. No one to assist me but the scurrilous, clever groom. And so I told your father . . . tales. I said you had begun to be hysterical. That, in your rages—revealed only to me—you spoke ill of him, stupid, dreadful things. I saw him look askance. You were, I said, disobedient, and unwomanly, in one, spoiled. And he—he came to accept all this. Did he ever question you? If he did, no doubt my warning to you had made you evasive, awkward as in nothing else, and this fueled the unsavory fire. Then he was wary of you. He fondled you less or not at all. And this you felt as a rebuke. So it increased, until you were strangers to each other. As, of course, you had always been. Even so I was not done. Day by day, your loveliness shone out of you. It was impossible to keep such light under any ordinary bushel. In the end, he would not resist. And you, loving him, trusting him, maybe you would permit, and so go mad yourself. I said that *he* was mad. I said you must judge. I had made sure a selection of tender beauties came upon him wherever he went. And some even caused him to believe they were his by-blows. I paid them what I could from the money he allowed me. He never noticed my gowns were made over, or that his enamouratas were professional. They are talented, such girls, needing to be. Meanwhile I said to him that there had been a child like you in the household of my aunt. And, although it was kept secret, a way had been found to bring the fool to her senses. "Let her," said I, "realize what you have given her as your daughter, by allowing her to go without it." He assured me I should have my way. He was even pleased with it.

So, you went down and down the house. I had you dressed in rags that stank. I had you smeared with filth. I let the sluts of the kitchen teach you dirty ways and words. I had them smother you up in that place below, among the greasy spits and smoking hearths. I made you as unappetizing as I could, and oh, my dear, that was very difficult, but in the end, I had succeeded. And so I invited him to spy on you, just once. And you were, no longer to his taste, the madman. "No daughter

of mine." These words he actually vocalized. He liked his
women clean and couth. Educated and gentle. Never swear-
ing, perfumed with roses, not the cinders of the fire.

But you, too honorable to speak ill of me, you pined for
him. You pined for your loving father who, if he had had one
clear thought, would have rescued you, bathed you, dressed
you in silk—and raped you over and over.

You thought I was a witch, and my daughters, who sobbed
for you every night—I had no need to lie to them—were
creatures of the Pit—your tormentors. Obviously, being so
ugly, they had nothing to fear. I could let them walk about the
upper house in the finest raiment. And I could let them, when
they were eighteen and you sixteen, go to a ball.

If you have read so far, and I pray you have, and not
thrown my letter in your winter fire, you will now perhaps
await, scornfully, bitterly, my excuse for keeping you from
that ball of state where, it was said, the roving eye of the
glamorous prince might light on any girl, so ostentatious egal-
itarian is your kingdom.

To be plain, at first I thought that here might be the answer. I had mused on plans to get you from your father's
hands, but there was no one I might rely on, or so it seemed
to me, who might assist you. But now, here was this. For you
were yet so beautiful, and I could allow you to become more
beautiful, if away from the sight of your father. And I had
heard of this prince, I had once met him, and he was young
and straight, handsome, a warrior and a scholar, a paragon.
How could he fail to notice you? How could you fail to respond to him? And so you would escape that dire house
where you had been made a slattern rather than an unpaid
and incestuous whore.

Yet I had to meddle, had to be certain.

And so I turned again to my clever groom.

Yes, in reply to your question, perhaps your accusation, I
paid him with my body. That grimy, cranky little man, always
to the windward of the law. And do you know, my Princess,
this villain was gentle. He had no imagination as a lover, but
also he wished to play no games. He took his pleasure politely, and after it said that he had been proud to have access

to my flesh. But also he confessed he loved truly a woman of the slums. I had seen her. She is ten years his senior, with fallen breasts, but when she beholds him, her face lights like the face of a girl. He said he would marry her if ever he had money enough. He had never asked me for a single coin, and refused the little I could offer him.

He, then, made investigation of the paragon, and soon enough I was brought word. The prince was another of a kind. Well, do I need to tell you now? You have, so the servant girl has whispered to me, the marks of his whip engraved upon your back, and where they cut the ring from your finger, after he had broken the bone, there is now another ring of white.

Could I have warned you of it? Only as I had tried to do in the matter of your father.

Instead, I kept you close. I locked you in. You were a slut in the kitchen. How could you go to the ball of the prince who was a beast?

You found a way. I had mislaid, thinking of your loveliness and your vulnerability, that you were intelligent, and, like me, devious after your own fashion.

You wrote to your godmother, that icy ambitious woman, and when she consented to interview you, you found a means to reach her. She saw at once, with her gimlet gaze, your potential under my disguise. So then she had you washed and garnished, and put on you a gown made in a single day by those seamstresses who work until they go blind. It was a sorcerous gown, pure white, and threaded with silver. How many lost the last of their eyesight over it? It was meant to dazzle only one.

She took you to the ball in her own carriage. She introduced you as a relative from a far country. Did she say that, when you were settled, she expected a gift? Perhaps she was more subtle. And any way, you were grateful, were you not, for he saw you, the beauteous royal young man, and he danced with you. Did his warm possessive hands remind you of the loving touches of your father? And when you kissed, hidden in the vines upon the balcony, were his lips a little parted?

She was very wise, your godmother, whisking you away so

decorously on the stroke of midnight. It is said you left him a
token, a small glass brooch shaped like a dancing slipper. I
imagine that was also her idea. The shoe of a woman is the
symbol of her sexual part. That into which one may slip and
be a perfect fit.

The rest is well known about the kingdom. That he sought
you, claimed you. That he wedded you.

And after that did you hear—I expect they kept it, protec-
tively, from you—that your mad father grew more mad? That
he went to the king's court and shouted there that you were
a minx and a harlot, and the prince a lecher. Those loyal to
the kingly house pursued your father. No one knows who. It
was in an alleyway. They cut his throat. And I, of course, was
disgraced, because I had ill-treated you. They sent us away, I
and my daughters, into exile, beyond the border. But they let
me keep a share of widow's money, which was to me a for-
tune, and we have done very well. It may amuse you to
know—or anger you—or gladden you, how can I tell—that
both my daughters have married. Their husbands are good
men, and very rich. It happened in strange fateful ways. I will
not tax you with it, in case I should offend. But, one of these
husbands is even handsome, and both value laughter and
sweetness. My daughters have blossomed in their care. They
do not look ugly any more, I can even see in them—my
younger self. Or, sometimes, you.

So as our path went upward, lovely girl, sad, lost girl, yours
declined. When did he begin to hurt you first? The female
servant who has helped me says that it was on your wedding
night. She says he chained you in a spiked collar like a dog,
and used his boots. And worse. Much worse. Does she lie?
How I hope so. Maybe they are even lies about the scars upon
you. Though once I came back, yes, hidden in my own disguise, and I watched on the street as you passed in the glass
carriage. And you were like a bird in a cage. Your hair so pale
a black—is there white in your hair? Your eyes that looked
about, seeing nothing. Just a glimpse, then gone, like a spring
flower, the snow-drop, that is swallowed by the mud.

Listen to me.

Tonight the clever dirty groom will be at your door, the

hidden door your husband uses, but not now, for he is away hunting, is he not, riding down other slender things with his whip and that sack of poison in him called by some his heart. Yes, the groom will be there, and he will have a cloak for you, and papers. And if you go down with him, he will guard you like a child. He knows how, for he too has a daughter now, by his wife that he loves, in their fine house that I have been able to buy for them. You should witness him with this girl child. I think in him, for the very first, I have seen the proper, golden, everyday love of a *father*. Trust this man, if you will trust me. If ever again you can trust anyone. The border is near, and it is lightly snowing now. By dawn, when you can be far away, the snow will be thick as a wall between you and your hell.

I have bought a house for you, also. It is in a valley. A fountain falls from a cliff, and there are pines that smell of balm. In the summer there was never anywhere a sky so blue. And in winter, the sun is like silver. Even if you never live in it, this place is yours.

You need never see me, never look at me. Of course, of course, I love you. I always have. It is the selfish love that finds in another its own self. But I ask nothing of you, only that you will let me set you free. That you will let me set free the one I might have been, the one I was, the one you are.

There is everything I can say. I will put down my pen. The groom takes this to the girl, the girl gives this to you. And now, through the hours of the silent night, I will wait, wondering if you are on the road, flying at midnight, leaving not only a provocative shoe of glass, but all the false and empty dreams behind you, the dreams which became nightmares. Or, since I hid you in cold cinders, have you thrown my letter in your burning fire?

Midnight

ABOVE THE GLITTERING ballroom, the gilded clock hung like a baleful planet. The hands on the face of it showed ten minutes to midnight.

Only ten minutes more. Then, she must be gone. But the girl—how could she bear to leave? She looked away from the clock, back at the face of the young prince who was dancing with her, over the marble floor.

They fitted together like hand and glove. Both so young, so beautiful, and so wonderfully dressed. For not only the prince was clad as one would expect, in garments of silk and velvet, so was the girl. She too looked like royalty.

How strange it had been. The old woman the girl had sometimes helped, giving her scraps from the kitchen, nice things when possible, though the girl herself got little enough. Then suddenly, this very night, when the evil, tyrannical women of the house had flounced away to the ball, the old woman entered—not by the door, but out of the *fireplace*—shedding her rags, her old age, becoming a shining creature. "Bathe yourself," the being had said to the astonished girl, "wash the soot from your hair. Then you will find there are garments for you, and everything else, to show your beauty as it truly is."

Bemused, indeed under a *spell*, the girl obeyed. Stepping from the tub, she found herself at once both dry and scented, and she was next instant dressed, in the whitest silks, whiter than new-polished stars—her hair plaited with diamonds. And on her feet two shoes of such lovely peculiarity, she stood gazing at them.

Then the being was beside her again. "They are not made of glass—you will be well-able to dance in them."

The girl saw then the shoes were only stitched over, each of them, with a hundred or so tiny sparkling crystals. And taking a step, found she was already gliding—dancing as if in a dream.

"Outside," said her benefactor, "a carriage awaits you. I made it"—a little, perhaps boastful, laugh—"from a pumpkin—but now it is formed of gold. The six white horses are mice, but no one will know—not even they. Go to the palace, and win the heart of the handsome prince. You will find it quite easy, as now you are."

The girl—who in her recent awful years of ill-treated slavery, had been called in mockery, *Ashy*—murmured, "But these are faery gifts. They will vanish away at morning."

"True. The very first moment of morning, which comes when night turns back to day—at midnight. Thus, before the in rags fatal hour strikes, you must depart or be seen in rags and ruin."

"But then," whispered Ashy, turning ashen under all her beauty, "what use is any of this?"

"He will love you. You must trust in that. Love is *never* blind. He will find you, even after midnight has struck. Do you understand?"

"No, Lady," said Ashy. But her own real name came back to her at that second. It was Elvira. She bowed to the one who had been an old beggar woman, and who could walk out of a fire. "But I thank you. Even if this night ends for me in tragedy, to taste the joy of it will be worth any later pain."

Then Elvira went out and found the incredible golden carriage and the white horses, and stepping inside the vehicle, was carried faster almost than light—which she now resembled—to the palace of the prince.

Through all the crowds, he saw her at once. As she saw him.

Like two magnets, one of stellar silver, one of flame-lit steel, they flew together.

"I thought the moon had fallen on the terrace," he said, as he led her out across the gleaming floor. "But it was you."

What had they said to each other, after that? Beginning with courtly phrases, presently the passionate desire, the deep tenderness each had at once conceived for the other, spangled in their brains, more vital than champagne, and sprang from their lips like arrows. There among the host of other dancers, they spoke of love—shameless, precipitous, sincere.

But, for all their bond of truth, Elvira told him nothing of who she was, of what had happened to her, the jealous wickedness of false family. Nothing of her station now in life, that of a girl smudged with filth and living among gray cinders.

She could not bring herself to do it. She was afraid. Love is *never* blind? Yet he saw her now in a gown of moonlight, with diamonds in her hair and shoes that seemed magically made of glass. He thought her the daughter of a king, just as he was the son of a king.

And so she had arrived with him at ten minutes to midnight.

Yet now—oh now—the hands of the gilded clock had leaped forward impossibly. Eight minutes were *gone*. Only two minutes were left. She must fly—she must run away for her very life.

Let me stay one minute more. Only one—

For after this—no, he would never find her. How could he? She would be hidden again in darkness. And then he would forget her completely. Or else his heart would break as her heart already broke, thinking of the empty desert of despair beyond this night.

A single minute now, all that was left. How slowly the hands of the clock crept—how swiftly.

If only Elvira might freeze time. One *half* minute all that remained—to make that half minute last another night—another hour—at least . . . at least another ten minutes—

"My love," Elvira said to the prince. There on the gleaming floor, among the crowds, they ceased to dance. Seeing this, the other dancers also stopped dancing. The orchestra fell silent in a sudden phantasmal flowing away of sound.

"My love—I must—"

The clock *struck*. The first stroke of the terrible twelve—an ax-blade that cracked asunder the pane of night.

Elvira stared up into the face of her, lover. She saw how his laughing delight was altering to bewilderment—dismay.

She drew her hand from his. She drew away from him.

The clock *struck*. The second stroke. Already smashed, the night scattered in bits like black and golden snow.

"I—" she said.

"Never leave me," he said.

"I—"

The clock *struck*. The third stroke. The palace and the city reeled.

Elvira's feet in the shoes of glass—were lead. She must gather up her glimmer of skirts and run—*run*—before the glory of the spell of illusion deserted her.

Four, struck the clock, five, six, *seven*—

Like a statue, Elvira. Turned to stone.

Already it was too late.

The crashing ax-blows had become a thin honed sword, which sliced away the imagery of enchantment. Eviscerated, the white gown, foaming up like feathers, *melted*—the diamonds, shed like rain, *dried*—even the peerless shoes—for how could they remain, when all else that was sorcerous vanished? The shoes were two puddles of mirror. Then a mirror's double shadow. Then—nothing at all.

Eight, nine, ten, eleven.

Twelve, roared the clock, the voice of judgment: *Twelve-twelve-twelve*. The echo continued forever. But after forever, silence returned.

Elvira had not run away. She stood there in the midst of strangers, three of whom—though she could not see them—she knew to be the enemies from her own house. These people had not lost their finery. They bloomed in it, and bloomed also with eyes stretched wide with shock, disgust, or fear.

And there before her, he—her lover, her prince, also changed at last to expressionless pale stone.

The girl wore only her dirty shift. Her hair hung down her back, thick with kitchen grease and cinders. She smelled no more of flowers and essences, but of sweat and toil, ash and agony.

Love is not blind. No, love sees too much. Love sees and becomes a whip with thorns in it. Oh, she had already learned as much, when her stepmother and stepsisters first turned upon her like starving rats.

Elvira waited, her head still raised, too shamed to be ashamed, her tears now the only jewels she wore.

And he, the prince, stretched out one hand, as if to push her away.

Instead, his hand clasped hers. He looked into her face, and suddenly the sun rose behind his eyes. He smiled at her gravely. "Now I understand," he said.

"But," she faltered, "do you still know me—even *now*?"

"Just as I knew you at first sight," he said. "It is still you. And how courageous you are, to have stayed. How you must love me, Elvira—perhaps even as much as I love you. Ladies and gentlemen," said the prince, turning to his astounded court, Elvira's dirt-blackened hand clasped firmly in his own, "Here is my future wife."

Empire of Glass

ONE DAY THE Prince decided he must choose a wife. The prospect filled him neither with interest or pleasure. There was no shortage of appealing women available when he was in the mood for them, and his daily life, he felt, went on perfectly well without irrevocably attaching a female human to it. Generally he preferred hunting, and liked the company of horses, strong and spirited, bloodhounds, swift and acutely-nosed, and quantities of other animals freshly killed and ready to be cooked.

The Prince's princedom, lying southeast in Europe, and landlocked but for a single seagoing river, was one of those Ruritanian ones. For the sake of convenience it will, therefore, be known in this account as Turitrania. In some respects it was an idyllic place, especially for the Prince. However, as the century drew to its close, he had found himself increasingly worried by those events which swept the outer world — revolutions, wars, the rise to eminence of commoners, and establishment of empires. There was, too, the fast progress of science, which had already accessed the military potential of the hot-air balloon. Not to mention awful rumors of enclosed ships, that might travel *below* the waters, and so pass, unseen and crammed with invaders, into any harbor.

The Prince's marriage plan was accordingly based on the idea of a very rich wife, having extremely powerful connections. In return she would gain status, for his line was historically ancient and noble; plus the prize of himself. He was, in his looks, not so bad as princes went, and reasonably amiable as they went, too.

A ball was arranged. It was to be magnificent, and invitations were sent far and wide. Late summer decorated the forests of Turitrania in silk foliage, and elaborately velvety flowers; and the mountains, visible from all the terraces of the palace, gilded themselves obligingly early in crests of silver snow.

Similarly overdressed, the Prince pulled the ears of his favorite bloodhound, Snouter, one last pre-betrothal time. Then strode manfully to the ballroom.

Between the hours of eight and ten-thirty, an evening passed which was both glamorous and loud. A huge orchestra bellowed dance music, dancing feet pranced; champagne fountains erupted and crystal goblets fragilely clinked. Young women flung themselves, or were flung by eager sponsors, upon the Prince. He greeted them, danced with them (as princes also went, he was not too bad a dancer), and questioned them intently. Many were rich, several absurdly so, most had connections, some even powerful ones. Some chattered, some were deliberately enigmatic, some were tongue-tied. *Some* were even beautiful—but the Prince tended to prefer prettiness to beauty, and besides, looks were not the prime objective.

By a quarter to eleven he was feeling rather tired. He yearned to leave the ball, have a swig of brandy, and go to bed—alone. To make a decision was, he began to think, beyond him. He could no longer see the *wife* for the *women*, as it were. As for their credentials—none of them had, he found, quite what he had hoped for: some whiff of true difference—the means whereby to make Turitrania omniscient, the foundation not only of security, but an empire of the Prince's very own.

The ballroom clock struck eleven.

Exactly then, through the vast doors, came stalking a tall female figure in a beaded white gown.

There was at that moment a brief interval without music, and so the exclamations of the crowd became particularly notable. The Prince peered the length of the room at the bold young woman. What had excited everybody so? An aide presently informed him. The newcomer was not only uninvited, she was quite unknown. And she had arrived, it seemed, in an extraordinary vehicle—a coach of glass. "But I have a glass coach," replied the Prince. *Ah*, hers was not the same.

The Prince's coach, a relic which had been in the royal family for a hundred years, only had large glass windows, and these were cracked. The young woman's coach was entirely *formed* of glass. It was quite transparent, and sound as a bell.

Just then she reached the Prince, and addressed him directly. "Perhaps you should ask me to dance," she said. "You'll note, I have put on my dancing shoes." She was not unattractive, if rather tall and slender for the Prince's personal taste, but when he looked at her feet, his heart bolted into a mad gallop. Without a word, he held out his arm. The orchestra struck up a waltz, and they took the floor.

"You dance well," said the Prince. "How is that feasible, in *those*?"

"They're perfectly comfortable," said the young woman, and whirled him round—she had already taken the lead—so his head echoed.

"Where did you come by them then?" the Prince asked, when he had regained his bearings.

"My godmother. The same as the coach. She makes things, you see."

Evidently both the godmother and her charge were cast in a modern mode.

The waltz, itself a modern dance that no one was quite yet used to, ended. The Prince and the woman in white stood alone on the floor, while everyone else stared from the sidelines, with their mouths open like those of horses after a stiff ride.

"But I suppose," said the Prince, attempting to be jocular and casual, "if you were to dance really *quickly*, or, say—jump about somewhat—they might . . . break?"

"Of course not," snapped the young woman. "I'll show you." And signaling audaciously to the conductor, she shouted, "A tarantella, if you please!"

The Prince understood why, though uninvited, she had been admitted to the ball, and his wildly thudding heart was sinking in inevitable resignation. Such was her aura of command, the orchestra meanwhile did as bidden. And in another second, she was dancing boisterously, spinning around, kicking her heels, leaping and stamping, and all the time the light of the chandeliers splintered and exploded like white fire, from her high-heeled slippers of transparent glass.

When the tarantella was done, the ballroom applauded to a man (if not always to a woman), the air ringing to screams of *Brava!* and *Encore!* But the girl only bent and took off her shoes. One she left lying, the other she grasped firmly in her hand. "I shall be going now," she said. "If you should want to look me up, that's for you to see to."

"But I don't even know your name," cried the Prince.

"Cindy," said the young woman carelessly. And the clock struck midnight. And then—and then a swirling seemed to surround her, her garments vanished and she with them in what appeared to be a fall of glass leaves caught in a tornado. This next dazzled away through the room, the alarmed crowd parting before it. She was gone. And soon after, from far across the regal park, there came the strange tinkling sprinting noise of a speeding coach of glass.

"You see," said the Prince to his ministers, "at all costs, she must be mine. Take note," and here he flung the single glass slipper with great force against a marble pillar of the parliament building. The slipper slipped to the ground, immaculate. The marble showed a thin injurious crack. "With such a material," the Prince continued, "Turitrania need fear no aggressor by land, sea, or air. With, also, such affiliated secret weapons as my future wife's device for swirling concealment, we will be the most mighty power on earth!"

The ministers, pale with savage greed, nodded like puppets. Until at last, one ventured: "But how, sir, seeing the young lady has vanished, and no one knows her, or from whence she came—how is she ever again to be found?"

The Prince uttered a bark of laughter. "How do you think? I've got her *shoe*. Go and fetch me Snouter, my best bloodhound."

Rapunzel

NOT FOR THE FIRST TIME, a son knew himself to be older than his father.

Urlenn was thinking about this, their disparate maturities, as he rode down through the forests. It was May-Month, and the trees were drenched in fresh young green. If he had been coming from anywhere but a war, he might have felt instinctively alert, and anticipatory; happy, nearly. But killing others was not a favorite pastime. Also, the two slices he had got in return were still raw, probably inflamed. He was mostly disgusted.

It was the prospect of going home. The castle, despite its luxuries, did not appeal. For there would be his father (a king), the two elder sons, and all the noble cronies. They would sit Urlenn up past midnight, less to hear of his exploits than to go over their own or their ancestors': the capture of a fabulous city, a hundred men dispatched by ten, the wonderful prophecy of some ancient crone, even, once, a dragon. There may have been dragons centuries ago, Urlenn judiciously concluded, but if so they were thin on the ground by now. One more horror besides was there in the castle. His betrothed, the inescapable Princess Madzia. The king had chosen Madzia for Urlenn, not for her fine blood, but since her grandmother had been (so they said) a fairy. Madzia had thick black hair to her waist, and threw thick black tempers.

After the battle, Urlenn let his men off at the first friendly town. They deserved a junket, and their captains would look out for them. He was going home this way. This *long* way home. With luck, he might make it last a week.

After all, Madzia would not like—or like too much—his open wounds. They ran across his forehead and he had been fortunate to keep his left eye. Doubtless the king would expect the tale of some valiant knightly one-to-one combat to account for this. But it had been a pair of glancing arrows.

Should I make something up to cheer the Dad?

No. And don't call him 'the Dad', either. He's king. He'd never forgive you.

Urlenn found he had broken into loud, quite musical song. The ditty was about living in the greenwood, the simple life. Even as he sang, he mocked himself. Being only the third son had advantages, allowing for odd lone journeys like this one. But there were limits.

Something truly odd happened then.

Another voice joined in with his, singing the same song, and in a very decent descant. A girl's voice.

The horse tossed its head and snorted, and Urlenn reined it in.

They sang, he and she (invisible), until the end. Then, nothing. Urlenn thought, *She's not scared, or she would never have sung.* So he called: "Hey, maiden! Where are you?"

And a laughing voice—you could tell it laughed—called back, "Where do you think?"

"Inside a tree," called Urlenn. "You're a wood-dryad."

"A *what*? A dryad—Oh, Gran told me about those. No, I'm not."

Urlenn dismounted. There was, he had come to see, something gray and tall and stone, up the slope, just showing through the ascending trees.

He did not shout again. Nor did she. Urlenn walked up the hill, and came out by a partly ruined tower. Sycamores and aspens had rooted in its sides, giving it a leafy, mellow look. A cottage had rooted there too, a large one, also made of stones, which had definitely been filched from the tower.

Before the cottage and tower was an orchard of pear and apple trees just losing their white blossom. Chickens and a goat ambled about. The girl was hanging up washing from the trees.

She was straight and slim, with short yellow hair like a boy's. And yes, still laughing.

"Not a dryad, as you see, sir."

"Maybe unwise though, calling out to strangers in the wood."

"Oh, you sounded all right."

"*Did* I."

"All sorts come through here. You get to know."

"*Do* you."

"Sometimes I fetch the animals, and we hide in the tower. Last month two men broke into the cottage and stole all the food. I let them get on with it." She added, care less, "I was only raped once. I'd been stupid. But he wished he hadn't, after."

"That's you warning me."

"No. You're not the type, sir. You looked upset when I told you, then curious."

"I am. What did you do, kill him?"

"No, I told him I loved him and gave him a nice drink. He'd have had the trots for days."

Urlenn himself laughed. "Didn't he come back?"

"Not yet. And it was two years ago."

She looked about seventeen, three years younger than he. She had been raped at fifteen. It did not seem to matter much to her. She had a lovely face. Not beautiful or pretty, but un-expected, *interesting*, like a landscape never seen before, though perhaps imagined.

"Well, maiden," he said. "I'm thirsty myself. Do you have any drinks without medicine in them? I can pay, of course."

"That's all right. We mainly barter, when I go to town." She turned and walked off to the cottage. Urlenn stood, look-ing at the goat and chickens and a pale cat that had come to supervise them.

The girl returned with a tankard of beer, clear as a river, and cold from some cool place, as he later learned, under the cottage floor.

He drank gratefully. She said, "You're one of the king's men, aren't you, sent to fight off the other lot."

The other lot. Yes.

He said, "That's right."

"That cut over your eye looks sore."

"It is. I didn't want it noticed much and wrapped it up in a rag—which was, I now think, dirty."

"I can mix up something for that."

"You're a witch, too."

"Gran was. She taught me."

Presently he tethered the horse to a tree, and left it to crop the turf.

In the cottage, he sat watching her sort and pound her herbs. It was neither a neat nor a trim room, but—pleasing. Flowering plants burst and spilled from pots on the window-sills, herbs and potions, vinegars and honeys stood glowing like jade and red amber in their jars. A patchwork curtain closed off the sleeping-place. On the floor there were baskets full of colored yarns and pieces of material. Even some books lay on a chest. There was the sweet smell of growing things, the memory of recent baking—the bread stood by on a shelf—a hint of damp. And her. Young and healthy, fragrant. Feminine.

When she brought the tincture she had made, and applied it to the cuts, her scent came to him more strongly.

Urlenn thought of Madzia, her flesh heavily perfumed, and washed rather less often. He thought of Madzia's sulky, red, biteable-looking mouth.

This girl said, "That will sting." *It does*, he thought, *And I don't mean your ointment.* "But it'll clean the wound. Alas, I think there'll be a scar. Two scars. Will that spoil your chances, Handsome?"

He looked up and straight in her eyes. She was flirting with him, plainly. Oh yes, she knew what she was at. She had told him, she could tell the good from the bad by now.

I don't look much like a king's son, certainly. Not anymore. Just some minor noble able to afford a horse. So, it may be me she fancies.

Her eyes were more clear than any beer-brown river.

"If you don't want money, let me give you something else in exchange for your care—"

"And what would you give me?"

"Well, what's on the horse I need to keep. But—is there anything you see that you'd like?"

Was *he* flirting now?

To his intense surprise, Urlenn felt himself blush. And, surprising him even more, at his blush she, this canny willful woods-witch, she did, too.

So then he drew the ring off his finger. It was small, but gold, with a square cut, rosy stone. He put it in her palm.

"Oh no," she said, "I can't take that for a cup of ale and some salve."

"If you'd give me dinner, too, I think I'd count us quits," he said.

She said, without boldness, gently, "There's the bed, as well."

Later, in the night, he told her he fell in love with her on sight, only did not realize he had until she touched him.

"That's nothing," she said, "I fell in love with *you* the minute I heard you singing."

"Few have done *that*, I can tell you."

They were naked by then, and had made love three times. They knew each other well enough to say such things. The idea was he would be leaving after breakfast, and might come back to visit her, when he could. If he could. The talk of being in love was chivalry, and play.

But just as men and women sometimes lie when they say they love and will return, so they sometimes lie also when they believe they will not.

They united twice more in the night, while the cat hunted outside and the goat and chickens muttered from their hut. In the morning Urlenn did not leave. In the morning she never mentioned he had not.

When she told him her name, he had laughed out loud. "What? Like the salad?"

"Just like. My Ma had a craving for it all the time she carried me. So then she called me for it, to pay me out."

The other paying out had been simple, too.

"In God's name—" he said, holding her arms' length, shocked and angry, even though he knew it happened frequently enough.

"I don't mind it," she said. He could see, even by the fire

and candlelight, she did not. *How forgiving she is—no, how understanding of human things.*

For the girl's mother had sold her, at the age of twelve, to an old woman in the forests.

"I was lucky. She was a wise-woman. And she wanted an apprentice not a slave."

In a few weeks, it seemed, the girl was calling the old woman 'Gran', while Gran called *her* Goldy. "She was better than any mother to me," said the girl. "I loved her dearly. She left me everything when she died. All this. And her craft, that she'd taught me. But we only had two years together, I'd have liked more. Never mind. As she used to say, *Some's more than none*. It was like that with my hair."

"She called you Goldy for your hair."

"No. Because she said I was *good as gold and bad as butter*."

"*What?*"

"She was always saying daft funny things. She'd make you smile or think, even if your heart was broken. She had the healing touch, too. I don't have it."

"You did, for me."

"Ah, but I *loved* you."

After an interval, during which the bed became, again, unmade, the girl told Urlenn that her fine hair, which would never grow and which, therefore, she cut so short, was better than none, according to Gran.

"It wasn't unkind, you see. But pragmatic."

She often startled him with phrases, words—she could read. (Needless to say, Gran had taught her.)

"Why bad as butter?"

"Because butter makes you want too much of it."

"I can't get too much of you. Shall I call you Goldy—or the other name?"

"Whatever you like. Why don't you find a name for me yourself? Then I'll be that just for you."

"I can't name you—like my dog.'"

"That's how parents name their children. Why not lovers?"

He thought about the name, as he went about the male chores of the cottage, splitting logs, hunting the forest, mending a scythe. Finally he said, diffidently, "I'd like to call you Flarva."

"That's elegant. I'd enjoy that."

He thought she would have enjoyed almost anything. Not just because she loved him, but because she was so easy with the world. He therefore called her Flarva, not explaining yet it had been his mother's name. His mother who had died when Urlenn was only six.

Urlenn had sometimes considered if his father's flights of fantasy would have been less if Flarva had lived. The Dad *(yes, I shall call you that in my head)* had not been king then. Kingship came with loss, after, and also power and wealth, and all the obligations of these latter things.

Other men would have turned to other women. The Dad had turned to epics, ballads, myths, and legends. He filled his new-sprung court with song-makers, actors, and story-tellers. He began a library, most of the contents of which—unlike this young girl—he could not himself read. He inaugurated a fashion for the marvelous and magical. If someone wanted to impress the Dad, they had only to "prove," by means of an illuminated scroll, that they took their partial descent from one of the great heroes or heroines—dragon-slayers, spinners of gold, tamers of unicorns. Indeed, only four years ago, the king had held a unicorn hunt. (It was well attended.) one of the beasts had been seen, reportedly, drinking from a fountain on the lands of the Dad. Astonishingly, they never found it. Rumors of it still circulated from time to time. And those who claimed to have seen it, if they told their tale just in *that* way, were rewarded.

Was the king mad? Was it his brain—or only some avoiding grief at the reality of the brutal world?

"Or is it his genius," said the girl—Flarva—when he informed her of his father's nature. "When the dark comes, do we sit in the dark, or light candles?"

How, he thought, *I love you*.

And strangely, she said then, "There, you love him."

"I suppose I do. But he irks me. I wish I could go off. Look at me here. I should have got home by now."

He had not, despite all this, yet revealed to her that the Dad was also the king. Did she still assume Urlenn's father was only some run-down baron or knight? Urlenn was not sure. Flarva saw through to things.

"Well, when you leave, then you must," was all she said in the end.

He had been up by now to the town, a wandering little village with a church and a tavern and not much else. Here he found a man with a mule who could take a letter to the next post of civilization. From there it would travel to the king. The letter explained Urlenn had been detained in the forests. He had only one piece of paper, and could not use it up on details—he begged his lordly sire to pardon him, and await his excuses when he could come home to give them.

Afterward, Urlenn had realized, this had all the aura of some Dad-delighting sacred quest, even a spell.

Would he have to go to the king eventually and say, "A witch enchanted me?"

He did not think he could say that. It would be a betrayal of her. Although he knew she would not mind.

There was no clock in the cottage, or in the village—town. Day and night followed each other. The green thickened in clusters on the trees, and the stars were thinner and more bright on the boughs of darkness. Then a golden border stitched itself into the trees. The stars waxed thicker again, and the moon more red.

Urlenn liked going to the village market with Flarva, bartering the herbs and apples and vegetables from her garden plot, and strange patchwork and knitted coats she made, one of which he now gallantly wore.

He liked the coat. He liked the food she cooked. He liked milking the adventurous goat, which sometimes went calling on a neighbor's he-goat two miles off, and had to be brought back. He liked the pale cat, which came to sleep with them in the hour before dawn. He liked wood-cutting. The song of birds and their summer stillness. The stream which sparkled down the slope. The gaunt old tower. Morning and evening.

Most of all, he liked her, the maiden named first for a salad. Not only lust and love, then. For liking surely was the most dangerous. Lust might burn out and love grow accustomed. But to like her was to find in her always the best—of herself, himself, and all the world.

One evening, when the lamp had just been lit, she straightened up from the pot over the fire, and he saw her as if he never had.

He sat there, dumbfounded, as if not once, in the history of any land, had such a thing ever before happened.

Sensing this, she turned and looked at him with her amused, kindly, *feral* eyes.

"Why didn't you tell me, Flarva?"

"I was waiting to see how long you'd take to notice."

"How far gone is it?"

"Oh, four months or so. Not so far. You haven't been too slow."

"Slow? I've been blind. But you—you're never ill."

"The herbs are good for this, too."

"But—it must weigh on you."

"It—*it*—"

"He, then—or she, then."

"They, then."

"*They?*"

"Twins I am carrying, love of my heart."

"How do you know? Your herbs again?"

"A dowsing craft Gran taught me. Boy and girl, Urlenn, my dear."

He got up and held her close. Now he felt the swell of her body pressing to him. *They* were there.

She was not fearful. Neither was he. It was as if he knew no harm could come to her. She was so clear and wholesome and yet so—yes, so *sorcerous*. No one could know her and think her only a peasant girl in a woods cot. Perhaps it was for this reason too he had had no misgivings that he abused, when first he lay down with her. He a prince. She a princess. Equals, although they were of different social countries.

However, what to do now.

"I've grasped from the beginning I'd never leave you Flarva. But—I have to confess to you about myself."

She looked up into his eyes. She had learned she had two children in her womb. Perhaps she had fathomed Urlenn, too.

"Have you? I mean, do you know I am—a king's son?"

She smiled. "What does it matter?"

"Because—"

"If you must leave me, Urlenn, I've always left open the door. I'd be sorry. Oh, so very sorry. But perhaps you might come back, now and then. Whatever, love isn't a cage, or if it is, a pretty one, with the door undone, and the birds out and sitting on the roof. I can manage here."

"You don't see, Flarva. Maybe you might manage very well without me. But I'd be lost without you. And those two—greedily, I want to know them as well."

"I'm glad. But I thought you would."

"So I must find a way to bring you home."

"Simple. I shall give this cottage to our neighbor. The goat will like that. The neighbor's good with fruit trees and chickens too. As for the cat, she must come with us, being flexible and quite portable."

"No, my love, you know quite well what I mean. A way to bring you into my father's castle, and keep you there. And selfishly let you *make* it home for me at last."

They sat by the fire—the evenings now were cooler than they had been. Side by side, he and she, they plotted out what must be done. The answer was there to hand, if they had the face, the cheek for it.

It had been a harsh, white winter. Then a soft spring. Now flame-green early summer lighted the land.

Amazed, the castle men-at-arms, about to throw Urlenn in the moat, recognized him.

"I'm here without any state."

"*In* a state," they agreed.

But then some of the men he had led in the war ran up, cheering him, shaking his hand.

"Where on God's earth have you been? We searched for you—"

"A wild weird tale. Take me to the king. He must hear first."

Urlenn had been driving a wagon, pulled by two mules, and his war-horse tied at the back. One or two heard a baby cry, and looked at one or two others.

Prince Urlenn went into the king's presence just as he was,

in workaday colorful peasant clothes, and with two white
scars glaring above his shining eyes.

The king (who did not know he was The Dad) had been
on a broad terrace that commanded a view of the valleys, and
the distant mountains that marked his kingdom's end. The
two elder sons were also there, and their wives, and most of
the court, servants, soldiers, various pets, some hunting dogs,
and Princess Madzia, who, for motives of sheer rage, had not
gone away all this while.

Urlenn bowed. The king, white as the paper of Urlenn's
last—and only second—letter, sprang up.

They embraced, and the court clapped (all but Madzia).
Urlenn thought, *I've been monstrous to put him through this.
But surely I never knew he liked me at all—but he does, look,
he's crying. Oh, God. I could hang myself.*

But that would not have assisted the Dad, nor Urlenn, so
instead Urlenn said, "Will you forgive me, my lord and sire. I
was so long gone on the strangest adventure, the most fearsome
and bizarre event of my life. I never thought such things were
possible. Will you give me leave to tell you the story of it?"

There followed some fluster, during which Princess Madzia scowled, her eyes inky thunder. But these eyes dulled as
Urlenn spoke. In the end they were opaque, and all of her
gone to nothing but a smell of civet and a dark red dress.
Years after, when she was riotously married elsewhere, and
cheerful again, she would always say, broodingly (falsely),
"My heart broke." But even she had never said that Urlenn
had been wrong.

Urlenn told them this: Journeying home through the forests, he had come to an eerie place, in a green silence. And
there suddenly he heard the most beautiful voice, singing,
Drawn by the song, he found a high stone tower. Eagerly, yet
uneasily—quite why he was not sure—he waited nearby, to
see if the singer might appear. Instead, presently a terrible
figure came prowling through the trees. She was an old hag,
and ugly, but veiled in an immediately apparent and quite
awesome power which he had no words to describe. Reaching
the tower's foot, this being wasted no time, but called out

thus: *Let down your hair! Let down your hair!* And then, wonder of wonders, from a window high up in the side of the tower, a golden banner began unfolding and falling down. Urlenn said he did not for one minute think it was hair at all. It shone and gleamed—he took it for some weaving of metal threads. But the hag placed her hands on it, and climbed up it, and vanished in at the window.

Urlenn prudently hid himself then more deeply in the trees. After an hour, the hag descended as she had gone up. Urlenn observed in bewilderment as this unholy creature now pounced away into the wood.

"Then I did a foolish thing—very foolish. But I was consumed, you see, by burning curiosity."

Imitating the cracked tones of the hag, he called out, just as she had done: "Let down your hair!"

And in answer, sure enough, the golden woven banner silked once more from the window, and fell, and fell.

He said, when he put his hands to it, he shuddered. For he knew at once, and without doubt, it had all the scent and texture of a young girl's hair. But to climb up a rope of *hair* was surely improbable? Nevertheless, he *climbed.*

The shadows now were gathering. As he got in through the window's slot, he was not certain of what he saw.

Then a pure voice said to him, "Who are you? You are never that witch!"

There in a room of stone, with her golden tresses piled everywhere about them, softer than silken yarn, gleaming, glorious, and—he had to say—rather untidy—the young girl told him her story.

Heavy with child, the girl's mother had chanced to see, in the gardens of a dreaded, dreadful witch, a certain salad. For this she developed, as sometimes happens with women at such times, a fierce craving. Unable to satisfy it, she grew ill. At last, risking the witch's wrath, the salad was stolen for the woman. But the witch, powerful as she was, soon knew, and manifested before the woman suddenly. "In return for your theft from my garden, I will thieve from yours. You must give me your child when it is born, for my food has fed it. Otherwise, both can die now." So the woman had to agree, and when she had borne the child, a daughter, weeping bitterly she gave it to the witch. Who, for her perverse pleasure, named the girl after the salad (here he told the name) and kept her imprisoned in a tower of stone.

"But her hair," said Urlenn, "Oh, her hair—it grew golden and so long—finer than silk, stronger than steel. Was it for this magic, perhaps imparted by the witch's salad, that the witch truly wanted her? Some plan she must have had to use the hapless maiden and her flowing locks. I thwarted it. For having met the maid, she and I fell in love."

Urlenn had intended to rescue his lover from the tower, but before that was accomplished, he visited her every day. And the witch, cunning and absolute, discovered them. "You'll realize," said Urlenn, "she had only to look into some sorcerous glass to learn of our meetings. But we, in our headstrong love, forgot she could."

"Faithless!" screamed the witch, and coming upon the girl alone, cut off all her golden hair. Then the witch, hearing the young man calling, *herself* let the tresses down for his ladder. And he, in error, climbed them. Once in the tower's top, the witch confronted him in a form so horrible, he could not, later, recall it. By her arcane strengths, however, she flung him down all the length of the tower, among great thorns and brambles which had sprung up there.

"Among them I almost lost my sight. You see the scars left on my forehead. Blinded, I wandered partly mad for months."

Beyond the tower lay an occult desert, caused by the witch's searing spells. Here the witch in turn cast the maiden, leaving her there to die.

But, by the emphasis of love and hope, she survived, giving birth alone in the wilderness, to the prince's children, a little boy and girl, as alike as sunflowers.

"There in the end, sick, and half insane, I found her. Then she ran to me and her healing tears fell on my eyes. And my sight was restored."

Love had triumphed. The desert could not, thereafter, keep them, and the prince and his beloved, wife in all but name, emerged into the world again, and so set out for the kingdom of the prince's father.

He's crying again. Yes, I should hang myself. But maybe
not. After all, she said I might make out her Gran was wicked—
said the old lady would have laughed—all in a good cause. A
perfect cause. They're all crying. Look at it. And the Dad—he
does love a story.

"My son—my son—won't this evil sorceress pursue you?"

Urlenn said, frankly, "She hasn't yet. And it was a year ago."

The king said, "Where is the maiden?"

Oh, the hush.

"She waits just outside, my lordly sire. And our children,
too. One thing—"

"What is it?"

"Since the witch's cruel blow, her hair lost its supernatural
luster. Now it's just . . . a nice shade of flaxen. Nor will it grow
at all. She cuts it short. She prefers that, you see, after the use
to which it was last put. By her hair then, you'll never know
her. Only by her sweetness and her lovely soul, which shine
through her like a light through glass."

Then the doors were opened, and Flarva came in. She wore
a white gown, with pearls in her short yellow hair. She looked
as beautiful as a dream. And after her walked two servants
with two sleeping babies. And by them, a pale stalking cat
which, having no place in the legend, at first no one saw. (Although it may have found its way into other tales.)

But the king strode forward, his eyes very bright. Never,
Urlenn thought, had he seen this man so full of life and fasci-
nated interest. Or had Urlenn seen it often, long ago, when he
was only three or four or five? In Flarva's time . . .

"Welcome," said the king, the Dad, gracious as a king or a
father may be. "Welcome to the wife of my son, my daughter,
Rapunzel."

Open Your Window, Golden Hair

AT THE POINT where the trees parted, he saw the tower. It seemed framed in space, standing on a rise, the pines climbing everywhere toward it in swathes, like blue-black fur, but not yet reaching the top of the hill. A strange tower, perhaps, he thought. The stone was ancient and obdurate, in the way of some old things—and these not exclusively inanimate. He could remember an old woman from his youth, that everyone called a witch, crag-like and immovable in both grim attitude and seeming longevity. Someone had said of her that she had never been younger than fifty, and never aged beyond seventy—"But in counted years she's easily ninety by now." The tower was like that.

Brown raised his binoculars, and studied it attentively, rather as he had so many landmarks on his excursion through Europe; he did this more as if he should, than because he particularly wanted or needed to.

But the tower *was* rather odd. Caught in that mirror-gap of spatial emptiness, only the cloudless sheet of earliest summer sky behind it, turning toward late afternoon, a warmly watery, pale golden blank of light. The tower was nearly in silhouette. Yet something hung down, surely, from the high, narrow window-slits. What was *that*? It had a yellowish effect, strands and eddies—creepers, perhaps.

Should he check the tower in the guidebook? No. He must make on to the little inn which, he had been told, lay just above the road to the west. It would take about half an hour to reach it, and by then the sun would be near to setting. He did not fancy the woods after nightfall, at least, not alone.

He was not sure about the inn. They were so welcoming

and kindly-spoken he suspected at once they might be planning to rob him, either directly or through the charges they would apply to his bed and board.

But the evening went on comfortably enough, with beer and various types of not unpleasant food. There was a fire lit, too, which was needed, since, with sunfall, a slight but definite chill had seeped into the world. Brown had selected and retained a good seat to one side of the hearth. Here, after his meal, he smoked and wrote up a few brief notes on the day's travel. This exercise was mainly to provide something with which to regale acquaintances on his return. He sensed he would otherwise forget a lot. The general run of things did not often linger very long in his mind. Having, then, made a note on it, he asked the so-genial host about the tower.

"Oh, we do not speak of it," said the host gravely. "It is unlucky."

"For whom?" bantered Brown.

"For any. An old place, once a witch's fortress."

"Witches, eh?"

The host, having refilled Brown's tankard, straightened and solemnly said, "It is unlucky even to look at it. To go there is most inadvisable." And after this, rather belying his previous assertion that one had better not talk about the tower, he announced: "Long whiles ago, back in times of history, it was said a creature also lived in the tower, the servant of the witch. She had bred it by force on a human woman, they say, and all the while the mother carried this monster-child, the witch fed the woman special liquids and herbs of power from her own uncanny garden. When the baby came forth, the mother, not to surprise us much, died. The creature then grew in the charge of the witch, and did her bidding for evil, and for all manners of ill."

"A fascinating story," said Brown, who thought he was actually quite bored.

"There is more," said the host, now gazing starkly up at the inn's low, smoky rafters. "Men were drawn to the tower, and somehow clambered up there. They were lured by the vision of a lovely young woman with golden hair, who would lean out the narrow window and flirt with and exhort them. But when they reached the stony place above and crawled in at the window—Ah!" exclaimed the host quite vehemently, making Brown jump and spill some of his beer—perhaps a ploy, so he would have to purchase more—"Ah, sweet Virgin and Lordship Christ, protect and succor us. No one must look at the tower, or venture close. I have said far too much, good mister. Forget what I have uttered."

Brown dreamed. He had gone back to the tower.

However, he was much younger, maybe eighteen or seventeen years of age. And his father was standing over Brown, as so often Mr. Brown senior had been, admonishing his son. "Don't touch it, boy. It isn't to be touched."

Yet surely—it *was.* All that golden floating fluff-like golden feathers escaping from a pillow full of swansdown—which down had come from golden swans.

"But it's so sweet, Father," said Brown.

And frowningly woke in the tiny bedroom up under the roof at the forest inn.

Midnight, harshly if voicelessly declared his watch.

Now he would be awake all night.

Next moment, Brown was once more fast asleep and dreaming . . .

Treacle goldenly flowed. Of *course* it was *sweet.* He tasted it, licked it up, swallowed and swallowed, could not get enough. He had been deprived of confectionary when a child, his strict father had seen to that.

The only difficulty was that the treacle also spilled all over him. He was covered in the stuff. There would be such trouble, later. Better then enjoy himself while he could. Brown opened his mouth wider, and held out both his eager, clutching hands.

The next day dawned bright as any cliché, and Brown got up with the abruptly, rather dreary awareness he must now go on with his exciting, adventurous journey across Europe. What, after all, was the point, really? Had he been a writer he might have made something of it, some book. Or a playboy would have used the time pretty well, though in a different way and through an unlike agenda. But Brown. What could Brown do with it? Bore people, no doubt, with badly recollected snippets of this and that. Even snippets like the tall tale the inn-host had cooked up last night. It had caused some funny dreams, that. What had they been? Something about sweets, was it, and—gold? Ridiculous.

Brown ate his breakfast in an ordinary silence, which the host respected. If the man felt either embarrassed or scornfully amused at his previous story-telling, one could not be certain. He might even, Brown decided, have forgotten it. Conceivably, he subjected every traveler who spoke of *anything* to some such dramatic recital.

After breakfast, Brown paid his bill, and left the inn.

His next stop was to be a town by a river, both with unpronounceable names. It should take about four hours to reach the unpronounceable town. If everything ran to plan.

Presently, Brown, striding through the sun-splashed blackness of the forest, realized he must have taken the wrong track. For it seemed to him the landscape was familiar. That leaning sapling, for example, and the fallen pine beyond— and then that break in the trees, through which the daylight currently streamed so vividly.

Brown halted, staring out with disfavor and a degree of annoyance. And there, sun-painted now on the sky, stood up again the old tower, with the pines still climbing toward it, and the yellow weeds still hanging down by the windows.

For a long while Brown paused, gazing at the tower. It was not a great distance away, perhaps a couple of miles, or not so much. He noticed a slender path of trodden earth ran down through the forest here, that seemed to lead directly to the foot of the hill, which really, itself, was not significantly steep.

He found he had walked forward without noticing it, and was on the beginnings of the path, descending toward the shallow valley that lay below the hill. See what sheer indolence, mere indifference, could lead to! Did he truly want to go in this direction? Did he *want* to climb up and gape at a nondescript ruin—which probably it *was,* a ruin, when one saw it close to? Then again, why not? It was all the same to him. One more rather pointless episode. *Climbed up to tower,* he mentally penned in his notes. *Nothing much to look at. Perhaps dating from the fifteenth century; creepers all over it. Not much of a view, as surrounded on all sides by the forest.*

As he had believed the path, and the subsequent climb, were not overly taxing for a man who had, so far, mostly walked through two or three countries already.

Well before noon, he had come up and out just below the hill top, and the stonework loomed in front of him.

Something about the tower was after all rather interesting—but what? It was lean, which had made it look taller, though it was not in fact high—perhaps thirty-five feet? Its construction had been from a darkish, smoothish stone, polished subsequently by weather, like the carapace of some hard, smooth, rugged sea-creature, possibly. The narrow window-slots appeared quite a way off from the ground, but were, of course, only some twenty-eight or thirty feet up. Nor would they be so narrow, one reasoned, when viewed at their own level. Something he would not be able to do. It was not a tower to climb, not in any way. Nor did he wish to. What besides could be up there—an empty stone space—or else it was full of the wrecked debris from some previous era, only left unthieved because it was so worthless.

But there was a curious and strangely pleasant smell that hung around the tower. It did not resemble the balsamic fragrance of the pines, let alone their other flavors of dryness and wetness, fruition and fading death. On the contrary, the tower had a—what was it? A sort of *honeyed* scent, like the tempting sweetmeats of the Middle East.

Were they the peculiar hanging creepers that gave off this aroma? There seemed to be nothing else that would do so.

Brown was reluctant to go nearer and sniff at them. They were doubtless full of insects, and might even have tiny thorns. One could never tell with alien species. Their color, however, was really after all quite beautiful. Less yellow than a golden effect, a shining *radiant* hue.

There now, despite his caution, he had approached very close. In fact, there seemed nothing remotely injurious about the plant. It was, if anything, extremely *silken,* and totally untangled—as if, fanciful notion, *combed* by careful and loving hands. And yes, the perfume was exuded by these multiple 'locks'. Irresistibly, Brown leaned forward, and drew into his lungs the delicious scent. What *was* it that this recalled for him? *Was* it confectionary—or flowers? Exactly then, something gleamed out above him. Involuntarily, Brown's neck snapped back. He found he gaped up the stem of the tower at the single window-slot directly above. He noted as he did so that oddly the creeper actually seemed, instead of having grown about the stone embrasures, to be extruded from their openings, hung *out* of the windows like some weird and ethereal washing, falling free thereafter down the tower wall.

But what had *that* been meanwhile—that glimpse he had had—something which passed across the slot thirty feet above; something white and vivid and—surely—alive—?

Arrested there, straining his neck, Brown was aware in that moment of a wild memory, the line of some poem, or of a song made from one, a piece by a well-known and respected poet and novelist—Thomas Hardy, was it?—Golden hair—open your window—Golden Hair—

Something shifted, some loose array of pebbles, or a rock, under the sole of one of Brown's boots. Losing his balance, instinctively he grabbed for the side of the tower. But his hands missed their purchase, and met instead the warm waterfall of the creeper. How strong it was, yet exquisitely silky and soft, vibrant with its own aureate and glowing life-force. A delight to touch, to hold. And the perfume now, pouring over him, wonderful as some mysterious drug.

He sensed he could fall forward, and the creeper would respond. It would catch him and lull him, support and caress him; he need fear nothing. With a startled oath, Brown sprang backward. An icy sweat had burst from every pore of his body. The world rocked beneath him and all about. He was— quite *terrified.* What in God's name had happened—?

"Damnation!" Brown exclaimed.

How absurd—the creeper—the creeper had attached itself to him, to his fingers, hands and arms—a rich swathe had
folded itself against his chest, nestling there on his clothing,
on the skin of his neck, *stuck fast.* For it was *sticky.* Sticky as
some ghastly glue—

Struggling, writhing and floundering, he shouted and
swore and tore at the encumbrance, trying exasperated, and
next with all his strength, to pull free—how stupid, how *silly.*
He was a fool—but how, *how* to release himself? The more
he pulled and fought, the more it wrapped itself against, onto
and *around* him—Now it had somehow got up into his hair,
dislodging his hat, and it had wound about his throat—like an
expensive muffler—and the scent, *too* sweet finally, cloying,
sickening—he retched, and chokingly bellowed for help to
some nonexistent fellow human, to the sky, and to the tower
itself, to God—None and nothing replied.

Silence then. A hiatus. Brown had ceased to resist, since resis-
tance seemed futile. Through his mind went a jumble of the
words of the inn-host: "To go there—inadvisable. Even to
look at it—unlucky." So no one would come in this direction,
and if they must, they would not look. Nor listen and heed,
presumably, should they hear anyone calling or crying out for
assistance—

In the name of Heaven, what was he to do?

Brown tried to collect himself together. The situation was
fantastic, but had to be rectifiable. He was a grown man, not
unstrong. True, he could not reach his pocket knife, the only
cutting implement he possessed, aside from his teeth and
nails—which would inevitably be inadequate. And the
creeper had roped him round very securely. But there must
be some way! Stay calm, and *think.*

Thoughts came, but they were no help. He saw himself
instead held here for weeks, months, as he slowly died of hunger and thirst, or was poisoned by the stenchful sweetness.

So horrible was this, and so unusually sharply imagined,
that for a moment he missed the other, newer sensation.

But then the faint quiver and tensing grew more adamant,

and next there was a solid jerk that tipped him off his feet.
Tangled in the weedy net he did not, of course, fall. Or rather,
he seemed to be falling *upward*—

For several seconds, Brown did not grasp what went on.
But soon enough reality flooded in. It would have been hard
to ignore, indeed, as the ground dropped away, the hillside
too, the forested valley, even the lower pines on the surround-
ing heights. The old stones rubbed slickly against him as he
slid. The sky seemed to open, staring eyeless yet intent at his
incongruous plight, while the creeper, muscular as the arms
of a giant, dragged him without any effort up the stalk of the
ancient tower.

Perhaps he lost consciousness for a minute. That was what
had happened. He was only dimly aware of the rough tugging
and squeezing that shoveled him in at the thin, hard window-
slot. His knees and left shoulder were particularly bruised.
But they were minor concerns, given the rest.

Spun up in the golden creeper-mass, coughing and retching still, the spasms uncontrollable if intermittent, Brown lay
in a sort of knotted ball on a floor of bitterly cold stone. He
was not able really to move, for the slightest motion, even the
helpless oesophagal spasms, seemed to glue and mesh him
more, and so confine him further.

The internal atmosphere was dark, though not lightless.
The day poured through at the narrow slot and lit his golden
chains heartlessly. Here and there patches of light also
smudged the stony inner walls. They comprised a room he
supposed, a guard-post, one assumed, centuries before. But
now nothing was there, only himself, and the restraining weed.

Inadvertently almost, Brown thrust and rolled and kicked
at his binding—or attempted to do so. It was, as earlier, to no
avail—in fact, again, it made things somewhat worse.

Brown started to sob, but managed to subdue this. If he
lost a grip on himself, he would have nothing left. Nothing
at all.

Someone had hauled him up here. That much was self-
evident. They had used the creeper, which must have been
treated in some bizarre way, and had therefore become both

lure and trap. Then they had dragged him in like any hapless fish on a line. Soon enough, no doubt, the villain—or villains— would return and hold him to account, maybe requiring a ransom. Brown groaned aloud, thinking of his two maiden aunts, neither wealthy, or the feckless uncle whom Brown had not seen for over fourteen years. But maybe there would be some other way. Or he might even escape, when once he was unbound.

Brown desperately longed then for his enemy to come back, to free him at least, if only partially, from the net. Presently he called out, in a stern although deliberately non-angry manner, firstly in English, then in the correct local vernacular.

No answer was proffered. There was no sound at all— aside, naturally, from the occasional brush of the breeze beyond the window-slit, the pulse of a bird's wings.

Once he thought he heard a hunter's dog bark two or three times, in the woods below. If only they would come this way—if only he might call again and be heard.

Brown composed himself on the hard, frigid floor, and in his cramped discomfort and bruised pain. He would have to be patient and stoical. Pragmatic.

The spasms had eased. The perfume reek seemed less. Conversely, he sensed the quietly dismal fetor of an enclosed and poorly ventilated place where beasts had died, and too many years stagnated.

He closed his eyes, for the constricted light dazzled, and the contrasting darkness was too full of cobwebs and shadows and *shutness*—except *there,* just beyond where his vision, his head being so constrained from movement, could reach— over *there,* in that wall, something that might be a very low doorway, a sort of arch . . . or maybe not.

Brown's watch had stopped—some knock against the window embrasure. But the clock of the day had gone on, and now the evening arrived. The sky outside the tower was turning a soft, delicate mauve, with vague extinguishing tints of red toward what must be the west. It would be very dark soon. It would be night.

Had anyone come in to inspect their catch? He believed

not, though somehow it seemed he had fallen either into a
stifled doze, or else some kind of trance.

The choking and nausea had passed, but he could not now
have moved, or struggled, even if the web containing him had
permitted it. How curious, Brown mused, deep in his haphaz-
ardly self-controlled, near anesthetic misery, a *web*. For was
not the creeper very like that, a web? Tempting and beautiful
in its own way, but sticky, a snare, and the means to an ultimate capture. And storage.

Should he call out again? If anyone had entered the tower,
and was below, they must definitely come up to see to him.
There might be threats, or violence, but then, if they wanted
him for ransom, at least for a while they would try to keep
him in one piece—or so he must hope. If he could talk to
them, make promises—however rash or implausible—exhort
them to see reason—He was not done for yet! He shouted, as
loudly and *calmly* as he was able. And, after a minute, again.

And—*yes*. There was at last a faint yet quite distinct movement that he had heard, a little below and behind him. If only
he could turn his head—Brown endeavored to, and his neck
was spitefully wrenched. He gave out a quickly mastered yelp
of physical hurt, protest, and frustration.

But the movement, the *sound,* was being repeated, over
and over. Steps, he thought, soft, careful, rather shuffling
steps, as of a person elderly, or somewhat infirm, climbing
now up, toward this room.

Thank God, Brown thought. *Thank God.*

"Good evening," said Brown, urbane yet cool, the proper
tone, he had judged, in which to greet his lawless captor. The
steps had taken a long time to reach him, and once during
their progress he had called out again, but now having spoken, he lay bunched and dumb, tense in every fiber and nerve,
awaiting a response—of any kind. Because he could not turn
and *see,* Brown was visualizing myriad versions of the one
who had so astonishingly made a prisoner of him. A bandit,
or merely a peasant driven into crime, or some eccentric
landowner, a savage *child*—but disabled, certainly, to assess

those footfalls; nevertheless obviously dangerous and conceivably lunatic. Brown must proceed very prudently. Yet even as he speculated on and guessed at all this, he sensed the *other* behind him, not moving now, needing a pause to recover, maybe, from the climb, although there was no noise of labored breathing, or other token of distress. Perhaps some old wound had discommoded him, nothing recent, something to which he was accustomed. And now he only stood at the entry to the room, gloating. Or . . . unsure—could it be *that?* A robber regretting his act, or nervous that its victim, under his shackles, looked far from weak, or himself unable—

"What did you say?" asked Brown. His voice came out far too urgently, and frightened in tone. "I didn't hear you," he added firmly, now much too like a schoolmaster, he thought.

But the visitor had only made one small extra sound. Not a word, no, it had not been conversation. A type of whispering, wheezing, *murmur.*

"You'd better," said Brown, "tell me straight out—"

And this was all he had time to say, before the one who had come in moved suddenly forward, and was against, and over, and *on* him.

Where he had had a glimpse of something gleaming and white high above, when he stood outside and below the tower, he had the impression now of a mask, pale as marble, yet glistening and streaming with an oily moisture that came from nowhere but itself. Nor was it any mask that resembled a human face. It was long and snouted and somehow *blind*—and yet—it could see—and there were huge long, slender needles—that might be teeth—and the large body was stretched out, horizontal, *heavy,* made of flesh but also hard and pale and gleaming-moist, and *stinking,* and there—hands—so many dead-white hands, each with just four fingers, and they flashed, *flashed,* and things tore at Brown, too fast to hurt, and then the hurt came, in long, openwork waves, and he screamed and thrashed in the ever-tightening ropes of the golden-yellow web, that was like hair, and would not give, or break, but Brown must give and Brown must break, and he gave and broke, and his screaming sank to a dull and mindless whining, and then to nothing at all, as the venomous fangs and the thirty-two claws of the creature the witch had raised from the womb on rampion and murder and darkness, began to prepare and present and devour its slow and thorough dinner. As already they had done, so many, countless times before.

Kiss Kiss

YOU SEE, I was only eleven when it began. I'm twenty-three years of age now. Just over twice that lifetime. But did I know more when I was younger? Was I more wise then than now?

The estate was small, and although my father was a prince, we were by no means rich. That is, we had fires in winter, and furs heaped on the beds. There was plenty of game in the forests for my father and his fifteen men to hunt and bring home as dinner. We had wine and beer. And in the spring the blossom was beautiful. And all summer there was the wheat, and afterward the fruit from the orchards. But I had holes in all but my best dress, as my mother did. One day, I would have to have something fine, because I would need to be married. I didn't question this, the only use I was, being a girl: the princess. Sixteen was the normal age. My mother said I was pretty, and would do. It was all right. And on my eleventh birthday, he gave me, my father, this incredible present. Since we didn't have so very much, seeing it, I knew, despite appearances, he must think I had a proper value. My mother gasped. I stood speechless. I really didn't need him to say, "It's gold. Gold over bronze. Be careful with it."

I said nothing. My mother said, "But, dearest—"

He cut her short, as usual. "It can be part of her dowry. They're popular in the city. They're lucky, apparently. You may," he said, "throw it up and catch it. Don't roll it along. It would get scratched."

"Thank you, Papa."

I held the golden ball in utter awe. It was very heavy. It was, I think, for strong young lordlings to throw about. My slender wrists ached from its weight.

But I took it out through the neglected garden, and walked

with it down the overgrown paths, to the lake among the pine trees where, in the worst winters, the wolves came, blue as smoke, and howled.

I've heard it said that sometimes when a man stands near the brink of a cliff, he may think, What if I step over? Just such an awful thought came to me as I stood by the lake, which was muddy and rushy in the summer evening. Suppose I let go the golden ball, and let it roll, scratching itself, over into the deeper water?

No sooner had I thought it, than a bird screeched in the trees of the forest on the lake's far side. And I started, and the ball dropped from my tired hands.

It rolled, flush, through the grass, in through the reeds with their dry, brown-purple flowers. I ran after it all the way, calling to it, stupidly crying, *No, no—*

And then it slid over the water's edge, straight in and down. Under the surface I saw it glimmer for one whole second, like a drowned sun. And then I saw it no more.

What could I do? I didn't do anything. I stood staring after the lucky golden ball, lost in the brown mirror of water, sobbing.

My father hadn't ever beaten me, at least, not with his hands. He had a hard tongue. I dreaded what he would say. I dreaded what I'd done. To be such a fool.

Gnats whined in the air. One stung me, and I scratched my neck, still crying. The scratching made a noise in my ear that suddenly said, "Little girl, little princess, why are you weeping?"

I stopped in amazement. Had I imagined it? The voice came again, "Can I help you, little princess?"

No one was there. Only the gnats furled over the dry flowers. At the edge of the water, in the shallows, something was stirring.

The sun was among the pines now, flashing. It caught the edges of the ripples in brassy rings. And two round eyes.

"Have you lost something precious?"

What was it? A frog . . . no, it was too big. The round eyes, colored like the duller flashes of the sun.

"Yes—I've lost—my golden ball."

"I saw it go down. I know where it is."

I thought, blankly, I've gone mad. It's the fright. Like the girl last year when the wild horse ran through the wedding party. She went mad. She was locked away. They'll lock me away.

I turned, to rush off up the sloping ground, toward my father's disheveled towers.

The voice called again. "Here I am. Look. You'll see, I'm well able to go after your precious ball."

Then I stopped and I did look. And it came out of the water part of the way, and I saw it.

I gave a squeal.

It said, "Don't be afraid. I'm gentle."

It *was* like a frog. A sort of little, almost-man thing that was a frog. Scaled, a pale yet a dark green, with round, brownish glowing frog's eyes. It had webbed fore-feet that might be hands. It held them up. They had no claws. And in its open mouth seemed nothing, but a long dark tongue.

I was terrified. It was a sprite, a lake-spirit, the sort the old women put out cakes for in the village, to stop their mischief.

It said, plaintively, "Don't you want your golden ball, then?"

My first adult decision, perhaps, was between these two evils. My angry father, and the uncanny creature from the lake.

"I want the ball."

"If I fetch it," said the frog-demon, "I must have a favor in return."

"What do you want?"

"To be yours."

It was so unequivocal—and yet, as I found out soon enough, so subtle. "Mine? How?"

"To belong to you, princess."

Was it pride or avarice, a desire for some power in my powerless existence? To have a spirit as my slave. No. I think I only knew I had to get back the ball. And because it hadn't said to me, I must have your virtue, or, I must have your first-born child, as in the stories they do, I was just relieved to say, "All right. You can be mine. Please fetch it me!"

After it had gone down, with one treacly little *plop*, I

stood there thinking I'd been dreaming. I even started to
search about for the golden ball, in case that too was a dream,
a bad one.

The sun went into the blacker lower third of the forest,
and the sky above grew coppery. Crickets started across the
fields. An owl called early for the shadows.

Then the water parted again, and up came the necessary
golden ball, real and actual and there. It was clasped by two
scaly frog hands.

I went gingerly down and took the ball, snatched it. I held
it to my breast with all my fingers.

Then the frog-thing's face broke the water. Even then, I
could see how sad its face was, the way certain animal faces
are. Its eyes might have been made of tawny tears.

"Remember your promise."

"Yes."

As I hurried back toward the pile of the house, I heard it
coming, hopping, after me. Not looking, I said, "*Go away!*"

"If I belong to you," it said, "I must be with you. Every
minute. Day and night."

Then I saw, the way the maiden does, always too late, in
the tale, what she has agreed to.

"You can't! You *can't!*"

"You promised me."

I started to pray then to God, in whom I believed, but
from whom I expected nothing, ever. He'd never answered
any of my youthful prayers. And didn't do so now.

But the frog-thing came to me, quite near. It stood as high
as my knee. It had frog legs, huge webbed feet, without claws.
Sunset gleamed on its scales. In its scratch of a voice it said,
"I won't speak to them. I won't tell them you lost the ball. I
can do things they'll like. Find things. It will be all right."

But I ran away. Of course. Of course, it ran after.

In the garden, by the broken statue of a god, an old god
even more deaf than God, I had to stop for breath. The golden
ball had weighed me down. I hated it. I hated it worse than
the frog-demon. In that moment I knew, too, how much I
hated my father.

The frog had reached me without trouble. It hopped high,

right up on the stone god's arm. And out of its mouth it pulled a most beautiful flower. Perhaps it had brought it from the lake. Creamy pink, with a faint perfume, thinner and more fresh than roses.

The demon leaned, and before I could flinch away, it had put the flower in my hair.

I thought, out of my new hatred for my father, Anyway, he'll kill this thing as soon as he sees it.

I tossed my head, and the flower filled the air with scent. I hated everyone by now, and all things. Let them all kill each other.

"Come on, then," I said, and went toward the house, and the frog-thing hopped along at my side.

They called it Froggy. That was their way. They used to throw it scraps from the table. It wouldn't ever touch meat. It had a little fish, and it liked green things, and fruit, but I don't know how it ate for it seemed to have no teeth. And this I never learned.

In the beginning, they were more circumspect with it — after, that is, the first outburst.

When I came into the hall, the women were at the hearth, and the boy was turning the smaller spit for the dead hares my father had taken in the forest. The house had a kitchen, but it was only used when there were guests. Half the time the bread was baked here, too.

The owl-shadows were gathering, red from the fire, and one of the men was lighting the candles. In all this flicker of red and dark, no one saw the frog for some while.

I got up to my mother, who was wearing her better hall-dress that had only one darn in it. She took hold of me at once, and called her maid to comb my hair.

It was the maid who saw the frog first. She screamed out loud and pulled out a clump of my hair.

"Uh — mistress — ah! What is it?"

I was too ashamed to speak. My mother naturally didn't know. She peered at the thing.

It stood there patiently, looking up at her with its sad face. It had vowed not to speak to anyone but me.

The maid was crossing herself, spitting at the corner to avoid bad luck.

At the fire they had turned and were gawping. And just then my father stormed in with his men, and three of the hunting dogs, stinking of blood and unwashed masculinity. One of the dogs, the biggest, saw the frog at once. He came leaping for it, straight up the hall. As this happened, the frog gave a jump. It was up a tree of lit candles, wrapped there about one of the iron spikes, and the wax splashed its scales, but it didn't make a sound.

The dog growled and drooled, pressed against the candle-tree, its eyes red, its hair on end.

My father strode over at once.

He said to me, as I might have known he would, "Where's your golden ball, girl?"

"Here, Father."

He looked at that. Then up the candle-tree. My father frowned.

"By Christ," said my father.

Although I hated him, hate can't always drive out fear, as love can't. In terror I blurted, "It came out of the lake. It followed me home. I couldn't stop it. It wants to be with me."

My mother put her hand over her mouth, a gesture she often resorts to, as if she knows she might as well not cry out or talk, since no one will bother.

My father said, "I've heard of them. Water demons. Why did it come out? What were you doing?" He glared at me. This must be my fault. And it was.

"Nothing, Papa."

He folded his arms, and lowered at the frog. The frog eased itself a little on the stand. Leaning over from the waist, it bowed, like a courtly gentleman, to my father. Who gave a bark of laughter. Turning, he kicked the dog away. "It's lucky. They bring good luck. We must be careful of it."

He ordered them to carve some of the half-raw hare, and offered it to the frog, which wouldn't have it. Then one of the women crept up with a cup of milk. The frog took this in a webbed paw, and had a few sips. Despite its frog mouth, it didn't slurp.

Once they had driven the dogs off, the men stood about

laughing and cursing, and the frog jumped on to the table. It got up on its hands and ran about, and the men laughed more, and even the women slunk close to see. When it reached the unlit candles at the table's center, it blew on them. They flowered into pale yellow flame.

This drew applause. They said to each other: See, it's *good* magic. It's funny. And when it scuttled over to me and jumped out and caught my girdle, hanging on there at my waist so I shrank and almost shrieked, they cheered. I was favored. They'd heard of such things. It would be a *good* year, now.

It was. It was a good year. The harvest was wonderful, and some gambling my father did brought in a few golden coins. Also, the frog found a ruby ring that had been lost or hidden— by an ancestor in the house. All this was excellent. And they said, when they saw me coming, the demon at my side, "Here's the princess, with her frog."

But that was after. It took them a little while to be so at home with it. And that first night, after my father encouraged me to feed it from my plate, let it share my cup of watered wine, when it started to follow me up the stone stair, where the torches smuttily burned, he stood up. "Put it outside your door," he said. "We don't know it's clean in its habits." This, from one who had, more than once, thrown up from drink in my mother's bed. Who defecated in a pot, who occasionally pissed against indoor walls. The servant women being expected to see to it all.

When we reached my room, I tried to shut the frog-demon outside in the passage. But it slipped past.

"I must be with you," it said, the first time it had spoken since we came in. "Day and night. Every minute."

"Why?" I wailed.

"Because I must."

"Horrible slimy thing!"

I tried to kick it aside. Did I say I was a nice girl? I hadn't learned at all to be nice, and was almost as careless and cruel to servants and animals as the rest of them.

But it eluded my foot, which anyway was only in a threadbare shoe, not booted like the feet of the always-dog-kicking men.

It wasn't slimy. I'd felt it. It was dry and smooth, its scales like thin plates of polished dull metal. When it sprang lightly on my bed, I took off my so far useless shoe, and flung it. But the frog-demon caught my shoe, and put it on its head like a hat.

At that, finally, I too laughed.

I didn't want it on my pillow. But on to my pillow it came. Its breath was cool and smelled of green leaves. In the dark, its eyes were two small lamps.

It sang to me. A sort of story. At last I lay and listened. The story was the accustomed kind my nurse had told me, but I was not yet too old for it. A maiden rescued from her brutal father by a handsome prince. Even then, even liking the tale, I didn't believe such men existed. I knew already what men were, and, without understanding, what they did to women, having seen it here and there, my father's men and the kitchen girls. It had looked and sounded violent, and both of them, each time, seemed to be in pain, scratching and shaking each other in distress.

Even so. No one had sat with me and told me a story, not for years.

In the night, I woke once, and it was curled up against my head. It smelled so green, so clean. I touched its cool back with my finger. It was mine, after all. Now I too owned something. And it would only talk to me.

Already when I look back, my childhood seems far away, my girlhood even farther. Old women speak of themselves in youth as if of other women. I am so old, then?

During the time they all came quite round to it, and called it Froggy, and the Princess's Frog, I must have been growing up with wild rapidity, the way the young do, every day a little more.

While it performed tricks for them, found for them things that had been lost, seemed to improve the hunting, the harvests, and the luck, I became, bit by bit, a woman. You see, I don't remember so much of it, because so much was always the same. It's all, in memory, one long day, one long night. The incidents are jumbled together like old clothes in a chest.

I recollect my bleeding starting, and the fuss, and how I

hated it—I do so still, but the alternative state of pregnancy appeals less. I recall the bear in the forest winter who mauled one of the men, and he died. I remember the priest coming on holy days, and blessing us, and that he too liked to touch the buttocks of the maids, and once of the kitchen boy, who later ran away.

The priest looked askance at Froggy. He asked was it some deformed thing from a traveling freak show, and my father prudently said he had bought it for me, since it was clever and made me laugh. Also, he said, it was fiercer than the dogs and would protect me. That was a lie, too. The frog was only gentle. Although, in the end, the dogs respected it and gave up trying to catch it. The biggest dog would let Froggy ride him, and all the while Froggy would murmur in the dog's ear. This was after the big dog was bitten by a snake in the forest, and ran home yelping, with terror in his eyes, knowing he would die of snake-bite, or the men would cut his throat.

But Froggy, when the dog fell down exhausted, scuttled over and latched its wide mouth on the bite. Froggy sucked out the poison, and dribbled it on the floor with the blood. Everyone stood back in astonishment, one of the men muttering, stupidly, if the dog died it would be Froggy's fault. But the dog recovered, and never forgot.

The women took to tempting Froggy to lick cuts on their hands to make them better. Froggy never refused. They said it was because they rubbed on honey first. They called this a 'frog's kiss'.

It never spoke to anyone but me.

And I remember one afternoon, when I had the by-now familiar black pain of menstruation in my belly, and I was lying in the spring grass, and Froggy was sitting quietly on my stomach, where the pain was, kneading me gently, until I was soothed and slept and the pain died.

The sun was in the orchard trees, that were just then losing their blossom, and all this yellow-white-green shone behind my frog, all puffed with light. The frog sang or chanted. Some old tale again. What was it? A knight who rescued a maiden. I saw for the first time how beautiful it was, this creature. Its amber eyes like jewels, the smooth pear shape of its body, like burnished, carven, pale, dark jade. The paws that were webbed hands and feet, and had no claws. The sculpted mouth, with its rim of paler green, toothless and fragrant. The healing tongue.

I smiled at the frog, not from amusement, but from love. I loved it. It was my friend.

After this, I seemed to learn things. The meanings of bird-song. The ways of animals, and of weather. I was more gentle, too. Who had I learned that from but Froggy? There was no one else.

My mother pulled me to her about this time. She was, despite the luck, still unchilded, and my always-displeased father had slapped her. There was a bruise under her eye where one of his rings had cut her skin. She seemed proud of the bruise, often touching at it in the hall, as if to show off that her husband still paid her attentions.

"Look at you, such a big girl. You must have more binding for your bosoms. And you mustn't run about so much." Sometimes I would receive these lessons, no one else took any notice of her. Finally neither did I. But now she added, playfully tweaking my ear, "You must have earrings. He'll want to find you a husband soon. He's mentioned it. A man with land and soldiers. You're a pretty girl, if only you'd leave off these sluttish ways. Do you ever comb your hair? I'll send you the girl to brush it every night with rose oil."

I thought of my father, planning to marry me to some large, uncouth and appalling landowner, someone like himself. From my thirteenth birthday, until now, I'd tried never to think about it. But I was fifteen. The awful appointment approached.

I ran off as soon as I could, the frog bouncing after me like a jade ball—the golden one had long ago been put into a coffer.

In fact, I don't remember I ever spoke of my troubles to Froggy. He was always there. Every minute. Night and day. He knew. And when my stomach hurt he kneaded it, or when I woke crying from a nightmare he comforted me, or made me laugh. I'll say He, now. I might as well.

I sat on the old stone horse statue at the foot of the

garden, which now I was tall and agile enough to climb, and Froggy sat in my lap, plaiting for me, web-fingered, a crown of red daisies. Butterflies danced, and the willows by the lake looked very bright. Later there would be a summer storm.

Froggy told me a story. It was new. A prince was cast into a dungeon. His lady came to find him and rescued him by putting magic on the bars.

At first I didn't know why the story was so strange.

Then I said. "But it's the man who rescues the maiden. She's weak and helpless. She can't do anything. He's strong and clever. It has to be him."

"Oh, no," said Froggy. "Not always. A man may be made weak, and overthrown. And do you think men are so clever, then?"

I shook my head. I gabbled, in sudden horror and fear. "I'll have to marry one of them. He'll take me away." And then I said, "He may be unkind to you as well."

"But I shan't be with you," said Froggy softly. "If you marry this man."

Astounded I stared. He raised his wonderful topaz-amber eyes. "Not be with me—but you're always there."

"Then, it would be impossible. He'd kill me, you see. Or I'd die."

I put my arms round Froggy and held him. He never struggled, as an animal, a puppy or a cat, would do. I laid my cheek against the crown of his head, the scales of smoky jade. "You're my only friend. Don't leave me."

"It must be. If you marry the man your father finds you."

My tears will have streamed over him. But I said, at last, "It won't happen. I'll stay here. I won't be married. Never."

I might as well have said, Night won't fall, or the sun won't rise tomorrow. Before when I first bled, and ran about screaming, thinking I was dying—no one had bothered to prepare me—Froggy had calmed me instead—before I bled, I'd never have thought such a filthy thing was possible. And with marriage, the threat had always been there, as long as I could recall.

My husband-to-be visited us just before Christmas that winter.

He was like the bear they said had killed my father's man, and clad in a black bearskin cloak, with clasps of gold. He had a gold stud in his ear, too. His boots were leather, his shirt embroidered. His men were well-turned-out and armed to the teeth. He stank of everything. I can't begin to itemize his smells. He was about forty, and I nearly sixteen.

I, contrarily, had been bathed in the porcelain chair-bath, and my hair had been washed and brushed with rose oil. I had on my best, newest dress, without darns, and earrings of gray-white pearl, and a ring of gold.

When he saw me, he struck a pose, my intended husband; he bowed and fawned, as if I were some great lord, or a bishop, or a king. Everyone laughed heartily, and he straightened up all good nature.

"You see, I like her. I'll take her." Then he kissed me. He had shaved, but already his skin was rough and he scraped my mouth. But that would be nothing.

The dinner was lavish. My frog did wonderful tricks, lighting the candles, cutting a fruit with a tap of his hand, finding things people had hidden, and juggling the bones of some poor little birds we had eaten.

In the end, we were able to go, the women and Froggy, to leave the men to get spectacularly drunk. My mother took me to her bower, the shabby room that led from the bedchamber. She sat me by the fire to pat my flushed face and feed me sugared walnuts.

"What a good girl. He liked you so. Oh it will be a lovely wedding. The church all hung with flowers. The day after your birthday. And you must have three new gowns, your father says. He's a generous man. And your husband will shower you with things in your first months. He's rich. Be careful to please him and you may even see yourself in silk!"

"How do I please him?" I asked, sullen with terror.

"It's simple, child. Never ever say no. God said women must be obedient. Do whatever your lord wants. And—well, I'll speak of that later, your wedding night. But you must always pretend that you like what he does. Recollect always, he's your superior. You owe everything to him."

I couldn't say that he made me sick, that I wished to throw

up from his kiss. I knew about sex, although she had tried to hide it from me, as she had successfully hidden menstruation. The thought of that struggling and grappling and the obvious pain, with *him*, repelled me so greatly I couldn't even think about it.

I said, "I see, Mama." And at my feet, the frog ate a little sugar, staring into the fire that made his eyes look, also, green.

When she sent me to bed—I must be at my best to see the monstrous husband off tomorrow; in fact she knew my delighted, drunken father would want intercourse with her tonight—I ran, Froggy in my arms, and shouted at the woman with the rose oil to go away.

Then, rocking Froggy, I wept, until needles seemed to be drawn through my eyes.

My own fire was out by then. It was growing stealthily and awesomely cold. I said, "Let's go into the forest. The wolves may kill us or we'll freeze. Let's do it. Anything. Anything instead of *him*."

There was a long silence. I heard the stars crackling like icy knives in the black sky. Then the frog spoke back to me.

"There's another way."

"No. No other way. Nothing."

"Yes. Do you remember the maiden who was rescued?"

"Oh, that story—"

"Do you remember the prince that the maiden saved with her love?"

"Shush," I said. I would say today: But this is true life. This is real, and inescapable. Here, there are no miracles or magic. Then I said, "Don't talk about those silly things. They can't help me."

"Yes. I'll tell you how."

I held him in my arms and he spoke and I listened. His voice—the very voice he used to charm the dog, to charm *them*—scratchy and little, mesmerizing in the silence.

"A spell can be broken so simply, princess. Do you love me by now?"

"*Yes*."

"Then all you need do is kiss me. On my frog's mouth. Is that unthinkable?"

"I had to kiss *him*."

"I'm not like that."

I looked down at him, my slumbrous, umbrous jewel. His holy frog face. My friend. "I'd have done it—I just thought you might not like me to—"

"*I?*" He couldn't smile. His eyes smiled, half closing, like a cat's. "Do it now," he said.

I never in my life did anything more easily. I lifted him up, and kissed him. His mouth was like a summer leaf, cool, a little moist, smelling of fresh salad, and with a crumb of sugar from the walnuts—*sweet*.

When I opened my eyes it was because my hands and my arms were empty.

"Who are you?" I said. I was so afraid, I was numb.

He said, "My God, it hurt so much. Worse than before. Oh God."

He leaned on my wooden chair, and then dropped into it. His shining golden hair fell long over his pale face. I had never seen a man who was so beautiful. He wasn't like a man. An angel, perhaps. I heard him breathing. Presently, in his musical voice, he said to me, "Little princess, my enemies worked against me. They changed me to the form—of what you saw. But your loving kiss—has brought me back. Now I'm yours for ever, and you're mine."

His eyes, as he looked at me, were not amber or green. They were very dark, the color of night, just as his hair was the color of day. His garments too. Fur, gold, steel, gems.

What did I feel? I was excited. I tingled all over. The fairy story had come true.

I didn't need to hear the sound of hoofs below, galloping, bells ringing from the village, to know his men were coming, all glorious as he was, washed, perfumed, and brave, armed to the teeth. Spell broken, he could drive the unwanted husband away. And my father—he would never cease to be grateful to me for the alliance I had brought him instead, this other husband, a prince who had been a frog.

And yet, I only went back to him slowly. He was now far larger than I. My head, when he stood up, reached just below his shoulder. The enormous rings on his fingers were icy. He had a smell like fire not water. But it was very cold.

My arms were empty, but he took me into his instead. What was wrong? What did I miss?

Oh, I missed my friend.

There was never such a wedding. They still talk about it, seven years after. Of course, I left my father's house. A bride does. She belongs to her husband. But he owns a princedom. My father cried large tears of greed as he bade me farewell.

There's everything here. A bed all my own, with a canopy shaped like a firmament and stitched with diamond stars, a different bath for every day of the week, marble, rose-quartz, cinnabar, and so on. There are foods, and drinks, I'd never heard of. He has a menagerie, with lions. His people, now he has come back, worship him like a god.

It was almost a year before he began to eat meat again. This was advised, to make him strong, and it worked, because soon after I conceived a child and it was a son. I've given him three sons now, and my body has changed shape a little. This happens. A woman's lot. Sex remains a mystery to me. But yes, it does hurt.

In our third year together, he struck me for the first time. It was over some small quarrel—I'd forgotten my mother's rule of obedience. I mean, God's rule. My husband was gracious afterward, said he was sorry, and sent me a rose made of rubies, just the color my blood had been from the broken tooth.

Despite the baths, he's just a little understandably lax that way. He smells of health and meat and wine, sweat, lust, sometimes of other women. From politeness, he says, he shuns me during menstruation. He never sings to me, or tells me stories, being very busy. He kicks the dogs.

I don't know why he changed so much, changed spiritual shape as pregnancy and birth physically have altered me. Was he always this way, when human? Yes, naturally. A fine, noble virile man. A prince. He doesn't juggle, never lights candles himself. Evidently, he's mislaid all the magic.

Every night, when I'm alone, as increasingly now, thank God, I am, in my heavenly bed, I say a prayer for the one I had. He taught me so much. He was my friend, my frog. He never left me. I loved him. Not like a baby, or a pet, not like a man. A unique and crystal love, all shattered now in pieces. I didn't know what was happening, and he must have suffered, being that other one. And so we wasted it, that perfect time. Now, it's forbidden to all of us to speak of it, the period of his life when he was enchanted. When he was a frog.

Nevertheless, I dream of it still. Sometimes. All that we did, when I was slender, young and free, and how I loved him so. And how I lost him for ever to that hateful betrayal of a kiss.

Into Gold

1

UP BEHIND DANUVIUS, the forests are black, and so stiff with black pork, black bears, and black-gray wolves, a man alone will feel himself jostled. Here and there you come on a native village, pointed houses of thatch with carved wooden posts, and smoke thick enough to cut with your knife. All day the birds call, and at night the owls come out. There are other things of earth and darkness, too. One ceases to be surprised at what may be found in the forests, or what may stray from them on occasion.

One morning, a corn-king emerged, and pleased us all no end. There had been some trouble, and some of the stores had gone up in flames. The ovens were standing empty and cold. It can take a year to get goods overland from the river, and our northern harvest was months off.

The old fort that had been the palace then for twelve years, was built on high ground. It looked out across a mile of country strategically cleared of trees, to the forest cloud and a dream of distant mountains. Draco had called me up to the roof-walk, where we stood watching these mountains glow and fade, and come and go. It promised to be a fine day, and I had been planning a good long hunt to exercise the men and give the breadless bellies solace. There is also a pine-nut meal they grind in the villages, accessible to barter. The loaves were not to everyone's taste, but we might have to come round to them. Since the armies pulled away, we had learned to improvise. I could scarcely remember the first days. The old men told you everything, anyway, had been going down to chaos even then. Draco's father, holding on to a commander's power, assumed a prince's title which his orphaned warriors were glad enough to concede him. Discipline is its own ritual, and drug. As, lands and seas away, from the center of the world caved in, soldier-fashion, they turned builders. They

made the road to the fort, and soon began on the town, shor-
ing it, for eternity, with strong walls. Next, they opened up the
country, and got trade rights seen to that had gone by default
for decades. There was plenty of skirmishing as well to keep
their swords bright. When the Commander died of a wound
got fighting the Blue-Hair Tribe, a terror in those days, not
seen for years since, Draco became the Prince in the Palace.
He was eighteen then, and I five days older. We had known
each other nearly all our lives, learned books and horses,
drilled, hunted together. Though he was born elsewhere, he
barely took that in, coming to this life when he could only just
walk. For myself, I am lucky, perhaps, I never saw the Mother
of Cities, and so never hanker after her, or lament her down-
fall.

That day on the roof-walk, certainly, nothing was further
from my mind. Then Draco said, "There is something."

His clear-water eyes saw detail quicker and more finely
than mine. When I looked, to me still it was only a blur and
fuss on the forest's edge, and the odd sparkling glint of things
catching the early sun.

"Now, Skorous, do you suppose . . . ?" said Draco.

"Someone has heard of our misfortune, and considerably
changed his route," I replied.

We had got news a week before of a grain-caravan, but too
far west to be of use. Conversely, it seemed, the caravan had
received news of our fire. "Up goes the price of bread," said
Draco.

By now I was sorting it out, the long rigmarole of mules
and baggage-wagons, horses and men. He traveled in some
style. Truly, a corn-king, profiting always because he was
worth his weight in gold amid the wilds of civilization. In Empire days, he would have weighed rather less.

We went down, and were in the square behind the east
gate when the sentries brought him through. He left his people out on the parade before the gate, but one wagon had
come up to the gateway, presumably his own, a huge convey-
ance, a regular traveling house, with six oxen in the shafts.
Their straps were spangled with what I took for brass. On the
side-leathers were pictures of grind-stones and grain done in

purple and yellow. He himself rode a tall horse, also spangled. He had a slim, snaky look, an Eastern look, with black brows and fawn skin. His fingers and ears were remarkable for their gold. And suddenly I began to wonder about the spangles. He bowed to Draco, the War-Leader and Prince. Then, to be quite safe, to me.

"Greetings, Miller," I said.

He smiled at this coy honorific.

"Health and greetings, Captain. I think I am welcome?"

"My prince," I indicated Draco, "is always hospitable to wayfarers."

"Particularly to those with wares, in time of dearth."

"Which dearth is that?"

He put one golden finger to one golden ear-lobe.

"The trees whisper. This town of the Iron Shields has no bread."

Draco said mildly, "You should never listen to gossip."

I said, "If you've come out of your way, that would be a pity."

The Corn-King regarded me, not liking my arrogance — though I never saw the Mother of Cities, I have the blood — any more than I liked his slink and glitter.

As this went on, I gambling and he summing up the bluff, the tail of my eye caught another glimmering movement, from where his house wagon waited at the gate. I sensed some woman must be peering round the flap, the way the Eastern females do. The free girls of the town are prouder, even the wolf-girls of the brothel, and aristocrats use a veil only as a sunshade. Draco's own sisters, though decorous and well brought-up, can read and write, each can handle a light chariot, and will stand and look a man straight in the face. But I took very little notice of the fleeting apparition, except to decide it too had gold about it. I kept my sight on my quarry, and presently he smiled again and drooped his eyelids, so I knew he would not risk calling me, and we had won. "Perhaps," he said, "there might be a little consideration of the detour I, so foolishly, erroneously, made."

"We are always glad of fresh supplies. The fort is not insensible to its isolation. Rest assured."

"Too generous," he said. His eyes flared. But politely he added, "I have heard of your town. There is great culture here. You have a library, with scrolls from Hellas, and Semitic Byblos—I can read many tongues, and would like to ask permission of your lord to visit among his books."

I glanced at Draco, amused by the fellow's cheek, though all the East thinks itself a scholar. But Draco was staring at the wagon. Something worth a look, then, which I had missed.

"And we have excellent baths," I said to the Corn-King, letting him know in turn that the Empire's lost children think all the scholarly East to be also unwashed.

By midday, the whole caravan had come in through the walls and arranged itself in the market-place, near the temple of Mars. The temple priests, some of whom had been serving with the Draconis Regiment when it arrived, old, old men, did not take to this influx. In spring and summer, traders were in and out the town like flies, and native men came to work in the forges and the tannery or with the horses, and built their muddy thatch huts behind the unfinished law-house—which huts winter rain always washed away again when their inhabitants were gone. To such events of passage the priests were accustomed. But this new show displeased them. The chief Salius came up to the fort, attended by his slaves, and argued a while with Draco. Heathens, said the priest, with strange rituals, and dirtiness, would offend the patron god of the town. Draco seemed preoccupied.

I had put off the hunting party, and now stayed to talk the Salius into a better humor. It would be a brief nuisance, and surely they had been directed to us by the god himself, who did not want his war-like sons to go hungry? I assured the priest that, if the foreigners wanted to worship their own gods, they would have to be circumspect. Tolerance of every religious rag, as we knew, was unwise. They did not, I thought, worship Iusa. There would be no abominations. I then vowed a boar to Mars, if I could get one, and the dodderer tottered, pale and grim, away.

Meanwhile, the grain was being seen to. The heathen god-offenders had sacks and jars of it, and ready flour besides. It seemed a heavy chancy load with which to journey, goods that might spoil if at all delayed, or if the weather went against them. And all that jangling of gold beside. They fairly bled gold. I had been right in my second thought on the bridle-decorations, there were even nuggets and bells hung on the wagons, and gold flowers; and the oxen had gilded horns. For the men, they were ringed and buckled and roped and tied with it. It was a marvel.

When I stepped over to the camp near sunset, I was on the lookout for anything amiss. But they had picketed their animals couthly enough, and the dazzle-fringed, clink-bellied wagons stood quietly shadowing and gleaming in the westered light. Columns of spicy smoke rose, but only from their cooking. Boys dealt with that, and boys had drawn water from the well; neither I nor my men had seen any women.

Presently I was conducted to the Corn-King's wagon. He received me before it, where woven rugs, and cushions stitched with golden disks, were strewn on the ground. A tent of dark purple had been erected close by. With its gilt-tasseled sides all down, it was shut as a box. A disk or two more winked yellow from the folds. Beyond, the plastered colonnades, the stone Mars Temple, stood equally closed and eye-less, refusing to see.

The Miller and I exchanged courtesies. He asked me to sit, so I sat. I was curious.

"It is pleasant," he said, "to be within safe walls."

"Yes, you must be often in some danger," I answered.

He smiled, secretively now. "You mean our wealth? It is better to display than to hide. The thief kills, in his hurry, the man who conceals his gold. I have never been robbed. They think, Ah, this one shows all his riches. He must have some powerful demon to protect him."

"And is that so?"

"Of course," he said.

I glanced at the temple, and then back at him, meaningly. He said, "Your men drove a hard bargain for the grain and the flour. And I have been docile. I respect your gods, Captain. I respect all gods. That, too, is a protection."

Some drink came. I tasted it cautiously, for Easterners often eschew wine and concoct other disgusting muck. In the forests they ferment thorn berries, or the milk of their beasts, neither of which methods makes such a poor beverage, when you grow used to it. But of the Semites one hears all kinds of things. Still, the drink had a sweet hot sizzle that made me want more, so I swallowed some, then waited to see what else it would do to me.

"And your lord will allow me to enter his library?" said the Corn-King, after a host's proper pause.

"That may be possible," I said. I tried the drink again. "How do you manage without women?" I added, "You'll have seen the House of the Mother, with the she-wolf painted over the door? The girls there are fastidious and clever. If your men will spare the price, naturally."

The Corn-King looked at me, with his liquid man-snake's eyes, aware of all I said which had not been spoken.

"It is true," he said at last, "that we have no women with us."

"Excepting your own wagon."

"My daughter," he said.

I had known Draco, as I have said, almost all my life. He was for me what no other had ever been; I had followed his star gladly and without question, into scrapes, and battles, through very fire and steel. Very rarely would he impose on me some task I hated, loathed. When he did so it was done without design or malice, as a man sneezes. The bad times were generally to do with women. I had fought back to back with him, but I did not care to be his pander. Even so, I would not refuse. He had stood in the window that noon, looking at the black forest, and said in a dry low voice, carelessly apologetic, irrefutable, "He has a girl in that wagon, Get her for me."

"Well, she may be his—" I started off.

He cut me short: "Whatever she is. He sells things. He is accustomed to selling."

"And if he won't?" I said. Then he looked at me, with his high-colored, translucent eyes. "Make him," he said, and next laughed, as if it were nothing at all, this choice mission. I had come out thinking glumly, she has witched him, put the Eye on him. But I had known him lust like this before. Nothing would do then but he must have. Women had never been that way for me. They were available, when one needed them. I like to this hour to see them here and there, *our* women, straight-limbed, graceful, clean. In the perilous seasons I would have died defending his sisters, as I would have died to defend him. That was that. It was a fact, the burning of our grain had come about through an old grievance, an idiot who kept score of something Draco had done half a year ago, about a native girl got on a raid.

I put down the golden cup, because the drink was going to my head. They had two ways, Easterners, with daughters. One was best left unspoken. The other kept them locked and bolted virgin. Mercurius bless the dice. Then, before I could say anything, the Miller put my mind at rest.

"My daughter," he said, "is very accomplished. She is also very beautiful, but I speak now of the beauty of learning and art."

"Indeed. Indeed."

The sun was slipping over behind the walls. The far mountains were steeped in dyes. This glamor shone behind the Corn-King's head, gold in the sky for him, too. And he said, "Among other matters, she has studied the lore of Khemia — Old Aegyptus, you will understand."

"Ah, yes?"

"Now I will confide in you," he said. His tongue flickered on his lips. Was it forked? The damnable drink had fuddled me after all, that, and a shameful relief. "The practice of the Al-Khemia contains every science and sorcery. She can read the stars, she can heal the hurts of man. But best of all, my dear Captain, my daughter has learned the third great secret of the Tri-Magae."

"Oh, yes, indeed?"

"She can," he said, "change all manner of materials into gold."

2

"Sometimes, Skorous," Draco said, "you are a fool."

"Sometimes I am not alone in that."

Draco shrugged. He had never feared honest speaking. He never asked more of a title than his own name. But those two

items were, in themselves, significant. He was what he was, a
law above the law. The heart-legend of the City was down,
and he a prince in a forest that ran all ways for ever.

"What do you think then she will do to me? Turn me into
metal, too?"

We spoke in Greek, which tended to be the palace mode
for private chat. It was fading out of use in the town.

"I don't believe in that kind of sorcery," I said.

"Well, he has offered to have her show us. Come along."

"It will be a trick."

"All the nicer. Perhaps he will find someone for you, too."

"I shall attend you," I said, "because I trust none of them.
And fifteen of my men around the wagon."

"I must remember not to groan," he said, "or they'll be
splitting the leather and tumbling in on us with swords."

"Draco," I said, "I'm asking myself why he boasted that
she had the skill?"

"All that gold: They didn't steal it or cheat for it. A witch
made it for them."

"I have heard of the Al-Khemian arts."

"Oh yes," he said. "The devotees make gold, they predict
the future, they raise the dead. She might be useful. Perhaps
I should marry her. Wait till you see her," he said. "I suppose
it was all pre-arranged. He will want paying again."

When we reached the camp, it was midnight. Our torches
and theirs opened the dark, and the flame outside the Mars
Temple burned faint. There were stars in the sky, no moon.

We had gone to them at their request, since the magery
was intrinsic, required utensils, and was not to be moved to
the fort without much effort. We arrived like a bridal procession. The show was not after all to be in the wagon, but the
tent. The other Easterners had buried themselves from view.
I gave the men their orders and stood them conspicuously
about. Then a slave lifted the tent's purple drapery a chink
and squinted up at us. Draco beckoned me after him, no one
demurred. We both went into the pavilion.

To do that was to enter the East head-on. Expensive gums
were burning with a dark hot perfume that put me in mind of
the wine I had had earlier. The incense-burners were gold,

tripods on leopards' feet, with swags of golden ivy. The floor
was carpeted soft, like the pelt of some beast, and beast-skins
were hung about—things I had not seen before, some of
them, maned and spotted, striped and scaled, and some with
heads and jewelry eyes and the teeth and claws gilded. Despite all the clutter of things, of polished mirrors and casks
and chests, cushions and dead animals, and scent, there was a
feeling of great space within that tent. The ceiling of it
stretched taut and high, and three golden wheels depended,
with oil-lights in little golden boats. The wheels turned idly
now this way, now that, in a wind that came from nowhere
and went to nowhere, a demon wind out of a desert. Across
the space, wide as night, was an opaque dividing curtain, and
on the curtain, a long parchment. It was figured with another
mass of images, as if nothing in the place should be spare. A
tree went up, with two birds at the roots, a white bird with a
raven-black head, a soot-black bird with the head of an ape.
A snake twined the tree too, round and round, and ended
looking out of the lower branches where yellow fruit hung.
The snake had the face of a maiden, and flowing hair. Above
sat three figures, judges of the dead from Aegyptus, I would
have thought, if I had thought about them, with a balance,
and wands. The sun and the moon stood over the tree.

I put my hand to the hilt of my sword, and waited. Draco
had seated himself on the cushions. A golden jug was to hand,
and a cup. He reached forward, poured the liquor, and made
to take it, before—reluctantly—I snatched the vessel. "Let
me, first. Are you mad?"

He reclined, not interested as I tasted for him, then let him
have the cup again.

Then the curtain parted down the middle and the parchment with it, directly through the serpent-tree. I had expected
the Miller, but instead what entered was a black dog with a
collar of gold. It had a wolf's shape, but more slender, and
with a pointed muzzle and high carven pointed ears. Its eyes
were also black. It stood calmly, like a steward, regarding us,
then stepped aside and lay down, its head still raised to watch.
And next the woman Draco wanted came in.

To me, she looked nothing in particular. She was

pleasantly made, slim, but rounded, her bare arms and feet the color of amber. Over her head, to her breast, covering her hair and face like a dusky smoke, was a veil, but it was transparent enough you saw through it to black locks and black aloe eyes, and a full tawny mouth. There was only a touch of gold on her, a rolled torque of soft metal at her throat, and one ring on her right hand. I was puzzled as to what had made her glimmer at the edge of my sight before, but perhaps she had dressed differently then, to make herself plain.

She bowed Eastern-wise to Draco, then to me. Then, in the purest Greek I ever heard, she addressed us.

"Lords, while I am at work, I must ask that you will please be still, or else you will disturb the currents of the act and so impair it. Be seated," she said to me, as if I had only stood till then from courtesy. Her eyes were very black, black as the eyes of the jackal-dog, blacker than the night. Then she blinked, and her eyes flashed. The lids were painted with gold. And I found I had sat down.

What followed I instantly took for an hallucination, induced by the incense, and by other means less perceptible. That is not to say I did not think she was a witch. There was something of power to her I never met before. It pounded from her, like heat, or an aroma. It did not make her beautiful for me, but it held me quiet, though I swear never once did I lose my grip either on my senses or my sword.

First, and quite swiftly, I had the impression the whole tent blew upward, and we were in the open in fact, under a sky of a million stars that blazed and crackled like diamonds. Even so, the golden wheels stayed put, up in the sky now, and they spun, faster and faster, until each was a solid golden O of fire, three spinning suns in the heaven of midnight.

(I remember I thought flatly: We have been spelled. So what now? But in its own way, my stoicism was also suspect. My thoughts in any case flagged after that.)

There was a smell of lions, or of a land that had them. Do not ask me how I know, I never smelled or saw them, or such a spot. And there before us all stood a slanting wall of brick, at once much larger than I saw it, and smaller than it was. It seemed even so to lean into the sky. The woman raised her arms. She was apparent now as if rinsed all over by gilt, and one of the great stars seemed to sear on her forehead.

Forms began to come and go, on the lion-wind. If I knew then what they were, I forgot it later. Perhaps they were animals, like the skins in the tent, though some had wings.

She spoke to them. She did not use Greek anymore. It was the language of Khem, presumably, or we were intended to believe so. A liquid tongue, an Eastern tongue, no doubt.

Then there were other visions. The ribbed stems of flowers, broader than ten men around, wide petals pressed to the ether. A rainbow of mist that arched over, and touched the earth with its feet and its brow. And other mirages, many of which resembled effigies I had seen of the gods, but they walked.

The night began to close upon us slowly, narrowing and coming down. The stars still raged overhead and the gold wheels whirled, but some sense of enclosure had returned. As for the sloped angle of brick, it had huddled down into a sort of oven, and into this the woman was placing, with extreme care—of all things—long scepters of corn, all brown and dry and withered, blighted to straw by some harvest like a curse.

I heard her whisper then. I could not hear what.

Behind her, dim as shadows, I saw other women, who sat weaving, or who toiled at the grind-stone, and one who shook a rattle upon which rings of gold sang out. Then the vision of these women was eclipsed. Something stood there, between the night and the Eastern witch. Tall as the roof, or tall as the sky, bird-headed maybe, with two of the stars for eyes. When I looked at this, this ultimate apparition, my blood froze and I could have howled out loud. It was not common fear, but terror, such as the worst reality has never brought me, though sometimes subtle nightmares do.

Then there was a lightning, down the night. When it passed, we were enclosed in the tent, the huge night of the tent, and the brick oven burned before us, with a thin harsh fume coming from the aperture in its top.

"Sweet is truth," said the witch, in a wild and passionate voice, all music, like the notes of the gold rings on the rattle. "O Lord of the Word. The Word is, and the Word makes all things to be."

Then the oven cracked into two pieces, it simply fell away from itself, and there on a bank of red charcoal, which died to clinker even as I gazed at it, lay a sheaf of golden corn. *Golden* corn, smiths' work. It was pure and sound and rang like a bell when presently I went to it and struck it and flung it away.

The tent had positively resettled all around us. It was there. I felt queasy and stupid, but I was in my body and had my bearings again, the sword-hilt firm to my palm, though it was oddly hot to the touch, and my forehead burned, sweatless, as if I too had been seethed in a fire. I had picked up the gold-work without asking her anything. She did not prevent me, nor when I slung it off.

When I looked up from that, she was kneeling by the curtain, where the black dog had been and was no more. Her eyes were downcast under her veil. I noted the torque was gone from her neck and the ring from her finger. Had she somehow managed her trick that way, melting gold on to the stalks of mummified corn — No, lunacy. Why nag at it? It was *all* a deception.

But Draco lay looking at her now, burned up by another fever. It was her personal gold he wanted.

"Out, Skorous," he said to me. "Out, now." Slurred and sure.

So I said to her, through my blunted lips and woolen tongue, "Listen carefully, girl. The witchery ends now. You know what he wants, and how to see to that, I suppose. Scratch him with your littlest nail, and you die."

Then, without getting to her feet, she looked up at me, only the second time. She spoke in Greek, as at the start. In the morning, when I was better able to think, I reckoned I had imagined what she said. It had seemed to be: "He is safe, for I desire him. It is my choice. If it were not my choice and my desire, where might you hide yourselves, and live?"

We kept watch round the tent, in the Easterners' camp, in the market-place, until the ashes of the dawn. There was not a sound from anywhere, save the regular quiet passaging of sentries on the walls, and the cool black forest wind that turned gray near sunrise.

At sunup, the usual activity of any town began. The camp

stirred and let its boys out quickly to the well to avoid the town's women. Some of the caravaners even chose to stroll across to the public lavatories, though they had avoided the bathhouse.

An embarrassment came over me, that we should be standing there, in the foreigners' hive, to guard our prince through his night of lust. I looked sharply, to see how the men were taking it, but they had held together well. Presently Draco emerged. He appeared flushed and tumbled, very nearly shy, like some girl just out of a love-bed.

We went back to the fort in fair order, where he took me aside, thanked me, and sent me away again.

Bathed and shaved, and my fast broken, I began to feel more sanguine. It was over and done with. I would go down to the temple of Father Jupiter and give him something—why, I was not exactly sure. Then get my boar for Mars. The fresh-baked bread I had just eaten was tasty, and maybe worth all the worry.

Later, I heard the Miller had taken himself to our library and been let in. I gave orders he was to be searched on leaving. Draco's grandfather had started the collection of manuscripts, there were even scrolls said to have been rescued from Alexandrea. One could not be too wary.

In the evening, Draco called me up to his writing-room.

"Tomorrow," he said, "the Easterners will be leaving us."

"That's good news," I said.

"I thought it would please you. Zafra, however, is to remain. I'm taking her into my household."

"Zafra," I said.

"Well, they call her that. For the yellow-gold. Perhaps not her name. That might have been *Nefra*—Beautiful . . ."

"Well," I said, "if you want."

"Well," he said, "I never knew you before to be jealous of one of my women."

I said nothing, though the blood knocked about in my head. I had noted before, he had a woman's tongue himself when he was put out. He was a spoiled brat as a child, I have to admit, but a mother's early death, and the life of a forest fortress, pared most of it from him.

"The Corn-King is not her father," he said now. "She told me. But he's stood by her as that for some years. I shall send him something, in recompense."

He waited for my comment that I was amazed nothing had been asked for. He waited to see how I would jump. I wondered if he had paced about here, planning how he would put it to me. Not that he was required to. Now he said: "We gain, Skorous, a healer and diviner. Not just my pleasure at night."

"Your pleasure at night is your own affair. There are plenty of girls about, I would have thought, to keep you content. As for anything else she can or cannot do, all three temples, particularly the Women's Temple, will be up in arms. The Salius yesterday was only a sample. Do you think they are going to let some yellow-skinned harlot divine for you? Do you think that men who get hurt in a fight will want her near them?"

"You would not, plainly."

"No, I would not. As for the witchcraft, we were drugged and made monkeys of. An evening's fun is one thing."

"Yes, Skorous," he said. "Thanks for your opinion. Don't sulk too long. I shall miss your company."

An hour later, he sent, so I was informed, two of the scrolls from the library to the Corn-King in his wagon. They were two of the best, Greek, one transcribed by the hand, it was said, of a very great king. They went in a silver box, with jewel inlay. Gold would have been tactless, under the circumstances.

Next day she was in the palace. She had rooms on the women's side. It had been the apartment of Draco's elder sister, before her marriage. He treated this one as nothing less than a relative from the first. When he was at leisure, on those occasions when the wives and women of his officers dined with them, there was she with him. When he hunted, she went with him, too, not to have any sport, but as a companion, in a litter between two horses that made each hunt into a farce from its onset. She was in his bed each night, for he did not go to her, her place was solely hers: The couch his father had shared only with his mother. And when he wanted advice, it was she who gave it to him. He called on his soldiers and his priests afterward. Though he always did so call, nobody lost face. He was wise and canny, she must have told him how to be at long last. And the charm he had always had. He even consulted me, and made much of me before everyone, because, very sensibly he realized, unless he meant to replace me, it would be foolish to let the men see I no longer counted a feather's weight with him. Besides, I might get notions of rebellion. I had my own following, my own men who would die for me if they thought me wronged. Probably that angered me more than the rest, that he might have the idea I would forego my duty and loyalty, forget my honor, and try to pull him down. I could no more do that than put out one of my own eyes.

Since we lost our homeland, since we lost, more importantly, the spine of the Empire, there had been a disparity, a separation of men. Now I saw it, in those bitter golden moments after she came among us. He had been born in the Mother of Cities, but she had slipped from his skin like water. He was a new being, a creature of the world, that might be anything, of any country. But, never having seen the roots of me, they yet had me fast. I was of the old order. I would stand until the fire had me, rather than tarnish my name, and my heart.

Gradually, the fort and town began to fill with gold. It was very nearly a silly thing. But we grew lovely and we shone. The temples did not hate her, as I had predicted. No, for she brought them glittering vessels, and laved the gods' feet with rare offerings, and the sweet spice also of her gift burned before Mars, and the Father, and the Mother, so every holy place smelled like Aegyptus, or Judea, or the brothels of Babylon for all I knew.

She came to walk in the streets with just one of the slaves at her heels, bold, the way our ladies did, and though she never left off her veil, she dressed in the stola and the palla, all clasped and cinched with the tiniest amounts of gold, while gold flooded everywhere else, and everyone looked forward to the summer heartily, for the trading. The harvest would be wondrous too. Already there were signs of astounding fruition. And in the forest, not a hint of any restless tribe, or any ill wish.

They called her by the name *Zafra*. They did not once call her "Easterner." One day, I saw three pregnant women at the gate, waiting for Zafra to come out and touch them. She was lucky. Even the soldiers had taken no offense. The old Salius had asked her for a balm for his rheumatism. It seemed the balm had worked.

Only I, then, hated her. I tried to let it go. I tried to remember she was only a woman, and, if a sorceress, did us good. I tried to see her as voluptuous and enticing, or as homely and harmless. But all I saw was some shuttered-up, close, fermenting thing, like mummy-dusts reviving in a tomb, or the lion-scent, and the tall shadow that had stood between her and the night, bird-headed, the Lord of the Word that made all things, or unmade them. What was she, under her disguise? Draco could not see it. Like the black dog she had kept, which walked by her on a leash, well-mannered and gentle, and which would probably tear out the throat of anyone who came at her with mischief on his mind—Under her honeyed wrappings, was it a doll of straw or gold, or a viper?

Eventually, Draco married her. That was no surprise. He did it in the proper style, with sacrifices to the Father, and all the forms, and a feast that filled the town. I saw her in colors then, that once, the saffron dress, the Flammeus, the fire-veil of the bride, and her face bare, and painted up like a lady's, pale, with rosy cheeks and lips. But it was still herself, still the Eastern Witch.

And dully that day, as in the tent that night, I thought, *So what now?*

3

In the late summer, I picked up some talk, among the servants in the palace. I was by the well-court, in the peach arbor, where I had paused to look at the peaches. They did not always come, but this year we had had one crop already, and now the second was blooming. As I stood there in the shade, sampling the fruit, a pair of the kitchen men met below by the well, and stayed to gossip in their argot. At first I paid no heed, then it came to me what they were saying, and I listened with all my ears.

When one went off, leaving the other, old Ursus, to fill his dipper, I came down the stair and greeted him. He started, and looked at me furtively.

"Yes, I heard you," I said. "But tell me, now."

I had always put a mask on, concerning the witch, with everyone but Draco, and afterward with him too. I let it be seen I thought her nothing much, but if she was his choice, I would serve her. I was careful never to speak slightingly of her to any—since it would reflect on his honor—even to men I trusted, even in wine. Since he had married her, she had got my duty, too, unless it came to vie with my duty to him.

But Ursus had the servant's way, the slave's way, of holding back bad news for fear it should turn on him. I had to repeat a phrase or two of his own before he would come clean.

It seemed that some of the women had become aware that Zafra, a sorceress of great power, could summon to her, having its name, a mighty demon. Now she did not sleep every night with Draco, but in her own apartments, sometimes things had been glimpsed, or heard—

"Well, Ursus," I said, "you did right to tell me. But it's a lot of silly women's talk. Come, you're not going to give it credit?"

"The flames burn flat on the lamps, and change color," he mumbled. "And the curtain rattled, but no one was there. And Eunike says she felt some form brush by her in the corridor—"

"That is enough," I said. "Women will always fancy something is happening, to give themselves importance. You well know that. Then there's hysteria and they can believe and say anything. We are aware she has arts, and the science of Aegyptus. But demons are another matter."

I further admonished him and sent him off. I stood by the well, pondering. Rattled curtains, secretive forms—it crossed my thoughts she might have taken a lover, but it did not seem in keeping with her shrewdness. I do not really believe in such beasts as demons, except what the brain can bring forth. Then again, her brain might be capable of many things.

It turned out I attended Draco that evening, something to do with one of the villages that traded with us, something he still trusted me to understand. I asked myself if I should tell him about the gossip. Frankly, when I had found out—the way you always can—that he lay with her less frequently, I had had a sort of hope, but there was a qualm, too, and when the trade matter was dealt with, he stayed me over the wine, and he said: "You may be wondering about it, Skorous. If so, yes. I'm to be given a child."

I knew better now than to scowl. I drank a toast, and suggested he might be happy to have got a boy on her.

"She says it will be a son."

"Then of course, it will be a son."

And, I thought, it may have her dark-yellow looks. It may be a magus, too. And it will be your heir, Draco. My future prince, and the master of the town. I wanted to hurl the wine cup through the wall, but I held my hand and my tongue, and after he had gone on a while trying to coax me to thrill at the joy of life, I excused myself and went away.

It was bound to come. It was another crack in the stones. It was the way of destiny, and of change. I wanted not to feel I must fight against it, or desire to send her poison, to kill her or abort her, or tear it, her womb's fruit, when born, in pieces.

For a long while I sat on my sleeping-couch and allowed my fury to sink down, to grow heavy and leaden, resigned, defeated.

When I was sure of that defeat, I lay flat and slept.

In sleep, I followed a demon along the corridor in the women's quarters, and saw it melt through her door. It was tall, long-legged, with the head of a bird, or perhaps of a dog. A wind blew, lion-tanged. I was under a tree hung thick with peaches, and a snake looked down from it with a girl's face framed by a flaming bridal-veil. Then there was a spinning fiery wheel, and golden corn flew off clashing from it. And next I saw a glowing oven, and on the red charcoal lay a child of gold, burning and gleaming and asleep.

When I woke with a jump it was the middle of the night, and someone had arrived, and the slave was telling me so.

At first I took it for a joke. Then, became serious. Zafra,

Draco's wife, an hour past midnight, had sent for me to attend her in her rooms. Naturally I suspected everything. She knew me for her adversary: She would lead me in, then say I had set on her to rape or somehow else abuse her. On the other hand, I must obey and go to her, not only for duty, now, but from sheer aggravation and raw curiosity. Though I had always told myself I misheard her words as I left her with him the first time, I had never forgotten them. Since then, beyond an infrequent politeness, we had not spoken.

I dressed as formally as I could, got two of my men, and went across to the women's side. The sentries along the route were my fellows too, but I made sure they learned I had been specifically summoned. Rather to my astonishment, they knew it already.

My men went with me right to her chamber door, with orders to keep alert there. Perhaps they would grin, asking each other if I was nervous. I was.

When I got into the room, I thought it was empty. Her women had been sent away. One brazier burned, near the entry, but I was used by now to the perfume of those aromatics. It was a night of full moon, and the blank light lay in a whole pane across the mosaic, coloring it faintly, but in the wrong, nocturnal, colors. The bed, narrow, low, and chaste, stood on one wall, and her tiring table near it. Through the window under the moon, rested the tops of the forest, so black it made the indigo sky pale.

Then a red-golden light blushed out and I saw her, lighting the lamps on their stand from a taper. I could almost swear she had not been there a second before, but she could stay motionless a long while, and with her dark robe and hair, and all her other darkness, she was a natural thing for shadows.

"Captain," she said. (She never used my name, she must know I did not want it; a sorceress, she was well aware of the power of naming.) "There is no plot against you."

"That's good to know," I said, keeping my distance, glad of my sword, and of every visible insignia of who and what I was.

"You have been very honorable in the matter of me," she said. "You have done nothing against me, either openly or in secret, though you hated me from the beginning. I know what this has cost you. Do not spurn my gratitude solely because it is mine."

"Domina," I said (neither would I use her name, though the rest did in the manner of the town), "you're his. He has made you his wife. And—" I stopped.

"And the vessel of his child. Ah, do you think he did that alone?" She saw me stare with thoughts of demons, and she said, "He and I, Captain. He, and I."

"Then I serve you," I said. I added, and though I did not want to give her the satisfaction I could not keep back a tone of irony, "you have nothing to be anxious at where I am concerned."

We were speaking in Greek, hers clear as water in that voice of hers which I had to own was very beautiful.

"I remain," she said, "anxious."

"Then I can't help you, Domina." There was a silence. She stood looking at me, through the veil I had only once seen dispensed with in exchange for a veil of paint. I wondered where the dog had gone, that had her match in eyes. I said, "But I would warn you. If you practice your business in here, there's begun to be some funny talk."

"They see a demon, do they?" she said.

All at once the hair rose up on my neck and scalp.

As if she read my mind, she said:

"I have not pronounced any name. Do not be afraid."

"The slaves are becoming afraid."

"No," she said. "They have always talked of me but they have never been afraid of me. None of them. Draco does not fear me, do you think? And the priests do not. Or the women and girls. Or the children, or the old men. Or the slaves. Or your soldiers. None of them fear me or what I am or what I do, the gold with which I fill the temples, or the golden harvests, or the healing I perform. None of them fear it. But you, Captain, you do fear, and you read your fear again and again in every glance, in every word they utter. But it is yours, not theirs."

I looked away from her, up to the ceiling from which the patterns had faded years before.

"Perhaps," I said, "I am not blind."

Then she sighed. As I listened to it, I thought of her, just for an instant, as a forlorn girl alone with strangers in a foreign land.

"I'm sorry," I said.

"It is true," she said, "you see more than most. But not your own error."

"Then that is how it is." My temper had risen and I must rein it.

"You will not," she said quietly, "be a friend to me."

"I cannot, and will not, be a friend to you. Neither am I your enemy, while you keep faith with him."

"But one scratch on my littlest nail," she said. Her musical voice was nearly playful.

"Only one," I said.

"Then I regret waking you, Captain," she said. "Health and slumber for your night."

As I was going back along the corridor, I confronted the black jackal-dog. It padded slowly toward me and I shivered, but one of the men stooped to rub its ears. It suffered him, and passed on, shadow to shadow, night to ebony night.

Summer went to winter, and soon enough the snows came. The trading and the harvests had shored us high against the crudest weather, we could sit in our towers and be fat, and watch the wolves howl through the white forests. They came to the very gates that year. There were some odd stories, that wolf-packs had been fed of our bounty, things left for them, to tide them over. Our own she-wolves were supposed to have started it, the whorehouse girls. But when I mentioned the tale to one of them, she flared out laughing.

I recall that snow with an exaggerated brilliance, the way you sometimes do with time that precedes an illness, or a deciding battle. Albino mornings with the edge of a broken vase, the smoke rising from hearths and temples, or steaming with the blood along the snow from the sacrifices of Year's Turn. The Wolf Feast with the races, and later the ivies and vines cut for the Mad Feast, and the old dark wine got out, the torches, and a girl I had in a shed full of hay and pigs; and the spate of weddings that come after, very sensibly. The last snow twilights were thick as soup with blueness. Then spring, and the forest surging up from its slough, the first proper hunting, with the smell of sap and crushed freshness spraying out as if one waded in a river.

Draco's child was born one spring sunset, coming forth in the bloody golden light, crying its first cry to the evening star. It was a boy, as she had said.

I had kept even my thoughts off from her after that interview in her chamber. My feelings had been confused and displeasing. It seemed to me she had in some way tried to outwit me, throw me down. Then I had felt truly angry, and later, oddly shamed. I avoided, where I could, all places where I might have to see her. Then she was seen less, being big with the child.

After the successful birth all the usual things were done. In my turn, I beheld the boy. He was straight and flawlessly formed, with black hair, but a fair skin; he had Draco's eyes from the very start. So little of the mother. Had she contrived it, by some other witch's art, knowing that when at length we had to cleave to him, it would be Draco's line we wished to see? No scratch of a nail, there, none.

Nor had there been any more chat of demons. Or they made sure I never intercepted it.

I said to myself: She is a matron now, she will wear to our ways. She has borne him a strong boy.

But it was no use at all.

She was herself, and the baby was half of her.

They have a name now for her demon, her genius in the shadowlands of witchcraft. A scrambled name that does no harm. They call it, in the town's argot: *Rhamthibiscan.*

We claim so many of the Greek traditions; they know of Rhadamanthys from the Greek. A judge of the dead, he is connectable to Thot of Aegyptus, the Thrice-Mighty Thrice-Mage of the Al-Khemian Art. And because Thot the Ibis-Headed and Anpu the Jackal became mingled in it, along with Hermercurius, Prince of Thieves and Whores—who is

too the guide of lost souls—an ibis and a dog were added to
the brief itinerary. Rhadamanthys-Ibis-Canis. The full name,
even, has no power. It is a muddle, and a lie, and the invoca-
tion says: *Sweet is Truth.* Was it, though, ever sensible to claim
to know what truth might be?

4

"They know of her, and have sent begging for her. She's a
healer and they're sick. It's not unreasonable. She isn't afraid.
I have seen her close an open wound by passing her hands
above it. Yes, Skorous, perhaps she only made me see it, and
the priests to see it, and the wounded man. But he recovered,
as you remember. So I trust her to be able to cure these people and make them love us even better. She herself is immune
to illness. Yes, Skorous, she only thinks she is. However, thinking so has apparently worked wonders. She was never once
out of sorts with the child. The midwives were amazed—or
not amazed, maybe—that she seemed to have no pain during
the birth. Though they told me she wept when the child was
put into her arms. Well, so did I." Draco frowned. He said, "So
we'll let her do it, don't you agree, let her go to them and heal
them. We may yet be able to open this country, make something of it, one day. Anything that is useful in winning them."

"She will be taking the child with her?"

"Of course. He's not weaned yet, and she won't let another
woman nurse him."

"Through the forests. It's three days ride away, this village.
And then we hardly know the details of the sickness. If your
son—"

"He will be with his mother. She has never done a foolish
thing."

"You let this bitch govern you. Very well. But don't risk
the life of your heir, since your heir is what you have made
him, this half-breed brat—"

I choked off the surge in horror. I had betrayed myself. It
seemed to me instantly that I had been made to do it. *She* had

made me. All the stored rage and impotent distrust, all the bitter frustrated *guile*—gone for nothing in a couple of sentences.

But Draco only shrugged, and smiled. He had learned to contain himself these past months. Her invaluable aid, no doubt, her rotten honey.

He said, "She has requested that, though I send a troop with her to guard her in our friendly woods, you, Skorous, do not go with them."

"I see."

"The reason which she gave was that, although there is no danger in the region at present, your love and spotless commitment to my well-being preclude you should be taken from my side." He put the smile away and said, "But possibly, too, she wishes to avoid your close company for so long, knowing as she must do you can barely keep your fingers from her throat. Did you know, Skorous," he said, and now it was the old Draco, I seemed somehow to have hauled him back, "that the first several months, I had her food always tasted. I thought you would try to see to her. I was so very astounded you never did. Or did you have some other, more clever plan, that failed?"

I swallowed the bile that had come into my mouth. I said, "You forget, Sir, if I quit you have no other battalion to go to. The Mother of Cities is dead. If I leave your warriors, I am nothing. I am one of the scores who blow about the world like dying leaves, soldiers' sons of the lost Empire. If there were an option, I would go at once. There is none. You've spat in my face, and I can only wipe off the spit."

His eyes fell from me, and suddenly he cursed.

"I was wrong, Skorous. You would never have—"

"No, Sir. Never. Never in ten million years. But I regret you think I might. And I regret she thinks so. Once she was your wife, she could expect no less from me than I give one of your sisters."

"*That bitch,*" he said, repeating for me my error, woman-like, "her half-breed brat—damn you, Skorous. He's my son."

"I could cut out my tongue that I said it. It's more than a

year of holding it back before all others, I believe. Like vomit, Sir. I could not keep it down any longer."

"Stop saying *Sir* to me. You call her *Domina*. That's sufficient."

His eyes were wet. I wanted to slap him, the way you do a vicious stupid girl who claws at your face. But he was my prince, and the traitor was myself.

Presently, thankfully, he let me get out.

What I had said was true, if there had been any other life to go to that was thinkable—but there was not, anymore. So, she would travel into the forest to heal, and I, faithful and unshakable, I would stay to guard him. And then she would come back. Year in and out, mist and rain, snow and sun. And bear him other brats to whom, in due course, I would swear my honor over. I had better practice harder, not to call her anything but *Lady*.

Somewhere in the night I came to myself and I knew. I saw it accurately, what went on, what was to be, and what I, so cunningly excluded, must do. Madness, they say, can show itself like that. Neither hot nor cold, with a steady hand, and every faculty honed bright.

The village with the sickness had sent its deputation to Draco yesterday. They had grand and blasphemous names for *her*, out there. She had said she must go, and at first light today would set out. Since the native villagers revered her, she might have made an arrangement with them, some itinerant acting as messenger. Or even, if the circumstance were actual, she could have been biding for such a chance. Or she herself had sent the malady to ensure it.

Her gods were the gods of her mystery. But the Semitic races have a custom ancient as their oldest altars, of giving a child to the god.

Perhaps Draco even knew—no, unthinkable. How then could she explain it? An accident, a straying, bears, wolves, the sickness after all . . . And she could give him other sons. She was like the magic oven of the Khemian Art. Put in, take out. So easy.

I got up when it was still pitch black and announced to my body-slave and the man at the door I was off hunting, alone. There was already a rumor of an abrasion between the prince and his captain. Draco himself would not think unduly of it, Skorous raging through the wood, slicing pigs. I could be gone the day before he considered.

I knew the tracks pretty well, having hunted them since I was ten. I had taken boar spears for the look, but no dogs. The horse I needed, but she was forest-trained and did as I instructed.

I lay off the thoroughfare, like an old fox, and let the witch's outing come down, and pass me. Five men were all the guard she had allowed, a cart with traveling stuff, and her medicines in a chest. There was one of her women, the thickest in with her, I thought, Eunike, riding on a mule. And Zafra herself, in the litter between the horses.

When they were properly off, I followed. There was no problem in the world. We moved silently and they made a noise. Their horses and mine were known to each other, and where they snuffed a familiar scent, thought nothing of it. As the journey progressed, and I met here and there with some native in the trees, he hailed me cheerily, supposing me an outrider, a rear-guard. At night I bivouacked above them; at sunrise their first rustlings and throat-clearings roused me. When they were gone we watered at their streams, and once I had a burned sausage forgotten in the ashes of their cook-fire.

The third day, they came to the village. From high on the mantled slope, I saw the greetings and the going in, through the haze of foul smoke. The village did have a look of ailing, something in its shades and colors, and the way the people moved about. I wrapped a cloth over my nose and mouth before I sat down to wait.

Later, in the dusk, they began to have a brisker look. The witch was making magic, evidently, and all would be well. The smoke condensed and turned yellow from their fires as the night closed in. When full night had come, the village glowed stilly, enigmatically, cupped in the forest's darkness. My mental wanderings moved toward the insignificance, the smallness, of any lamp among the great shadows of the earth. A candle against the night, a fire in winter, a life flickering in eternity, now here, now gone forever.

But I slept before I had argued it out.

Inside another day, the village was entirely renewed. Even the rusty straw thatch glinted like gold. She had worked her miracles. Now would come her own time.

A couple of the men had kept up sentry-go from the first evening out, and last night, patrolling the outskirts of the huts, they had even idled a minute under the tree where I was roosting. I had hidden my mare half a mile off, in a deserted bothy I had found, but tonight I kept her near, for speed. And this night, too, when one of the men came up the slope, making his rounds, I softly called his name.

He went to stone. I told him smartly who I was, but when I came from cover, his sword was drawn and eyes on stalks.

"I'm no forest demon," I said. Then I asked myself if he was alarmed for other reasons, a notion of the scheme Draco had accused me of. Then again, here and now, we might have come to such a pass. I needed a witness. I looked at the soldier, who saluted me slowly. "Has she cured them all?" I inquired. I added for his benefit, "Zafra."

"Yes," he said. "It was—worth seeing."

"I am sure of that. And how does the child fare?"

I saw him begin to conclude maybe Draco had sent me after all. "Bonny," he said.

"But she is leaving the village, with the child—" I had never thought she would risk her purpose among the huts, as she would not in the town, for all her hold on them. "Is that tonight?"

"Well, there's the old woman, she won't leave her own place, it seems."

"So Zafra told you?"

"Yes. And said she would go. It's close. She refused the litter and only took Carus with her. No harm. These savages are friendly enough—"

He ended, seeing my face.

I said, "She's gone already?"

"Yes, Skorous. About an hour—"

Another way from the village? But I had watched, I had skinned my eyes—pointlessly. Witchcraft could manage anything.

"And the child with her," I insisted.

"Oh, she never will part from the child, Eunike says—"

"Damn Eunike." He winced at me, more than ever uncertain. "Listen," I said, and informed him of my suspicions. I did not say the child was half East, half spice and glisten and sins too strange to speak. I said *Draco's son*. And I did not mention sacrifice. I said there was some chance Zafra might wish to mutilate the boy for her gods. It was well known, many of the Eastern religions had such rites. The solider was shocked, and disbelieving. His own mother—? I said, to her kind, it was not a deed of dishonor. She could not see it as we did. All the while we debated, my heart clutched and struggled in my side, I sweated. Finally he agreed we should go to look. Carus was there, and would dissuade her if she wanted to perform such a disgusting act. I asked where the old woman's hut was supposed to be, and my vision filmed a moment with relief when he located it for me as that very bothy where I had tethered my horse the previous night. I said, as I turned to run that way, "There's no old woman there. The place is a ruin."

We had both won at the winter racing, he and I. It did not take us long to achieve the spot. A god, I thought, must have guided me to it before, so I knew how the land fell. The trees were densely packed as wild grass, the hut wedged between, and an apron of bared weedy ground about the door where once the household fowls had pecked. The moon would enter there, too, but hardly anywhere else. You could come up on it, cloaked in forest and night. Besides, she had lit her stage for me. As we pushed among the last phalanx of trunks, I saw there was a fire burning, a sullen throb of red, before the ruin's gaping door.

Carus stood against a tree. His eyes were wide and beheld nothing. The other man punched him and hissed at him, but Carus was far off. He breathed and his heart drummed, but that was all.

"She's witched him," I said. Thank Arean Mars and Father

Jupiter she had. It proved my case outright. I could see my witness thought this too. We went on stealthily, and stopped well clear of the tree-break, staring down.

Then I forgot my companion. I forgot the manner in which luck at last had thrown my dice for me. What I saw took all my mind.

It was like the oven of the hallucination in the tent, the thing she had made, yet open, the shape of a cauldron. Rough mud brick, smoothed and curved, and somehow altered. Inside, the fire burned. It had a wonderful color, the fire, rubies, gold. To look at it did not seem to hurt the eyes, or dull them. The woman stood the other side of it, and her child in her grasp. Both appeared illumined into fire themselves, and the darkness of garments, of hair, the black gape of the doorway, of the forest and the night, these had grown warm as velvet. It is a sight often seen, a girl at a brazier or a hearth, her baby held by, as she stirs a pot, or throws on the kindling some further twig or cone. But in her golden arm the golden child stretched out his hands to the flames. And from her moving palm fell some invisible essence I could not see but only feel.

She was not alone. Others had gathered at her fireside. I was not sure of them, but I saw them, if only by their great height which seemed to rival the trees. A warrior there, his metal faceplate and the metal ribs of his breast just glimmering, and there a young woman, garlands, draperies, and long curls, and a king who was bearded, with a brow of thunder and eyes of light, and near him another, a musician with wings starting from his forehead—they came and went as the fire danced and bowed. The child laughed, turning his head to see them, the deities of his father's side.

Then Zafra spoke the Name. It was so soft, no sound at all. And yet the roots of the forest moved at it. My entrails churned. I was on my knees. It seemed as though the wind came walking through the forest, to fold his robe beside the ring of golden red. I cannot recall the Name. It was not any of those I have written down, nor anything I might imagine. But it was the true one, and he came in answer to it. And from a mile away, from the heaven of planets, out of the pit of the earth, his hands descended and rose. He touched the child and the child was quiet. The child slept.

She drew Draco's son from his wrapping as a shining sword is drawn from the scabbard. She raised him up through the dark, and then she lowered him, and set him down in the holocaust of the oven, into the bath of flame, and the fires spilled up and covered him.

No longer on my knees, I was running. I plunged through black waves of heat, the amber pungency of incense, and the burning breath of lions. I yelled as I ran. I screamed the names of all the gods, and knew them powerless in my mouth, because I said them wrongly, knew them not, and so they would not answer. And then I ran against the magic, the Power, and broke through it. It was like smashing air. Experienced—in-experiencable.

Sword in hand, in the core of molten gold, I threw myself on, wading, smothered, and came to the cauldron of brick, the oven, and dropped the sword and thrust in my hands and pulled him out—

He would be burned, he would be dead, a blackened little corpse, such as the Semite Karthaginians once made of their children, incinerating them in line upon line of ovens by the shores of the Inner Sea—

But I held in my grip only a child of jewel-work, of pore-less perfect gold, and I sensed his gleam run into my hands, through my wrists, down my arms like scalding water to my heart.

Someone said to me, then, with such gentle sadness, "Ah, Skorous. Ah, Skorous."

I lay somewhere, not seeing. I said, "Crude sorcery, to turn the child, too, into gold."

"No," she said. "Gold is only the clue. For those things which are alive, laved by the flame, it is life. It is immortal and imperishable life. And you have torn the spell, which is all you think it to be. You have robbed him of it."

And then I opened my eyes, and I saw her. There were no others, no Other, they had gone with the tearing. But she— she was no longer veiled. She was very tall, so beautiful I could not bear to look at her, and yet, could not take my eyes away. And she was golden. She was golden not in the form of metal, but as a dawn sky, as fire, and the sun itself. Even her black eyes were of gold, and her midnight hair. And the tears she wept were stars.

I did not understand, but I whispered, "Forgive me. Tell me how to make it right."

"It is not to be," she said. Her voice was a harp, playing through the forest. "It is never to be. He is yours now, no longer mine. Take him. Be kind to him. He will know his loss all his days, all his mortal days. And never know it."

And then she relinquished her light, as a coal dies. She vanished.

I was lying on the ground before the ruined hut, holding the child close to me, trying to comfort him as he cried, and my tears fell with his. The place was empty and hollow as if its very heart had bled away.

The soldier had run down to me, and was babbling. She had tried to immolate the baby, he had seen it, Carus had woken and seen it also. And, too, my valor in saving the boy from horrible death.

As one can set oneself to remember most things, so one can study to forget. Our sleeping dreams we dismiss on waking. Or, soon after.

They call her now, the Greek Woman. Or the Semite Witch. There has begun, in recent years, to be a story she was some man's wife, and in the end went back to him. It is generally thought she practiced against the child and the soldiers of her guard killed her.

Draco, when I returned half-dead of the fever I had caught from the contagion of the ruinous hut—where the village crone had died, it turned out, a week before—hesitated for my recovery, and then asked very little. A dazzle seemed to have lifted from his sight. He was afraid at what he might have said and done under the influence of sorceries and drugs. "Is it a fact, what the men say? She put the child into a fire?"

"Yes," I said. He had looked at me, gnawing his lips. He knew of Eastern rites, he had heard out the two men. And, long, long ago, he had relied only on me. He appeared never to grieve, only to be angry. He even sent men in search for her: A bitch who would burn her own child—let her be caught and suffer the fate instead.

It occurs to me now that, contrary to what they tell us, one does not age imperceptibly, finding one evening, with cold dismay, the strength has gone from one's arm, the luster from one's heart. No, it comes at an hour, and is seen, like the laying down of a sword.

When I woke from the fever, and saw his look, all imploring on me, the look of a man who has gravely wronged you, not meaning to, who says: But I was blind—that was the hour, the evening, the moment when life's sword of youth was removed from my hand, and with no protest I let it go.

Thereafter the months moved away from us, the seasons, and next the years.

Draco continued to look about him, as if seeking the evil Eye that might still hang there, in the atmosphere. Sometimes he was partly uneasy, saying he too had seen her dog, the black jackal. But it had vanished at the time she did, though for decades the woman Eunike claimed to meet it in the corridor of the women's quarters.

He clung to me, then, and ever since he has stayed my friend; I do not say, my suppliant. It is in any event the crusty friendship now of the middle years, where once it was the flaming blazoned friendship of childhood, the envious love of young men.

We share a secret, he and I, that neither has ever confided to the other. He remains uncomfortable with the boy. Now the princedom is larger, its borders fought out wider, and fortressed in, he sends him often away to the fostering of soldiers. It is I, without any rights, none, who love her child.

He is all Draco, to look at, but for the hair and brows. We have a dark-haired strain ourselves. Yet there is a sheen to him. They remark on it. What can it be? A brand of the gods— (They make no reference, since she has fallen from their favor, to his mother.) A light from within, a gloss, of gold. Leaving off his given name, they will call him for that effulgence more often, Ardorius. Already I have caught the murmur that he can draw iron through stone, yes, yes, they have seen him do it, though I have not. (From Draco they conceal such murmurings, as once from me.) He, too, has a look of something hidden, some deep and silent pain, as if he knows, as youth never does, that men die, and love, that too.

To me, he is always courteous, and fair. I can ask nothing else. I am, to him, an adjunct of his life. I should perhaps be glad that it should stay so.

In the deep nights, when summer heat or winter snow fill up the forest, I recollect a dream, and think how I robbed him, the child of gold. I wonder how much, how much it will matter, in the end.

Blood-Mantle

FEBRUARY, THE WOLF month, is also the color of wolves. And through the pale browns and grays and whites of it, something so very red can be seen from a long way off.

In that fashion then, he saw her, coming down among the slopes of the damp and leafless woods. She passed by the old altar with its wrapper of ivy, the strips of hide hanging over it from the trees above. She crossed the stream by the old stones, carefully, so as not to get her little shoes wet. But the rain, which had earlier drenched the woods, beaded her long dark hair, and the fine palla she wore. The palla was so dense and rich a red, sight seemed to sink into it, it drowned and made vision drunk, as only natural colors were supposed to do. It was altogether of a hue that had no place in the wood, making everything else dim and unreal.

Having come over the stream, she could not avoid seeing him in turn as he emerged between the trees and stood there, looking at her. She was not apparently startled by him, though he was an interesting apparition, clothed, in the wintry day, only in hairy skins that were belted by a twisted briar. His own hair was long and shaggy, but his face clean-shaven and beautifully chiseled, as was his body. He too was the February color, silver-brown, his skin, his hair, and his eyes like brown water with a silver rim.

"Where are you going?" he said to her, "And why did you dye your cloak with blood?"

"Not blood," she answered haughtily, "scarlet that the ships bring from the East."

"I serve the god in the woods," he said.

"I know you do," said she.

"You must submit."

"No," she said.

"Then you offend the god."

"I care nothing for your god. I have my own. I am a Christian," said the girl in the red palla.

"Yes, I have heard of him," said the young man who served Lycaean Pan. He spoke indifferently. The priests had marked him, he had a wolf soul that had shown itself during the ritual, grinning like a wolf with strong white teeth. He roamed through the woods, sacred to Faunus Lupercal, sleeping in dead trees, bathing in dew, shaving with slate, eating beetles, and hares with the life-hotness still in their meat, drinking from the fountains of the rocks, dancing under the full moon with wild hoarse howls and shrieks. It had always been this way, his kind in this place. And if she did not know it, the girl, she was a fool. And if she did know, why else was she here save to tempt her fate?

"Come now," he said, "submit. Or I can pull you down and have you anyway."

She neither ran nor trembled; she went no nearer to him. So then he came up to her.

"What does the needle do with the pin?" he said. "The pin has a round knob and a piercing shaft. The needle has an eye. One goes through the other. Thread the needle with the pin."

"Very well," said the girl, "but you will be sorry."

Then she opened her scarlet mantle. She was naked under it. She lay down on the ground on her hair and the red stuff, and he lay down on top of her. No sooner had he possessed her—with difficulty, for she was a virgin, and hurt him—than something terrible occurred. The folds of the palla began to move and stretch and reach out, and before he knew what was happening, they had folded up over him and covered him and buried him, like the petals of some huge poppy.

The sensation was at first not unpleasant, then it became horrible and fearful. The great palla settled down on him and all his energy was drawn away into it, as into the body of the girl. They were together a blood-red plant that consumed him. . . .

Later, much later, when the sun was going down through the woods, only a patch of rusty moisture showed on the earth, and by moonrise, this too was gone.

*   *   *

"The lupin is the wolf flower. Why?"

"Because it's hairy. And once there were blue wolves. They were born in nests high in the trees."

"Men," said my grandmother, "and wolves, were all one race, in the beginning. Then there had to be changes. There began to be a tribe that had only the heads of wolves, and the bodies of men, though they were shaggy-haired all over. But all wolves have human eyes. That's the difficulty. Men see it and they say, These are men disguised as animals. Men have always been afraid of their own kind, but daren't admit it. Then they see the wyes of wolves and it gives them an excuse. That is why men hate wolves."

"I think wolves are handsome," said my young cousin, George. "I wouldn't mind being a wolf. Could I be?"

"Very likely," said my grandmother, spending her double meaning only on me.

"But you didn't finish the story," I said. "What happened to the wolf-boy? And the girl in the red cloak?"

My grandmother shrugged. "Where's your imagination gone? That was in the days when the beast gods were respected, although the Christians were driving the old ways out. That girl wasn't a girl, but a demon conjured up by some priest. The boy thought he had the protection of his own god, Wolfish Pan. But Pan was already dead. The Christians killed him. And that's another story. Now, off home, before it starts to get dark."

My smaller cousin, Bettany, began to cry. She said there would be wolves in the wood, and they would devour her.

George, a cruel pretty child, sly, looking under his lashes, declared it was the demon girl who would cause us trouble.

Grandmother said there were no such things any more as demons, and that otherwise, there had been no wolf seen in our countryside for fifty years. Besides, wolves ran away if you shouted at them. She had done this as a girl.

I held Bettany's hand, though it was wet from her snifflings. But George skipped ahead of us, slashing viciously at various bushes. The shadows were lengthening, but the wood was still bisected with broad avenues of light. It was April weather, not February, birds sang and waking squirrels sprang over the budding branches. We crossed the stream by the bridge, and I looked for an altar the other side but of course there was nothing left of it. It was easy to fancy, for all that, a slim brown shape now here, now there, between the tangle of trunks and sprays of wild vine.

Beyond the wood, the lane ran on across the fallow fields, by the deserted park and the dilapidated houses of rich people long since dead and forgotten, and so uphill to the outskirts of our town.

During the night, I dreamed that a wolf had given birth to me, high up in a tall tree of colossal boughs. By moonlight, the wolf was a soft milky blue, with wonderful sad eyes.

It was a melancholy, almost a mystical, dream.

Near morning, something very dreadful happened. I was roused by an awful crying note, over and over, so repetitious I thought it was something mechanical. The whole house seemed in uproar. Then, through the window, I saw one of the men rush out, and presently return with the doctor. George was very sick, my aunt told me, and put weeping Bettany, whom I was irritatedly powerless to comfort, with me into my room. Endless comings and goings next, we excluded from them, and finally silence.

A week later, I, with the rest, was dressed in black and taken to a grave-side along the hill. Little George had died of an unpronounceable illness that years subsequently I discovered to be meningitis.

In the following months, the family cracked like a trampled eggshell. Soon I was sent away to school. Other things, events, and my maturity, drove me further and further off to exile, to the cities and the south.

I did not visit the town for many years, by which time not one of my kindred remained there, and my rather improper, story-telling grandmother had herself died. The ancient wood had been felled for the timber mills, and the encroaching roads and buildings of the town rolled over it.

*   *   *

"You've come back at a bad time," said the old man, who thought he remembered me, but in fact only remembered the little girl I had been. "Something going on now, not nice."

"What is that?"

But he would not tell a little girl. Later on, over midnight glasses of hot chocolate at the hotel, a sinister gossiping began between staff, regular guests, and the itinerants, among whom now I was numbered.

"There's been another."

"So there has."

"Oh where?"

"The same area as last time. But worse, much worse, this one."

"Is it true that they—?"

"Oh, yes, quite true." Then, seeing me lean closer: "The throats are torn out and the bodies mauled. Dogs, you might say, or something escaped. But there's the other thing—they wouldn't do that. Or if it is, not an animal. Or if it is, then that's not all it is."

Although there are streets now, and hard concrete, over the wooded tracks, and the stream runs in a canal with seats on the banks and refuse in the water, and the trees have gone to copses on neat lawns, even so, the town keeps its dreams and nightmares of legends. They know what they think this is. Only the alien traveler would scoff.

"A month to the day they moved the cemetery. Lifting the stones. . . . Everything was done properly, the priests saw to it. But there. The old Vaudron family, they were here from heaven knows when. The old lady, you knew her? Some of her tales, now, the children used to shake with fear for weeks—"

"And him only seven years of age, and dead in a night, calling out in pain. Awful cries, like something lost, or a whistle—"

The Vaudron family was my uncle's; they were talking about my little cousin, George.

"Well," said the receptionist, the doors being closed, coming to drink her own chocolate beside me. "There's a police patrol now every night, and a lot of good it does. Last month, they saw someone, a man, very late, along by the canal. They're not sure, he may be innocent, but they've found a dead woman—and there's something about him. They follow. Then he passes under a street lamp. Now there is a girl, looking out of her window, waiting for somebody, maybe. He goes by, across the street, under the lamp—and she starts screaming. He vanishes down an alley. The police run after him, can't find him. Some of them go up the stairs and hammer on the door of the girl's room. Was it a signal? It seems not. That girl, all she can say. A man, but he had the *face of a wolf*. And they have to take her to the sanatorium, where she is to this minute. She lies there and screams that she saw a man with a wolf's head and a wolf's face."

"Do you believe she saw that, really, Madame?" I said.

The receptionist shrugged. "Why not? Is it so strange? In my grandmother's day it wouldn't have surprised a soul. Now we have television, which would have upset her no end."

I thought about my own grandmother, just young enough to have seen such witchcraft as television in. She was still renowned, it would seem, for her stories. I thought about little Cousin George, dying of meningitis. I couldn't accept that if any essence of us persists after death, it could degenerate into something so arcanely banal as a murdering ghost or werewolf. But on the other hand, perhaps some sort of subsidiary impression had been left over from the physical energy of the male child who liked wolves. Like a paw-print in wet cement.

A couple of nights later, I happened to run out of cigarettes, and so I walked down to the neon café and bought a packet, and drank a *fine*. Then, not wanting to go back to read or sleep, I began to stroll along by the canal. It was just after midnight, but the moon was high, completely round and slicked with white, so the street lights were nearly superfluous. A clear-edged bluish glow lay everywhere, and the shadows were only transparently black. Stars stung the sky. There was nobody about, not here, away from the cafés of the main street. It had occurred to me that, in the era of my childhood, this must have been the route to my grandmother's house in the wood: This the stream, though the old bridge was gone and I had already crossed over by the new one, and trees invisibly all round, in the blue light. Plowed under now, everything, house and all, along with the rich people's villas, and the concrete poured over, paw-marked or otherwise.

I smoked a cigarette, and when I finished, tossed the butt into the moon-slit water. Then, turning, I saw a man under one of the lamps, leaning there, watching-me.

I walked over to him. Perhaps he was looking for company, but the prostitutes who might occasionally have touted here, no longer did so. Then, without shock, I recognized him. It was not from the past, but the story.

Of course, I had never believed my little cousins would grow up, either of them, any more than I thought I should myself. This may be the reason why children are often not offended by the death of their peers. Five years older than he, I had found him easy to leave behind. Yet, there was a family resemblance; mostly he looked like the wolf-boy in the legend. Handsome and curious, those ash and amber colors, veiled by moonlight, and the pale beautiful lupine eyes. It was a human head, if less human than anything I had ever seen before, less human than the face of an animal. Nor was he dressed in skins, but as one would expect of a poor young man, perhaps a student. Was he nineteen years old? Probably. I was twenty-four, that would be right.

I went up to him, and I said, "Good evening, George."

He smiled, gorgeously. The hot eyes did not join in, but all the rest of the face, the body muscles, seemed to do so.

"You know me?"

"We're related, shall I say?"

"Is that," he asked, "why you're wearing red?"

It had happened, as it happened I had run out of cigarettes, that the coat I had brought with me was of the reddest, most scarlet wool, a coat of blood.

"Whatever do you mean?" I said.

"Remind me of your name, since you know mine," he said.

I told him, adding that until I was twelve, we had lived in the same house, with my uncle, his father. He looked uninterested rather than dismayed. He said, "Ah, that. But that's past. Well, will you come and have a drink with me?"

I said I would.

Naturally he did not, taking me lightly by the arm, walk me back toward the bright busy cafés, but away along the canal, and down a side-street. Soon we had reached some closed shops and then a rough empty lot with a ruined, boarded house, and many trees. He led me to the house, through the thickets, which were full of fallen stones. I had no notion who it belonged to, it had been built, and abandoned, after I left the town. Several had bivouacked there since. We crept through some loose boards into a cold, moon-stripped salon. A fire was ready-laid from branches, cones, newspapers, in the grate, regardless of the state of the chimney. This fire he immediately lit with matches. From under some bricks he took two bottles of wine, a cheese wrapped in oil-cloth, and a bag of apples. We feasted solemnly. We had done so as children.

"Didn't the police come here?"

"It goes without saying," he said.

"But you were away, and had left no trace."

He grinned at me slowly.

"And the smoke. Doesn't anyone see?"

He said: "There's always that." He seemed to think he was protected, and conceivably he was.

"Tell me," I said at last.

"Why should I?"

"I thought you might like to."

"Confession?"

"Or boast. Who else would listen?"

"Plenty of people would listen."

"Do you remember any childhood?" I asked him.

He looked at me a long while, as if gaging the limits of my understanding. Then he shook his head. His hair was a shaggy flamy thing in the firelight. His brown-silver eyes shone, when they were in the dark out of the fire, hard and flat and green. Human eyes do not do this. Wolf eyes, however human, do.

"Then, when did it begin? When they dug up the grave?"

"Yes." He moved closer—we were both seated on the floor. He touched my face gently, with his long-fingered, long-nailed hand. "After all," he said, "you remember your childhood, but you don't feel, do you, it was truthfully you? *That* was someone else."

"Yes, that's so."

"Well. I know he was a child. Another person. I simply recognize that it wasn't myself at all. I'm George here and now. I'm here, I'm now."

"And the grave—"

"Like lifting the lid of a kettle. The lid, down, gives the illusion of suppression. But I was there, underneath."

He said there was a darkness and he came out of the darkness in the way one comes out of sleep. There might have been dreams, or not. He said, had I ever woken up and for a while not known where I was, or the day or date even, not minding it, knowing I would recall, but not yet recalling. I had, and said I had. Well, he said, it was like that for him. Then, he found himself walking through the town. It was quite unfamiliar, yet—like days and dates—he realized it would *become* recollected, he had only to wait. And then he saw a girl, by the canal. Probably she was soliciting. He went up to her and asked her for a cigarette (George had seen his father and brothers smoke. It would be normal for him to assume that he, when an adult, would smoke also). The girl gave him the cigarette. (He asked me if I knew the prostitutes in Roman times had been called 'she-wolf'—not as an insult, but to indicate their honorable usefulness, linked to the motif of the wolf-mother of the city, and the werewolf festival of Lupercalia.) Then she suggested he might like to go with her, to a café, but instead he took her into an alley he had already found, and there he killed her. It seemed perfectly natural to him, he was excited but competent, knowing instinctively, as with sex, what should be done. In fact, it was like sex, and afterward he was sorry he had not possessed her before killing her. He did not abuse the corpse. The ethics of the bourgeois Vaudron family intervened. He found another girl to satisfy concupiscence, and then arranged to meet her again the next night. When he met this second girl this second time, he first made love to her and then tore her to pieces. He killed her in the middle of orgasm, both hers and his own. This was highly fulfilling, it seemed, and became thereafter his modus operandi. Sometimes he fed at these times. He also ate other food. The cafés and hotels threw things out, or gave them to him, or he stole them.

It came to me that the town had remained a wood for him, and in a way I wondered if he even saw the buildings and the roads as such, or if they were somehow caves and trees, and savage woodland glades. By this formula, too, he might have his uncanny protection, making himself in turn invisible to the town, and to its police force. Seeing him quite frequently, as they must do, they had never seen *him*.

The fire sank. It was cold in the boarded house, February weather.

"Sometimes I go to a church," he said. "Once, I did make confession. But not the killings. You see, for me, the killing is not a sin."

"No, I understand that."

As he moved to put more cones and branches on to the fading fire, I told him the dream I had had, the night he—no, George—had died. About the blue wolf who gave birth to me in the great tree, and her sad eyes. I mentioned the idea to him that the mother-birth is the second birth, that the ejection of the seed the paternal birth—precedes it. I wanted to inquire after the metamorphosis he himself underwent, perhaps during this ejection, or directly before. Presumably, it did happen. But how did he accomplish it? He seemed totally physically real, and if he was, such a displacement of atoms must be impossible.

"Well, maybe the wolves did birth you," he said. "You arrived at the house an orphan."

"I don't remember my parents," I said.

"I remember mine," he said. "*His*."

"Do you remember our grandmother?"

"A big mouth, always telling us things she shouldn't have. But you were a strange child. That's how I see you now. I wonder what happened to that other girl. . . ."

"Bettany?" I paused. Bettany had married a handsome

Jewish banker, and become another woman who ate choco-
lates and produced children. I had not met her for years. Neither of us now wanted to talk about Bettany. I think it was
only some associative memory stirring in George's brief past,
like a nerve. Eventually, I pushed her right away, and said,
"And you remember the story our grandmother told us?"

"The girl with the mantle made of blood," he said. "Like
you."

"Do you worship the old gods? Do you make sacrifices
to Pan?"

He laughed. The laugh was wonderful. He sat back on his
heels, laughing, warm February fire all over him. He ate life.
It had filled him. He was unlike anything, human or beast.

"No. Pan? Pan is dead. Or is that a pun—*Pan*—du *pain*—
bread—*peine*—pain—the body of Christ?"

"I meant, how do you effect the transformation?"

He lowered his eyes—with a dagger-green flash—like a
modest girl who has been asked by a man if he may touch,
very politely, her breast.

"What is that?" he said.

"Man into wolf. Is it possible?"

"Of course."

"How?"

"Do you want me to show you?" he said, looking at me
now in the old sly way, under his lashes.

"No," I said. But I did want him to. "Could you not simply
describe for me—"

"If I do it," he said, "you may be frightened. You may go
mad. Or, I may kill you."

"You would stop being yourself."

"I should become myself."

"There's no self to become," I said. "Whatever you are, not
really. So, I suppose you could become anything. Is that what
the answer is?"

"I remember the girl in the story," he said. "She wouldn't
submit."

"Then she did."

"Yes. Then she did. Do you actually think," he said, "that
any one of us is truly what we're pleased to call 'Real'? All

matter, flesh, skin, trees, stone, bricks, blood—it's all illusory, fluid, non-existent, formed from nothing—therefore capable of any alteration, and of complete change. Wouldn't you say? Where else do the woods go to, when they turn into concrete? How else? And the bread that's a body, and children who grow up or turn into a heap of calcium in the ground?"

"What about the needle and the pin?"

"There's no choice between them. They're the same. They both pierce and they both join together."

"Is that what it meant?"

"In the story she told us."

"Show me, then," I said.

"Look at me, then," he said.

So I did look. I looked hard, too hard. And then I let myself relax, even my eyes, I allowed them to unfocus a little, just a very little, and gradually, by the broad gusts of fire through the shadow, I began to see the wolf. There was no violence, no tearing or twisting, no flare up of pelt, the skull re-shaping itself, a howling frenzy. Frankly, it was all already there. By allowing myself to see, I merely saw it. Then again, the terror of it, for it was quite terrifying, was all because it was *not* a wolf at all, but some intrinsic fear-thing that was to do with man's phobia at wolves, primeval, matted, dark, fathomless. It was the head of a creature that was the head of fear, and with a man's body, a man's long wolfish hands, with which to work the horror out.

Presently I looked away, and opened my purse and took out a cigarette. When I had struck the match and lit it, I offered the packet to him, and he had become a young man again, a wolf-boy, much more wolf-like in his human form. The werewolf was only the image, the *icon* of the nightmare.

We smoked our cigarettes in silence, and then he lay down, his head in my lap. The fire played on the planes of his face. I watched him, trying to memorize his beauty, as one does with some work of art one may never see again. After a while, he said that he often slept here, but he was cold tonight, did I feel the cold as he did? He thought not. His blood was hotter than mine. So then I took off my red coat and laid it over him, drawing it up to his chin.

He slept after an interval, and I, my back propped against the rotted boards, also slept a few moments. I dreamed I was in the tree again, in the act of birth from the belly or the penis of the lupin-blue wolf. I thought: That's the riddle, then. Not to find the bestial in humankind, but this constant thrust to be born free of it, the coming out from the beast, the ancestor in his sheath of hair and hunger. Then I woke, and he slept, still. I got up carefully, not to wake him, I did not want to make him start. But as I moved to the fire, I half believed I caught the flash of his eyes, watching on under their lashes. Yet who goes in the wood, knowing the wood, is there to tempt his fate. He recalled, he had told me so. I pulled one of the last twigs out of the grate, and carried the bud of February fire back to him. I even still waited an instant, letting the glare and heat of the burning twig flicker above his face, as Psyche did, when she stared down on her shape-changer monster-god in the legend of love. But now he did not open his eyes, if he ever had.

I put the flame to the edges of my coat, all the way around, then threw the last smolder of the twig down into his hair.

At first, there was nothing, just a ripple, sparks, smoke. Then suddenly, all of it went up, the coat, the wolf-mane, and he too, a spasm of fire, scarlet on the shadow, the color of blood, redness covering him, obliterating him. He gave no cry, and scarcely changed position, only rolling a little, as if to be one with the warmth and comfort.

I found it very cold outside, after the fire. The house was burning by the time I reached the canal, I could see the light on the sky, and the smoke going over the sinking moon.

My grandmother's grave, in the transported cemetery, has flowers growing on it, and ivy, but no lupins. I took photographs of that, and other Vaudron graves. That was really all modernization had left me. The dwellings and landmarks of my childhood were gone. There was some excitement in the town that day, about a derelict house which had caught on fire in the night. Tramps had been using it, and no one was astonished that the cooling clinker revealed the remains of a man. Then again, however, they were not sure it was a man, or anything, for that matter, ever alive. At the correct temperature, even bones will melt. You can rely on the constancy of nothing.

Having to buy a coat, I was disconcerted by the women in the shop. They were so interested in all the other aspects of their lives, that for them I hardly existed. I had become a sort of ghost. I left the town near evening, by the night train for the south. In the city I knew I would be recognized, and spoken to, I knew I should be perfectly alive and real.

Wolfed

UNDER THE GLITTERING cliffs of skyscrapers, in the tangled night wood of neon, concrete, glass, and steel that calls itself New York City, he strayed from the path, and went into a little bar.

He was twenty-six years old, six foot four in height, and he weighed around one hundred and seventy-two pounds. He had the kind of face sometimes seen on celluloid, but once, that very year he thought he might make it as an actor, the middle-aged woman in the casting office had said to him, "Oh, honey. You're just too good-looking. That blond hair and those *black* eyes—be warned. You'll have a bad time here." She then suggested something else. And when he did that, she was very generous, both with her surprisingly pretty body, and with the wad of bills he found later in his car. It was this that had started him on his present career, the one he should have been pursuing right now, since he was down to his last twenty. So maybe the bar was a fine idea ... or not. Really, it was the girl. She was the reason he came in. And she was not the sort of girl to be any use. Because she wouldn't *need* him, not at all.

As he sat down on the chromium stool at her side, practiced, he took her in, through the low, cave-dim light. But practice had not prepared him. He liked women a lot. Their voices, their bodies—oh, yes, those—their clothes and how they wore them. Their cosmetics even, jewelry, lingerie—everything about them. And this one—

She had a burnished hood of claret-red hair, matched neatly by her velvet gown, which being tight, backless and nearly frontless, gave him an exquisite view of several rich curves, and a faultless pearl-cream skin. Then, imagine a deer in the wood who is truly a wicked—but beautiful—witch in disguise. That was her face. She had no makeup but for the black kohl round her eyes and on her lashes, that looked real and a full inch long, and the ripe scarlet on her full, smooth lips. No jewelry, good or cheap, on her slim arms, at her long, delicious neck, or in the lobes of her alabaster ears. However, where her shorter than short skirt rode up, just above the black lace of her long-legged stocking-tops, he noted a garter with a golden rose. And five years of having to do with gold, though seldom in the way of ownership, suggested the golden rose, like her lashes, was quite real.

He did not speak, but he saw from his vision's corner, that she had turned to frankly study him. Perhaps she liked the look of him. Most women did. Suddenly she laughed, a great laugh, appealing, not too loud, not ugly, and *not* irritatingly coy. Lashes, gold, laugh—all genuine?

He turned too, and gazed at her full on.

Oh, yes.

Her teeth were white, and her eyes the shade of green found in Han jade. She smelled faintly, warmly, of some smoky flower, perhaps not of the earth. Was that the catch— she was an X-File alien?

"Thank you for laughing at me."

"I'm sorry."

"No, I liked it."

"Why?"

"It means I've amused you. And I didn't even have to tell a joke."

She smiled now, and raising her glass—of some green cocktail less convincing than her Han-green eyes—she said, "I laughed because you're so handsome."

"Oh, I see."

"Do you?"

"Well . . . maybe. Shall I do it at you?"

"If you want."

The few other customers were far off along the room, but now a waiter was floating down the bar counter, and the girl signaled, and he floated right over.

He knew now she would buy him a big drink, and she did, and when it had been served on its little white paper Undependable, she said to him, "Will you tell me your name?"

"Sure. It's Wolfgang. But you'll believe I prefer to be called Wolf."

"So we don't gang up on you," she said.

"Yeah, that's it. And I guess they call you Red," he added, guessing that he doubted that.

"Rose," she answered.

She leaned a fraction toward him, and the white fruits of her breasts moved gently in the red velvet, just enough he understood that she had on no brassière, and probably no underclothes at all, apart from the stockings with the garter.

"Rose," he repeated. He let her hear it, that he was aroused. From the warm fragrance of her, the darkening of her eyes, he was suddenly recklessly banking on the fact that she was, as well. You had to take a chance sometimes. But you had to be careful too. There had been that girl in Queens who looked like five million dollars, and turned out to have a habit, and a worse habit—which was a knife.

"Are you hungry?" said Rose.

"I'm always hungry." He paused, "Not always for food."

"Me neither," said Rose.

Wolf glanced at those other customers. No one was looking at Rose, or himself, they were all lost, as most persons were, in their own involving lives. Just as well, perhaps, for she had put her slim white hand now on his crotch. It was the mildest, almost, you could say, the most *tactful* caress. But he came up like a rock against her.

"You're interested," she said.

"My. You can tell."

"I'm so glad. Because you're perfect, Wolf."

"That's nice."

"I hope so."

"What," he said, as she removed her cruel, tender little hand, "did you have in mind?"

"Well, you see, it's not really for me." She watched him, watched his face change down, cool an iota. "No, this isn't some trick, Wolf. It's just, you see, I promised to take my grandmother something."

"Your *grandmother*."

Rose laughed, differently now. This was exuberant, even coarse, and yet, she could get away with it entirely. Muscles rippled lightly under red velvet dress and white velvet skin. Despite all his years of experience, he wanted badly to pull her close, and open his mouth, let out his tongue against her ear, her throat, to taste the heat of her under her succulent sheath, and then he would like—

"It sounds unattractive, I know. But it isn't. *She* isn't. Grandmothers aren't always elderly any more. I'm nineteen, and my grandmother—Ryder, that's her name—is just, well, in her early forties."

"That doesn't sound like it's legal."

Rose shrugged.

"Or quite truthful," he amended, sternly.

Rose picked up a little ruby purse, and slid out of it a small photograph. She held this out. When Wolf took it from her, he saw it showed a most beautiful, lion-maned woman, in a skin-tight leotard. Not young, but nevertheless voluptuous, limber, strong, and highly enticing.

"This is Grandma?" he said.

"That is she. And honestly, Wolf, the picture hasn't been retouched."

"You'd swear that on your mother's life."

"Can't. No mother, now. I'd swear it on mine."

Wolf emptied his glass. The girl raised her hand and the waiter stirred. Wolf said, "Maybe not. I don't want you to waste your money."

"I haven't. Look, we'll take a cab over there. Go up, and see. I know, when you meet Ryder, you'll want to go in ... if you take what I mean."

"And if not?"

"No hard feelings. Make some excuse to her—wrong floor, wrong apartment. If you come straight back down, well I'll wait around a while, and let's say two hundred dollars for your wasted time. How's that?"

"You guessed. Aw shucks."

Rose leaned forward again. For a blissful moment, as she adjusted one crimson pump, he caught, in the scoop of neckline, the peek-a-boo flicker of an icing-sugar-pink nipple. The colors didn't clash at all. And then her soft lips were on his, and her narrow tongue darted in and out and was gone.

"I did so want to give her something lovely for her birthday," said Rose. "And you are, Wolf, lovely as lovely is."

The elevator had gold inside, not solid this time, but not bad: gold-plated.

When he alighted, and rang the gold-plated bell, her intercom came on.

"Is that you, honey?"

Ryder's voice was low and sweet—and dangerous.

Wolf said, "I guess not."

"Oh," said Granny's intercom. "Then what?"

"Rose—sent me up."

"Rose did? Do I know a Rose?"

"She says she's your granddaughter."

"Oh, that Rose. Okay."

The jet-black shining door opened wide, and showed him an enormous reception area, with black and white marble underfoot and on the walls, golded mirrors, a skylight set with milky glass shot by red jewels that threw down rosy blood-drops all over everything. There were no other furnishings, and just two engraved glass doors, opening somewhere else, presently closed. You couldn't see through the engraving, not properly. But inside it looked fairly impressive.

After all, he had been let straight in and he hadn't seen Granny yet, in order to back off nicely if he didn't care for her. But then, anyway, the elevator was a private one and this was the penthouse suite, so it would be kind of unlikely he had taken the wrong route, or made any mistake at all.

Just then the glass doors were pushed decisively open.

And there stood—Granny.

"What a wonderful voice you have," said Granny. "Trained, yes?"

"I was an actor."

"Not anymore? No more acting?"

"Not on a stage."

She grinned. She had perfect teeth, the teeth the best sort of predator would have. Which was about right. She definitely did exude the aura of a lioness. Even a lion. Almost as tall as Wolf, in her high-heeled slippers, and with a mane of gleaming platinum-to-silver hair, she wore otherwise a completely transparent robe, tied tight to her tightly muscular waist by a thin rope of Cartier gold. She was muscular all over, the way a dancer is, and maybe she was a dancer. On the muscles had been smoothed a satin padding of flesh, and over that a lightly tanned skin like honey. Her breasts were heavy, but edible. The urge to weigh them in the hands was overwhelming. And she had done just what they did in books, gilded her nipples. Under her round and muscular belly, which gave a little ripple even as his eyes irresistibly went there, a sort of little *wave* to him, her bush was of the same metallic effect as her mane.

She gave a kind of kick with one long, long, *long* leg. That was like a horse. But no, she was simply kicking out of the way a champagne cork lying on the mosaic—it *was* a mosaic—floor.

"My birthday party," she explained. "They drank and drank. They all brought me presents, so I couldn't turn them out. Would you like to finish the Dom Perignon? A couple of bottles still half full, I think, and I don't drink alcohol on weekdays. It would be a kindness."

"I guess I can force myself."

"Then come on in."

She turned and moved away. Her bottom was a stimulating sight. Yes, a dancer must be it—perhaps with a giant snake, winding and coiling about her amber body, caressing, slipping, its incredible muscles matched by her own.

The room was about two blocks big, with carpets on the walls that might have come from Ancient Persia, and a single statue in bronze, of a girl holding up a dish, and in the dish lavish fruit, oranges, peaches, grapes—the proper stuff of an epic lust-scene.

Had Rose already called up? She must have told Granny

that she would like *this* present. Or why else had Granny come to the door clad fit to wake the dead?

She was returning with a large, sparkling crystal goblet about a foot long, somewhat the way he was feeling in a particular part of himself right now, and full of bubbling silvery-golden something.

"Wolf—that's right, is it?"

Rose had called.

"Yes, ma'am."

"My name is Ryder. I don't look a day over forty-three, and I'm not."

She deserved an accolade, though she probably received them always. "You don't look more than thirty-three to me." She didn't, or not by very much. And though she had expression lines by her mouth, which was large and marvelously shaped, and had the faintest gilded glisten on it, and by her eyes, which were as dark as his own, and also gilded—they were of the variety of line that made you want to deepen them through laughter, and through loud cries that had nothing to do with sorrow or dismay.

"The trouble is," said Ryder, putting her hand lightly on his shoulder, huge eye to eye with him, her slight, clean breath just blowing over his lips, scented by silk, musk and savannah, "I didn't know about you, when I took the two herbal tablets. They're terrific. They make you sleep for six hours. It's been a tiring day. I calculate I have about forty minutes, before those pills work. Do you think we could find something to kill forty minutes?"

Interestingly, her personal bathroom was even bigger than the two block sitting room. And in the midst of its Grecian glacier of tiles and friezes, its ten and twenty foot, emerald colored plants that thrived on heat and steam, lay a very special Jacuzzi of ink-black marble.

"I love to get wet," said Ryder. Then she added, "Do you mind short hair?" And drew off the mane, just as she had discarded her transparent robe and golden tie. Her own hair was also silver, a thick short fur over her head leading into a serpentine coil along her neck. This way, she looked more cat-like, more chancy even than before.

She stepped down into the tub, and lay along a marble ledge just under the water. There were a pair of black marble nymphs here too, naked and glowing. Ryder lifted her arms and wrapped her hands loosely around their hips.

"Come in."

So far, the water moved only gently, and through the little liquid thrills, her breasts, lifted by her arms, golden nipples glinting, bobbed and trembled as the water came and went. The way the water ran, he noticed; the nipples were getting particularized attention. That must feel good, and obviously the ledge had been arranged for exactly this position and this treatment.

He took off his clothes, and Ryder watched him through half-lidded eyes. He could see she was pleased with him, very pleased. She wriggled her legs as he descended into the pool, and a spray of delicate cool-warm drops hit the surface of his chest and thighs, sprinkling like diamonds his already enormous erection.

"You're a little ahead of yourself there," she said.

He laughed.

The water was at a clever temperature, warmed enough to be comfortable but cool enough to brace. He eased on to the ledge beside her, and bent to her mouth. They kissed, tongues entwining like the serpent dance he had visualized, while his left hand and the water played over and over her big cushiony breasts, and her hard little nipples eagerly nosed after his fingers, wanting to be tickled. She made a deep luxurious moaning sound, again and again into his mouth.

When he lifted his head, a soft flush was on her face, making her look younger than ever. She pulled him over and on top of her, his penis lying delightfully trapped between their bellies, quivering uncontrollably with its own life.

Ryder polished his back with her hands, and slid them into the groove between his buttocks. She too began to play, while the water lapped with its own caress, creating a melting fire that trickled ever more strongly through into his loins, and until she had drawn out of him in turn a murmur of tortured pleasure. But he was now so hard that pleasure was stealing close to pain. He eased himself away from her.

"Step back off the ledge, but stay close," she whispered. "Kneel facing me, where the groove is. Trust me, you'll like it there. The water does something—special. Custom built." He did what she said, and as he knelt on the smooth marble between her legs, she glided them up on to his shoulders, and her hands clasped firmly on the black stone nymphs. The speed and direction of the water intensified at once. It became insistent, *skillful*. It was probing at him in exactly the most apt of places, bubbling around and around his balls, and stroking, fierce, rhythmic, at his stem, while at the hugely engorged tip of him there began a ceaseless, miraculous suction, like that of the most amazing and cunning and unavoidable mouth in the world.

He said, ". . . Ryder—"

"Oh Mr. Wolf," she gasped. Her calves slid on his back. "Will you eat me?"

As the wicked water deliriously stroked and taunted and urged him, he bent into the wet sweet core of her vulva to kiss her better and better. Her hair here was coarse and aromatic as summer grass. Her clit was small but totally erect, standing up to him like a pearl on fire. He licked her, licked her, to the tempo of the inescapable ecstasy chasing up and down along his spine, mounting like architecture in his groin, and felt the long quivers of a glorious complementary agony vibrating through her legs, as he clasped her jerking hips in both his hands.

She lay spread before him, and he glimpsed her as she writhed, panting, clinging and squeezing at the nymphs as if she drowned, so that the jets of water they controlled were increasing, going wild, roiling over the maddened gems of her nipples, and working upon his penis like five or six desperate tongues and one starving loving mouth. He could feel Ryder's tension churning and swollen beneath his grasp, banked up against her clit as if behind a dam, galloping in her vagina, the whole golden pulsing hill of her pelvis.

Her eyes were fluttering. Her vulva was fluttering.

And he had only moments left to him.

She heard him groan aloud, and she breathlessly teased like a naughty little girl, "Oh, he's starting to come—he can't resist—he's going to, he's going to come—" But then her breathing and voice broke entirely in her first soaring scream.

A spasm as huge as the whole sky-scraping tower that contained him shook Wolf to his roots. He roared, arching against her, smothered in her, even as the lights exploded, frantically, gaspingly, swirling and slapping with his tongue on and on upon that burning orgasmic pearl of hers, to hear her screaming, to keep her screaming, so the marble room rolled and boomed like a bell, and her golden heels beat against him like the drums of paradise.

To his amazement, when he was only fourteen, Wolf had learned that there *was* life after orgasm. Heaven knew how.

He had to admit he was sorry, however, that Ryder had had to go and sleep off her two herbal sleeping capsules. There were lots of things they could have done, after an interval. Instead she had left him the run of her apartment, all the rooms excluding her bedroom, dressing room, and the bathroom with the fascinating jacuzzi.

So he wandered a while through her studio, which was indeed equipped for dancing and exercise, and also partly as the most economical, effective—she proved it—and *female* gym he had ever seen. He viewed the study, the swimming-pool of chartreuse water in the conservatory, the music and book library, with a piano, and a music system that had spread gold-rimmed speakers all through the apartment, the *computer* room—small, yes, but *astounding*—guest rooms, eating rooms, roof garden, three more bathrooms out of *Spartacus* or *Jupiter's Darling*, and so on. And . . . so forth.

The kitchen was the tiniest room. Even so, it had everything the health-or-diet conscious—or even the simply greedy and thirsty—could wish for.

Ryder was opulent, but trusting. Which was warming. Wolf had always had his own code, and behaved well, which he had not always been credited with. A meeting of social graces.

He ate some smoked salmon, and some creamy chicken, a

poppy-seed bagel, and a salad of dark green cress, frilly let-
tuce and yellow tomatoes. He finished the first of the three
half-empty bottles of champagne.

It was back in the sitting room that he found her note. It
was to him, and he didn't know when she had written it. Possibly, even before he had arrived at the apartment.

*Wolf, once we part, I'll be out, dead, for six or seven hours.
So, I'll see you tomorrow, if you care to stay over. (The guest
rooms have everything.) Meanwhile, I think Rose may be coming back, around midnight. She's been very sweet to me, and
I'd like to be really sweet to her too. I'm not actually her
grandma. You may have guessed. That's a little—how shall I
say?—joke. Did you like Rose, too? I hope you did. I'm sure
you did. You have, I think, Excellent taste. Yum. So, let me tell
you what Rose really likes. Get ready:*

Wolf read on. He raised an eyebrow, recalled he was not
on camera, raised both eyebrows.

He laughed again. "Oh, boy."

Then he sat down, to consider.

Twenty minutes later, at ten fifty-one precisely, he strolled
into the second dressing room that led from the closed bedroom of his sleeping hostess.

It was like stuff he had seen back-stage, and in the cara-
vans of the movie lot. Only a deal more generous, and expensive to the point of being fabulous, the essence of *fables*.

At least two hundred gowns. At least a hundred and fifty
wigs. All of them the most beautiful, the most realistic, the
most exclusive. And in drawers, when he opened them, smil-
ing, and already aware of something else, all the pure Indian
and Chinese silk, and handworked lace, all the patterned and
mist-sheer stockings, garter-belts, waspies, buttoned gloves,
that any woman of that turn of mind could have conjured. All
the makeup, too, every lip-paint, blusher, mascara, shadow,
tint, texture, contour, high-light . . . A Garden of Eden for any
girl who liked these things.

Or any man who liked them, too.

It had been a revelation, the first time. The rich girl in
Idaho who, in her long white house, had dressed them up
together, saying, when she had finished painting him, lacing

him, putting on his costume, "Well, just look at you." "I'm way too tall," Wolf had commented, staring at himself, or rather at this new *herself* in the mirror. "Sugar, I just don't think," said the rich girl, "that anyone'd mind that. The hell of it is, you're prettier than *me*."

Not since then. Not quite. Though now and then ... just flirting with a pair of panties, hose, softly silicone-padded bra ...

He liked women. The look and feel of them. He liked making love to them. He liked what they wore, their perfumes, and the unguents they stroked on to their faces and over the curves of their breasts. And the stockings they drew up their legs, and the lisping of the silky stuff over their bodies. Once or twice, just ... once or twice. He dreamed of it. She, and he, also a she.

Apparently, it was just this very thing that turned Rose on. A slim, handsome man, disguised — as a woman.

He was erect again. He was thinking of Rose now. Rose, all freely moving and warm and white and spilling over in her red dress, and the stocking-tops, and the garter, and he, Wolf, perhaps in that one, there, the black number. Because it was a fact, the garments that fitted Ryder's big firm body, would fit him just as neatly.

He'd need the bathroom with its razor for guests and its creams and glosses. He'd need some more champagne, too. And it was already eleven. He would have to hurry.

But then, the actor is expert at changing costume fast, and everything else that goes with it.

Rose let herself into Ryder's apartment at a quarter past midnight. The lights were low, and the softest music was playing. As she opened the two glass doors into the vast sitting room, Rose called quietly, "Ryder? It's me, are you around?"

"I'm afraid she's dead," said a low, light, husky voice from the couch.

"*What*?" said Rose.

"Sorry. I mean she's dead to the world. Herbal sleeping tablets."

"Yeah," said Rose. "And who are you?"

The tall and beautiful woman on the couch re-crossed, with an electric rasp, her sheerly stockinged legs, revealing, as she did so, the long black tongue of a garter-belt, under the black satin hem of her dress. Her hair was a mane of foaming black curls, just lit with a streak or two of silver. She was big, but slender, her stomach flat, her breasts, under the high-necked gown with its collar of black sequins, rather small. Her face was truly something, smooth as bone china, with a crimson mouth and somber velvet eyes.

"Who am I? You can call me—Nana."

"Oh, *Nana*." Rose smiled. She leaned right down to adjust her pumps, and as she did so, she put her hand against her bosom, so that only the upper swell of her breasts was visible. She tossed her claret hair. "My," said Rose, "what big eyes you've got, Nana."

"Research shows," said Nana, idly, standing up and bringing the champagne, "that the larger your eyes are, the better you can see."

"Really." Rose took the glass, and extracted a few sips. "And does research tell me why you're wearing my grandmother's French perfume?"

"It tells *me* she's not your grandmother. Way too young."

"True. It's our joke, hers and mine. When we met, you see, she said, Now, Rose, stop that—I'm old enough to be your grandmother—Now you understand. So, tell me why the perfume?"

"Because she left it for me, in the guest bathroom. Along with the nail gloss."

Rose observed the nails of Nana. "'Savage Sunset,'" deduced Rose. "Like the lips. Blood red. Mmm. Have you been biting and clawing? Have you been *eating* someone?"

"I admit, I like to eat women."

"Poor, helpless, older women, all alone in their humble homes."

"And little girls in short red dresses."

"Oh, Nana, what big teeth you have."

"Forget about the teeth. Look at the tongue."

Rose lowered her eyes.

Nana, in her high black heels, now towered over her. Rose swayed toward Nana, pliant, almost confiding.

"Do you know, Nana, there's this bulge—just *there*. Yes, just where I have my hand. Are you pleased to see me?"

"Extremely pleased."

"Yes, you do seem pleased."

Rose slipped her hands around Nana's buttocks, and massaged them, and pulled them inward. She rubbed against the mysterious bulge in Nana's satin groin, back and forth, back and forth.

Nana tilted back her head and closed her eyes.

Nana was feeling very near the edge again.

It had started as she shaved herself and creamed herself, and it got more and more as she dressed in the cool shivery silk and it slithered and shivered all over her, and kept on slithering and shivering and slithering, teasing at her, and then the warm, tactile silicone padding of the brassière rubbed on her nipples, her male nipples, which were the nipples of none other—what a shock!—than Wolf. And by the time the stockings were hooked to the garter-belt, it was with enormous—enormous being the absolutely right word—difficulty that Wolf packed his rampant and colossally aroused penis into the satin and lace modesty pouch.

"If you keep on at that, Rose, I'm not going to be able to hold on to myself—"

Rose shook her head with surprise, and ran her arms all up him, all up Nana, and lifting herself up his body, by some magical acrobatic feat, somehow lifted up Nana's skirt as she came, and wriggled down the pouch, so out popped the gigantic rearing waving almost howling snake, red-hot to bursting. And supporting herself on his shoulder, while Wolf-Nana held her up by his hands cupping the smooth round little curves of her bottom, Rose sank on to the snake, absorbed it deep within her divine recesses, and so began to dance.

"Oh Nana—how big—how *big*—"

Wolf pushed hard against and into her. He must think of other things. Not silk, not being danced upon. Not her wonderful enfolding vagina, that had him now as if it would never

let him out. And not—*decidedly* not—about the white breasts
rising up now from the neck of the dress, blinking their two
adorable shy pink eyes at him, going in again, creeping up
again, *appearing*, vanishing, and creeping up—

Think about the wood.

Think about the city.

Think about the stars.

But the wood is all thick and twinkling with white, half-
naked young women, their breasts playing hide-and-seek,
their naked bottoms filling the hands, and their legs wrapped
tight about the waist where the corset is, and the silk, and the
brassière above, tweaking him innocently so two ravenous
little stars ignite there, and Rose is throwing back her head,
her neck is arched, her breasts rise like two moons, first with
a faint flush, and then with her nipples all bare and upright,
and he is going to, again—going to—

Think of the moon.

The moon is a *breast*.

Think of—think—of—the subway—

A tunnel, lined with wet eager velvet—*clinging, surging*—
the train is—*coming*—

Think—

"Oh Wolf—*faster*—"

He is on the couch—did they fall?—and she is on top of
him, and he is thrusting, and thrusting her home upon him,
with his hands on her bottom, and her dress is just a red rope
round her middle, and her breasts tickle his lips, and he is
nuzzling them, and now she is gasping, and now giving a little
sound nearly like the start of the first word of a sentence—Oh
come, Rose, come, oh, come into the garden, Maud—oh,
Rose, Rose, come, before it's too late—

And then she comes.

She makes a noise like laughter, and she shudders all over,
again and again, and he sees her, shuddering, laughing in ecstasy, her breasts and her hair, and he rushes her body up and
down the length of him, and tingles and rills and impossible
yawns of unbelievable pleasure tumble up his spine and
across his blood and through his penis, until he detonates, in

what must be the firework display of the century, but, alas, all invisible inside her.

In the early morning light, punctual as a clock, after her six or seven hours, Ryder wakes and joins Rose and Wolf-Nana, and they shower together and eat a small but healthy—and nourishing—breakfast, and go back to bed, which is Ryder's bed, all lambent with her scent and the size of Central Park. And here the two women praise all Wolf and Nana's virtues, which are many, and play games all over him, until in the end, in a knot of limbs and hair and laughs and shudders and spasms and shrieks, they are coming together, and coming apart, and coming and coming and coming.

And perhaps, being so well-suited as they are, at the top of that cliff in the city wood, they *will* live happily ever after.

My Life as a Swan

1

MY FATHER DIED. That was the end of us, my mother and me — she too old and I too young, so we counted for nothing. Bitter was the cup of my youth. Never shall I try to recapture the beginnings of my human life.

But neither, ever, even in the silver hell to which I shall finally fall, can I forget when first I saw him: Hrothgar, the Enchanter. My Fate.

The dark lake spread so far, and was like a sea, or so I thought, then. For of course, I have never seen the ocean.

Others, who had beheld such things, compared the lake to an iron mirror. Black, yet polished and therefore reflective, it stretched from the skeins of trees, tumble of rocks, away and away.

The sky was dusken. To the east, several of the bird-white stars were beginning to show. And I, the stupid one, a woman yet a child of perhaps seventeen years — for how could I then, or can I now, be sure — stood on the brink, staring out toward the coming night.

How slender and determinate, however, the night.

It sped toward me. I realized, in fear naturally, since anything unusual was probably a threat, that a part of the darkness had come away from the fastenings of the sky. It had wide wings, and a body with a curious shape, a face, and two eyes that were stars. These stars were not pale, but red.

Obviously I had been instructed in the idea of evil gods and entities. And, evidently, I had taken such ideas into my mind.

So, during those moments, I turned to run.

One wing brushed my head. It seemed to comb the very top of my skull. I felt the contact of it all through my scalp, and through my hair to its ends.

But it was warm, *living*. It was vital yet caressive. Oh, what had I known? Many blows and scratchings, wicked words, and the tongue of a whip. This was unlike any of these.

In wonder I gazed upward, and as it sailed on along the hem of the darkness, the great owl, whose eyes were forges of red molten gold, glanced back at me.

I fell in love with it, the owl. How not? Of them all, of all things, what else, *who* else, had *looked* at me? Who else — what else — had *I* to love?

Soon there was discussion of the owl all along the lake shore. The two villages talked of it, and all the cots and hovels scattered about. Owls were birds of ill-omen. Their cries indicated bad news, tidings or warnings of death. They were the familiars of witches. Worse, perhaps, they skimmed other birds and small game from the forests, that was there only to feed men. Such a large owl, too, some of the men said, might pick off even hares, even a lamb. For they had watched the owl intently by that time, as it was flying in the dusk of night or dawn. Never had so great a flying creature been seen in this locality. The wing-span, they said, was wide as that of two full-grown men placed head to foot.

In fact the owl became ever larger and more terrible, in their talk, as the days fell from the month.

Meanwhile it was heard crying, in the strange somber pipe of its voice, above the woodcutters' hutment — and next morning a man let slip his ax, and his arm was cut open to the bone. He would never work ably again. Also a young woman had heard the owl three nights together, calling from the trees by Second Village. On the fourth evening she bore a stillbirth.

The hunters came together. They would go out with bows and knives, fire at the owl and bring it to earth, where they would kill it. They would burn the body, but offer the tawny smoky feathers to the hunter god.

So for several sevens of days they went after the owl, shot at it with bows, even thought once they had winged it — but never brought it down. Never killed it at all.

And then simply it went away. It was nolonger seen by anyone, and not heard once. The summer began to vanish too.

A child wandered off and failed to return, and they blamed this on the deep lake, or an early wolf. No blame now for the owl of ill-omen. Almost, it was forgotten.

Although not by me, for I mourned it, in my helpless and powerless way. I had lost most things or never had them. To mourn, then, was my sole luxury.

And I dreamed of it. I was used to dream of its touch, and of its flying away from me, and looking back with its fiery eyes. As if it called me to fly up in the air and to follow it. But where? And how . . .

My mother's hut lay back from the shore, many steps up into the trees, as if to hide itself, poor, lonely, unworthy hovel, from the more deserving people round about.

It was a sorry shack certainly. Half the roof was down, and in the coming winter only the snow would seal it when the world froze. My mother did not stay in the hut with me by then. Since two years ago she kept outside, under a pine. I had had to ask a man of First Village to help me dig the grave, as I had not the strength to make it deep enough the wolves, or other beasts, should be unable to get in at her. And she had had a morbid dread of that. I paid him with fresh rabbits from the traps and went hungry a little while. I hated trapped meat in any case. I would much have preferred to kill outright and swift, but none had taught me the skill. Only sometimes I managed to catch a lake fish and smash it dead instantly on a rock. That was better. I could eat that if I must.

The man had told me actually, he would settle for something else. I was surprised he wanted me for that, but I was young and put his lust down to my age. I told him I had an ailment there, it would be wrong to risk infecting him. He said I was a filthy bitch, dug the grave, and took the rabbits instead.

All those years I had remained a virgin. My mother had said I must, and examined me now and then with her bruises of fingers. She whipped me often as a child. Then, when she was too old to do that, she said I must whip myself, it was a good thing to do, the gods liked it. So I would pretend, taking the whip off among the trees, striking it on things, and groaning. If she wanted evidence I showed her marks made from berry juice. Her sight was dim. She was satisfied. After her death I put the whip in her grave, thinking she might want it elsewhere. But sometimes in the winter storms I imagined I heard it slashing inside the wind, doing her penance, or seeking for me and mine.

The owl had been gone thirty days and nights and a stray premature snow had come down. I was digging the last gourds from the hard ground. I looked up in the bloodless past-noon light to see a man, treading through the forest toward the lake.

Due to the twists of the path between the trees, I saw him oddly, first from the back.

He was tall, or looked to be, though not as tall as some. Yet how he moved and held his body, which was lean and graceful, made him seem the taller. Long black hair, thick as poured honey, hung over his shoulders, and it had a mellow color in its blackness too, when the sunlight altered. The sun came out as he turned along the track. And then I saw him sidelong. His face was not like any I had ever seen. Not among men, nor even among the old carved images of the gods. Yet his face did seem to have been carved, *fashioned* more than randomly produced from flesh and bone. A straight nose he had on him, and a high bone in the cheek, and a high noble forehead off which the dark hair ran. Then the path brought him round and he was full face. His brows were arching and black, his eyes deep-set and black also. He had a beautiful mouth, slim and couth. There were no such mouths among the men I had met by the lake. But he was unlike any of them anyway, and in one further curious manner. For I could see he was older yet young. By which I mean he might be some ten years older than I. Among the lake people, either they were young, or then suddenly they grew old. Their faces and their bodies became too spare or heavy, crumpling and crumbling as if a loose earthwork sagged and came down. There is no middle country for such men, nor women either. But this man, he was both older and young. And his face, his throat, even his body as he walked, even his hands, were fine. His face was full of

the knowledge of wisdom. His age was this too. For every
year he had lived, perhaps for every instant, he had learned.

Then he walked by the hut, and he glanced at me. The
slant of the sun lit a moment red in the dark of his eyes.

His look was playful. His clever beautiful mouth partly
smiled. He said to me nothing at all. But his eyes said, *Do you
not remember, then*?

And after that he was past and gone, his boots wounding
the thin white skin of the snow.

When I could nolonger see him for the trees, I went out
and stood looking down at the marks his boots had left, till
the sun slid behind a wide-winged cloud.

Generally I had little to do with the villagers in the social way.
That is I very seldom sought them, while they avoided me.
Now and then I overheard, or glimpsed one or other, or some
group of them at a slight distance, and then normally I would
turn aside where I could not be seen, even back into the hut,
if I was near enough. Part of me though now longed to go
down into both the villages, to look about and try to find if he,
the man I had watched on the path, had gone there. Yet such
an act had no point. Even if he had entered the villages, he
would never have stayed. What had he been? Some traveler . . . a strange traveler, however, who traveled not only on
foot, but apparently without any baggage. Nor had he seemed
to be armed in any way. I had noted neither a knife nor a stick
in his possession. His clothes had been ordinary, I thought,
some rough tunic and leggings, cloak, boots. Yet I was unsure,
really, what he had worn, and whether the garments were
sturdy or impoverished. I had only noticed—*him*.

The next evening I went out over the crackle of snow to
set a rabbit-trap up by the big white birch. Lightning struck
this tree when I was only an infant, I could remember the
terrible crack and flash, as if the sky had split. Rather than
destroy the tree, the lightning made it stronger. Now it towered on the hill above all the rest.

As I was kneeling there, a man spoke quietly behind me.

I nearly sprang from my body. I was well used to being
wary, and knew the usual sounds both of animals and people

if they approached. This one, whatever he—it—was, had made none.

What had he said? He said the words again. "Leave that. I've two here already."

Then I jumped up and round and saw it was the man I had seen the previous day.

There could be no mistaking.

I could not speak, had forgotten language.

But he held up before me a pair of large brown rabbits, both fresh-slaughtered, their necks loose. They had been killed, each of them, with a single clean blow.

"You'll like this better," he said, "I think."

I said, "I haven't any money to pay you." I barely knew though what I said.

And he said, "Did I ask money? We'll share the meat, you and I."

I thought I had gone mad and was imagining this, as sometimes I *did* imagine things, and did think myself mad. Was I frightened? Yes, quite an amount. But I did not shake from fear, although I shook. Turning again I bent and undid the trap and left it lying, and looking back saw he had walked down the slope toward my hut, so I must go after him.

At the door he waited. Less courtesy it seemed than some other, more savage thing.

I did not believe he was truly there. Once I went in at the door he would vanish. He was an illusion of the forest, or some elemental.

I should fetch an amulet, put it between him and me. Did I have any?

After a second I went into the hut and he walked in after me, and put the two rabbits down at once on the log that was my table.

Not knowing what to do, I took my knife and set to work, my hands trembling as all of me did. There was a spinning at my center. I did not know if I hated or liked it. He only stood, and watched me.

When I had botched up the job of getting off the fur, and jointing the carcasses, I put the iron pan on the fire, and threw in some herbs that I kept to dry by the hearth. He watched that too. But when I picked up both rabbits he said, quietly, as before, "Cook yours. I will eat mine raw."

Then I knew he was unhuman. It is unlawful to eat raw meat, the gods forbid it to men, even I knew that.

But I put the larger of the skinned rabbits back on the log, and dropped my own portion, if mine it was, in the pot.

I thought then I had better offer him a drink. I had only water, or the thin beer I brewed as my mother taught me.

So I offered, and asked what he would have.

Then he smiled at me.

His smile burned me like a flame. And his eyes, that all this while I had not quite met, black as the wood of the forest, did they burn too, and worse? "Look there."

On the log stood a tall gray jug. I had never seen it before. And there seemed to be blood in it. Why not, if he ate his meat raw?

Then he held out a shiny gray cup to me, and the blood too was in that. But I realized quite well there had been nothing in his hand a moment before—empty, his hand. And the cup was not gray but old metal, silver. And it was full of red wine, that the high classes and the priests drink only.

"Taste it," he said. I only stood there, and then I found the cup was in my hand, not his, though he had not stretched out to put it there, nor had I taken it. "Why," he said, "is your hair that shade?"

I heard myself answer from far off, as if I were really in the corner among the shadows. "When I was small, it grew out white." So it had, about a month after the lightning split the birch tree. As if the lightning had run also into my hair.

"Your hair shone on the shore," he said, "like the moon fell there. Your skin's as white. But your eyes are black."

I had never seen in a mirror to know the color of my eyes. I wondered if they had *not* been black before, but only altered to it since having been looked at by his.

And all this while he looked at me.

None ever had, except my dead mother now and then, when she poked at me or whipped me.

His eyes were like the black lake. But they would not let

you drown in them. They lured you in only to push you weightlessly away, only then to lure you back again.

He was an Enchanter. Of course by now I knew. A red glint of the departing sun had stayed caught under the black of his hair, and in the black water of his eyes.

And I could see myself reflected in his eyes after all, tiny and pale, like a water-bird that drifted on their surface.

We shared the wine, passing the cup back and forth, or rather the cup moved from me through the air to him, then back to me. I could taste the fire where his mouth had scorched the rim. The silver jug meanwhile had less and less wine in it, as we emptied the cup two or three times over. Then the jug was full to the brim again. Yet no one had poured from the jug, or refilled it. We said nothing else, and then the rabbit in the pot was savory and done, and I put it on the log in the wooden dish, and the dark bread to one side.

We sat, he on the other log, I on my heels on the floor.

He tore the uncooked rabbit in three and ate it without ceremony, but also without any uncouthness. He ate the eyes and tongue, and the bones too he ate, I heard them crunch between his teeth. Even the teeth of the rabbit his teeth crunched and he swallowed them, those teeth of the rabbit.

Perhaps I ate. I think so.

The wine was sweet and strong, I had never tasted wine before. Perhaps, I thought without much awareness, this was *not* wine anyway.

The shadows deepened in the hut, but the fire kept bright and warm without any attention. And then four moths came in and perched, one against each of the four walls. They were little double flying flames. He must have made them, or summoned them.

All his meal was gone. Not a trace. Instead a tawny, barred feather lay on the log. This feather did not amaze me.

"I'll tell you my name," he said. "Hrothgar. Say it back to me."

I said it back to him.

He did not ask my name, I had none, not really, just some scrap my mother and some of the villagers called me by. It had never been mine, and for myself I had never invented one.

"I will call you," he said, "Otila. It's a lucky name."

I should have asked him why he gave me a name, and a rabbit to eat, and wine. Why he sat here.

He said, "Well, now I'll be on my way."

I said nothing. On the walls the lights faded. The jug and the cup were gone. On the dish were only the bones of the cooked rabbit that perhaps I had eaten, and a crust of the bread. No feather lay on the log.

Outside something called through the darkness with a wild unholy bubbling note.

I had the impression of shadowy flight, and twice red amber fire, heartless, soulless: two eyes. Was I still reflected in them, still swimming on their surface like a water-bird? I seemed to feel myself for a moment carried up into the sky, and all the night opening around me like a limitless roof stabbed with stars.

When I woke the night was nearly done.

I lay by the table, with my head on my arm. It was cold and the fire was out.

I put four young winter cabbages and some of the gourds into a sack, and some of the thin beer in the leather skin. I walked down with them, which took perhaps an hour, and into First Village.

A horrible place. Seldom had I been there, but the muck of it had, apparently, never quite been rubbed off from my mind. It stank too, of men and their dirt, and ill-kept beasts. Gray, tusked swine rooted in the alleys that were presently floored with hard snow. Smoke rose from chimney holes and murked the pale sky.

People rambled about, seeming busy and important in that slack aimless way they have, that way I have never grasped—either its reason, or how to pretend I am the same and so pass as human.

The upper village, built on an earthen terrace and now paved white, had the gods-house, a long low wooden shack. I went by and tried the mortal houses with my wares. I had never bothered with the lower alleys. I thought he would not be down there.

Six days had passed since the night when we ate the rabbits, and he ate one and its teeth.

In all the nights I had heard the owl call only once.

Yet I knew he had not left the vicinity of the forest, still haunted it.

Of course, he might be anywhere. But then, why not here?

As to why I *sought* after him I had no idea.

When had I *ever* had one? It was only that seek him I did. He had told me his name.

At some of the doors where I rapped with my knuckles, they shouted me away. One, a rough-haired woman, came out, snatched up and threw a clod of hard snow at me. It glanced off my hip.

Then I turned a corner, and a man walked up and bought two of the cabbages and took a drink of the beer. He gave me a brown misshapen coin—not often had I beheld true money.

When the man was gone I put the coin in the pouch in my skirt, and looking up I saw an old humped man, unlike the other, crouching along the street. Deformed, with a great broken hill seeming to rest on his back, his gray hair straggled down like cord. Less gray this hair than silver. And looking up and out, from his face all bones and ridges and age-lines that were like knife-cuts, *his* eyes. It was him. It was the Enchanter.

Having sought him and found him, now I stood powerless and speechless on the snow. In that narrow crowded space between the walls of rotted houses, he moved up to pass me. He was bent so much his head reached only to my breast, but his eyes laughed at me, cruel black as the lake of drowning, where my image had swum. "Oh, so you stirred yourself to look for me, then?" he said.

But before I could answer, to agree or deny, round the shank of a wall he went. And going after, he was gone. As I had known he must be.

So I went away, back through the village, lugging the heavy sack and the skin with me, not seeking custom, getting none.

I had seen him, and been seen.

*   *   *

That night in the hovel I made my own magic.

Did I know what I did? Know? I *knew* nothing at all.

I threw torn bits of my hair on the fire and splashed my blood
on it from a shallow cut I made across my arm. I called his
name, on and on. I wept, too. I wept because I was lonely and
had nothing beautiful, even if I did not know I was alone, nor
did I understand what beauty was.

And I cursed him later, when the moon rose and not a
sound in the forest, not a shadow, not a feather.

In the end I lay on my back on the floor and put my hand
between my legs, as sometimes I had since childhood, somehow discovering that not all touches there must be painful,
obscene, deathly, and meaningless.

The fire came off the hearth, with my blood and hair and
tears in it, and burst in my body, and I screamed, and yet his
name still was in the screaming.

Then I fell asleep, and in my sleep dreamed the owl had
entered the room and stood on me, its claws planted on my
breasts like hard bone hands, and with a dead hare in its beak.

When I woke, stiff and sore at sunrise, there was a tiny
scratch on my left breast. But perhaps *I* had made it by accident.

The fire, though, had not gone out. It blazed. There was
wood in the middle of it burning. And on the log-table was
the hare, headless, bloodless, boned, and peeled of fur, all
ready for the pot.

"Where's the old cripple with the humped back?"

"Ah, he's to the out-farm." This, from some man.

It was his woman who demanded, suspicious and glaring,
"Why'd you ask it, white-face girl?"

"I have a pot needs mending," I replied.

For by then, here in Second Village, and three hours' walk
from the hovel, I had heard tell of the old fellow with gray
hair, who could heal the animals of sodden feet and the rash,
and also mend household items.

I had come all this way on this occasion without anything
to sell or barter.

"White *scut!*" spat the woman, as I went off.

The out-farm was a holding up a hill, with the skulls of foxes and even three wolves hung on cords, to clack in the wind and scare off others.

The poor sheep huddled by the bare trees, plucking at a bundle of dried grasses left there for them. Their coats were thick, but winter came, was arrived.

Was this the first I ever felt any pity? Even for myself I never had. Only variable hurts had I ever felt, and not known what to do with them.

He was with the sheep, too, the old cripple man that was Hrothgar the Enchanter's disguise. I saw what he did.

He must have told those in the house not to watch, frightened them with some sorcerous formula. The gods know what.

He was straddling the sheep, and for a moment I thought something else went on, as it does here and there. But no. Clamping them between his thighs with a strength and control few men, even when young, could call on, he made much of them, stroking and patting them, and singing words whose sounds did not *resemble* words. Each animal was let go from his clutch, glowing. Then they shone, in the wet white sun, like the palest gold—a metal then I had never seen.

I stood by the fence, and he paid me no attention. Nor did he shout I must go away.

In the end he was done, and all the sad sheep were shining and frisking about. *Then* he came crouching over to the fence posts.

"Why follow me?" he said.

"To see you." I was bold with exhaustion, and also amazement, and—gladness. I liked how he had made the sheep better.

"Well. I'm seen."

"Visit me," I said, "this night."

"So forward," he said. "Not tonight. I have things to steal tonight."

Now I was really astonished. Why need *he* steal?

"What?" I said. And stupidly, or maybe not stupidly, "I have things you can steal, too."

"Oh, you do. But think of this. Hrothgar steals also from himself."

Then—he did send me away.

I cannot describe how he did it. Did he ask or tell or command me to go? I found myself back among the trees, walking into Second Village.

I felt leaden as if the mud and snow and filth weighed me to the earth. Yet also, how curious it was, alight and clean.

In the iron tub I washed myself and my hair with water that was chill, for I could only take the edge from its cold with the heated panful from the hearth. A little stream ran behind the hovel, not quite frozen. I had carried off so much I had thought I would drain it dry. In my mother's time we had used this tub on only a few occasions every year, and then always she first, so I washed myself in water already shallow and thickened from her cleansing.

After the bath I did not want to put on the clothes I had worn. I found the other garment, the long shapeless, colorless dress of coarse wool that had been in our family, so my mother said, since my great-grandmother's time. It was for the use of any female who must go to the gods-house, to swear hand-lock pledge, or answer for some misdeed, or show a baby to one of the gods. It fit me well enough, but at first I thought I would take it off, for it itched. But then the wool seemed to settle.

I combed my hair by the crackling fire, drinking a little of the beer.

I said to the sparks as they flew up, sizzling at the wet drops that dashed from the comb, "If you won't come to me I shall curse you properly. I know how to do it." I did not know. There had been little cunning, or craft of any kind, in my family. Yet at this time I felt a sudden power on me. It was the power of desire, which I recognized but had no name for. Except, it had *his* name. "Hrothgar," I said to the fire. "Tonight you will come here. Or I shall break your wings and you'll die."

Only the madness in me made me say such things, to threaten an Enchanter of such might. Love drives out fear, they say. Or makes fear only the servant of love, and both fools.

But he did not come. Oh, of course he did not.

A light woke me.

I could not, waking up, think where it might be from. There was no moon, and clouds were all across the stars.

The fire was out. I had smothered it down to keep the wood for morning.

Usually by night in winter my bed was cold, but I was used to that. Now my bed was warm.

I turned and looked into the source of the light, which was his eyes, the whites of them so clear, and the dark lit within like two black lamps that hold a russet fire.

Did I have the sense to be afraid?

Yes.

But I put out my arms and my hands and took hold of him.

Under the cover of the old wool blanket and the older pelts, he was bare as I.

He laughed. Musical, his laugh. Never had I heard a laugh like music.

"It seems you expected me."

"I cast a spell to make you visit."

"So you did. But was it worth, your little spell, more than a shriek or a single tear?"

He was warm, hot as flame, and smooth as metal—yet not like that. The lightest hair ran over his breast—feathers—running to a gradual, denser fur along his belly, thick at his loins, thick as the rich hair on his head.

"How quick you go," he said, amused.

But I would not stop.

I cared nothing. Perhaps I did not reckon him real at all, but a dream, a phantom come to me in sleep, to give me what life never would.

Unlike the front of him, his back and backside were naked, and hard smooth nearly as marble, though then I did not know what marble was. Yet malleable, too, for muscles moved in his back and chest and all his body, fluent as I have felt in feral animals.

Then I felt the rod of his sex tap against my thigh. I could not help but touch it, clasp it. It was like a separate thing, large and strong, a beast itself that I had interested and that now quested, blindly yet sure, coming to find me out even as I tried to discover him, and he while *he* lay there on his side, and only looked at me, removed.

I had once or twice seen the things of men, if never wanting to, been shown them. They were ugly, wrong-shaped, foul and senseless. But this of his not like that, and itself coaxing and eager, and I wanted, having put my fingers on it, not to let it alone.

But then gently he slid my hand off him. And I thought I had angered him, and was also myself angered—as how had I ever been angry or dared to be?—but instead he roped me with his arms and drew me in.

I lay held fast against him as his kisses opened my mouth.

What is this pleasure? Pleasure then exists—there is joy in the world—

No it is not pleasure or joy. It is some state that has no name, as none of us have names, even when named. Even he does not have any name.

Nor is this any world I have known, and no one has known it. Or, if ever they have, not as *I* do.

This, is *mine*.

Mine, his long back, his hair, his skin, his taste, and the thrust of him that breaks me undone and spills my blood on the straw mattress under us. Mine, the sense of his wings that bear us upward. Mine the little cry of pain, and then the cry of delight, and now mine too the wings—the wings—and I alone am flying upward, straight through my body and his, and through the wreck of the roof, and out into the clouded darkness of the night.

Which is where next I find myself. In the night sky above the forests, flying to the slow drum of wing-beats, and truly they *are* mine, and truly all things are altered.

When I lived by the other shore, I was brought gifts. I had a velvet gown, dark blood red, and a necklace of dull gray-green stones that were, I learned, polished emeralds. I had silk shoes, too. And boots with fur for the winter. And a cloak of fur, and a mirror, not of iron but burnished silver, and in that mirror I lost myself, for it was no longer myself I saw there, by whatever name I went. For it seems I had thought of myself one way, and even *his* descriptions of me had only added themselves to my comprehension of self. But she in the mirror was a stranger. I remember, too, in the mirror her hair turned to darkness, and her red dress to black.

That night, after he took me and tore me and had me and possessed and ruined and remade me, I was changed. And soon I glimpsed the whole width of the black water of the lake, below.

Miles of it there are, whole days and nights of journey and time. It is a sort of sea, though tideless, but then no one had ever told me of sea-tides and I only heard those things mentioned in the place where I later lived, on the farther shore, and most of them from him. That is, the *other*. I do not mean Hrothgar. Hrothgar taught me nothing, thereby everything.

Below, on the black mirror of the water of the lake then, I see my white reflection, and high above I am, close to the misty moon, which has come out of cloud and sheens the sky, the earth, and me.

I see myself reflected there, far down on the lake, just as in the mirror of his black eyes.

A pale water-bird, flying.

For I fly.

I fly.

I *feel* the tug and pull of the muscles in my body, the white wings that lift and sink and lift again.

Power.

So *strong*.

And this—is myself.

Otila—so he called me. Then maybe that is the true name of what now I am as first I fly.

I know my shape, for once long before I have seen one.

Not an owl, a predator of amber and red and flame.

I am white as the snow, as my riven hair that the shock of the shock-struck birch turned ashen.

My long smooth throat stretches.

From sideways eyes, black as the lake, I see two sides of everything, and both sides make one for me, one thing, that finally, at *last*, I understand.

I am a swan.

A swan.

I am a swan.

2

Waking, I thought I had dreamed it all. And then I saw the reed-bed that stood out on the water. Everything was gray and rose in the sunrise-twilight. The dead and frozen reeds stuck up sharp as long knives, and rattled with the dawn wind.

And I sat on the shore, where trees came down to the water. But this was not the part of the lake I knew. And I did know that area of the shore quite well. It was where I came to catch fish, and where, too, now and then, reluctantly I had seen village men also fishing, or the woodcutters chopping down a tree.

But this though, here, was a secretive place. It had been curved in by an arm of the land, and hooded over by the low-hung trees in their weight of dead snow.

As the light grew more clear, a smudge of constant smoke far along the shore, revealed where must be one at least of the villages familiar to me.

I was miles away.

Having decided this, I stood up, shaking myself. I was human enough, nolonger an avian creature. What had happened then? I had told myself a story in which Hrothgar became my lover, I had reached the peak of pleasure ... then slept, or entered some other stranger state. During which, it seemed I had walked far around the rim of the lake, believing all the while I flew.

I stared out.

The water was silkily ruffling, pleating and unpleating. It was now not very dark, only reflecting the filmy pinkness of a lifting sky.

Not quite meaning to, perhaps, I pictured the swan I had been, as if I had witnessed her arrival here, rather than accomplished it, sailing in on the air, skimming the water with extended feet, settling in a surge on its cool, unstable constant, that held no coldness for any part of me, next swimming with deft swift little kicks, until reaching the shore —

I had stepped off on the land, and after a moment was a swan no more.

Yet — and now I noticed insanely for the very first — I was naked. I had left my mattress and walked here, and lain down and slept here, on the bare earth, bare and white as *it*.

Why had I not died? Should I die now, of exposure to the deep white cold, since finally I had *realized*?

I did not *feel* cold. The atmosphere, the ice under my soles, they were only cool, like the water.

I took a step and oh —

Again everything changed.

Between a pair of heartbeats I had become the other. Now I walked, still two-legged, but balanced on a different center, and at an altered angle. I blinked and my doubled vision drew together within some miraculous gem in the middle of my brain.

Like a thrown spear, light and sure, yet heavy and potent with the power of essential velocity, I ran and launched myself skyward.

How huge, that sky. I did not think of magical, holy spaces, or gods who might dwell there, up behind the layers of the light. I thought only of flying.

But even so, nothing was lost on me, the wisps of cloud dissolving to the west, the tiny flecks of smaller birds.

Below now, the water shone a silver mirror. Again I saw from shore to shore. Clusters of life were dotted here and there. Deer were feeding on bark, a savage pig was trotting between the stems of trees. Little ungainly boats unseamed the fringes of the water. Fish glinted, too, deep down, these seen by me in some way I cannot describe. I had no caution or doubt at flight, as I had had none in the darkness. I did not think or feel, or reason or *know* as a human does. Although some nebulous invisible cord must still have bound me to what I had been, and would be again.

I made my landing some quarter mile from the area of my mother's hovel, at the place I had gone formerly to fish.

Swooping low, alighting on the ripple-floor of the lake, I fished once more. I snapped up the shiny trophy and broke it clean of pain and horror in one faultless snap. Down it fell into my long dense body, under the firm pads of flesh and snow feathers. Bones too I ate. I drank a little of the lake.

Two men were out along the shore. In my human guise I would have known them, but now did not, they had no interest for me, were like rocks that moved about. To be avoided, discarded. Only after would I recall.

One pointed to me. They paused, anxious lest I take or disturb anything they might want. But they did not attempt to kill me. There was a law everywhere in these regions against the killing of such birds. Even I had known, only lords might hunt swans, pluck, eat them. The swan did not know, and cared nothing. Men were rocks.

I turned away, floating among the brown grasses decaying by the water. Dipping my head I saw my reflection, but it meant nothing wondrous or significant. It was the normal state of my life, to see myself, as flying was. I thrust my long neck deep in the shallows, and fished again for a water plant.

When I stepped this time ashore, I trampled my way up between the pines. And here it came to me I was a woman, and so I became one again. And then, though I felt no harm at all from the cold day, and no one else was about, I fled to the hut, got inside, and slamming the rickety door, let down the bar, and leaned there on the timbers. I wept. I had and have no grasp of why. Or, if now I do, it is redundant.

And soon anyway I made up the fire and put on some beer in the pan to warm. I had eaten and needed nothing else. Nor was I thirsty, and still not chilled. Yet I required the beer, as I did the clothes I slung on myself, and the comb I pulled through my hair.

*   *   *

It is impossible for me, sensibly and convincingly, to detail how it was for me to change my shape, either from woman to bird, or back again.

There was nothing tangibly physical in the transference. No muscle or sinew stretched or worked oddly, my breathing did not seem to become alien, nor the beat of my heart quicken. My hair—or feathers on me—did not stir. I experienced, after that second time, no transitional sense of occlusion or perspective. I was one being. Then another, I *melted* from one condition to the next. It seemed to happen only with a slight overview, something to do with my whereabouts or my consciousness when on land or water, or looking at such external or internal things. I was never, even so, to alter to a woman when on the wing high in the air. Nor half drown as a woman when adrift on the lake. Nor either did I ever change to my form of swan when inside a human habitation.

I felt no sorcerous impulse, and no coercion. It was not some spell or curse he had put on me. I believed initially, and long after again I believed, it was my own gift that somehow I had found. And even as I sat by my human fire in the hovel thinking of it, less frightened than puzzled, nearly sad, I did not really think we had joined in sexual congress. There was no trace of him left in the hut, and despite the burned mark of blood on the mattress, I guessed I had imagined him. *That* therefore had been the dream. To shape-shift was the reality, and all my own.

Here then began my life as a swan. Or, should I say, as a woman who might become a swan—at will, presumably, a swan who likewise might re-become a woman. Some will envy me, I know, some fear me and some hate. And many will not credit a word.

Hrothgar I did not see again for the thirty-three days of that long winter month.

Snow fell thick.

I became a swan as the mood or reverie took me. Which was quite often. One day I was humanly gathering blackened berries as a condiment from the shrubs up among the birches,

and heard ducks calling as they sheered over the water. I let
the berries fall and next moment found myself—my other
self—running, leaping from the path among the thinner trees,
springing upward and gliding free. The bluish tawny ivory of
my beak was striped, I think, with the congealed juice of the
berries. I had been chewing some. I did not return until the
next frozen dawn, and by then little animals, or ice, had consumed the shriveled fruit.

As a human too I continued impervious to the temperature.

My hair had thickened, and my skin seemed to be more
white. My hands did not chap or split in blains.

Sometimes I found one of my own blanched feathers lying
by the doorway of the hut. Once I found one in my own hair.

One morning too I saw, near the hut, the tracks of a solitary wolf. It had drawn close, then sped away. I never saw it,
but suspected it had seen me fly down, after which the rest
had alarmed it.

Did I rejoice in my talent?

Of course. My life had been till then walled in.

Sometimes, when a woman, I sat by the hearth and domes-
tically mended my garments or broke wood for the fire. I
thought I must use my genius for flight to take me to those
distant shores I had, by now, so often observed from the air.
But at this era I never, when a swan, was tempted to do that.
For, as a *swan*, I had slight concern with it. I preferred the
nearer verges of the lake, even if I ranged somewhat further
afield than ever I had as a girl. The shallows were perfect for
feeding, plants still to be reached with my long and supple
neck and selective beak. Even when ice formed like paving at
the margins, I did not swim so much out away from shore.
And sometimes, as a human, I took the ax and smashed the
ice, so that I, the swan, could sail off more easily and briefly.

Sunrise was pale yellow now, sunset dark red, and the sun
looked old.

Some had said the sun always slowly died in winter, returning as a fresh new orb between the midnight and dawn of
a single early day of spring.

Did all things alter their shape, being, and nature? Aside

from birth, old age, and death, of what else were mortals capable?

And did I miss the presence of the Enchanter who had so curiously enchanted me?

When a woman I missed him. I thought of him by night, if in the hut, and skillfully conjured for myself the pleasure I had now determined I never received from his body. Should I remember him I yearned after him, *burned* after him—but in the most inchoate way. I had other concerns. I had other employment.

When a bird I thought of nothing but what I did. *I*, the swan, was paramount.

Is it of interest that, as a woman, I always recollected my swan-life vividly—while as a swan, I more and more forgot my human form?

For after each excursion I examined what I had seen and done. Always it thrilled and excited me. The peculiar grieving I felt at first was all dispelled. And as it was only in human form that I could *humanly* relish my swan-times, I was nolonger isolate, or dully sullen during my mortal life.

The owl began to perch, high on the lightning-stricken birch tree.

I heard it. I heard him.

The cry now was particularly cruel and heartless, a deviant demonic cry that made the hearth fire crawl down under the wood.

I did not go to see save once. It had been full moon that night, and the owl a black shadow on the pallid tree, and its own shadow reeling as it raised now one fretted wing or the other, with a single sudden ignition of red eyes.

Was I ensnared?

Maybe. I was unsure.

I knew besides I could not keep the Enchanter out, should he choose to enter the hovel. He had come in through wall or barred door or too-narrow window in the past. It abruptly seemed to me, only now, that I had not dreamed our union. Or, if only a dream was all it was, then what called in the tree was only an owl.

As a swan, I had never flown where the owl was. Nor did I ever note the owl. Did I not then, at all, recall Hrothgar when I was a swan? I cannot say, even now. How curious, how bitter.

No more snow descended, but there was an early morning—I had just come into the hut—when the frost that formed was so fearsome it had turned the world white-black, with crusts of tin. Things died everywhere about, or were already dead, and the old dying sun dragged itself out of the east the color of stale bladder-water.

That was the hour he returned, Hrothgar.

I had just started the hearth to life. I put on the beer to heat, and saw him entering through the wall.

Through the wall, as I had suspected he could if he wished, he idled in to the enclosed room. And as he came in, he was changing, owl to man, that very second.

So I saw, for he showed this to me, what I too, no doubt, resembled and was, in that metamorphosis that seemed to me, once it had happened, only inevitable, almost rational.

The owl was nolonger quite a creature—but more like a mantle the Enchanter had put on, one that wore threadbare instant by instant, and frayed off from him. At first too it seemed the mantle of the owl was larger than a man, a giant, but as rapidly it vanished, it grew also less. *Its* body then rivered away through *his* body, leaving momentarily an impression of itself. So I saw a naked man with feathers on his skin the knotty wood-like bird legs branched down through his own, its claws turning to vapor against the bones and muscles in his thighs. The wings of the owl, its head, went last of all. Then he was, for a single heart-beat, a man *masked* as a bird, his black eyes looking through its golden ones, the wide wings ranging out behind his back. But after this, he was solely a man. And from his nakedness only a rusty down of its eclipsed feathers drifted to the floor.

This act took no more than it would be to count to seven or nine. Yet had seemed to last many minutes. Ever after when I thought or think of it, it will seem to last an hour or longer.

I did nothing. What could I do?

Except I gazed at him. I had not before seen him clad only

in his body, since in the other undream visit, when he deflowered me, we had lain in the dark. I had only *felt* of him.

Seeing him I desired him. And I knew we had been lovers. For the desire was greedy, practiced.

Where I knelt by the fire, his shadow fell.

I looked away from him, and put out one hand and touched the shadow, at the center of its loins, and watching only the shadow, saw the shadow weapon raise itself at once, engorged and ready. He had been quiescent before. Then I turned and glanced back at him in the flesh, and he had not roused, the blade of his sex lay sleeping.

"Well, Otila," he softly said to me, "if you can provoke a shadow by fingering it, don't you think you will be able to wake me as I am?"

He played with me, clearly.

"As you were," I said, "you were the owl."

Then for the moment of a moment, the mask of the owl glared down at me from behind his face, this time its golden eyes *inside* the black of his own.

And then—he was clothed. Fully dressed, like one of the richer travelers I had seen, if rarely, in leather and good wool and furs.

I knew I could never have made garments for myself out of the thin air, even though I might become a swan.

The beer was heated. I got up, and taking it to the log-table found two cups of earthenware standing ready to receive it.

When the beer poured it was hot wine, blond in color, and with a scent and taste of spice.

He drank, and so did I.

"You never thank me," he said, "for my gifts. Aren't they to your liking?"

I could not answer. It seemed then I must accept my shape-changing came only from him. I knew without he told me. Had always suspected, no doubt, and so hidden it from myself. Lacking him I should be nothing once more. What payment did he demand?

"I never thought them gifts," I said. "I thought you pleased yourself. If I am gifted, you make me your debtor."

"Why should I do that?"

"You pray to a god of sorrow and darkness."

He smiled. "I pray to nothing. I'd not waste my time on it."

"Why," I said, "are you here with me? Why have you *gifted* me with—this magic that—makes me—another creature—?"

"Oh," he said. "That little deed. Did I do *that*?"

And then there was the movement of his dark furs and hair, like a cloud, and I dropped the cup but it never reached the floor to shatter. It must have disappeared. He had hold of me, bent me round in a painless twining, so I let go even of the ground under me.

We were on the mattress, where I had not-dreamed we were before.

Now the sere light of winter day poured through the narrow windows, the broken roof, all over us.

How thoroughly he investigated me at this meeting. He *sampled* all the country of me. His tongue was like a wolf's, burning and harsh, then limpid between my legs. This was horrible, then a wonder. His sharp teeth nibbled my flesh and ran along my cheek, and bit away little snippets of my hair. He ate my hair, swallowed it. His face was full of thought as he did this—I saw it plainly in the light. He licked all my skin also, leaving behind a scent of fire and frost. When I slid my hands over him now, sometimes I felt the quills of feathers under *his* skin as perhaps he could, under mine. Several times he mounted me, and twice turned me and had me that way, from the back. Once he lifted me on to the smooth tower of his blade, and danced me there, I with my head thrown back, crying.

Light dripped on over the room, moving from one end of it to another.

I had no space to be afraid, barely even to be surprised. I knew that what we did was unholy. The pleasures of it were very great. But at the bursting climaxes of each action my body still did not change. It seemed I did not need to shapeshift here, having learned how during our first congress, and having done so independently since. Our confluence now was simply for itself.

In the end, the last light had dripped all away.

We had not spoken ever once our flesh began its dialog, and only I had made true sounds.

I lay motionless, sore and shining in my inner parts, my breasts scorched where he had suckled at them. My bones had flowed to melted tallow, and did not harden. I could not anymore think of a life where he did not lie here beside or beneath or upon me.

As darkness, without any warmth of a sunfall however drained, began to soak into the hovel, I spoke his name.

To my ears tonight it had the noise of the quills of feathers brushing against harsh stone.

But he had already left my bed. As the blacker shadow came in and in, he clothed himself again in that. From the table he picked up the remaining cup. It still smoked with heat, though poured six hours before. And he drank it dry, as he had drunk my body, and my thoughts.

I did not believe he could go away. Or if he did, he would return to me.

Meanwhile of course I knew he would leave me now forever.

Nor could I say anything, other than his name — *Hrothgar* ... *Hrothgar* ... feathers, feathers against stone, stone —

Exactly when he went out of the hut I was unsure. He remained in human form certainly, but out through a wall he must have passed.

It was another spell on me, as it had been that time when he dismissed and sent me from him in the other village.

Only many minutes after was I able to realize I might get up.

Standing in the doorway I glimpsed, in fading dreary dusk, something great and black that winged off across the trees, over the unseen water below.

As if I *had* asked, and been answered, I knew very well he had flown to the farther shores of the lake. I knew he was gone. Only the winter would stay with me. I wept by the fire and my falling firelit tears shone red as blood, glamorously bright as gold.

Even in rejection and lament, I knew I should follow him. The swan, I thought, knew that. To follow is a natural thing.

Seasons follow each other, and sun and moon, and beasts and birds. And mankind follows each some other also, through birth and life and love and death and silence. It is how we exist, moving always on, even into emptiness, one behind another. There is no choice.

It is how we exist. And how we perish.

3

The place where first I lived, on the lake's far, other side, was a box of broken stones. It was, I believe, the shrine to an ancient god. No one cared for it now. Nor did I. I made now and then a superstitious sign of respect at the old granite block which, probably, had been an altar. But I sensed no presence. There was nothing left in that space either to be entreated or feared.

No human beings came there ever. New gods replace old always, and are often jealous.

It provided me a roof and walls—despite their rents and lapses, stronger and more secure in fact than those of my mother's hovel.

Besides, anyway, I never now felt the cold injuriously. I had arrived on that bleak snow-shore at sunfall a swan, and moving up from the water—where I had found in the mud small shelled creatures that I ate—I became a woman, naked as before, and the icy dark fell on me like the softest of soft rains.

Even so, inside the shrine I discovered some pieces of sacking, and cobbled them together with yarn and a long hooked needle left in a stone cupboard by someone. This then was now my clothing. In the cupboard too was a broken lamp, but I made it burn from a store of sticky black oil left by. While the fire itself I struck with a shard on the altar. These things are not so difficult to accomplish, when one lives as I had.

My flight over-water to get there was of a different sort.

It began, as I said, in passionate desperation.

But, once I had changed, though the abstract motive to follow remained constant, it was charged only with a kind of complacence.

Which left me, as the white wind came driving from the winter's core, and struck my wings. Then I must battle as I never had, nor could I have done when human. Many times I was cast down as if by violent fists, to the midst of the lake, far from all land. Below me I could keenly sense the alien depths of black water. Not a single island broke the surface, only thin rifts of ice floated free from shores which, in the beginning, I could no longer make out on either or any side.

After a score of attempts I rose again and rejoined my war with the wind. Until thrust down again, and again. Night and day passed.

How long the fight lasted I neither knew nor cared. My strength lessened but did not fail. But I must fly low. At last I sighted the perimeter of the other land, through darkness, as the wind itself began to weaken. I alighted, ate, came ashore, and by then the wind was dead.

Yet maybe I had need, in the shrine, of my cobbled-together mortal comforts—shelter, garment, lamplight—in no physical way at all. But only for their normalcy.

I was there a long while.

My life was uneventful, apart from its one iridescent and enormous sorcerous ingredient.

As does the least of humanity, I lived, just as I had previously. Sometimes humanly I even caught and killed fish from the water, and cooked them on a makeshift hearth I constructed in the shrine. Sometimes I went up into the forest of larch and birch, and found branches and cones for the fire. As I always had.

I did not try to brew beer. I had here no means to do it. Perhaps I thought, when spring returned, I would gather wild salad among the trees, and later in the year berries and sloes . . .

People I *never* much thought of. Never needed.

People, to one such as I, were unreal, irrelevant, important only in their threats and unkindnesses. Another race, presumably greater and more valued than my own, whatever race mine was or had been. The Enchanter was not human, however, to me. I thought of *him*. I thought of him so much and with such desire, both of my heart and my sex, but also of such emotions as I possessed, that for me he grew almost present, nearly tangible, there in that box of jagged stones.

I believed always still I should find him, yet did not anymore seek him. Sometimes I dreamed of him, too. He was at his most actual then, there with me, mine.

But when I was a swan, then I was one of the winged race, the race of flying spirits. And even if Hrothgar, as an owl, was also too of this divine people, I did not think of him save as some detached, ascendant being, omnipresent, omnipotent, therefore forgettable.

Spring did come back. It has seemed to me it always does. Though one day I may be proven wrong.

It flooded among the trees. The darker were overtaken by the greener. Flowers opened on forest floors. The reeds sliced from their mummification, they tore wide their dead encasing, each with a green lance.

When a swan, I grazed on the tough bright grasses that now filled the meadows inland.

I saw no other of my avian kind. But one afternoon near sunset, I heard the crying of swans away along the shore. I had never heard this in my life, either life. Indeed, before I received my enchantment, I had seen a swan only once, and that far out along the lake.

What did hearing this crying wake in me? Not so much, though I knew it instantly, and was for a moment alerted, intrigued—partly drawn. As the noise of humanity would conversely have made me, human or swan, seek cover.

There dawned a day of liquid light when I paddled steadily over the lake, feeding in the shallows, but venturing out a little to deeper water after the friskier fish. I traveled quite some distance from the shrine and up the shore-line then, further than I had ever gone in the winter. So I came to a spot where willows, translucent yellow, trailed to the lake. Beyond a thick bank of reeds, glancing sidelong from the tiny snails I feasted on, I saw the nest.

As with their calling I had, I knew the nest at once. A swan's making.

None were there. And what I should have done, had I come on my other kind in that instant, I can never know.

But I slipped in nearer, dividing the reeds, food forgotten.

It had all the vacancy, the nest, of neglect, of abandonment. Why, having built it, had they gone away?

Then I was near enough that, dipping my long neck, I beheld the empty vessel was also filled. Six objects lay within it. In my human mode I might have taken them for smooth stones, even strange large sullied gems of some sort.

But I was a swan. I lifted myself up into the nest, and stood there, gazing on what remained. Two of the egglings were dead, their faint pulse of sentience ebbed away. Four, lying close together as if for company and consolation, retained their inaudible beating of thin life.

The nest was spiky with snapped reeds and twigs, on some of which unborn buds had expired, ciphers for the other unborn deaths that came after.

A swan, I did not ponder. And I cannot, even in this, present my feelings. I was only sureness and decision.

I placed myself gently, thoroughly, my lower body set down and enfolding, and warming, the egglings. How cool and *alive* they felt to me now. Gradually, as I sat there, I was conscious their pulses modulated, grew attuned to mine. Now all five of us sang together. It was *like* a song, like music. There is music. In the voices of birds and animals, of rain and the flicker of leaves, in laughter. Or, in the Enchanter's laughter there had been, that single earlier time.

The day went over, a golden wing, a scarlet one, a silver one, one black — as night.

They and I kept rhythm together. Waking and sleeping.

At some time during the dark, turning a little, carefully, I tipped the two dead eggs from the nest. They fell into the water and sank, leaden with their necrosis. Heartless, I. Indifferent, rather. I was a swan.

*   *   *

Yet—did I conserve and choose to nurture these beings from some mindless *human* urge? Had his possession of me made me aware that I might have borne a child—children? Was it, for me, in some deepest recess of my brain—far deeper than any dungeon deeps of the lake—that these creatures would stand for our non-existent progeny, a proof that he had taken me and I him? To me, at this later time, it seems it may be so. But I can never swear to it.

I did not leave them, save for a moment now and then, to dipper up for myself swift food from the lake margins. There was by then an abundance, and as the spring went on and the warmth began, insects swarmed flying even in among the reeds where I sat. I was able to feed myself with ease, snapping glittering jaws-full of them from the air. In the nights moths visited me to die, meat and nectar. I dined on them, while nightingales whirred from their throats of loose pearls.

My swanlets hatched one by one.

The first of the two males came out like a warrior, cracking the shell, barely assisted by me. Then the two females, more insistent and busy, more *thorough*. The second male tapped and tapped like a miniscule hammer on his cell-wall, till in the end I freed him with a light skimming blow of my beak.

They were speckled and gray as cobwebs, bemused and foolish. They tumbled about. I brought them plants to eat and bullied them into the water, which they were afraid of—until in, when they fell into a deep love with it. They worshipped the lake, staring down at their reflections, which evidently the water had created for them, to make them know themselves and become happy.

I sipped small flies from the air.

My children followed me along the line of the shore.

Summer bloomed.

I had not been human by then for more than three months.

Did I recall my humanness? Or him?

I recalled . . . something. Something. What? I do not know.

But *they* were bigger now, long-necked already, their dusty, spotted sheaths under-patched by the promise of pure white.

How I loved them, but it was love by another name and nature.

The first male was certain and strong. The two females were by turns serious or playful. The last of them, the second male, younger than the others by half a day, was placid, and more slow. If he had been a mortal son, I now believe, I would have thought him due to enter some temple of a mild god, for he was quiet, and clove to me more than did the rest.

I taught them by example, as a parent always does. They learned and began to tend very much, and ably, for themselves.

I remember an evening, when I was solitary, and feeding in the long crimson of the afterglow, and stars burned through the sky. I saw my children meandering some way off, a chain of starry whiteness. They were suddenly fledged, all but the finest last residue of their feathery down. They were nearly grown, nolonger mine. I never minded that. But in those moments the last one came back to me over the evening water, calling very softly. He swam about me, butted me in the side. He was now almost my own size, and must grow to be a fraction bigger. He rubbed his long head under mine. The velvety, scratchy perfection of the touch remains curiously with me as a human woman. It was a caress, I think, I know, although at the time I did not notice it as such, then it was only a greeting, an avowal. He would, I do suppose, have become my lover, since I had no mate. They pair for life, so I have been told, swans. Then the moon rose, also swan-white. A swarm of spangled dragonflies cascaded by. We raised our beaks, he and I, and supped, while the final fire smoked out in the lake.

And now a man, this other *he*, enters my world. This one is very different from Hrothgar—who anyway I cannot state was mortal. His name is Signian, which at first I could not pronounce. But then, during that renewal of my human life, I found great awkwardness with speech for a while, and even with the simple acts of walking, and standing, becoming seated, or lying down. I had been only a swan by that hour for almost five months.

*   *   *

They approached the shore with a stealthy and studied tenseness. They were very loud, thundering through the trees and shrubs, storms of leafage and small branches bursting about them, and flies swirling up, and little birds in a clatter of frenzied wings.

Then they stood along the border of the water, all facing out toward the wideness of the lake.

Human—they were human things. I did not recollect what they were, yet I shied from them, and so my children too flinched back. Unrecognizable but steeped in some awfulness: they stank, they were too colorful in their green and brown clothes meant to conceal them, and raucous in their cunning stealth.

What I did now my children would copy. I stood upright and raced along the lake, flaring my wings, propelling myself skyward in a collision of breaking water and undone light.

Then they did as I had, my two sons, my two daughters.

White as secret truth, we seared from lake to sky, our fire of wings spread like sails, our necks stretched. As we rose and fled we were already forgetting the vile things on the shore.

It was a summer noon. So sheer and shining, faintly tinted with red. The season was ending, the time of falling leaves drew near.

I heard then the music of humanity. Like sick harps. A twisting strummed note, over and over. A twang.

In the air all about me, more little birds. How sharp and narrow they were. So slender, their beaks made of flint, and feathered only at the tail—*wingless*—

He made no sound. My son. My lover who was to be.

The arrow from the man's intelligent bow had pierced his sun-white throat.

He fell.

I saw him fall. White leaf out of season.

Ah, then I was a swan nolonger even in midair, or my mind nolonger was a swan, nor my heart.

I veered about.

Past me, reckless and unreckoning, my other three airborne children rushed, rising on into the light, leaving us behind, celestially gone.

But *he* sank downward, fast as a stone.

There. I saw him meet the land, directly where the human things stood. I saw him smash, shattered, and untrue. A lie. His feathers scattered, like fresh snow.

No. I was not a swan anymore. Though still I kept the shape of one. For I too dropped toward the men, oblivious of their twanging kill-harps.

There is this, of course, had I been a woman exactly then, never would I have dared—surely I should have run away. Nevertheless as my feet hit and scalded and broke the reeds and water, already my physical alteration was erupting from me. A swan, I had reached the shore. Next instant I was a woman, naked and white, her hair flying, her arms raised even then like wings, her neck arched, racing toward the hunters and their bows, murderously hissing her rage and grief—

And they darted away. Some of them were shouting, one screaming. They ran, for they had seen a demon, a bird translated abruptly into woman's form.

Only one man stayed. Rooted to the spot either with terror or surprise, I will never know, nor will I ever care.

For when I reached him, and brought forward my beating wings to shatter in turn his bones, my neck and beak to tear him into bits, a weighty darkness came from him, and covered me up. Was this too sorcery? No, only his long cloak, that he had swept off and over me.

Could it be that, even at such a moment, he found my public nudity unsuitable? The gods he and his revered were strict and disapproving. Perhaps that then, but mostly I believe now he was afraid, and meant to distract and net me, like the flying thing I had been only a breath before. He credited, too, all that he had seen. Swan to woman. Where his huntsmen would come to say they had been mistaken, or seen nothing odd, this one would always grasp the fact of my transformation. He liked such ideas. In childhood, he had been told stories of them.

When the cloak smothered me I was lost. I rolled on the earth in its folds—it stank of his kind—retching and shrieking, trying to rip myself free with teeth and nails, all that was left to me as armament.

At last my consciousness went out.

They came and picked me up, for he had called his followers back by then. They picked up the body of my dead son also. But I was spared seeing this, spared knowing quite then that he was taken next to the kitchen of the great royal house, slung down, stripped of his plumage, and cooked for their table. It was surely these beasts, too, who had slain the birth-parents of my other children. Being of the high human class, it was allowed them even by the gods, particularly those pale, prim gods they kneeled to, that they shoot with arrows, pluck, roast, and devour swans.

For a while I lay like the dead, in a little building devoted to the female god of their pantheon. I was tended there by the veiled faceless women who served this deity.

No doubt they expected violence of me when I revived, for I had been bound to the hard couch. But I was no longer passionate or volatile. I had been returned into my former self, cautious and nervous, cringing and placatory. Though I had some trouble in speaking the human tongue for a while, I quickly came to understand it again. This, despite the differing accent and mannerisms of the priestesses, and presently the other humans who appeared. I did therefore exactly as I was bid.

Each of the priestess-women recalled to me my mother. They were ignorant, sly and spiteful, authoritarian—and cringing, too, as I was once more. And they would regularly beat themselves for penances. Sooner almost than all else, once I had woken, been bathed and clad, they took me to gaze on their goddess. She was an upright, slender, shapeless stone, stood on an altar, and veiled over as they were, but for a fine golden crown set where her head must be. The women were the ones who boastfully educated me in the rich substance of gold. The Prince's mother, they said, had donated the crown to their goddess-house.

As I was so obedient and docile, and even acted out praying, once they advised it was best I should pray, they seemed better pleased with me. They asked my name. And when I managed to tell them it, that is the name Hrothgar gave me, the only one I could now recall, they were both pleased *and* sullen. Apparently they thought the name meant I was, notwithstanding other evidence, of high birth, perhaps even royal myself, though foreign. This was Hrothgar's joke, of course. To give me such a name. Or had he foreseen I should require it later? Again, I do not know, nor shall I, now. I think it does not count.

The leaves were dropping in the woods, and on the yard where I was put out to sit on sunny days, and sew long shapeless garments of the order.

Here too he visited me after some nineteen days.

Signian. I had been told his name as well by then. *Prince Signian.* Son of a dead lord and the lord's still-living wife, the Princess Orjana.

When he came into the yard, the priestesses fluttered.

He was thought very handsome. So it was continually announced.

He had long yellow hair, wide shoulders, and a strong stocky frame. His eyes were narrow and light-colored in his broad, sun-browned face.

Perhaps he was handsome. To me he was ugly. He reeked of his sweat and eating, of kennels and closed rooms. Of murder. It had been his shot that pierced my son and smashed him on the earth. And he had eaten of him too.

Now he sat and looked at me, deep in my black eyes, black enough to resist him, as the lake mirrors, but conceals what lies beneath its surface.

The priestesses had heard the tale of my shape-shift. I could discern, despite their faultless belief in their goddess, they did not believe *this*. The young men had been hunting, when they drank deeply. The shadows had deceived them then, some trick of midday summer light. The priestesses would not quite say this, but they knew it to be so. And they only liked him more, their darling Prince, for his little fallibility. That he had faith in magic meant too he kept his faith in the miracles of the gods. Which could only be virtuous and benign in so noble a master.

He asked me if they were kind to me in the goddess-house.

Naturally I said they were.

He asked me if I yet remembered where I had come from,

anything of my past—for already the women had asked that, and I had said I had no memory at all before I woke here. To him I gave the same falsehood over.

Then he put his hand out, and stroked and fingered my hair, that my first lover had compared to the moon.

After this Prince Signian left me.

But the next day I was taken, under guard, to another house, one which belonged to him and was very different.

As the winter came back, I was growing used to the new phase of my life.

I hated it, it goes without saying. I was in despair.

This may seem very peculiar. I had never had much, and lacked all comforts save the most basic, and those wrested by me from a harsh environment. But I would gladly have taken my old life on, more than gladly if I might have gone back into its last stages, when I had been a bird, and had my children. Had my son, my lover.

Now, in the grand lodge just inside the wall of the Prince's town, I was given every material thing that might be wanted or wished. Fires burned hot for me, lit and maintained by servants. I had a wooden bed with linen pillows, and pelts of bears and wolves. I had a blue gown, and later another the red of blood. I could wash and bathe myself in warm scented water whenever I chose. There was food, meat and white bread, and wine to drink. After the first thirty days, he gave me a little silver ring to wear on my thumb. He said I should study it, and think how the silver circlet of my quim ringed round his manhood. To begin, I only wore it when he came to see me. Then he grew petulant, and after this I wore it always.

I was a prisoner. I do not exaggerate. I would not take on my other form, for I could not fly the house. And why was this? Something so paltry. I was never let out, always in some kind guarded, indeed watched, women to walk behind me, men to undo doors. Only into a tiny garden might I go, and that always accompanied, among the clipped bushes soon salted with snow. To get beyond the outer doors was not allowed. He had told me straightly. I was too precious, he said, too necessary to him to be risked. I had no memory, was frail.

In the spring perhaps, he said. Then he might take me up into the town to see its stupendous sights of lofty buildings and gloomy byways. Even there I should, I knew, be trapped.

Yet, as a swan, I could escape instantly—Ah no. The answer to the riddle has a terrible simplicity. A swan must run and launch itself into the air, its body large and wings so big. Unlike the smaller birds it cannot spring straight up, even from the ledges of the wider windows. Even in the little garden, where there was no space to run at all. I had no room anywhere to begin my flight. It had been the same in the goddess-house.

I dreamed of flight, that was the sum of it. In dreams the roof blew off and the inside walls collapsed. Then I evaded my jailors, dashed through the leveled chambers without impediment, leaped and spread my wings—and was gone.

He had a story he told me, that I had been under a spell, locked into the form of a bird by an evil Enchanter. But his love—that is, Signian's love for me—had broken the sorcery.

I do not say he loved me.

I know he lusted for me, or rather perhaps for what he had seen I was. He often remarked on the whiteness of my skin, my uncanny hair.

He did not take me until I had been examined intimately by an old woman, brought in by one of the priestesses. I loathed but was not unprepared for her disgusting investigations. I had had my mother to put up with in the past, after all.

But I knew the examiner would soon find I was not a virgin, and would this put off the Prince? For of course I knew also *why* I was being examined.

No one, however, said anything to me of my state, until Signian appeared that evening.

He gravely gazed at me then, as we sat before the great dinner that had been laid for him and, I suppose, for me—I barely touched it—amid the blazing forest of candles.

"I've been informed, Otila, of your misfortune. I shall not be the first with you."

Should I seem startled, shocked? Contrite? What use? I had anyway no heart for the game.

I said, "That is true."

"*Sir*," he said softly, kindly. "You must always call me that."

"Very well."

He sighed and ate more of the greasy meat, chewing and frowning with thought. At least, the dish was not of roasted swan.

"Otila, I recall your memory has failed you, yet do you have any notion how this came about, that you lost your maidenhead?"

Modestly I kept my eyes on the table's red shawl, trimmed with beads. "Sir, it is my one dim memory."

"You were forced?" he asked, hopefully it seemed—but whether from stricture or prurience who could say.

"I was wedded."

Where this lie had found its origin I stay unsure. It entered my brain, slipped out upon my tongue.

"Wedded?" He had laid down the joint. He must be enraged or perturbed, which was it? I had already seen he had only a limited number of expressions, and one might often have to serve the purpose of two or three moods.

"Yes. My father gave me to a man. The gods witnessed our union. We were together a little while—I forget how long . . . and then—then too, I forget."

"*Sir*," he instructed, absently now. He thought once more. He said, "Your husband—was it *he*, do you think, who aborted you from being one of the gods' creatures to a spiritless bird?"

"I can't say, sir."

"Yet you were wedded. And you recall no other detail—even his looks—his name?"

I shook my head.

He banged the table with his fist. On their bronze spikes, shaped like the branches of thin trees, the candles trembled warningly.

I said, "Sometimes—I seem to think—he was tall, and dark-haired . . ."

What else, of course, could I summon. The Prince resettled himself.

"I must speak to the priests. Your previous union must be

properly dissolved. It's unlawful I bed another man's wife. Unless I have killed him in battle."

Maybe I had trusted I could evade his carnality if I made out I was that, a wife. Really I think I had known he could convince himself, always, of some acceptable path whereby he could gratify his needs.

In any case, after he had eaten he drew me to the bed in the corner, pulled my dress both down and up, wadded my flesh and bit at my breast, before cramming his piece inside me. He was a fair size, and would have hurt me if I had not been undone. He demanded little of me but compliance, though now and then instructed, as he had instructed me to call him *Sir*, to tickle or pinch him here or there. His wants were minimal. Yet he rode some while, a slow and lumbering journey during which he grunted, and at the climax of which he gave a tiny squeal.

He had me only twice, and was quicker the second time, if less vocal.

My distaste was really beyond words, even thought.

I can compare it only to the unpleasantness of certain bodily reactions, a short flux of the bowels, or vomiting. It was vile, but unimportant. Meaningless in the scheme of my severed life.

After that congress a servant brought me, the following day, the silver mirror, wrapped in silk.

This in some ways was almost worse than his utilizing me. To gape for the first at my own clear image, and know her for a stranger—more a rape even than Signian's. He had not touched, I thought, my soul.

Oh, I was a swan, a swan. I had looked at my reflection then and known it for my own. A swan.

Beyond the lodge, the town climbed ungainly up the hill to a terraced palace. From the highest window of my prison I could see this grandiose and insignificant dwelling, his home, where he lived with his mother, the Princess. The palace was constructed of hefty stones, and banners tipped with metal flailed about its roofs. The town itself was morose and dirty. The sort of pigs that wandered the village streets, ambled here also, through filthy alleys and along the wider lanes— that were less than the width of the lodge's main chamber, and frequently blocked by refuse.

Outside the walls of this extended jail of a town, the forest had been cut away, for reasons of defense.

Further down the trees began again, around a broader road, up which wagons and carts, and even boats mounted on wheels, sometimes toiled, and men and women trudged.

Last of all, about a mile off, I might see the lake.

Long hours I spent at the window, staring out. My mind spread its wings and spurred me from this alien body I did not recognize, and fanned away, away.

I never thought of the Enchanter Hrothgar, at the window when I watched the lake. Never once, I am prepared to vow before any god, even the unkind measly gods of Signian's town.

Only in my room, when Signian was gone, after I had washed his slime and reek away from me, only then did I think of Hrothgar. And I cursed him. I wished him in agony and dead, or in some molten pale hell, to which the worst of the wicked are consigned.

But I dreamed of him most awfully after Signian's visits. As if that thrusting bulb of meat had stirred me up to lasciviousness in turn for my other, occult lover.

I never dreamed of my dead son. Never fantasized as to what *our* love-making might have been, the rasp of feathers, flare of wings, a land-flight. As a woman, I could not picture— let alone experience—what that could be, only that it must and would have happened, and that then, from him, my lover the swan, my own true progeny would have been born, laid like ghostly opals in our nest, brought by us to life.

Spirits of the air.

The winter scraped and sharpened its scythes on the four winds, and mowed down the year. In the town, the palace, even in my prison, we must celebrate, now the longest month of the cold season was done.

Seven little house statues had been brought out of Signian's people's gods, six of them shapelessly male, and one a version of the shapeless veiled goddess I had been shown in the goddess-house.

They were lined up on the great hearth-lintel, given crowns of gilded straw, and candles lit to them and ribbons hung over them—as if for infants who must be kept amused. Boughs of evergreen, lugged in from the despised wood, were raised along the beams, with painted wooden bees on strings, to ensure plenty.

I was sent the red gown. And when Signian arrived, he delivered to me, in person, in a long box of carved wood, the necklace of polished emeralds.

He often harangued me now with a history of his ancestors, all of which I forgot instantly. He spoke of travels, too, not his own, I believe, and so had taught me something of items and materials, jewels and sea-tides, for these things lingered in my mind—they were not human, therefore perhaps retainable. Now, he told me this:

"These emeralds are a minor treasure of my house. My father gave this necklet to his mistress once. But she died, in childbed—only a daughter. My mother, the Princess, thinks it seemly now I award it to you, even though you've borne me no children yet, and the old wisewoman—" He meant the old woman, who now examined me always once a month. "—says you are still not in that condition."

What could I say to this curious speech? I thanked him, of course. Ill-omened jewels, formerly dragged from the coffer of one dead. And he wished me fecund? I knew in the heart of my womb that it was my shape-shift that would deny always any human child, wanted or not. Just as I had come to be sure I could bear the children of swans. After he had laid me and finished, and gone away, I considered Signian's second speech to me that night. I was to be presented to the Princess Orjana. She had said she must judge me fit for my apparently enduring role as her son's plaything. So I was to go up to the palace. To the stone heap on the hill.

4

Complex preparation preceded my entry to the palace. I was
soaked in a bath of honey and curd, laved in scent. I fasted for
a day, drank only water. My hair was washed and dressed in
six long plaits. I was told I must call the Princess *Royalness*.
They clothed me in the red garment. I was not permitted to
walk, as I had not been permitted when brought to the lodge.
I traveled in another closed cage, this on wheels, drawn by
two small horses thick with hair, in the manes of which bits of
gold were wound, just as bits of bronze and silver had been
wound in my plaits.

"I have been hearing tales of you," she said, the moment she
was seated, and the others had withdrawn to the ends of the
long, chill room. One there played a stringed instrument, perhaps further to obscure our words. The Princess motioned I
might sit on a stool. I did so. "My son supposes you were enchanted under some spell, which his care of you has broken.
Can this be true?"

"I don't know, Royalness."

"No. They say too you recall nothing of your past—only
some hint you were wedded, or think you were. Or is that
merely a little fib, to hide an immorality?"

I said nothing. I gazed only at her hands, which lay together in her lap like two discarded yellowish gloves. They
had mentioned, to look too often in her eyes would be an
impertinence.

She also was an old woman, but old in a manner I had
never, until now, ever seen. Hers was a *preserved* age. Her
parchment skin and skull-like face had been rubbed with unguents, and lightened with powder. The thin wither of her lips
was touched with soft rose. Her hair, gray where mine was
white, had been burnished to a shine and intricately dressed,
and she wore a little circlet of gold in it, reminding me of their
ghastly faceless goddess.

"Well," she said, "my son is fond of you, and you please

him. For now therefore it seems best you live here with us, in the high house. One day Signian must marry. He will choose two wives. Then it will be necessary for you to go away, perhaps even from the town. But don't be downcast. Though your heart will break, you will be respected among our people for your service, and will receive, in addition, a small amount of money, to keep you till your death. Any offspring you may produce will likewise be maintained. He may gain a good position either in the Prince's guard, or the god-houses, wherever it is judged most suitable. A daughter can gain, if diligent and couth, a station among the lower ladies here, a nurse to the children or somesuch. You see. We are fair enough." Still I said nothing. What must I say? Something, apparently: "I trust you're grateful," she suggested, "for my care of you?"

"Thank you, Royalness."

She refolded her thin, flaccid hands.

"Meanwhile, I should like you to tell me how you think it is my son, usually so sturdy in his commonsense, credits he witnessed your change from a white swan into a woman?"

Jolted, I stared after all into her deadly face. Her eyes were narrow and pale like his. But—unlike his—full of a dire, nearly sub-human intelligence.

"Royalness—how can I know? I remember nothing of it—"

"Yet you remember a wedding to another man. The priests here will dismiss any possible prior union this very evening. Do you accept such a thing?"

"Yes, Royalness."

"Of course. My son must be preferable. You are not quite an imbecile, I think. But now I shall tell *you* something of my own." She leaned forward slightly. Was she so eager? I felt I would recoil, but knew I must instead keep motionless, and now was expected to meet her eyes. "My son was told, when a child, stories by his nurse, legends and ancient tales. In you he believes he's glimpsed something especial. But naturally you are nothing of the kind, only a young woman with strange coloring, and a mysterious, shall I say, past. Be thankful, Otila, if such is your name, at our sophistication. But let me warn you, too. *I* have heard such myths of transference and shape-shift, when a girl. I do remember one particular old yarn . . . A maid that a prince fancied, who crept every night out of his bed to a burial-mound, and plucked the plants there, and wove them into a dress which, if putting it on, made her become a wild swan. But they discovered her and knew her for a witch, and burned her to death, so not the slightest morsel of her, flesh, hair, nor bone, remained. Do not, Otila, however flighty or forgetful your mind, lead me to imagine *you* are a witch."

I sat, caught in the trancing, lizard-like glare of her eyes.

It transpired I need say nothing now.

"One further matter," the Princess Orjana added, sitting back. "You will have your hair darkened. And your skin, a little. You are too unusual. Oh, he prefers you pale, but my son always heeds my advice. Certainly *you* will do so."

She sent two of her women. They stained my hair with a stenchful paste which stung my head, and turned my tresses, as the women called them, black.

It was powder I must use on my skin.

They powdered my face and neck, my hands, to show me how I must go on. Now I had a tawny skin.

My mouth they tinted with a red salve, not rose but carmine.

When he came later, and pushed me over on the bed, he decided aloud that I stayed pale below, both flesh and hair. He seemed to like this discrepancy. He took me twice, as only the first time had he, and made louder noises. He told me after I would not mind this changing a little, to delight him and to avoid undue comment in the palace. He said I must own, his mother was wise. An outstanding woman. He hoped one day he might find a wife to help him who was half so clever, but he doubted it. And then he commented that he liked me very well for being only simple, a creature of the senses. But then, I was really a swan, was I not? Only he, like a god—*that* he did not quite say—had converted me back into a human thing.

*   *   *

There, in the lodge, I had neither physical space nor mental space to race and spring and shape-shift and be free. I could not even cry out and be left in peace. Someone slept by my door, a woman. Servant, jailor—

But the next day following the interview with the Princess, I was carted off again to the palace, and put into a pair of chambers inside the round flank of a tower.

It was a fortress, the palace. It was thought I needed, here, fewer guardians. The palace women who were meant to serve or contain me, besides, were always slipping away about their own business. The single guard in the place beyond the outer door, liked to drink deep. He often slept. Yet he had the knack too of fully waking always at those times when the Prince arrived.

Outside the window of the room in which my bed was set, I could see only sky, and a long area where a roof extended. It was long enough, perhaps, if I could only step out on it, I might race and transform and fly. The window, however, was a little too thin for me to pass through it, either as woman or bird.

I began to starve myself.

When one of my supposed attendants remarked that I left my food untouched, and out of date the old woman examiner came to poke my openings for signs of pregnancy, I next burned each of my meals on the fire when I was briefly alone, leaving my plate empty enough, as if I had eaten my fill.

But also, alone, I did what I had done before. I tore off pieces of my hair—now black, but with roots like ice, and flung them too on the flames. I used the blunt table knife to release drops of my blood. I called to *him*, to the other he—to Hrothgar, the Enchanter.

I lay on my back, and stroked my inmost part, but found now it was like a fine instrument dulled. It could yet be musical, but nolonger fully answer.

Even so.

I had summoned him back to me before.

I, even *I*, who counted for nothing, I had brought him into view like my shadow.

He would not know me, I thought, if he beheld me now,

black-haired and swarthy, in my blood-red dress that the silver mirror showed much darker.

I do not know why I had not properly called to him before. Perhaps only I had been sure he would never hear me, or if he did he would refuse me. As if I had not, till now, suffered enough to give my outcry credentials. As if my soul must shrivel and my heart bleed, before any might notice my plight.

Each day, alone, I tried to squeeze out through the narrow window. It was almost possible, that was the worst of it. If it had been less so, doubtless I would not have tried so desperately, so repeatedly.

But I had always been slight, and starving only made me weak, very little thinner.

One night I dreamed the walls melted away from the window-space and enlarged it. I dreamed an owl flew over the sky beyond, which was slate-blue with dusk of dawn.

Waking with actual dawn, I smelled the spring, sheer on the dark stone breath of the palace.

That morning I was restless. Signian had gone off again to hunt, as he did, and might be away several days and nights between. I went out of my rooms and walked about the byways of the palace, those which were allowed to me, the two women padding after me like sulky wolves, who did not want the prey they tracked.

People whispered as they passed me in the alley-enclosures of passageways. They had always done this, but now their mutterings were pronounced more clearly—I was meant to hear, it seemed. I was the Prince's whore. A foreign woman. I had been a wife, but the priests of the seven pallid gods had absolved me of that, so I could lie with their matchless Prince in lesser sin. What more could I crave than such happiness? Though some of them reckoned I would be damned despite the priests' efforts, punished after death. Signian, of course, was blameless. I had seduced him. Some said, I was a sorceress . . .

When the dark filled my window that evening, I heard an owl hooting far off in the forest, more than a mile away.

I visualized *his* eyes, looking at me, black then red-gold, through my fire.

By now I thought I barely remembered his face. Yet it at last occurred to me my falsehood of a wedding, to a dark-haired man, perhaps paraphrased his sexual acts with me and mine with him, which were as unlike the procedures of the Prince as *I* now was to my former self. I pictured Hrothgar's advent here, disguised as an old, hump-backed man, and how I would tell Signian that see—here was my husband—I rec-ollected him now I looked at him—an evil sorcerer—Oh kill him, Sir, destroy him! Save me from his clutches—

In my sickly fasting sleep, unheralded deep pleasure erupted inside my body. I woke dazed, and tried again to force myself through the narrow window. But could not, and now was certain that for every wisp of flesh my fast had shaved from me, a further chunk of stone had added itself to the embrasure. My sulky wolf-women found me lying there. I was ill for many days, during which the foul old woman exam-ined my blood on the linen sheet. She told me I had miscar-ried the Prince's seed and was a worthless dunce, but she would not tell him if I would give her a present. So then I got up, staggering and mad, and picking up the silver mirror I flung it at her head. It knocked her over, shrieking, and the wolves ran in and I laughed as they and the guard carried the hag out. I kept saying she must have the mirror, it was silver, and I wanted her to have it as a gift for her kindness to me. I did not know if she had lied, thought she had. I do not know either if she recovered from my present. None spoke of it. She never came in to me again.

After the event anyway all is blind, dumb, deaf, and noth-ing once more, for a while.

Hrothgar the Enchanter appeared at the palace in the short-est spring month of eighteen days.

There was a noise I heard, ringing round and round the shell of the house.

From my clamped rooms I could see nothing, only roof and sky.

In the corridors outside there seemed to be unusual activ-ity, and then this lessened. One of the wolves went to ask the

sentry, at the outer door of the apartment, if he knew what
went on. When he did not, sat there with his pot of wine, she
and the other stole off and left me.

I had no interest in the sounds in that house.

But then, I had not seen the company come up the road
from the shore. Some lord rode foremost on a jet-black war
horse, and behind him twenty grim faced men, some mounted
and some pacing in step. All of these wore dark plates of mail
and carried honed weapons, but the lord himself wore heavy
silk, and a cloak of the white and black furs of mustelids. A
sword was at his side even so, sheathed in velvet, leather and
gold.

His hair was black and chased, as his sword was, with fine
strands of aging silver.

Signian had come back from his hunt by then. He waited
in the larger hall to meet with this unlooked-for caller.

Who entered, and stood, lean and silent and tall, of a
daunting authority almost appalling in its unspoken, latent
power. He must be some mighty lord indeed, this man, or
war-leader, doubtless with hordes to follow him. Where then
were the rest of them? What did he want of the peaceful and
pious town?

"You have a woman here," the stranger said, in a flat and
unimpassioned voice. "She has white hair and dark eyes."

Signian seemed at a loss. The filled hall fidgeted and murmured.

The stranger said, ungiving as the bone mask of the moon,
"She is my wife."

I was told these things. They were described to me in some
detail, when Signian slammed unannounced into my cell. It
was shortly evident he blamed me. I had put on him some
allure so he called it, not daring quite to say I had enspelled
him, for strong men had now come to claim me, and besides
this Prince was not so puny a woman could ever work full
magic on him.

He ranted about the war-leader, and his black horse, and
his dire guard, who waited there, beak-nosed, their eyes
smeary glitterings behind the curious visors of their helms.

Feathers were fixed thickly on their helms and cloaks, he told me, all black. They had, these men, a distasteful odor, perhaps of ancient unwiped blood—

From what Signian recited, I thought that it *was* no other than Hrothgar. Who else would come here for me? Yet I did not entirely believe it. I felt neither relief nor hope.

When the Prince shouted I must remove the red and put on the other, insignificant gown, the bluish one, and that I must also take off the silver ring he had given me, since it might offend my husband, I did what he said at once. His eyes on my body, briefly bare between the garments, held no arousal.

His desire was only to have me gone.

"I have sworn to him, this man, I have kept you here for your own protection, and treated you always with respect."

I did not reply.

Signian added, abruptly almost as if he fawned on me, "See then, my girl, you won't want him to hear, will you, how you loved me so. Best say nothing of our meetings. I've held my tongue, to protect you. And he seems to accept you are still his wife, in deed as in name."

I did not ask of Signian what state—spiritual legal—I was *truly* in, since his priests had rinsed the former marriage off me before their disapproving gods.

Nor did Signian inquire if I was glad my unremembered spouse had come to get me back, nor either if I thought I might after all *recognize* my spouse. He did instruct me that the Princess, his mother, advised that I should greet the man joyously, as was proper.

With my recent illness, I had lost the savage and bitter fantasy of turning Signian against Hrothgar from spite. In fact, inevitably, given these circumstances, it would have proved both unworkable and immaterial.

I felt, as I say, no hope. Yet deep within myself did happiness begin to force up from the soil of my misery? Must I then disguise it? Or was I afraid? Should I disguise *that*?

I did not know. All was grayness in me.

As my wolf-women, the pair of them shivering in apprehension of the Prince's wrath and the threat of the invader in

the palace, conducted me to the hall, I could think only of my
dead son, the swan, my white darling with his long, strong,
slender throat that the arrow pierced, his feathers broken on
the shore. And I wept, how quietly.

Signian noted this.

He said, uneasy and approving together, "Yes, tears of delight at seeing him. But be careful he doesn't think they come
from any shame—any abuse I meted out to you."

The moment I entered the high and echoing hall, with all the
Prince's arrogant people huddling at its bannered walls, and
Hrothgar, of course Hrothgar, standing at the center of the
wide stone floor, his minions—they were not human and
barely looked it—poised at his back in their black feathers
and mail, my tears dried and left my eyes like pits of fire. He
spoke to me only a handful, not even that, of words. "Come
here to me," he said. And so I crossed the floor and went to
him. It was so ordinary, I might once again have dreamed it
all, but it was real.

Then Hrothgar turned to the Prince, and his mother, Orjana. Signian stood like a pole. She sat upright on her gilt
chair, not a hair uncombed, only her limp hands now grip-
ping, like claws, the chair-arms. She was quite terrified, I saw.
More deathly gray than the places within me.

"You have been generous to My lady," said Hrothgar. "I
would wish to reward you. I'll send something to you, befit-
ting your acts. Please receive these gifts, though you deserve
far more, as the payment of my debt."

Although he looked unlike himself, and yet exactly as I
had known him, in the way such things are known, I recalled
instantly on seeing his face, his body. His hair even lined with
the silver of faked age, and his face with a fakery of lines,
yet . . . I never knew him either. I had never known him. In
another past we had met, not he and I—another than he, another than I. He was a stranger also to me. But we went together from the hall, unhindered, his men-who-were-not
treading behind us. Outside one lifted me on to Hrothgar's
black horse. It was accurate to say the creature—both guard

and horse—had a feral smell—the smell of a large bird that lives on carrion. We rode away from the terraced palace, down the hill, out of the town walls, back into the forests below, toward the edges of the lake.

5

Certain was it he would never, now, possess me.

He did not.

Nor did he speak to me, had not even when I rode with him on the horse. After those first words, *Come here to me*, his silence.

By the shore he dismounted, and one of the non-men again assisted me, and set me on my feet.

Then Hrothgar whistled very low, and along the lake a sort of raft came drifting. By then it grew dusk. The raft was like a slice of twilight cut free. It slid in to the land, then stopped and waited there. He indicated, by a swift, not ungracious gesture, that I should step on to the raft. I did so. I thought he would leave me there. Set me too adrift. Instead he stepped lightly after me, and at once the wooden thing—or whatever type of thing it was—moved off again, and away, scudding now briskly out on the lake, into the dark.

Behind us, a great clattering of wings.

A thick, fluctuating shadow swirled over, and on into the east, letting fall as it passed countless black feathers. They had been crows, men and horses both. Nothing remained upon the shore but for the trees. And inland, unseen, the town and palace of the Prince and his mother.

Some many miles along the lake, the raft swam back in against the shore.

None had pursued him, nor would they find us now.

I was ashamed. As if I had been truly wed to him, a deliberately joined in sex with another chosen lover.

I could say nothing, and he did not speak to me.

A fire sprang up and burned with a curdled heat. Little

lights, like moths, evolved on the trees. Beer smoked in a
round iron pot. He dipped in a metal cup, and gave me the
drink, without a touch of his skin on mine.

Should I try to explain what had happened? Why had he
come to save me from that prison, if he did not know me innocent of blame?

Not once had he looked at me. He stared into the fire he
had created. Later he drew a loaf of dark bread from the
ashes at the fire's rim, broke off a piece and handed me it.
Gods can do such things, make men from birds and birds
from men, call fire out of the ground and baked bread, beer
or wine or water from the air. And the gods are always cruel.
We are nothing to the gods. Or perhaps they think us cruel to
them, we fail them so often, have no magic of our own to
enthrall them, disappoint, and finally die. Oh, we die.

"Let me tell you," he said, after the full moon rose, "how I
came to be a worker of spells, what your kind call an Enchanter. How the ability of shape-shift was mine."

I gazed at him.

In the naked moonlight all traces of age had vanished
from him. And I knew, though the evil mirror was no longer
mine, that this was not so for me. I should look the elder now.

So he told me, still not once resting his eyes on me, that he
had grown up in a sprawling town, not quite unlike the dun-
geonous heap of Signian. At thirteen years old, he was sold as
a kind of servant, to a man said to be talented in healing and
the minor arts of sorcery.

But the man was a cheat. He taught Hrothgar many
knacks of spurious magic and quackery, that might seem to
do good, but did nothing save deceive.

Hrothgar learned these things, having no choice. The man
beat him if he was inept, or even when he was not.

"His brain had rotted," Hrothgar told me. "At last it did
not concern him whether I was able or incompetent, servile
or trustless. One night he beat me, on and on, using for the
task a great staff he kept, normally, for his pretense of magery.
It had the head of an owl."

He paused. "At length," said Hrothgar, "I lay on the floor

of his house, dying I have no doubt. And he, to rest his tired arm, went pottering and muttering about, cursing and kicking me when he had to step over my body on the ground."

Hrothgar knew at that hour also that he died.

Of course, by then he did not care, wished only quickly to be gone.

And then—he was.

"Out of myself I lifted, on great red wings."

The shape-changing had come to him in brutalization and agony, and in death also, very likely. He did not remind me that I, otherwise, had become the swan in the throes of pleasure he had gifted.

Hrothgar flew out and off his body and circled the villainous healer's dirty room. The man watched, his mouth gaped open. "His horror," said Hrothgar, with neither passion or rage, "was a vision to me. An education I had never, till then, received."

Hrothgar, as an owl, put out the old man's eyes, then eviscerated him with his claws, and left him there. Next flying up to a window just broad enough to allow escape—for an owl's method of flight is that way easier—with one wing Hrothgar tipped a candle off its spike.

He left the house to burn, the town to burn if it would.

"I supposed my own human body would be burned up with it. But I was dead, and this my newest life. It suited me. You'll believe, I had never enjoyed my wretched slavery as a man."

A long way off, high among great trees, he watched and saw the scarlet smoke above the town. Then he flew on.

As an owl he lived a great while. Years, he thought, though keeping no calendar, he never afterward learned. He became a man again only when he saw a young woman that he fancied. It was not, he told me, myself. And I saw he did not say this to be harsh to me, merely to be factual.

When returned to the human form, he was full-grown and strong. Besides, he had acquired the talents of magic. He could accomplish much.

"Every useless lying conjure of my former master's in me became reality. It seems I knew what should be done, and therefore could do all. Like the sun will know when to rise, and when to set. And perhaps it knows this from watching other suns, in the time before time, that only seemed to do it."

After they had made sexual love, the girl he had taken and brought to ecstasy, changed into a bird. She might then alter at will and as she wished, or even to amuse Hrothgar. Later, some years later, the same skill was born in a young man that Hrothgar lay with. These two were the first lovers. But he had had many lovers since then.

It seemed to him, he told me, that he did not cast any spell upon them. Did not *infect* them with his sorcery. Instead, they themselves had attracted his notice and his desire through that very unknown, yet potent ability of shape-shift, carried dormant within their bones.

So it had been too, he said, with me.

When he told me that, I wept again. I could not help it. It was a foolish jealousy, in part. For he had never especially valued me as a woman, only noted and wished to let out my other self, the swan—which locked up inside me, must have cried out to him for rescue. Yet too, that inner life of mine, the swan, had been the best for me of all my existence. My *true* life. My *only* life.

I thought, if I had continued among the reeds of the lake, mated with my perfect, adopted son, borne others of our breed, I might have forgotten him, Hrothgar. And maybe that was how it always was. How it had been for all those others he had *fathered* of themselves. Even ultimately for him also, the Enchanter.

But he looked over at me when I cried my tears. For the first, and steadily.

"Otila," he said. His face was neither cruel nor kind. "Yes," he said. "Weep."

My soul knew what he meant by this. My soul then wept. Tears that were like fiery liquid glass ran out of my eyes. But my ignorant mind understood nothing. Until he drew close, and held me as the best of fathers will. And told me why I cried. Told me why I should, from that minute, inside the silence of my soul, cry forever, until my useless mortal time is worn away.

* * *

"To be this other, this true self, we must steal from ourselves. We must rob ourselves of humanness, and glory in the theft. So I, so you, Otila. For our humanity is also a thief." So he said, that night.

The gods decree it is a crime for humans to kill themselves. Even in extremity they must labor to survive.

By this it seems they wish further to punish us.

Maybe they are only sorry that we become dust after life, and so strive to keep us animate.

Or else we are fire and stars after life, and they are envious, and grudge us.

I discovered, when several of my years had gone by, that he did send rewards, as he had said he would, to Signian and the Princess, his mother. These were not gold or jewels. Signian, who bathed very seldom, took a bath that next summer, and was sinisterly drowned in the metal tub. He died thrashing and calling in front of his steward and servants, who tried frantically to save him. Something weighted him beneath the water, they said, struggle as he and they would to hoist him out. Orjana died of grief, or I have heard a tale she hanged herself. But self-murder is forbidden, as the killing of swans is forbidden, to any but the royal class.

"I can afford you sexual love," he said. "If you want. But you'll find only ashes in it now. We are nolonger of the same tribe, you and I, Otila, my poor Otila. All that, for you, is done."

It was love anyway that had destroyed me.

Not any love for my Creator, Hrothgar the Enchanter. No, it was my other love. My son—my lover—

In fury and despair I had run ashore, changing as I went from swan to mortal woman, and shown myself like this to the Prince who had slain my love. I had thought it was the courage of the swan that made me do this. But it was not the swan. It was my human fury and my mortal anguish, those sins which, though they may make us brave, we are ever warned of, for they destroy us.

He had no name, my son. Nor I, as a swan.

We had no need of names.

We had had no name even for love. For love is beyond all namings as all true things must be. Such is the most real nature of magic. It is *met* with, not taught or learned. It is ourselves. But these—we lose.

Hrothgar it was told me that, despite my own view, I had acted not as my actual self, who was a swan, but as my other, ingrained, thieving *unreal* self. A mortal thing. And by doing this, I smashed the enchantment. Gave everything away. And so the hunter captured me. And with his poisoned and filthsome and irrelevant sexual acts, he confirmed my wreck, scorched out of me what truly, truly only I *was*—as no fire or acid could have done. Had I been struck by whitest lightning, like the birch tree whose paleness changed my hair, or by the flaming spear of some downfalling star—or by the wrath of the gods themselves—I could not have been separated from the creature of the air, the spirit I had been. Live or dead, a swan I must have stayed.

And a swan, I would have mourned by loss, my beloved. I would have mourned him. But not been stripped of my *self*.

Never now could I shape-shift anymore. Never would I become again a swan.

All that while in the hell-house of the Prince, I had deceived myself, making out I was constricted, kept from change and flight by walls of stone. As I was. But the stone was my heart.

And there is no mourning either, as no penance or sweetness, that can bring solace for the loss of self.

There is no world in which to live thereafter, either this or another.

There is nothing. No thing. None.

And He? Hrothgar's action of seeking me in the palace, of setting me free, even of punishing my two principal jailors, his former action too, when he had killed the man who beat him—were these not the revenges and honor of a human man? I said no word of them to him, as already now I knew. For him it had been different. For he had gone *through* the lightning and the star, the wrath of gods—he had died, was dead. His body burned but he, having become his true self, might do as he wanted. He was an Enchanter. If of the same tribe, as he had said, he was of the royal class. A Prince. Having gained a privilege that could not be mine.

And he also, having told so much, said of this no word. He read my heart. My untaught lesson was over and complete.

He held me through the night, my father the Enchanter. I felt no hint of feathers under his tactful skin, no shift of wings at his back. In his black hair no redness shone, even from the clear fire. His eyes showed nothing amber, golden.

I thought of the black crows he had liberated, and with a dull start of the horses too, from which he must have liberated the selves of birds—perhaps not in any way of sex, but more as I had seen him do with the sheep whose fleeces glowed . . . What birds, then, would the sheep become?

But I recalled mostly the black crows, how they flew away into the moonrise. I thought of my three children who had lived, and who winged also away.

And I thought of my death, which now was all the life I had.

From one prison I had come. Yet out into the vast prison of the earth I must wander. Wingless. Alone.

When morning began, soft as flowers, Hrothgar left me and walked away. He showed me no sign of anything but his male humanness. I recall the path twisted there. I saw him last, as at the first, from the back.

There was even drink that stayed hot by the fire and a crust of the dark bread, as at our former meal. They did not vanish until I spoke to them, and said I would not eat or drink. And then I wept again, for with their going, the end began.

These were my last tears.

I have shed none since that can be seen. My weeping is tearless. What, after all, have I to do with water? It shames me that I breathe—for the gods know now, I can have nothing ever to do with the air.

Let me have only the earth. Or fire.

They are still mine. Burn or bury me.

Twice ten years are gone since that morning by the shore. I dwell far inland of the lake. I do not see the water. I whore for my food, if ever I want any. My hair, that was made black in that kennel of a palace, grows out now gray, as with the Princess it did.

Sometimes, in the blundering and unmusical assault of man-woman congress, I feel a faint fluttering at my womb, as if the soul of a bird flew there, trying to come in, to make itself within me, to be born of me. But I am barren, and now old.

In the winter dawns, above this ramshackle village of scavengers and thieves, sometimes I see swans fly over, not white but black on the golden sky. Then for the splinter of an instant, I spread my wings, and am among them. But this is not what occurs, and indeed, I never dream of it. Nor of the Enchanter. Nor ever, ever, ever of what I would wish to dream of most. My life. My life as a swan—

The Beast

WHEN HE SAW the rose, he knew that only one woman in the world could wear it: his daughter. The image and the certainty were so immediate; total. He stood staring.

It was made of amber, rich yellow amber, and the unfolded petals were smooth, translucent, without any of the normal bubbles, or trapped debris. Near the center hung a drop of "dew"—a single warm and creamy pearl. The necklace was a golden briar. It was perfect. And he visualized Isobel, her massy sweep of white blond hair swung loose from the icy line of its side part. Her pale skin, the mouth just touched with some pale color. The evening dress he had recently bought her in ivory silk. And the rose, on the briar, precisely under her throat.

"He has some fine things, doesn't he? Have you seen the jade horse?"

"Yes, I did." Always polite, and careful, he turned from his scrutiny and regarded the other man. They sipped from their glasses of some flawless champagne that came, not from France, but from the East.

"I've heard he collects anything exquisite. Will go to great lengths to get it. Even danger. Perhaps your own collection might interest him."

"Oh, I've nothing to match any of this." But he thought, *I have one thing*.

After the brief evening was finished, when they had regained their coats from the golden lobby and gone down the endless length of the glass tower, back into the snow-white city, he was still thinking about it. In fact, if he were honest, the thought had begun at the moment he met their host, the elusive and very private Vessavion, who had permitted them into his home, that mansion perched atop the tower of glass, for reasons of diplomacy. There had only been the six invitations, six men known for their business acumen, their wealth, their good manners. It had been meant to impress them, and because they were, all of them, extremely clever, it had done so.

He wondered, going over what he knew of five personal files in his mind, as his chauffeur drove him home, if any of them had a daughter. But even if they had, it could not be one like his. Like Isobel.

He had always given her the best. She was due only that. And Vessavion—Vessavion also was the very best there might be, Six and a half feet tall, probably about one hundred and eighty, one hundred and eighty-five pounds—this was not from any file, there were no accessible files on Vessavion— blond as Isobel, maybe more blond, the hair drawn back and hanging in a thick galvanic tail to his waist. Gray eyes, large, serious. A quiet, definite and musical voice, actor-trained no doubt. Handsome. Handsome in a way that was uncommon, and satisfying. One liked to look at him, watch his spare elegant movements. A calm smile revealing white teeth, a smile that had nothing to hide and apparently nothing to give, beyond a faultless courtesy amounting, it seemed, to kindness.

The car purred through a city made of snow. Lights like diamonds glittered on distant cliffs of cement. They came over the river into the gracious lowlands, and entered the robot gates of his house. It was a good house. He had always been proud of it. The gardens were exotic. But Vessavion, in the middle of that multitude of rooms, Vessavion had a garden that was like a cathedral, open to sky almost it seemed of space, flashing with stars.

She was in the library, sitting by the fire, an open book on her knee. She might have been waiting. He looked at her. He thought, *Yes*.

"Was it wonderful?" she asked, cool and sweet. There was a lilt to her voice that was irresistible, like the slight tilt to her silvery eyes.

"Very, I hope you'll see it. I left him a note. Something of mine that may interest him . . . The African Bible."

"You'd give him that?"

"In exchange—for something else. Perhaps he'll refuse. But he does collect rare and beautiful things."

She was innocent of what he meant. She did not know. He had begun to keep secrets, her father. It had started five weeks before in the doctor's office. Time enough for truth later. Truth was not always beautiful, or desired.

Vessavion's answer came the next day. It was as if Vessavion were somehow linked into his plan, as if this had to be. He invited the owner of the African Bible to a small dinner. The visitor had a daughter, Vessavion had heard. She must come too.

Conceivably, Vessavion had even known of Isobel. The father knew there were files also on him. Had Vessavion perhaps seen some inadequate, breath-taking photograph?

The dinner was set three nights before Christmas. It was well-omened, the city in a Saturnalia of lamps and fir trees, wreathes and ribbons. He said to Isobel, "Will you wear the ivory silk for me?" She smiled. "Of course." "And, no jewelry," he said. She raised her eyebrows. "Do you think he'll hang me with jewels?" "He may. He might." "I'm quite nervous," she said. "I've heard about him. Is he really—is he handsome?" "Tonight," he said, "you'll see for yourself."

The elevator took them up the tower of glass, and at the top the doors opened into the golden lobby, with its French gilt mirrors and burnished floor. A servant came, like all Vessavion's slaves, virtually invisible, and took away their outer garments. They walked into the vast pale room where the log fire was actually real, pine cones sputtering in it on apple wood. On the walls two or three beautiful paintings from other centuries, genuine, obscure, and priceless. Lamps of painted glass. Brocade chairs, *their* unburnt wood carved into pineapples. For the season, a small rounded tree had been placed, dark green, decked with dull sequins of gold, a golden woman on its top holding up a star of crimson mirror. And there were boughs of holly over the mantle of the fire, and tall, yellow-white candles burning. It was charming, childish, almost touching. But then, had it been done only to please Vessavion's guests? Perhaps even to please a woman?

On a silver tray by the fire were three long slender goblets of some topaz wine. Vessavion came in. Immaculately greeted father and daughter. They drank together.

But the father had noted Vessavion's face when he beheld Isobel. There was no subterfuge at all. Vessavion's face changed, utterly, as if a mask had lifted from it. Underneath it was just the same face, handsome, strong, yet now alive. And it was young. The father thought, *He's only two or three years older than she is. I can see it, now*. This delighted him very much.

Isobel had changed a little too. For the first time in a decade, she was blushing, softly, marvelously, like milk-crystal filled by sunlight. Her eyes shone. No man who liked women could have resisted her.

They ate the delicious meal—fish from somewhere cold, perhaps Heaven, a soufflé made of clouds—the invisible servants attending to everything, wines floating down yellow-green, red, and clear as rain. There was a blue liqueur.

All the time, he listened to them talking, the girl and the young man, without hesitations. He felt, the father, the pleasure of a musician, whose music plays at his will alone.

He thought, *I must relinquish that. Now they are each other's*. He was glad. He had not wanted to leave things in a muddle. It was not he felt she could not manage without him, not because she was a woman. No. Women were vital, survivors, even ruthless if they had to be. It was only, he had not wanted to *make* her work at things like *that*. She was meant to soar, not brood among the cobwebs and dusts. And it would be all right. Yes, now it would.

It came time to reveal the African Bible. Vessavion took the huge black book and opened its clasps of platinum with his strong, graceful hands. He read, his lips moving silently. Evidently he understood the esoteric language into which the Bible had been translated. When he glanced up, he said, "I do want it. But how can it be priced?"

The father said, "I would like you to have it as a gift."

Vessavion smiled. He looked at Isobel. His smile for her, already, was feral and possessive, eager and consumed—consuming. Isobel lowered her eyes. Vessavion said, "Then may I give your daughter something? I know what would suit her. Do you remember the amber rose?"

The father felt a pang of agony—it was jealousy, much, much worse than the clawing of the cancer that now, anyway, was kept dumb by drugs. But he was glad too of the jealousy. It confirmed he had been right.

They went among Vessavion's collection. It was rumored he had other things, hidden away, but here there was enough to astound. The Han horse, white as ice, the Roumanian chess pieces carved from a mountain, the banner from a war of 1403, the great unfaceted sapphire polished like a ball made out of the summer sea. And more.

Vessavion took the rose from its cabinet, and fastened the briar about Isobel's white neck, lifting away so gently her wave of blond hair. His hands were courteous, they did not linger, but his color too intensified faintly, for a moment. He was a young man.

They sat long into the night, over coffee and wine. Soft music played somewhere, and beyond the conservatory of enormous flowers, that garden, checkered by enormous stars.

Isobel and Vessavion talked on and on. If it was a melody they made, each knew it, where to come in, and where to wait. They might have known each other for ever, and been parted for a week. So much to say. How they had missed each other.

Finally, deliberately, he murmured that now they must go away. He relished his cruelty, seeing their eyes clouded, and hearing their voices falling from each other like caressing hands.

Vessavion rose. He named a fabulous production, drama, opera, something for which it was impossible to get tickets. He, of course, had them. Would they accompany him? The father liked, too, this old-fashioned kindness to himself. He declined graciously. He said that Isobel must go. That was all that was needed.

They descended in the elevator, down into the snow world. She was very quiet and still. Self-conscious even. She avoided his eyes.

When they were in the car, she said, shyly, "Is it all right?"

"Yes. Wonderfully all right."

"You're pleased?"

"Can't you tell?"

"You like him?" she said, hopeful as a child.

"Very much."

"But he's so mysterious. No one knows anything about him."

"Perhaps that's part of it."

"Do come to the theater," she said.

He said, laughing, "You'd kill me if I did."

He thought afterward, it was a pity he had said that, although she, too, not knowing, had laughed in turn. It was a pity to accuse her, *her*, even in a joke, of something which was already happening by another means.

He believed she did not sleep that night. Across the court, he saw her light burning on, as he sat through the dark.

Isobel had only been in love in childhood. With characters in books, with the characters that actors portrayed on a screen or a stage. Later, she lost her taste for this sort of love. She was fastidious, and her standards had been permitted to be extremely, impossibly, high. She had, now and then, liked men. But the conquest which her beauty always allowed her to make, sometimes brought out in them their worst—foolishness, bombast, even, occasionally, antagonism. Besides, she did not recognize them.

Seeing Vessavion, she recognized him at once. Not only his personal beauty, which was, if anything, greater than her own. Also his demeanor, and presently his manner, his mood, his mind. When they spoke, of trivial or important elements, they seemed to glide together along the same broad white road. Each found new things there, and sometimes the same things, or things of a fascinating difference which, once shared, were accessible to both.

However, to be realistic, she had fallen in love with him on sight. And in his eyes she presently saw the same had happened for him.

Beyond all this, there was his mystery, and even though, from the first evening of the dinner, he spoke to her of his life, of events in which he had participated, of childhood memories, his air of seclusion remained, sweet and acid at once, luring her on. Could she ever know him? Oh yes—and yet, to be possessed by a handsome stranger that she knew, that she could never know—He did not kiss her until their third meeting. By then she was weak with longing, confused, almost in pain. At the touch of his mouth, his tongue, the pressure of his body, safe tethers of steel gave way in her, she fell all the distance down into the heart of him, and lay there drowning.

She was a romantic who had dismissed her dreams, a young woman with a young woman's libido, who had found no stimulus, until now. She trusted him completely. Yet he was a shadow. It was more wonderful than anything of any sort she had ever had in her life before.

After their eighth meeting, he took her into a vast bedroom that was like a dark blue cave, and here all night, all day, they made love over and over, sometimes drinking champagne, sometimes eating food that magically arrived without trace of human participation.

At first her orgasms were swift and tenuous, flickers, shudders, butterflies of feeling. But he taught her, with his hands and his mouth, lips and tongue, every inch of his honed and subtle body, the sword of his loins, his white hair, his skin, to writhe and to wait, to simmer and to flame, so that ocean-rushes of pleasure dashed her up and up into a steeple, a vortex, where she screamed, where she died, and he brought her slowly back to life, gentle then as the mother that she did not recall.

After they had lain on that great blue bed, the few single silver wires of their separate hair, torn out in frenzy, lay like traceries. Once there was a broken nail, white as a sickle moon. Or a spot of silken fluid. Or only the impress of their bodies, one thing.

It was a winter wedding. Her father was there, and the witnesses, that she did not know and never saw again. They ate a sumptuous meal in a towering restaurant above an ice-blue sea that perhaps was not real, she did not know or care.

A few days later her father was gone. He vanished, leaving only a mild and friendly letter, which Vessavion read her as she wept. The house in the lowlands of the city was now hers, and once she went back to it, alone, Vessavion's man waiting for her at the outer door. But the house, where she had always lived since she could remember, seemed unfamiliar. She saw to her father's things, what was necessary. It occurred to her she did not weep enough. She tried to force out her tears by thinking of his goodness to her. He had been a dedicated yet not a passionate parent. He had made her too sure of herself. She found that this section of her life, her years with her father, was over, and she could fold it away, neatly, and now it did not matter.

Sometimes she and her husband were apart for an hour or so, or he might be absent for a portion of an evening or an afternoon. She assumed he must attend to his business interests, as her father had done. These separations were tantalizing, nearly enjoyable. Vessavion's mansion had, besides, so many rooms. She was always finding new ones. It was like him. In the winter garden grew winter flowers that burned and seemed to smoke. Rivulets flowed and tiny bells chimed among the hair of vines. Sometimes too Vessavion took her away to other places on a private plane. They saw enormous mountains clad in green fur, marble columns, and waterfalls that thundered. But generally they returned quickly from everywhere, back into the blue cave. They made love almost without cease. They made love as if famished.

She said to him one night, in the dark, chained by his hair, locked to him still, "Was there anyone before me? There must have been." "Why do you want to know?" he said, "surely you understand." "Then no," she said, "I'm the first for you as you were the first for me." "Exactly," he said. "How could there have been anyone? I was waiting for you." She said, "Will it ever end—this wanting—this electric *tingling*, this *hunger*?" "If we grow very old," he said, "perhaps." "Not till then?" she said. "I'm glad." They made love again and again. She was hoarse from her own crying. She said, "But won't you ever leave me?" "How can I leave you? You're myself." She thought, *Supposing the inconceivable took place—if I should leave him instead?* She said, "If someone made me go away from you—" He said, "I'd die. I'd stop like a clock." She recollected her father, whom she had left and who had disappeared. She believed Vessavion. She held him fast in her pale arms, wound him with her long pale legs and slender feet. Inside her body she held him. If they died, it must only be together.

In March the snow was still solid and thick upon the city. From Vessavion's high windows, she could see across a polar landscape, all ice and glass, broken only here and there by roadways and obstinate steel turrets.

He returned in darkness, her husband, and as he walked into the tawny chamber that was their drawing-room, she saw on his face, so white and calm from the snowscape he had been traveling through, a jewel of scarlet. It was on his cheek, like an ornament. She did not mention it at first, and then it trickled down like a tear.

"You're bleeding." She was concerned but went to him coolly; her frenzies were never for such things.

And he only smiled, and reaching up, wiped the scarlet tear away. "No."

"But it was blood."

"Was it? How strange."

"Did something happen—out there on the street?"

"It must have done. I don't know."

Carefully she led him to a couch and sat down beside him, examining his face that still was not familiar, although recognized from the first.

"Where do you go in the city?"

"All sorts of places."

"Please tell me," she said.

"No," he said, "it would bore you."

Isobel leaned close to him and breathed him in. He was scented by the freezing dark he had come from. And by something else which she had sensed before, but only once or twice outside a certain situation. Animal, the aroma, spicy and intent, not truly human. It was rather like the smell of him in sex. It aroused her and she put her hand on his breast. But when he moved to kiss her she said, "Not that. You have a secret." And she wondered if there could be another one, another woman or a man, someone he went to when he was not with her. But even as she thought this, she knew it was not credible, it was a lie. What then, the reason for this excitement?

"Tell me," she said.

"I tell you everything."

"Not this."

However, he took her to him, and there on the couch he undressed her, unsheathing her body like a flower from silver wrapping. He drew her up on to the blade of his lust, and they danced slowly in the rosy firelight. She stared into his face, remote with pleasure, taut with the agony of holding back.

"Where do you go?" she moaned.

But her blood curdled in fire and her womb spasmed open, shut, open, shut, and arching backward she knew nothing was of any consequence but their life together.

When they were eating dinner, the goblets of blond wine at their finger-tips, slivers of vegetable blossom and white meat lying on porcelain, then, he told her.

"I have an interest sometimes," he said, "in people. I watch them a little. Would you believe, I follow them."

"Why?" she said. She was puzzled. People did not really interest her, only he interested her. She had never found people equal to what she was. Only he was that.

He said, thoughtfully, "You see, you're perfect, Isobel. You're like—like the moon. You change, and yet you remain constant. Every line of you, angle of you, the turn of your head, the way you lift your eyes, your voice—all perfect. But most people have nothing of this. And then again," he hesitated, "sometimes there are attractive people who, without any true beauty, are quite marvelous. But, it isn't these that intrigue me. No. Now and then there is someone ... very ugly, who has one beautiful feature. Their eyes perhaps, or their hair. Their teeth. Their fingers even—Do you understand? The *discrepancy*."

Isobel realized that, all the while she had been with him, she had glowed. Glowed actually like the amber rose, the first thing he had given her. It was like a halo inside her skin. It warmed when she made love with him, soothed and turned darker when they were at rest, talking, or even apart. Yet now,

now the glow seeped out of her, and for a moment she seemed to see it shining in the air. And then she was cold.

"You always trust me," she said.

"Of course. Who else should I trust?"

"You shouldn't always trust me."

He paled at that, in the curious way of someone who is already pale. His eyes were somber, heavy. He said, "But why should it effect you, if I talk a little nonsense."

"It isn't nonsense. You meant what you said. That certain people, ugly people, intrigue you because they have one beautiful feature."

"And what does that matter?" he said, lightly.

"It matters to you."

"Isobel," he said, "let's talk of something else."

She smiled and drank her wine, nodding. It was the first falseness she had ever offered him. And he took it from her, without question.

She searched all through March, searched the mansion atop the tower of glass. At the beginning of April the snow held on, an ice-age, and she found it. The room. By then it hardly counted. She had been deceiving him all that while, betraying him. Pretending when they made love. Pretending when they talked. He had spoken of visiting some far off country, and she had pretended to be pleased. It seemed he was fooled by all her pretense, although his eyes had now a shadow in them. After all, probably he wanted her to find the room. He had not quite been able to tell her everything, and the room would do it for him. And it did.

A few days after their marriage, he had shown her the room of his hidden collection, the things he possessed which, until then, he had shown to no one—not from vanity, but more as if to protect his visitors. What he had was so fine, it might wound. But Isobel, his wife, now possessed these treasures, too; it would be safe for her to see. And there were panels from Medieval France, a painting by Leonardo da Vinci not reckoned to exist—a Madonna with sea-water skin and lilies in her hands. There were dolls made of emerald and gold, which moved. There were green pearls, and tapestries woven at the time of Christ, a dress of beads constructed for a child in ancient Rome, a shell that had formed in the shape of a castle, a statuette of an angel made from a single ruby. And—more. Much more.

She had liked it, his collection. She had played gently with a few of the items. She had worn the green pearls.

And in March, she searched out the other hidden room, and at length located it, behind a bookshelf which slid. There was a lock and Isobel broke this with an ordinary hammer she had asked one of the invisible servants to bring her. It was quite easy to break, the lock, it did not take much strength. Horribly, sadly, resignedly, she grasped all this was meant to be.

The room was quite small, and tastefully decorated, although not lavish like so many of the rooms of the mansion. There were no windows, only soft lighting, wisely placed, to point up the objects on display.

As with the other collections; everything was arranged exquisitely. Indeed, it was arranged tactfully. That, of course, was the whole substance of what he had done, what he had intended.

Isobel went about slowly, and thoroughly, an obedient child brought to a museum. She looked at everything. At the lustrous plait of red hair held in claws of gold. At the white teeth scattered, as the pearls had been, over a velvet cloth. At the two eyes gleaming in the crystal of protective fluid. At the small hand under its dome, one finger with a tarnished wedding ring. At the beautiful breasts, seeming to float like sweets. At the ears. The solitary foot. And—more.

When she had seen everything, Isobel went out. She closed the door, leaving the broken lock hanging, and drew back the bookshelf which slid. Then she went to her bathroom and bathed herself, and washed her hair and dried it. She dressed in her dressing-room. She packed her bag with the things which were only hers. And on the pillow in her bedroom, which she had never used, she left the amber rose.

She met Vessavion in the tawny drawing-room, as the gray wolf dusk filled up the sky, and turned the ice-age of the city to iron.

Vessavion looked at her, and she said, "I have seen it."

He bowed his head. He said, "What will you do?"

"I will leave you, obviously."

"Let me explain."

"What can you say?"

"Perfection," he said, very low, stammering. "Until I saw you, I had never come across it in a human thing."

"Even after you had me, you continued."

"Yes."

"Through the snow you hunted them and cut away what was beautiful, and their blood splashed you, and once you were careless, or uncaring, and I saw. But your money and your power protect you. No one will stop you."

"I put what's beautiful into its proper setting. I always have. It must be a mistake—when they have it."

She said, "Good-bye."

"If you leave me," he said, "then—"

She closed the door, and presently she was descending the glass tower in the elevator, down into the iron snow.

There was a week after that like a hundred years. She spent it in her father's house, safe behind the robot gates which would admit no one. She disconnected the telephones. When any mail fell through into the pillar at the gate, someone came and destroyed it.

She did things in that house she had not done for some while. She played the piano, and cooked cordon bleu meals she did not eat, and read books cover to cover, not knowing what they said.

In the evenings she drank wine, too much, but then that did not ever help and so she did not drink wine any more.

Spring began to come through the overgrown gardens, and small birds appeared, making nests, singing, as if the world existed. There were sunsets and sunrises, too. Laughable.

When the week was over, as she dressed one morning, she saw she had grown thin, had lost perhaps eighteen pounds. And when she combed her hair, some fell in a rain.

She was driven across the city to the tower of glass, and

went in, and rose up, and came out into the golden lobby, but it was not gold any more, the floor opaque, the mirrors misted, shadow in the air.

Isobel entered the mansion of her husband, Vessavion. She walked slowly through long rooms, and L-shaped rooms, and octagonal rooms. The fires were out, there was no light. Cobwebs hung on things. Dust spread over all. The invisible servants had vanished.

She found him in the blue bedroom that was a cave, on the blue bed that they had seeped in flame.

He was naked, lying on his back upon his own hair. His flesh and his hair, like hers now, did not have any luminescence. His light had gone out. She went close and gazed into his face.

Vessavion was quite dead. Quite blank. Empty. Useless. Over.

There was nothing about him to show what he had been. He was thin and worn, and there was already a line of gray in his hair. His face had fallen in. It was old. And it was very ugly, unnaturally so, hideous in fact. Like the face of some nightmare, some beast.

She wished that she could have said something, anything, to alleviate the awareness she had of the attenuated awfulness of pain, like an unfinished sentence caught up on nails in the atmosphere.

But it was no use at all. Nothing more could be said or done. She had loved him, she had betrayed him, she had killed him as no other had the power to do. And here he lay to rot on the bed of love. And he had the face of a beast.

The Beast and Beauty

WE SAW THEM married. We were all surprised, to various degrees; some of us were even shocked. She was so—we could hardly gloss over it among ourselves—so ugly, so graceless. And he was beautiful, such a handsome and couth young man, with his long, rich hair and slim, straight build. And this other—this *object,* standing there beside him.

To do her credit, if we can call it that, she seemed quite as amazed as we. But this only made her, we thought, less coordinated, more gauche and awkward. A parody. She was squat and short-legged, rather fat, and her wiry, frizzy hair hidden under a sort of exotic headdress, part hat perhaps, part bird's nest. She had small, pale, dull eyes, all of us noticed this, so unlike his own, that were dark, large, and luminous.

We knew he had not married her for her money. She had none, and he was well-off. Had she then some terrible and inexorable hold over him? Some of us, I do believe, were constructing plots by which we could find out how she had suborned and captured him. But—and here the strangest thing of all—he seemed *happy.* And when they kissed—well, for a fact, he kissed her tenderly, sweetly. Even with—and we were worse horrified of course by this—with an element of actual physical desire.

We will never forget it, that day.

Not one of us.

They had a small house on the coast, which had belonged to him for two or three years. They went to the house at once. He had said, being by the sea, and the countryside there so appealing, they had no need of a honeymoon holiday.

There they lived then, the two of them. The town, quite a well-built and sophisticated place, was only a twenty minute drive from the house—or an hour's walk. Sometimes they did walk, along the cliffs, with the brilliant shifting shelves of water below, and off across the sunlit meadow-paths, between the tall hedges, the fields, the banks of wild flowers and the woods. A cycle of perfect summers. Had either of them ever before been so wonderfully happy? They told each other, he most often in fact, that they never had.

And between the walks and luxurious meals, and everyday or eccentric duties of their house and gardens, between—others had to suppose—their times of romance and sexual love-making—they continued with their usual work, he creating his rather excellent yet very crowd-pleasing art, and she writing her rather—it was generally agreed—*ordinary* little novels. His successes had begun early and had continued but hers, though at first she had been quite popular and sold well, had fallen off. In the end she hardly published at all, but still went on writing. She was, it seemed, nothing if not stubborn. Had that been the secret of her success with *him?*

By the second year they did not often see people, beyond the occasional, normally unplanned meetings in the town, or the city inland. They seemed wrapped up in each other. No one else had or could fathom why. That was, the rest of the world could see easily how *she* might be wrapped up in *him.* While with him, naturally, it stayed a mystery.

He had never painted her, for sure. But then, he very seldom, or now ever, painted people. His subjects were landscapes, skies, seas.

Another year passed.

Another year.

Nobody genuinely had grown at all used to their extraordinary liaison. Now and then it was still commented upon in amused disbelief, or even in a type of moral outrage. But less and less. An *unanswered* mystery can be irksome when it unalterably persists.

He had had, and he was the first to admit it, a limpidly flowing and pleasant existence. Born into an emotionally and financially solvent family, blessed with great good looks, and strong yet accessible talent, he had prospered. His earliest memories,

even, were nice ones. Happy: he grew *up* happily; popular, protected, yet independent, self-assured and enjoying his creative
side, while reveling in friendships, not to mention love-affairs.
Although, he would sometimes ruefully admit, the end of love-
affairs, and exotic brief relationships, after say six months, a
year, were often less delightful. He hated to hurt these women.
But he had always had such luck with them. He need do very
little more than be his handsome, charming, easy-going and
gracious self, and girls cascaded from the boughs of earthly
heaven into his life and bed. Saying good-bye was mournful, of
course. It could sting. But quite frequently not only he, but a
former lover, were soon established elsewhere, completely un-
damaged. He was never harsh, never cruel. He tried always to
be kind. Kindness was—inherent in him, really. To distress another might distress him therefore. He liked the world sunny,
even in rain. Intelligent, he *knew* he had a splendid time of it.
And he honestly regretted the others, that he saw, heard of and
read of, all about him, who did not. Things were unfair. Had he
been able, he would have waved a magic wand, and put everything right. For this reason too, of course, he did not believe in
a God. But then, it seemed he hardly needed one.

When he met her, the woman who would become his wife,
he felt, immediately, compassion. She had just begun to
work—actually her writing had for a while ceased to be lucra-
tive enough to support her—in a small art shop in the back
streets. He went in there occasionally for a particular primer
not often available elsewhere. She served him politely and
fairly efficiently, though she was slightly clumsy in her movements. Her body seemed uncoordinated and not properly to
fit her psyche. He had noticed things like this before with
plenty of people.

It must be said that the fact she was not herself attractive
was *not* why he felt compassionate. Being himself so frankly
beautiful, he did not, as some beautiful persons do not, bother
very much with the looks either of others or himself beyond
the obvious matters of grooming, hygiene, and sanity. But he
could see she was miserable. And though this, he had found,
was often the case with people generally, he discovered her
dejection rather pointedly disturbed him.

Covertly, he watched her as she dealt with his purchase and its payment.

Then, something happened.

A flock of quite ordinary birds lifted from the street outside and flew upward through the last of the afternoon sunlight. As a painter, he liked the image, and watched it. Then, turning back to her, saw that she had, too. And—for a split second, already ephemerally fading—he saw her face had flooded with its own soft light. A look of—*joy*. Pure joy. At seeing something beautiful, however everyday, or transitory, or unmeaningful. As if, he thought at the time, she had looked through a window into some other world, more lucent, more lovely, and immediately recognized.

It was not until he was almost at his apartment that it came to him that, for just one single second, she had looked at him, also, in the same way. And *in* that second, as in the longer moments with the birds, the misery had of course quite vanished from her face.

Perhaps this was irresistible. He was, as has been noted, normally inclined to kindness. To be kind filled him with pleasure. He had now and then given away his toys as a child.

He did not need to go back to the shop, but found himself passing about a month later.

Going in, there she was. She seemed if anything even more worn down and melancholy. But when he greeted her and she glanced up at him—why, there it was again. The wonderful sunrise.

That then, her charm for him. Her enchantment. Better than any mirror, to which inanimate species he never paid much attention beyond obvious necessity. Unlike a *human* mirror, too, which only returns the object of desire as a sort of faulty replica.

It was not he thought: *I can make her beautiful*. It was more somehow *I can make her happy*. Besides, it was not, and never could be with him, a *conscious* thought. He was unincluded in that tribe.

Adamantly, at first she would not lunch or dine with him. When he asked, she seemed almost frightened. Yet, the glow of light in her face persisted, fluttering on and off as the wings

of the flying, sun-fringed birds had appeared to. After about
a week of his constantly entering the shop, buying something,
trying to persuade her, she agreed to drink a cup of coffee
with him.

The café was discreet and serene, the coffee it served very
good. They were there for half an hour.

It became a habit between them once, twice a week. After
four weeks they ate sandwiches and drank, each, a glass of
wine. They knew each other's names. They had started to discuss books, and plays. He took her to a play. He liked her reactions to such significant events.

She looked younger. Her cheeks had color and she had
had her hair cut more becomingly. Her eyes on him were always wide. Radiance existed in them. Her voice, though very
low, was of an even timbre, not inarticulate or unmusical
when she became animated.

They took a little holiday, four or five days in a quiet but
opulent hotel. She had told him, flat and downcast as she did
so, that her room must be separate. She was a restless sleeper,
she snored, so she told him. He replied, untruthfully, that he
too was, and did. On the third night he joined her for a drink
in her room. Presently she insisted that all light be extin-
guished. *I hate to be looked at,* she whispered. *My body, I
mean.*

He wondered what injury of birth or life had maimed
her—some swollen or shrunken part, hidden when clothed—
a rampant birthmark—a disease of the skin—but in the darkness she was simply a woman of short stature, clad in flesh
that was, depending on a companion's view, heavy, or voluptuous. There were no deformities or lesions of scars of which
he was made aware, nothing strange that, lacking full sight,
the other senses stumbled on. Her skin was smooth and soft,
her mouth tender, no part of her in any way offensive.

He knew as well, from her responses, what he would have
seen in her face. Light transmuted to ecstasy.

He had painted the picture of a violin, once. She was like
his violin. And her writing, too, for him, was like her music; he
had given it back to her.

She began to live with him for large amounts of each

month. Unreluctantly she left her job, no longer needing it, since by then he was funding all her expenses, both with and apart from him. She did not seem even properly to notice this, and he preferred that reaction in her, for gratitude would have grated on him. All he wanted in exchange he saw in her eyes and face, heard and held, and glimpsed finally, when he made love to her: by then, she would permit a vague lamplight. He had, in all his benign existence until this point, never so relished, so basked in, so *needed* anyone other than himself.

To marriage also she made, now, no objections. Perhaps, during the wedding ceremony and the lavish feast that followed, she did not fully notice anyone but her lover. And he, for his part, was lost in her. Or found.

She, until she met, and then lived with her husband, had never been with anyone. Which is to say, she *had* been thrown in among a *huge* number of others, but with none who were ever concerned about or interested in her, let alone loving toward her.

Her parents had been uncomely and loutish, and both inclined to violence. Her couple of older siblings took after them. At an immature age she was rescued, or so it was termed, and cast instead into a sort of state orphanage, where all the cruelties and bullying continued in more elaborate form, not to mention the physical hideousness of natures, ambitions, and surroundings, and the dearth of any food either for the heart or spirit; there was little enough for the stomach.

Somehow or other she had learned to read. Most probably this, and other more rudimentary knowledge, was beaten into her. But as she grew up, despite the menial factory work into which, at fifteen, she was processed, and the yet everexpanding callousness of everyone about her, somehow she learned, of her own instinctive volition, to grasp at literature and to hold on. A fluke of circumstance put her, at the age of sixteen, into the position of entering a short story competition. She won it unrivaled, and was taken then under the wing of a quite prestigious publishing house.

Initially thrilled at her potential money-making ability,

and her youth, they quickly lost momentum having once seen and met her. Gauche and awkward, clumsy and utterly un-pretty, she had in herself no marketing power, as they were soon agreed. Only her writing had any worth which, in an age of instant visibility and supposed communication, would *never* be enough.

Some listless attempts *were* made physically to polish her up. But the smart garments and trendy hair-dos, the cosmetic specialists and speech-trainers soon gave up on her in impa-tient revulsion.

It was true, she had always seen about her, particularly on a screen, but even among her hair-dying and lip-glossing fel-low citizens, persons who, lacking certain essential fleshly at-tributes, effected improvements. Some indeed underwent surgery, tooth-jobs, chin-jobs, face-jobs, body-jobs, gym ther-apy, hair transplants, wigs, waxes, revitalizations, skin-grafts. Though confused by all that, in her own muddled and entirely ineffectual way she had tried, or felt forced to try, to emulate the rest—who, she could see, did end up usually rather better for all the grueling, costly, painful work put in on them.

But it was soon clear to her, as to her publishers it had already been, and quite swiftly, that *she* was beyond assis-tance. A lost cause. A lump best left in a cupboard of un-forced privacy.

Lacking any solid publicity, and all promotion therefore, soon enough her talent too slid from the World Stage. At twenty she was a has-been. She retreated to a narrow one-room flat and various ill-paid employment and gradually, in exhaustion, smothered under that universal bucket, her light faltered down into coma.

It was he who woke her.

She had somehow, even bereft of so much, never been robbed completely of her fundamental passion for true beauty. Even for such as ill-made and crushed as she, stars and waves, leaves and lamps, sunrise, moonset, and the faces of non-human animals—all such abrupt and extraordinary miracles would drench her, for a few seconds, in the glow of paradise. Although a paradise from which she herself was for-ever banned.

She had seen, too, some naturally elegant and attractive people before, if normally from very far off. Confronted by him, so close, so apparent, she had been stunned.

Only her naivety later allowed her to give in to his persuasion. It was all a dream. She must start up from it soon enough, to find herself lying on a hot raw ground of reality and fact. Otherwise she could never have trusted the circumstance, let alone him.

Perhaps, *in* reality, she did *not* trust him. You are alone in darkness—a God or an angel appears. What map-reference is there, in such a case, to guide one? You can only give in.

But time ran by and over her, a clear river, all at once delicious and gentle. Amazement followed on amazement. The dream did not dissolve. It must, after all *be* real.

Of course, she had known one previous astonishment with her success in the competition. Maybe, even subconsciously, it had been *this* which soothed and lured her to accept a second gift. Choosing, as few would not, to forget how the first glory had been drained to dust.

In legends, even in contemporary stories such as she herself might have written, the gifts of gods are often suspect. Even if no evil plan of harm has been hatched against the recipient, *indigenous* to the glamor and wonder of the gift is its lethal flaw. The molten gold sears off the hand, the exquisite ring imparts a poisonous disease, the peerless wings are over-strong and hurl their wearer up against the sun. The kiss breaks the mirror.

We heard of it in disbelief. Where the marriage had shocked some of us in itself, the outcome, those five years later, sent us staggering.

Obviously, there was a lot of publicity, not least since he was so well-known and fashionable a painter. To the general public, of course, the blow was minimized by emotional distance. For us, however, particularly those of us who had never lost contact with him—even where keeping, when possible, out of *her* proximity—a kind of cloud of mourning settled. There was some anger as well. How not?

Inevitably, all the while, some of us had entirely foretold

a reversal. That he *must,* at some junction, emerge from his unreasonable trance and realize his peculiar mistake. Or, more likely yet, that he must see another, no doubt a woman, somebody gorgeous and couth, and fall in love more logically with her.

Several of us had remained shattered that so far he had not seemed able to. While a few of us, certainly, once or twice over the years, may have tried to *cause* this to happen: *Oh, have you met so-and-so, she is such a fan of your work*—but no scheme bore fruit. He had gone on with *her.* Until *this.*

If only we could have undone the knots of that wicked fate which had inconceivably ensnared him—

But that, as we soon learn in this world, is as a rule out of our remit.

We must all make our own way. To Heaven, or to the Abyss.

And who could have predicted such a dreadful, vile—yet nearly laughable—thing? It was—*absurd.*

They had been at their house on the coast that day, as so often they were. It was a day like many they had already spent there.

It seems he painted in the morning, at a place in their gardens that overlooked the sea. It was glamorous summer weather, the temperature warm but mild, and a soft breeze blowing through the cedars and the scented lavender bushes.

They ate lunch on the patio above, a fresh salad with locally caught fish, some wine and fruit. He had laid a rose by her plate.

About three o'clock they decided to stroll inland to the town, to buy a minor item necessary for the studio; this would then be delivered later in the week. After which they might take in a movie, dine early, and about ten be chauffeured home through the long blue dusk, the full moon out and stars glittering, all well with their world.

They never reached the town.

He was found on the beach, just above the tide-line, by that unlucky cliché—a person walking their dog. It was by then about six a.m., and the sun up and streaming clear over the water. Any error was impossible.

He was covered in blood, which was not astounding. Most of his bones were broken too, also hardly inappropriate, under the circumstances.

His beauty was impaired, if not totally eradicated. He had stayed recognizable. Even the dog-walker knew him at once, if only from photographs and clips of TV footage. It seemed the dog-walker had very good prints of three of his paintings, and cried, and so the dog howled, and they cried and howled again when the police arrived.

Not long after that the beach grew very crowded.

She did not attend the funeral. It would hardly have been feasible that she could. She had vanished, disappeared rather as spent liquid slides down a drain into the sewer beneath. Had she *been* visible, accessible, it went without saying she must instead any way have been shut in jail, on trial, there found guilty, and either dispatched, or incarcerated for the remains of her time alive. She had killed him, her lover-husband, the painter. But why was this? *Had* he betrayed her with another lover? Or merely begun to be cruel, scorning her, insulting, bullying, and abusing her, like all those others from her past? No, none of those. He had stayed faithful and adorable, ever cognizant of her, appreciative, eager to comprehend and interest, to make her smile or laugh, or sigh with pleasure. The perfect and most lovely of partners. Was it then *this* very thing—weird irony of an imperfect earth—this very faultlessness of his in his conduct, his charming attentions, his real care of her, his joy in bringing joy to *her*—had it somehow sickened or driven her away from him? Had he *smothered* her with his loving kindness? So that, only in order to breathe again, she had thrust out her sudden hand when they stood at the cliffs wild-flowery and unrailed brink, thrust out her graceless and stumpy hand and, catching him off-balance, spun him away and downward, his fine face looking only surprised, and not even that very much. He struck his head mere moments following, and so made no complaint at all, striking all of himself next, and repeatedly, on the cliff, and ultimately the rocky beach two hundred and seventy feet below. He was already mostly dead, a task the beach had completed in six further seconds.

Or could it have been an accident?

No, it could not.

If she ever wrote about what had happened, what she had done at about half past three on that summer day, it never came to light. What happened subsequently to her, or where she had gone to—despite numerous sightings of her, all of which proved either false or too imprecise or dilatory to be of help—has never been learned. Maybe she too has died by now. Or else she is flourishing somewhere, in some theoretical country of the blind where, by a quirk of life's madness, it turns out she, after all, has some advantage. But this seems so very unlikely.

You may still ask, nevertheless, why did she kill him?

Turn back the pages of the memory she herself had—or has. Look carefully at its pictures, which only resemble, and attain, anything beautiful when they do not deal at all with contact by actual human things: the flying birds, purring cats, bounding dogs, the leaves, the lit lamps, the mountains, the sea, the sky, the sun, the moon and the stars. Even a paper written on, perhaps, a play seen, a book read. Yes, but turn quite fast past all those. Look now as she has at the faces of humanity. Not, as you might expect, while they leer and snarl at her—but as they make those corrective attempts upon themselves. As they put on the face-pack or undergo the nose-job, as they paint in and paint out what is missing and what should not be there. Such effort. Always that effort, which sometimes somewhat, and sometimes vastly improves them, makes them so much better, appealing, silky creatures, lovable and valid. Until the mask comes off, the wig, the special brassière or controlling device. Out with the tooth-implants, the plastic breasts, wipe away the makeup. And then—they are so much less. So much more . . . *her* people, though they will never agree. They survive by hiding in disguise. Although she, poor ruin, so badly made—as they had always told her, and she learned *their* truth as she learned to read—beaten, beaten into her—she, she could never improve herself by such slender means. She had been thrown too far down that cliff of abysm. Nothing could *she* do. Her only consolation then perhaps, faint as a brush of pollen from some dying flower, to see that they at least must *work* at their survival.

But not so with everyone.

You will perhaps picture now how he was, her lover, her husband. Handsome, gracious, elegant—flawless. And to nurture this he need only—*be*. Asleep by night, waking in the morning, if a little unwell with a minor ailment, if sweating, hot and disheveled from too long in the sun at a painting, irritated by some difficulty in his work, or grubby from some chore, or in the paroxysm of lust, which does not always beautify its subject—then, as at all times, by dark, by light, in shadow or in glare—he—*he*—*always* perfect. And to maintain perfection, all he need do was—*nothing*. Nothing at all.

On that walk, at the edge of the ocean, the afternoon sun, the clarity of the air—he turned his head to look away toward the water, speaking no doubt in his beautiful voice about the picture he had been making. His shining hair, his eyes, his expression, every feature of face and body, even that half step he took, so graceful, like that of a dancer or a duelist, in utter poise, if not quite in balance, that strong and eloquent movement of his hand—do you see? Do you *see?* As if across vast distances, the shrill scream of the revelation must at last have reached her. All this he has, and is. Even goodness and kindness belong to him. He needs do nothing. He *burns* the world.

Her hand too springs out. And he—is gone.

Below the Sun Beneath

1

LIFE DROVE HIM into death, so it had seemed. It was the choice between dying—or living and *causing* death, to be corpse or corpse-maker. Perhaps Death's own dilemma.

He had joined the army of the king because he was starving. Three days without eating had sent him there; little other work that winter. And the war-camp was bursting with food; you could see it from the road: oxen roasting over the big fire and loaves piled high and barrels of ale lined up, all a lush tapestry of red and brown and golden plenty, down in the trampled, white-snowed valley. He had fought his first battle with a full belly, and survived to fill it again and again.

Five years after that. And then another five. Roughly every sixth year, the urge came in him to do something else. But he had mislaid family, and even love. Had given up himself and found this other man that now he had become: Yannis the soldier.

And five years more. And *nearly* five . . .

The horse kicked and fell on him just as the nineteenth year was turning toward the twentieth. Poor creature, shot with an arrow it was dying, going down, the kick one last instinctive protest, maybe.

But the blow, and the collapsing weight smashed the lower bones in his right leg, and he lost it up to the knee. All but its spirit, which still ached him inside the wooden stump. Yet what more could he expect? He had put himself in the way of violences, and so finally received them.

The army paid him off.

The coins, red and brown, but *not* golden, lasted two months.

By the maturing of a new winter he was alone again, unemployed and wandering, and for three days he had not eaten anything but grass.

*   *   *

Yannis heard the strange rumor at the inn by the forest's edge. The innwife had taken pity on him. "My brother lost a leg like you. Proper old cripple he is now," she had cheerily announced. Yet she gave Yannis a meal and a tin cup of beer. There was a fire as well, and not much custom that evening. "Sleep on a bench, if you want. But best get off before sun-up. My husband's back tomorrow and if he catches you, we'll both get the side of his fist."

As the cold moon rose and the frosts dropped from it like chains to bind the earth, Yannis heard wolves howling along the black avenues of the pine trees.

He dozed later, but then a group of men came in, travelers, he thought. He listened perforce to their talk, making out he could not hear, in case.

"It would seem he's scared sick of them, afraid to *ask*. Even to pry."

"That's crazy talk. How *can* he be? He's a *king*. And what are they? A bunch of girls. No. There's more to it than that."

"Well, Clever Cap, it's what they say in the town market. And not even that open with it either. He wants to *know*, but won't take it on himself. Wants some daft clod to do it for him."

Yannis, as they fell silent again, willed himself asleep. In the morning, he had to get off fast.

A track ran to the town. On foot and disabled, it took him until noon.

The place was as he had expected, huts and hovel-houses and the only stone buildings crowded round the square with the well, as if they had been herded there for safety. Even so, at his third attempt he got a day's work hauling stacks of kindling. He slept that night in a barn behind the priest's house. At sunrise he heard the priest's servants gossiping.

"It's Women's Magic. That's why he's afeared."

"But he's a *king*?"

"Won't matter. Our Master'll tell you. Some women still

keep to the bad old ways. Worse in the city. They're *clever* there. Too clever to be Godly."

Beyond the town was another track. At last an ill-made and raddled road.

He knew by then the city was many more miles of walking-limping. And all the wolfwood round him and, after sundown, as he crouched by his makeshift fire, the wolves sang their moon-drunk songs to the freezing sky.

On the third day, a magical number he had once or twice been told, he met the old woman. She was out gathering twigs that she threw in a sack over her shoulder, and various plants and wildfruits that she put carefully in a basket in her left hand. Sometimes he noted, as he walked toward her along the path, she changed the basket to her right hand and picked with the left. She was a witch, then, perhaps even knew something about healing. There had been a woman he encountered like that, before, who brewed a drink that stopped his leg aching so much. The medicine was long gone and the full ache had come back.

"Good day, Missus," he therefore politely said, as he drew level.

She had not glanced up at his approach—that confident then, even with some ragged, burly stranger hobbling up— nor did she now. But she answered.

"Yes, then. I've been expecting you, young man. Just give me a moment and I'll have this done."

He was well over thirty in years, and no longer reckoned young at all. But she, of course, looked near one hundred: to her the average granddad would be a stripling. And she was expecting him, was she? Oh, that was an old trick. *Naturally,* nothing could surprise *her,* given her vast supernatural gifts.

Yannis waited anyway, patiently, only shifting a little now and then to unkink the leg.

Finally she was through, and looked straight up at him.

Her eyes were bright and clear as a girl's, russet in color like those of a fox.

"This is the bargain," she said. "Some wood needs chopping, and the hens like a regular feed. You can milk a goat? Yes, I believed you could. These domestic chores you can take off my hands for two or three days. During which time I will teach you two great secrets."

He stared down at her, quite tickled by her effrontery and her style. She spoke like someone educated, and her voice, like her eyes, was young, younger far than he was. Though her hair was gray and white, there were strands of another color still in it, a faded yellow. Eighty years ago, when she was a woman of twenty, she might well have been a silken, lovely thing. But time, like life and death, was harsh.

"Two secrets, Missus?" he asked, nearly playful. "I thought it always had to be three."

"Did you, soldier? Then no doubt three it will be, for *you.* But the third one you'll have to discover yourself."

"Fair enough. Do I get my bed and board as well?"

"Sleep in the shed, eat from the cook-pot. As for your leg—don t fret. That comes included."

During that first day she was very busy inside the main hut that was her house, behind a leather curtain; at witch-work he assumed.

Outside he got on with the chores.

All was simple. Even the white goat, despite its wicked goat eyes, had a mild disposition. The shed allotted as his bedchamber was weather-proof and had a rug-bed.

As the sinking sun poured out through the western trees, she called him to eat. He thought, sitting by the hearth fire, if her witchery turned out as apt as her cooking, she might even get rid of his pain for good. Then some few minutes after eating he noticed his leg felt better.

"It was in the soup, then, the medicine?"

"Quite right," she said. "And in what I gave you at noon."

He had tasted nothing, and stupidly thought it was relief at this interval that calmed his phantom leg. He supposed she could have poisoned him too. But then, she had not.

"Great respects to you, Missus," he said. "I'm more than grateful. May I take some with me when I go?"

"You can. But I doubt you'll need it. There's another way to tackle the hurt of your wound. That's the first secret. But I won't be showing you until tomorrow's eve."

He was relaxed enough he grinned.

"What will all this cost me?"

"It will," she said, "be up to you."

At which, of course, he thought, *I'd best be careful then. God knows what she's at, or will want.* But the fire was warm and the leg did not nag, and the stoop of dark beer, that was pleasant too. Well, she had bewitched him, in her way. He even incoherently dreamed of her that night. It was some courtly dance, the women and the men advancing to and from each other, touching hands, turning slowly about, separating and moving gracefully on . . . There was a young girl with long golden, *golden* hair, bright as the candlelight. And he was unable to join the dance, being old and crippled; but somehow he did not mind it, knowing that come the *next* evening — but *what* the next evening?

The succeeding day, at first light, he noticed the large paw-marks of wolves in the frost by the witch's door, and a tiny shred or two that indicated she had left them food. There had been no nocturnal outcry from the goat or chickens. Another bargain?

Everything went as before. Today the goat even nuzzled his hand. It was a nice goat, perhaps the only nice goat on earth. The chickens chirruped musically.

When the sun set, she called him again to eat.

She said, "We'll come now to the first secret. It's old as the world. Older, maybe. And once you know, easy as to sleep. Easier."

Probably there was more medicine in the food — his resentful leg all day had been charming in its behavior — but also tonight she must have put in some new substance.

He woke, having found he had fallen asleep as he sat by her fire, his back leaning on the handy wall.

She was whispering in his left ear.

"What?" he murmured.

But the whispering had stopped. She stood aside, and in

the shadowy sinking firelight she was like a shadow herself. The shadow said, in its young, gentle and inexorable voice: "Easy as *that*, soldier. Nor will you ever forget. Whenever you have need, you or that wounded leg, then you can."

And then she slipped back and back, and away and away, and he thought, quite serenely and without any rage or alarm, *Has she done for me? Am I dying?* But it was never that.

He floated inward, deep as into any sea or lake. And then he floated *free* . . .

Children dream of such things. Had he? No, he had had small space for dreams of any sort. Yet, somehow he knew what he did. He had done it before, must have done, since it was so familiar, so *known,* so wonderful and so blessed.

He was young. He felt twenty years of age, and full of health and vigor. He ran and bounded on two strong, eloquent legs, each whole and perfectly able. He sprang up trees—*ran* up them, impervious to pine-needles and the scratch-claws of branches, leaped from their boughs a hundred feet above and flew—wingless but certain as a floating hawk—to another tree or to the ground below. Where he wished, he walked on the *air.*

The three gray wolves, feeding on bits of meat and turnip by the witch's door, looked up and saw him; only one offered a soft sound, more like amused congratulation than dismay Later a passing night bird veered to give him room, with a startled silvery rattle. A fox on the path below merely pattered on. Later he went drifting, careless, by three or four rough huts, where a solitary man, cooking his late supper outdoors, stared straight through him with a myopic gaze. Blind to nothing physical—he was dexterous enough with his makeshift skillet—the woodlander plainly could not detect Yannis, who hovered directly overhead. Even when Yannis, who was afterward ashamed of himself, swooped down and pulled the man's ear, the man only twitched as if some night-bug had bothered him. A human, it seemed, was the single creature who could not see Yannis at all.

He roamed all night, or at least until the fattening moon set and the sky on the other side turned pale. Effortlessly, he found his way back to the witch's house. A faint shimmering line in the air led him. He followed it, aware it was attached to him, and of its significance, without at all understanding, until at last he found it ran in under the shed-house door, and up to the body of the man who sat propped there, so deeply asleep he seemed almost—if very peacefully, in fact, nearly *smugly—dead—and* slid in at his chest. *The cord that binds me, while I live,* he thought. *And only I, or some very great witch, could see it.*

He paused a moment, too, to regard himself from *outside.* Rather embarrassed, he reassessed his value. Aside from the leg, he was still well-made. And strong. He had—a couthness to him. And if not handsome, well, he was not an ugly fellow. He would do. He was worth quite a lot more than Yannis, since his crippling and invaliding out of the army, had reckoned. Yannis gave himself a friendly pat on the shoulder, before pursuing the cord home into his physical body, and the warm, kind blanket of sleep that waited there.

"You will never forget now," she said, next morning. "Whenever you must ease the spirit of the leg, you need only release *your* spirit. Then the leg will never fret you, no matter that its physical self is gone and it sits in a jail of wood, just as you do in the prison of flesh we all inhabit till death sets us free."

"Is it my soul you've let out, then?" he asked her. Since waking up again he had been less confident. "Isn't that going to upset God?"

She made a noise of derision and dipped her bread in the honey. "Do you think God so petty? Come soldier, God is *God*! How could we get these skills if it weren't allowed? But no, besides. It's not the soul. The soul sits deeper. It's your *earthly* spirit only you can now release, which is why it has the shape of you and is male and young and strong. And too—as you've seen—nothing human, or very few, will ever espy you in that form. You will be *invisible.* Which, when you reach the city, can render you service."

"You think I'll use the knack to do harm."

"Never," she said. "Would I unlock it for you, if I thought so?"

Yannis shook his head. "No, Mother."

"And I am your mother, now?"

He said, quietly, "She was yellow-haired and pretty. I don't insult you, Missus. And anyway, I meant . . ."

"There," she said, and she smiled at him. She had a sunny smile, and all her teeth were amazingly sound and clean, especially for such an old granny as she was. "And now, Yannis, I will give you the second secret. Which is less secret than the first."

He sat and looked warily at her as she told him. "You'll gain the city by nightfall. There is a king there, who is a coward, a dunce, and as cruel as those failings can make a man. He has twelve girls by three different wives, all of these queens now dead, and mostly due to him. But the princesses, as we must call them, as we must call him a king—for they're all the royalty we'll get in such a land as this—are at a game the king is frightened of. He wants to be sure what they do, for *un*sure he is, and to spare. And when sure, to curb them. But he dares not take on the task himself."

"This is the tale I heard elsewhere," said Yannis, who had sat forward, partly eager to forget for a while about spirits and souls and God.

"You may well have heard it, for rumors have been planted and are growing wild. Already the king has hired mercenary men to spy on the girls and catch them out. These mercenaries were of all types, high, low, and lowest of the lowest, even one, they say, a prince, but doubtless a prince in the same way of this king being a king. All fail, and then the king gladly has them murdered. That is *his* bargain. The man who spies on and renders up the princesses, him the king will make his princely heir. But fail—and off with his head."

"If it's so hard to catch his daughters, then why try?"

"Because it is never hard at all. Those who watch the girls, or would do, the princesses drug asleep, being themselves well-versed in witchcraft. Whoever wants to find out anything must not taste a bite nor swallow a sip in that house, unless it be from the common dish or jug, and sampled by others. Or if he is forced, he must only pretend. And immediately after he must feign slumber or better—slip into a trance so sleep-like, so *deathlike,* it will convince the sternest critic. Then he may follow those girls as he wishes, and learn all and everything. Providing, of course, none can see him."

Yannis said, "For example, by letting his spirit free from his body."

"Just so."

Next a silence fell. It came down the chimney and through the two little windows with the shutters, and sat with the witch and the soldier, timing them on its endless noiseless fingers to see how much longer they would be at their council.

At last Yannis said, "Two secrets, then. What is the third?"

"I said already, *son,* you must find the third secret yourself. But some call it Courage and others Arrogance, and some blind fool Madness. You must *act* on what I have taught you, that is the third secret. Now, go milk my goat, who has fallen in heart's-ease for you, and bid my chicks good-bye. Then you shall set off again, if you're to reach the city gate by sundown."

Yannis stood like a man distracted. Then he said, "Either you want my death, and so have done this. Or else you mean me to prosper. But—if that—then *why*? I'm nothing to you."

"For sure perhaps, or not," she said. "But I have been something for *you.* For even when you were a warrior in the wars, you have cared for me."

"But Missus—never ever did I meet you before . . ."

"Not me that speaks these words, but so many others— *womankind.* My sisters, my mothers, my daughters, the daughters of my daughters—all of those. For the old woman and the young woman, they the rest of the soldiers might have killed for uselessness, or put to a use that would have killed them too. Those women that you helped, that you defended, and hid, that you gave up your food to. Women young and old are dear to you, and you in the midst of turmoiled men, blood-crazed and heartless, have where able been a savior to my kind. And so, also to me, Yannis, my son."

Then Yannis hung his head, lost for words.

But she, as she turned in at the leather curtain, said to him, lightly, "I will after all tell you a third thing. It is how the old beast of a king knows his daughters are at dangerous work."

Yannis shook himself. "How, then?"

"By the soles of their feet."

2

They used a different language in the city—in their buildings, their gestures. While their speech contained foreign
phrases, and occasional passages in a tongue that was so
unlike anything in the regions round about that it took him
time to fathom it. However, he came to realize he had
heard snatches of it before. It was an ancient and classic
linguistic of which, racking his brains, he saw he had kept a
smattering.

Most of the city was of stone. But near the center—where
a wide, paved road ran through—the architecture was, like
the second language, *ancient,* and some even ruinous, yet built
up again. Tall, wide-girthed pillars, high as five houses stood
on each other's heads. Large gateways opened on terraced
yards. A granite fountain played. Yannis was surprised. But
the metropolis had been there, evidently, far longer than
those who possessed it now.

On a hill that rose beyond a treed parkland, a graveyard
was visible, whose structures were domed like the cots of
bees. He had never seen such tombs before. They filled him
with a vague yet constant uncomfortable puzzlement. He did
not often turn their way. And he thought this reaction too
seemed apparent with the city people. Where they could, they
did not look into the west.

The sun set behind the hill about an hour after he had got
in the gates—he had made very good speed. But it was darkly
overcast, and the sunset only flickered like a snakeskin before
vanishing.

How strange their manners here.

The innkeeper that he asked for chances of work, or shelter, answered instantly, in a low, foreboding tone, "Go to the
palace. There's nowhere else."

"The *palace* . . ."

"I said. Go *there.* Now off with you or I call the dogs."

And next, at a well in the strengthening rain, the women

who cried out in various voices, *"Off* — go on, you. Get work at the palace! Get your bed there. There's nowhere else."

And after these — who he took for mad persons — the same type of reply, often in rougher form, as with the blacksmith in the alley who flung an iron bar.

All told, a smother of inimical elements seemed to lie over the old city, the citizens hurrying below with heads down. Maybe only the weather, the coming dark. Few spoke to any, once the sun went. It was not Yannis alone who got their colder shoulder.

The last man to push Yannis aside also furiously directed him, pointing at the dismal park, by then disappearing in night-gloom. "See, *there.* The palace. And don't come back."

To which Yannis, thrusting him off in turn, in a rush of lost patience answered, "So I'm the king's business, am I? Are you this way with any stranger who asks for anything? Go and be used and win — or die?"

But the man raised his fist. In a steely assessment of his own trained strength — which the witch's teaching had returned him to awareness of — Yannis retreated. No point in ending in the jail.

Black, the sky, and all of it falling down in icy streamings, which, even as he went on, altered to a spiteful and clattering hail. He thought of falling arrowheads. Of the horse which fell. Of the surgeon's tent . . .

At the brink of the park a black crow sat in an oak above. And Yannis was not sure it was quite real, though its eye glittered.

I *am here by Something's will.*

But the will of what? A king? A witch? Some unknown sorcerer? Or only those other two, Life and Death.

In the, end, all the trees seemed to have crows in them. Stumbling over roots and tangles of undergrowth, where rounded boulders and shards nestled like skulls, Yannis came out onto a flight of stony stairs. It was snowing, and the wind howled, riotously bending grasses and boughs and the mere frame of a strong man. And then a huge honey-colored lamplight massed above out of a core of towery and upcast leaden walls.

He judged, even clapped by now nearly double and blin-
kered by snow, that the palace was like the rest, partly ancient, its additions balancing on it, clinging and unsure. But it
was well-lit, and rows of guardsmen were there. One of them,
like the unwilling ones below, trudged out at him and caught
him, if now in an almost friendly detaining vice. "What have
we here?"

"I was *sent* here," said Yannis, speaking of Fate, or the
fools in the city, not caring which.

"That's good, then. Will cheer him up, our lord. Not every
day, would you suppose, some cripple on a stump can en-
hance the evening of a king."

His own king had once spoken to Yannis. The king had been
on horseback, the men interrupted, respectfully standing in
the mud, just after the sack of some town. The king had com-
mended them for their courage. It was ritual, no more, but
Yannis had been oddly struck by how the king looked not like
other men. That was, the king was not in any way superior—
more handsome, say, let alone more profound, yet *different* he
was. It had not been his fine clothes, the many-hands-high
horse. It perplexed Yannis. The king seemed of an alien kind—
not quite human, perhaps, but nor was it glamorous.

This king was nothing like that anyway. When Yannis first
saw him he was some distance off, but even over the sweep of
the tall-roofed, smoky, steamy, hot-lit hall, he appeared only
a man, aging and bearded between black and gray, and drunk,
possibly; he looked it.

The guardsman who brought Yannis in quickly pushed
him into a seat at one of the lower tables. Here sat a cobbler,
tellable by his hands, some stable grooms still rank from their
duties, and so on. A lesser soldier or two was in with the rest.
The guard said, "Eat your fill. Have a big drink and toast his
kingship. Don't get soused. He'll be talking to you later."

The tables where the king's court sat near him lay over an
area of painted floor just far enough off to indicate status. The
king's own High Table was up on a platform. It faced the hall,
but directly to its left side another table spread at a wide
angle. The king's table was caped in white cloth-of-linen,

hung with medallions of gold. It had utensils, beakers and jugs of silver and clear gray crystal. It was crowded, the Master occupying the central carved and gilded chair. The left-hand table meanwhile had a drapery of three colors, a deep red, a plum yellow, and a chestnut shade. But no medallions hung on it. The jugs were earthenware. It was also completely empty, but having twelve plain chairs.

An armorer next to Yannis asked questions and commented. Where did Yannis come from? Oh, *there* — Oh, *that little war*? A *horse* did for his leg? What luck! Try that pie — best you've tasted, yes?

Finally Yannis asked a question. "Why is that other table empty up there?"

"Oh, they'll be in."

"Who?"

"His girls."

Yannis, cautious, casual: "His wives, you mean?"

"No wives at present. He got sick of wives. His daughters. No sons — none of those useless women of his ever made him a son. Just girl after girl. Now look. Here they come. Do as they please. Women always will, unless you curb them."

Color. Like a bright stream they rippled into the basin of the big room, flowed together across the platform.

And if this king was only human they, Yannis thought — or was the idea only the strong ale? — *they* were *not*, not quite. Nor like that other unhuman king. These women, these girls, these twelve princesses ... like water and like fire, things which gleamed and grew and bloomed and *altered*, metals, stars, alcohol — the sun-wind in the wheat ...

Not beautiful — it was never that, though not *un*beautiful — graceful as animals, careless as ...

"Where are you off to?"

Yannis found he had half-risen. He sat again and said quickly to the armorer, "Pardon me, just easing my leg."

And looked away, then back to the platform and the twelve flames now settling on it like alighting birds. Because of the table's angle, he could see each of them quite well. They had no jewels, unlike their father. They wore the sort of dresses some not-badly-off merchant's brood might put on.

You could not but look. Their hair . . .

A hush had gone around the hall, and then been smothered over by an extra loudness.

Watching, very obliquely now, Yannis noted the king exchanged no words with any of these young women, not even she who sat down nearest to him.

None of them appeared particularly old. Yannis tried to guess their ages—a year, a little more or less between each one and her closest neighbor.

He had been dazzled. Enough.

Yannis took another draft of ale, and when he raised his head the armorer had shifted, and there was another man.

"Listen, and get this right. You're done dining. In a count of twenty heartbeats get up. Go out that door to the yard. Someone will meet you. You'll be going to see the king."

Then the man himself got up and went, and the armorer did not return, and Yannis counted twenty beats, rose, and moved out into the torch-scripted, black-white winter yard. The wind had dropped with the snow. Two new guards bundled him along to another entry, and up some miles of crooked steps. It was like being escorted to his own hanging. God knew, it might well be before too long.

The king stood in his chamber. He was a bloody king, lit by the galloping hearth.

The king scrutinized Yannis, unspeaking.

After which, the king spoke: "The Land of the Sun Beneath."

Yannis stared. He must be meant to—the king unsmilingly smiled: "Have you heard of such a land? No? But you're traveled. Where have you put your ears? In a bucket?"

Yannis had pondered what to do if offered a drink—in the light of the witch's advice to trust only the communal and well-patronized plate or jug, as in the hall. But this was not a hospitable king, either. It was a game-player, and—an enemy?

Something nudged Yannis's brain back to its station.

"Your Majesty means—the country into which the sun sinks at evening, in the tales . . . ? The lands beneath the world . . ."

"In the tales," said the king. "The sun goes under the rim of the earth. Where else can it go?"

Yannis stood there. He knew that many clever scholars had decided the earth was not flat, that the sun circled it. Others, however, remained stubbornly in the belief of a flat world with killing edges. It was, observing nature, difficult not to. And the roots of this city were ancient, primal.

"Yes, Majesty."

"Yes. The Land of the Sun Beneath, where the sun rules after darkness falls here. But there is a land beneath those lands, ever without the sun. Some call it Hell, and some the Underworld. What do you call it, Crank-Leg?"

Yannis thought the king did not anticipate a reply.

The king said, "I suppose, soldier, you'd call it death. Maybe, when they cracked your leg off, you even paid a little visit."

Yannis found he hated the king. It was a response that this king wished to foster in him. The king preferred to know how he weighed with common men, and to make men hate and fear provided an instant measure. Yannis had glimpsed traces of hate, fear, all over the court, both high and low exhibited signs. So the king knew where he was.

"Well," said the king, "you've few words. Do you know what you're to do here?"

Yannis did, of course. "No, sire."

"Then you are not like all the rest, all seven—or was it seventeen of them—those others who failed. Very well. My daughters, in my hall, those girls with their hair. Even *you* will have noticed them. On nights of the round moon they go to another place, the place we spoke of. Despite they sleep all together in their luxurious bedchamber, which every night is locked and guarded to protect and make sure of them—on those three nights they *slip through,* like water from a leaky bowl. At dawn, they come back. Do you know how this was discovered?"

Yannis heard himself say, "By the soles of their feet."

The king unsmiled. His eyes shone like scorched stones, cooling, cold. "So you *do* know."

"Only the phrase."

"Yes. The soles—not of their shoes, which are pristine as when sewn for them—but the skin of their feet. *That* is marked as if worn right through. Blemished, *black* and *red* and decorated in silver and sparkle, too. As if they'd bruised and torn them, then dipped them in rivers of moonlight and rime. You must follow these bitch-whores of mine, and see how they get out, and where they go, and if—*if*—it's to that hidden underland, and next—what goes on *there*. Things no man can see, of course, and keep his sanity. But you'll already have been there, as I said, when you lost half your leg. You'll already know. You're already partly mad. Why else are you here now?"

"And were the other men mad, sire?"

"They must have been, would you not say, old Crook-Shank?"

"Have you," said Yannis, "never yourself *asked* your daughters?"

"I?" The king stared at Yannis. "A king does not ask. He is *supplied*. Without asking. I set others to find out. And *now you* are here. If you succeed, you will be my son, and a prince, my heir, to rule after me. Any of the twelve whores you choose shall be your wife. Or all of them, if you want. I'll have someone fashion an extra-large bed for the sport. If you fail, however, your head shall be slashed from your body, as the best of your leg once was. Top to toe, soldier. That's fair. And now," said the king, "since this is the first of the moon's three round nights, the servant outside will show you the way."

It was rising in the long middle window, the moon, round as the white pupil of an immense dark eye. It watched him as he entered and was closed in, but it watched them, also, all twelve. Together, they and he made thirteen beings. But the moon perhaps made fourteen. Besides, there were the animals.

Three big, wolf-like dogs sat or stood, still as statues; a strange pale cat, with a slanted yellow gaze, lay supine. Additionally, there were little cages hung up, in some of which small birds perched twittering—and as the door of every cage stood open, several others flitted to and fro, while occasionally one would let loose a skein of lunar song, or a moon-white dropping would fall, softly snow-like on the floor.

The princesses were arranged, like warriors before a skirmish, some on the richly draped yet narrow beds, or they stood up, and two were combing their hair with plangent silking sounds, and drizzles of sparks that flew outward in the brazier-spread fire-glow. This combing and spark-making was like the playing of two harps, a musical accompaniment to the birds' descant.

A magical, part uncanny scene. It lulled Yannis, and therefore made him greatly more alert.

But he took time, as with the king, and since they stared full at him, even the dogs and the cat, and some of the birds, to study these women a while.

For a fact, though, he could not properly see past their hair.

Charms they had, and they were alike, all of them to each other—and unalike, too—but the hair was still, in each one her symbol, extraordinary, unique. Three colors, every time transmuted. For *she* had hair red as amber, and *she* hair brown as tortoiseshell, and *she* gold as topaz—and *she* red as beech leaves, *she* brown as walnut wood, *she* gold as corn fields—*she* red as summer wine, *she* brown as spring beer, *she* gold as winter mead, and *she* was red as copper, and *she* was brown as bronze. But she—Yannis hesitated between two flickers of the brazier-light—*She*—the youngest, there, there in the darkest shadow of the farthest bed—*she* had hair as gold as *gold.*

"Well, here's our father's latest guest."

It was the tallest, eldest girl who spoke, with amber hair. In age, the soldier thought, she was some years his junior, but then a wealthy, cared-for woman, he knew, could often look much younger than her years, just as a poor and ill-used one could seem older.

"There is a chamber set by for you," levelly said the girl with tortoiseshell hair.

"Every comfort in it," said the girl with topaz hair.

"But we know you won't enjoy that since—" said the girl with hair like beech leaves.

"You must watch us closely and follow behind so that—" said hair like walnut wood.

"You may report to the king what we do," concluded hair like cornfields.

"A shame," said Summer Wine.

"And unkindness," said Spring Hair.

"Every inch of your tired frame must protest," said Winter Mead.

"But such is human life," said Copper, tossing her locks as she stopped her comb.

"Alas," said Bronze, also stopping hers.

Then, in the sparkless gloaming, Gold-as-Gold said this: "We know you must do it, and will never deny you have now no choice. Come, join us then in a cup of liquor for the journey, and we'll be on our way, while you shall follow, poor soldier, as best you can."

The soldier bowed very low, but he said nothing, and when they poured out the wine, each had a bright metal cup with jewels set round the rim. But the cup they gave him was of bright polished metal, too.

Then the young women drank, and the soldier pretended to drink, because what the witch had told him was so firmly fixed in his brain he was by that instant like a fine actor who had learned his part to perfection. And presently he did speak, and said might he sit just for a minute, and the young women who were by then finishing putting on their cloaks and shoes for the outer world, or so it looked, nodded and said he might.

Yannis thought, *The draft came from the same pitcher. The drug must be in the cup—but no matter, I never even put my lip to it without my finger between.*

Next he plumped down the cup, spilling a drop. He let his head droop suddenly and seemed surprised. He smiled for the first, stupidly. Then he shut his eyes and thought, *God help me now,* but he had not forgotten the secret of the trance.

Another moment and Yannis himself sat upright in the chair, even as his body stretched unconscious across it. He was out of his skin. And oh, the moonlight in the chamber then, how thrillingly clear, a transparent silver mirror that he could see straight through. And the soul-cord that connected flesh and spirit, more silver yet.

He let himself drift up a wall, and hung there, and watched.

They came soon enough, and tried him, gently at first. Then they mocked, and Amber and Beech Leaves and Spring Beer slapped his face, and then Cornfields came up to him and tickled him maliciously. Walnut Wood kicked his sound ankle, and Bronze and Winter Mead spat on him. Tortoiseshell cursed him articulately, in which Summer Wine and Copper joined. Only Topaz stuck a pin into his arm and twisted it.

Sure he slept, they then turned together up the room to its darker end, where Gold yet stood, the youngest of them. She instead came down, and hesitated by him a second. Standing in air, the soldier thought, Now what will *she* do?

"Poor boy," said Gold, though her face was impassive, and she anyway half his age. "Poor boy."

"You silly," called one of the others. "Why pity him? Would he pity *us*? Hurry, so we can be off."

So Gold left him, or his body, sleeping.

But Yannis pursued all of them, unseen, up the room.

They spoke a rhyme in that ancient and angular other tongue, and then they stamped, each one, on a different part of the floor. At that, the dogs, cats, and birds—who had taken not much note of him—looked round at the far wall, which sighed and slowly shifted open. Beyond lay blackness, but there came the scent of cold stones and colder night. One by one the girls fluttered through like gorgeous moths. Yannis followed without trouble. Even though the hidden door was already closing, he strode on two strong legs straight through the wall.

3

Beginning with an enclosed stone stair, which did not impede the now-fleet-of-foot Yannis, the passage descended. Nor did the almost utter dark inconvenience him; his unbodied eyes saw better than the best. After the stair came a descent of rubble, but everything contained within the granite bastions of the palace. Here and there the accustomed steps of the princesses now did falter. Once, Yannis found to his dismay, he reached out to steady the youngest princess. Fortunately, she seemed not to realize. But he must be wary—her compassion might have been a trap.

He had learned her name, nevertheless. The eldest girl had called her by it. Evira. That was the name of the youngest princess, Gold-as-Gold.

Ultimately, the way leveled. Then they walked on in the dark until splinters of the moon scattered through. At last full moonlight led them out onto a snow-marbled height, far above the city. They were on the western hill, where massed the houses of the dead.

Yannis knew they must soon enter some mausoleum, and next they did, after unlocking its iron gate with a key the eldest princess carried.

Yannis had lost all fear. He had no need of it.

Within the tomb lay snow and bones, and the ravages of the heartless armies of death and time.

And then there was another door, which Yannis, as now he was, saw instantly was no earthly entrance or exit. And despite his power and freedom, for an instant he did check. But the twelve maidens went directly through the door, even she did, Evira. And then so did Yannis too.

Beyond the door lay the occult country.

It was of the spirit, but whether an afterlife, or underworld below the Sun Beneath—or an else-or-otherwhere—Yannis was never, then or ever, certain.

Although it was unforgettable, naturally. In *nature*, how not?

Should the sun have sunk into a country beneath the earth, then this land, lying below the other two, had no hint of daylight. Nor was the round full moon apparent. Yet light there was. It was like the clearest glass, and the air—when you moved through it—rippled a little, like water. The smell of the air was sweet, fragrant as if with growing trees and herbs. And such there were, and drifted flowers, pale or somber, yet they glowed like lamps. Above, there was a sort of sky, which shone and glowed also, if sunlessly. Hills spread away, and before them an oval body of water softly glimmered. Orchards grouped on every side, they too glinting and iridescent. The leaves nearby were silver, but farther off they had the livelier glisten of gold.

The moment this somewhere closed around them, the women discarded their cloaks and shoes, and shook out the flaming waves of their hair. Then they ran toward the lake.

As they ran, he saw their plain garments change to silks and velvets, streams of embroidery budding at sleeves and borders like yet more flowers breaking through grass.

And he was aware of his own joy in the running, and his lion-like pursuit, his joy in the otherworld, in life and in eternity. Strong wine. Strong as—love.

He did not glance after the spirit-cord, however. He sensed he might not see it, here.

When the women reached the lake, they were laughing with excited pleasure. Some of the silver and golden leaves they had sped under had fallen into their hair—ice on fire, fire on water—he, too, had deliberately snatched a handful of each kind of leaf. But the leaves of the lake-side trees were hard with brilliancy. *They* were diamonds; they did not deign to fall. Impelled he reached out and plucked one. It gave off a spurt of razorous white—like a tinder striking—filling the air with one sharp snap.

"Someone is behind us," said the eldest princess, amber-haired.

The others frowned at her, then all about them.

Yannis thought, *Strange, Amber is the oldest of them, yet she is young like a child, too. Perhaps in knowledge, soul-wise, the youngest princess of all . . .*

And I, he thought, *What am I? Perhaps in fact I am only drugged and dream all this—*

But the youngest princess, Evira, said quietly, "Who could follow here, sisters?" Trusting, and like a child as well.

They could not see him, he knew. Not even the silver and gold and diamond hidden in the pocket of his no-longer-physical shirt.

Then what looked to him at first like a fleet of swans appeared across the lake. Soon he saw twelve gilded boats, one for each princess. Who guided these vessels?

Up in the air, Yannis stood a pillar's height high. He scanned the vessels; each rowed by itself, and was empty.

Beyond the lake a palace ascended. It resembled the palace of the king in the world above, yet it was more fantastic in its looks, its towers more slender, more burnished—a female palace rather than male, and certainly young.

In the sunmoonless dusk, its windows blazed rose-red and apricot. Music wafted over water.

Oh, he could see: this country mirrored the country of Everyday, prettier, more exotic—yet, a match. Had *they* then instinctively created this otherworld out of its own basic malleable and uncanny ingredients? And was that the answer to the riddle of *all* sorcery?

In a brief while, the fast-flying boats beached on the near shore.

Then the princesses happily exclaimed, and flung wide their arms, as if to embrace lovers. And at that—at *that*—

There they are, Yannis breathed, in his unheard phantom's whisper.

For there indeed *they* were.

Begun as shadows standing between the land and the water, gaining substance, filling up with color, youth and life. Twelve tall, young, and handsome men were there, elegantly arrayed as princes. But their royal clothes no better than the panoply of their hair—one amber red, one brown as tortoiseshell, one gold as topaz, red as beech leaves, brown as walnut wood, gold as corn fields, summer wine, spring beer, winter mead; copper, bronze, and gold—*as gold.*

In God's name—could God have any hand in this? Yes, yes, Yannis's heart stammered over to him. A snatch of the ancient tongue came to him, from his own past, where he had known pieces of it—that the soul was neither male nor female, yet also it was *both* male and female. So that in every woman there dwelled some part of her that was her male other self. Just as, in every man—

The fine princes walked into the arms of their twelve

princesses. Why not? They were the male selves of each woman. Every couple was already joined, each the other, sister and brother, wife and husband, lovers for ever and a day.

Yannis stared even so as the princes rowed them all back across the lake to the palace of unearthly delights.

Invisibly, he sat in turn in every boat.

Was it heavy work for them? *No.* Yannis was lighter even than the light.

Nevertheless, they sense I am with them, he thought

He returned to the air and landed on the other shore first.

How long, that night? Dusk till dusk—so many hours. In the world they had left, he thought at last it would be close to dawn. But here it was always and never either night or day.

In the kingly great hall that far outshone that of their father above, the young women danced the often lively dances of their world and this one, forming rhythmic lines, meeting and clasping hands with their princes, parting again to lilt away, and to return. Sometimes the young men whirled them high up in their arms, skirts swirling, hair crackling. Wheels of burning lights hung from the high ceiling, which was leafed with diamond stars. On carven tables food had been laid, and was sometimes eaten, goblets of wine were to be drunk. Somewhere musicians played unseen. There were no other guests.

The soldier watched, and sometimes—the plates and cups were communal—he ate and drank. He wondered if the food would stick to him, or leave him hungry; it seemed somehow to do neither. He himself did not dance until it grew very late.

And then, as it had happened on the shore, and as he had known it must—turning, the soldier found another woman stationed quietly at his side. She at once smiled at him. He knew her well, though never had he seen her before. She might have been his sister.

"Come now," she said, soft as the silver and golden leaves in his pocket, and firm as the single adamant.

And onto the wide floor of the hall, which seemed paved with soot and coal and frost and ice and candle beams and sparks, she went. And somehow then she was dancing with the amber prince who had partnered the amber eldest princess. So then Yannis went forward, and took the princess's hand. While his spirit's sister danced with the prince, Yannis danced with Amber, who seemed then to see, if not to remember him.

"How lightly you step," he said.

"How strongly you lead," she answered.

After this, one by one, he danced with each of them, twelve to one, as his feminine aspect engaged their princes.

"How strongly you lead," said each princess, seeing him, too.

Until he came to the youngest princess, Gold-as-Gold Evira.

"How strongly you *step*," said she.

"How *lightly* you lead," said he.

And he looked into her eyes and saw there, even on that curious dancing floor, a color and a depth he had met seldom. And Yannis thought, *This after all, the very youngest, soul-wise is the eldest—*

And she said, "By a ribbon of air."

And he said, "But I must follow you."

"You," she said, "and no other."

"Are you so sure?" he said. He thought, *What am I saying?* But he knew.

And she smiled, as his soul-sister had, and he knew also her smile. And then his inner woman returned, and coming up to him she kissed his cheek, and vanished, and he, if he had grown visible, vanished also.

From high up he watched the princesses and the princes fly toward the doorway and hurry down to the boats. As they ran he saw the naked soles of their feet, and they were worn and bruised and in some parts bloody from so much dancing, and streaked with shines and spangles.

Yannis ran before them over the lake. He ran before them up the land beyond, missing the tender farewells. He bolted across the orchards of the Otherwhere, and behind him he heard them say, "Look, is that a hare that runs so fast it moves the grasses?" One thought it must be a wolf, or wildcat.

Then he fled to the mystic entry to the world, and unmistakenly rushed in like a west wind, and found instantly the silver spirit-cord flowing away through the mausoleum, and on. So out over the graveyard hill, and in at the secret corridor, and up inside the palace walls. Straight through the stone he dived. And stood sentry behind his body, sleeping tranced as death in the chair, until they came in.

"Look at him!"

Eleven sisters scorned and pinched him and made out he snored, the fool.

By then the Earth's own dawn was rising like a scarlet sea along the windows. It showed their dresses were plain again, and how weary they were, having danced in their physical bodies all night. But the body of Yannis the soldier had slept with profound relaxation. So in he stepped to wake it up at once.

"Never a hare, nor a cat, running. *I* ran before you, exactly as *I* followed you all night, my twelve dancing ladies." Just this said Yannis, standing lion-strong on his legs of flesh and wood, eyes bright and expression fierce. And he showed them leaves of silver, and of gold, and a diamond, taken now from his physical pocket. He told them all he had seen, and all they had done, every step and smile and sip and sigh. And he added he had not needed three nights to do this, only one. "Meanwhile, I will remind your highnesses, also, of mockery, pinches, blows—and a twisted pin."

Their faces whitened, or reddened.

But Evira Gold-as-Gold only stood back in the shadows, her cat and dogs and most of her birds about her.

"What will you do?" Eleven voices cried.

"Why, tell the king. And he will make me his heir, and you he will *curb*. Whatever that word means, to him."

Then some of them began to weep. And he said, "Hush now. Listen. What you do harms nobody. More, I believe you do good by it, keeping the gates oiled between here—and *there*. And he is a poor king, a coward and tyrant, is he not? His people sullen and afraid, his guards afraid, too, or arrogant and drunken. He's not how a king should be, his people's shepherd, who will die for them if needs must. Few kings are any good. Few men, few human things."

But still they sobbed.

Then Yannis said, "I tell you now what *I'll* do, then."

And he told them. And the crying ceased.

Down into the king's hall went Yannis, with the twelve princesses walking behind him on their bare and bruised and lovely feet.

And as he had suspected, the instant the court and soldiers saw the daughters walked meekly with him, everyone grew silent.

The king with his grayed black-iron beard and hair looked up from his gold dish of bloody meat. "Well?" he said.

"Their secret is this, sire," said Yannis, "they stay wakeful on full moon nights and do penance, treading on sharp stones, and praying for your health and long life, there in their locked room. Such things are best hidden, but now it's not, and the luck of it is broken. But so you would have it." And then he leaned to the king's ear and murmured with a terrible gentleness this, which only the king heard: "But they are, as you suspect, powerful witches, which is why you fear them; but the old gods love them, and you'd best beware. Yes, even despite all those other men you have allowed these girls to dupe, and so yourself had the fellows shorn of their heads: blood *sacrifices,* no less, to the old powers of Darkness you believe inhabit the lands below the Sun Beneath. This too shall I say aloud? Or will you give me what I'm owed?"

Then the king shuddered from head to foot. Top to toe, that was fair. And he told everyone present that the soldier had triumphed, and would now become a prince, the king's heir, and might marry too whichever of the daughters he liked.

"That's easy, then," said Yannis. "I'm not a young man; I'll take the oldest head and wisest mind among them. Your youngest girl, Evira." *And because,* he thought, *she is the golden cup that holds my heart.*

And gladly enough she came to him, and took his hand.

Less than half a year the iron king survived; maybe he destroyed himself by his own plotting. But by then Yannis was well-loved by the city, its soldiers loyal to him, for he had learned how to be a favorite with them, having seen other leaders do it.

Yannis, therefore, ruled as king, and his gold-haired queen at his side. Some say they had three children, some that they had none, needing none.

But it was not until after the burial of the cruel first king that Yannis said to his wife, "But did your white cat, at least, not protest?"

"At what, dear husband?"

"At your changing her, for however short a space, into a goat."

"Ah," Evira said. "Of course, you have known."

"And the dogs to wolves, and the birds — to chickens ..."

"They were glad," said Evira, coolly, "privately to meet with you. For I had sensed you were coming toward us all, and foresaw it was the only way that you would let me tell you and warn you and teach you — and so help me to save my sisters, who trust no man easily, from our fearsome and maddened father. The way matters stand in this world, it is men who rule. So here too it must be a man. But a man who is cunning, brave, kind — and with the skills of magic woken in him, needing only the key of one lesson."

And from this they admitted to each other that Evira had disguised herself as the elderly witch in the woods, and since she was far cleverer than her sisters, none had discovered her. Though at the last, as they danced, because of the russet radiance of her eyes, Yannis did.

To the end of their lives he and she loved each other, and Evira and her sisters went on dancing in the other country below the sun, even with Yannis sometimes. But he never betrayed them. Never.

It took storytellers, alas, to do that.

NOTE

Tanith Lee categorized the stories in this volume by the tales that inspired them. A list of the source tales with their stories follows:

Snow White
: Redder Than Blood. Snow Drop.

Pied Piper
: Magpied

The Sleeping Beauty
: She Sleeps in a Tower. Awake. Love in Waiting.

Cinderella
: The Reason for Not Going to the Ball. Midnight. Empire of Glass.

Rapunzel
: Rapunzel. Open Your Window, Golden Hair.

The Frog Prince
: Kiss, Kiss.

Rumpelstiltskin
: Into Gold.

Little Red Riding Hood
: Bloodmantle. Wolfed.

Swan Lake
: My Life as a Swan.

Beauty and the Beast
: The Beast. The Beast and Beauty.

The Twelve Dancing Princesses
: Below the Sun Beneath.

ACKNOWLEDGMENTS

"Redder Than Blood" © 2017 by Tanith Lee.

"Snow Drop" © 1993 by Tanith Lee, first published in *Snow White, Blood Red*, edited by Ellen Datlow and Terri Windling, William Morrow & Co.

"Magpied" © 2013 by Tanith Lee, first published in *Weird Tales* issue 361, edited by Marvin Kaye, Wildside Press.

"She Sleeps in a Tower" © 1995 by Tanith Lee, first published in *The Armless Maiden*, edited by Terri Windling, Tor Books.

"Awake" © 2003 by Tanith Lee, first published in *Swan Sister*, edited by Ellen Datlow and Terri Windling, Simon & Schuster Children's Publishing.

"Love in Waiting" © 2017 by Tanith Lee.

"The Reason For Not Going to the Ball" © 1996 by Tanith Lee, first published in this version in *The Magazine of Fantasy and Science Fiction*, edited by Kristine Kathryn Rusch, Mercury Press.

"Midnight" © 2004 by Tanith Lee, first published in *Weird Tales* issue 335, Terminus Publishing.

"Empire of Glass" © 2011 by Tanith Lee, first published in *The Immersion Book of Steampunk*, edited by Gareth D. Jones & Carmelo Rafala, Immersion Press.

"Rapunzel" © 2000 by Tanith Lee, first published in *Black Hair, Ivory Bones*, edited by Ellen Datlow and Terri Windling, Eos.

"Open Your Window, Golden Hair" © 2013 by Tanith Lee, first published in *Fearie Tales* edited by Stephen Jones, Jo Fletcher Books.

"Kiss, Kiss" © 1999 by Tanith Lee, first published in *Silver Hair, Blood Moons*, edited by Ellen Datlow and Terri Windling, Eos.

"Into Gold" © 1986 by Tanith Lee, first published in *Asimov's Science Fiction Magazine*, edited by Gardner Dozois, Dell Magazines.

"Bloodmantle" © 1989 by Tanith Lee, first published in *Forests of the Night*, HarperCollins.

"Wolfed" © 1998 by Tanith Lee, first published in *Sirens and Other Demon Lovers*, edited by Ellen Datlow and Terri Windling, Eos.

"My Life as a Swan" © 2008 by Tanith Lee, first published in *A Book of Wizards*, edited by Marvin Kaye, Science Fiction Book Club.

"The Beast" © 1995 by Tanith Lee, first published in *Ruby Slippers, Golden Tears*, edited by Ellen Datlow and Terri Windling, William Morrow & Co.

"The Beast and Beauty" © 2017 by Tanith Lee.

"Below the Sun Beneath" © 2013 by Tanith Lee, first published in *Once Upon a Time*, edited by Paula Guran, Prime Books.